A Darker Path to Justice

Book Two of the Psalms of Fire and Fury Book Series

A Darker Path to Justice

Copyright © 2025 Kristina M Barbee

All rights reserved.

Cover Art by Rachel Mcewan

https://rachelmcewandesigns.com/

Author Photo by NoxNichelle Photography

https://www.noxnichelle.com/

Map Illustration by Cassandra of Oakleaf Arrow Studios

https://www.https://oakleafarrowstudios.com/

ISBN 979-8-9886178-5-3 (Hardcover)

ISBN 979-8-9886178-7-7, 979-8-9886178-8-4 (paperback editions)

ISBN 979-8-9886178-6- (ebook)

1 2 3 4 5 6 7 8 9 10

www.kristinambarbee.shop

CONTENT WARNING

This book and the entire series contain threats of harm and torture of others, religious trauma, manipulation and abuse by the church, extreme violence, mentions of abuse, on page torture and bodily harm, PTSD, alcoholism, manipulation, mentions of suicide and suicide, depictions of Dermatillomania and Trichotillomania, Suicide ideation, suicide attempts, child death, violent pregnancy loss, depression, displays of medical insanity, drug use, drug trips, forced abortion, crude language, detailed (all consensual) sexual acts, and other subjects that may be triggering or harmful to certain readers.

Reader discretion is advised.

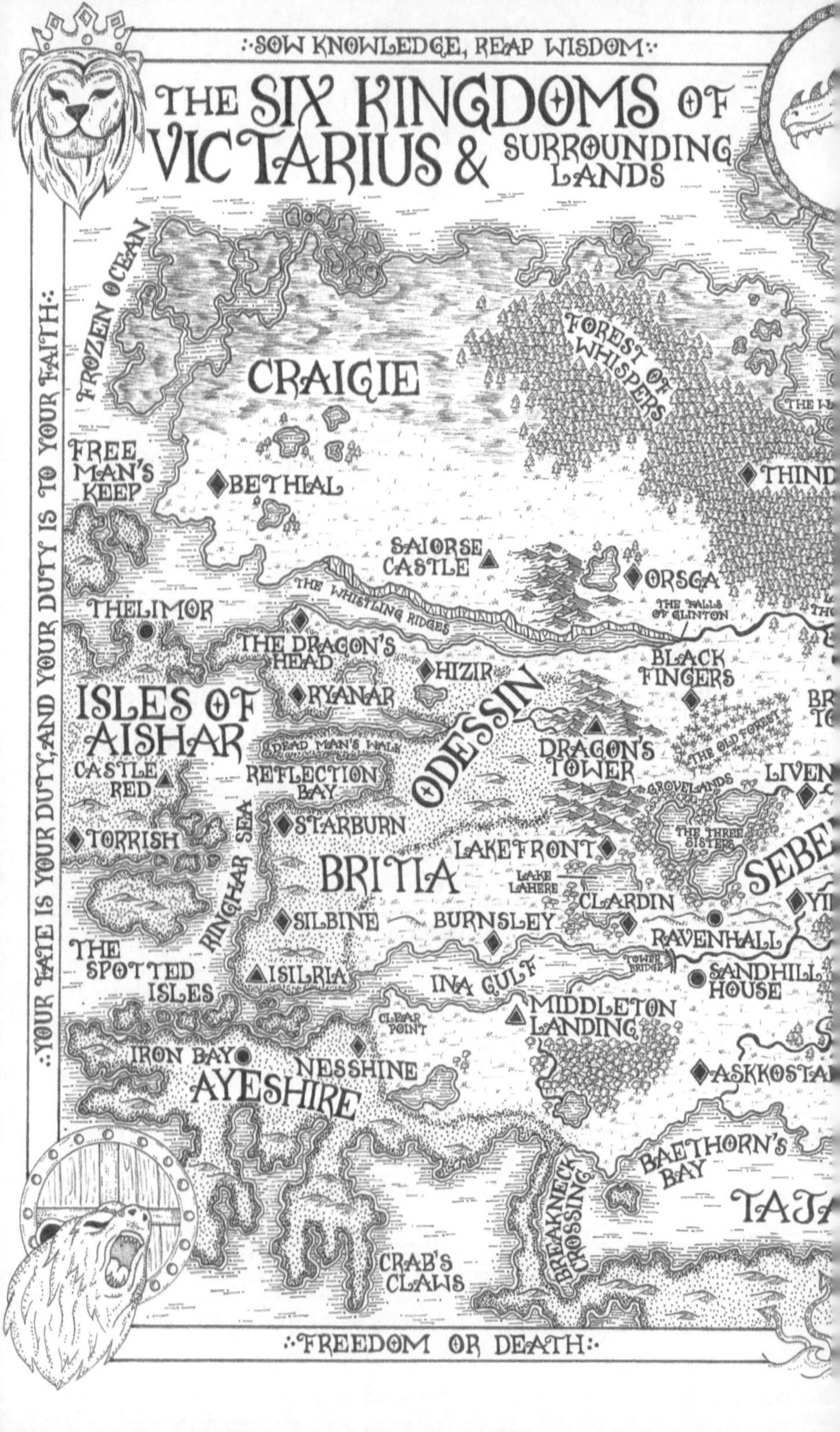

:·SOW KNOWLEDGE, REAP WISDOM·:
THE SIX KINGDOMS OF VICTARIUS & SURROUNDING LANDS
:·YOUR FATE IS YOUR DUTY, AND YOUR DUTY IS TO YOUR FAITH·:
FROZEN OCEAN
CRAIGIE
FREE MAN'S KEEP
BETHIAL
FOREST OF WHISPERS
THIND
SAIORSE CASTLE
ORSGA
THE FALLS OF CLINTON
THELIMOR
THE WHISTLING RIDGES
THE DRAGON'S HEAD
HIZIR
BLACK FINGERS
RYANAR
ISLES OF AISHAR
ODESSIN
DEAD MAN'S WALK
DRAGON'S TOWER
THE OLD FOREST
CASTLE RED
REFLECTION BAY
GROVELANDS
LIVEN
STARBURN
THE THREE SISTERS
TORRISH
LAKEFRONT
SEBE
BRITIA
LAKE LAHERE
RINGHAR SEA
CLARDIN
YI
SILBINE
BURNSLEY
RAVENHALL
THE SPOTTED ISLES
ISILRIA
TOWER BRIDGE
SANDHILL HOUSE
INA GULF
CLEAR POINT
MIDDLETON LANDING
IRON BAY
NESSHINE
ASKKOSTA
AYESHIRE
BAETHORN'S BAY
BREAKNECK CROSSING
TAJ
CRAB'S CLAWS
:·FREEDOM OR DEATH·:

·: PROTECTOR OF PEACE, KEEPER OF JUSTICE :·
THE ICE ISLES
THE UNCLAIMED LANDS
WINDELL SEA
N
THE SHATTERED STEPPES
FIND STRENGTH IN YOUR RESILIENCE, INTEGRITY IN YOUR ACTIONS & GRACE IN YOUR HEART
HIUS
EN
LE
FSDEN
THE FLOATING GRAVEYARD
UNTAMABLE COAST
DESERT
SEA OF SERPENTS
EMERALD OCEAN
·: WE ARE THE WATERS :·

DEDICATION

Dedicated to all the women who made this book happen.
And, of course, to me.

PROLOGUE

658 AC, Berren Castle, Thirty-two eons before the events of The Psalms of Fire and Fury

Lord Thillian Torrin, the Lord of Sebern, furrowed his brow as he surveyed his nephew, Captain Theodus Montarian, standing before him. The Lord of Sebern's knuckles turned white as he brought his hands together on the table, his fingers joined in a frustrated embrace.

"I have deliberated long and hard on your fate, nephew," Lord Thillian began, his voice heavy with sorrow and frustration. "And I have come to a decision that I believe befits the gravity of your transgressions... or should I say- crimes."

Captain Theodus attempted to interject once again; he always did that, but Lord Thillian's booming voice cut through the air like a thunderclap, his palm crashing down on the table in a burst of anger. "Quiet, Theodus! You have done and said enough, and I grow tired of constantly being forced to fix this court's never-ending problems. You will accept your punishment with honor, respect, and great humility," he paused and shook his head slowly, "You have cost our country much with your ego and have become this court's greatest disappointment."

Captain Theodus did his best to stand tall despite his desire to shrink and rage. Lord Thillian could see it in how his nephew's cheek twitched, and his breath huffed. Captain Theodus's hot-headed, short fuse still sparked, but he held back the fire as the guards around him tensed in preparation for another loud interruption by the young army captain.

"Yes, my lord," Captain Theodus replied, his voice strained with each word.

"Good. Bring them in." Lord Thillian jutted his chin at the door where his Lord's Guard stood watch. The doors rattled open, and their audience returned to the council room.

Lady Kathilla Edgel swept into the room like a tempest, her eyes flashing with storms in them as she prowled across the room, holding herself rigidly on the opposite side of the room as Captain Theodus. Her hands clenched into fists at her sides, never once unclenching to rest on her swollen belly or rise to wipe the tears missing from her face.

Lord Daveed Vegaria of Ayeshire sat beside Lord Thillian. He rested his cane on the arm of his chair and grunted at the pain in his knees as he moved his aging bones into the seat. The future Lord and Lady of Sebern- Lord William and Lady Catherin Torrin- sat nearby, their faces a mask of solemnity as they watched the proceedings unfold.

Lady Catherin let her solemn eyes fall to Lady Kathilla's belly before falling to her own pregnant belly. She raised her eyes to look at Lady Kathilla, hoping to find some memory of her late brother in them.

All she found was fury.

"I have deliberated long and hard," Lord Thillian continued, his gaze sweeping over the assembled company. "But apologies and title-stripping will not restore the honor our House has lost, nor will they bring back those we have lost at Broken Tower."

Lord Daveed nodded in agreement. Captain Theodus held his jaw shut so he did not speak.

"But what has occurred cannot go unpunished. We... regret how out of control the battle got in the end. Mistakes were made on all sides, and tempers flared even after swords were sheathed. The battle should have ended then- when Lord Edgel commanded his warriors to stand down. He knew his fight was lost, that his attempt to take the Land of a Thousand Rivers and the Falls of Glinton and place them under Craigie banners had failed. That our units, alongside Broken Tower's and Odessin's, outnumbered his greatly."

He paused to catch his breath that he lost in his long-windedness, "While my heart aches for all the lives lost, I am quite tired of the repeated history between your country," he flashed his eyes at Lady Kathilla, "-and that of Odessin. History that continues to cost many innocent lives. The Holy Lands were split between your countries as evenly as one could divide them many ages ago. I hope that is enough to end this back-and-forth someday. Perhaps, Lady Edgel, one might consider the loss of your husband and all his men as a blessing in disguise for you finally to end this generations-long rivalry."

"A lecture? Truly? I thought we were here to find some semblance of justice for what was done. My husband laid down his arms, and your soldiers slaughtered them all." Lady Kathilla snarled.

Lord Thillian let her get out her anger. She was still a young, passionate woman, fresh to her heirdom and responsibilities. He knew that girls like her, girls from Craigie, were never properly taught to calm down and act appropriately in places of court and meeting rooms. She would learn someday to behave appropriately, just like his daughter-in-law, Lady Catherin, had. Lady Catherin hailed from Craigie but knew that Lord Thillian held court differently than the northerners who plagued the corners of his mind with their brutishness. They lacked decorum, respect, patience, things he knew did not come naturally to them.

"As I said, tempers flared when swords were set down, likely due to the thrill of battle holding our men too much in its grasp, or perhaps comments were made that caused more anger once surrender occurred," Lord Thillian continued, his voice steady but tinged with aggravation, "Regardless, Captain Theodus has been stripped of his position within our army, his pension cut, and his family has been asked to relinquish their places and titles at our court."

Lady Kathilla's eyes widened in disbelief, her hands trembling with rage as she struggled to contain her fury. "That's all? Posterity and gold taken for his murder of surrendering lives?" she scoffed and started, her voice dripping with scorn.

Lord Thillian held up his hand to quiet her. He controlled his face despite wishing to roll his eyes at her outbursts. The experienced lord had learned proper decorum at a young age. He knew how to act appropriately and manage his emotions. He knew how to choose his words wisely and carefully: "And so long as I am alive and lord, he will never set foot on Sebern land again."

Lord William Torrin's mouth fell open as he shot his eyes between his cousin and father. "Father, what? You take titles from him and his family, and you take his homeland?" He jumped out of his seat. "Where will he go? The eastern mountains where the brutes and their monsters will turn him into one of them?"

Lady Kathilla smirked. "Sounds like justice to me."

"No." Lord Daveed Vegaria, the Lord of Ayeshire, gruffed. "He will come to our lands where he may start a new life in Ayeshire."

Lady Kathilla huffed. "You're joking? You have a new home and life ready for him already? Of course, you scheming men do. He gets barely any consequences while my husband is dead. While an entire unit of Craigie warriors lay slaughtered alongside him?"

"So, would you like his head—a death for a death then? More blood will not make this right," Lord Thillian said, his words sharp but his tone of experience trying to educate ignorance. "More blood will not lift the stain on these lands, my lady."

"No. Craigie will not stand for this," she threatened, her hand jabbing at the controlling men in the room. "Make the punishment fit the crime. Make his future match the slaughter he and his men committed against mine!"

"Are you calling for war?" Lord Thillian cocked his head at her like a sly fox outwitting its prey. "Our combined countries could easily turn Craigie into a memory, especially after losing many of your warriors. Your people do have a troubled history of losing fights you start, my lady."

Lady Kathilla stood her ground. Since its rebellious founding, the North had been anchored by three immutable principles: freedom, honor, and glory. And there was no honor in complicity in a room that benefited from silence.

"So, my husband's murderer loses his posting and is told to go live out his days in a different court? Meanwhile, my daughter waits at home for her father, who will never come back, and my unborn son will never learn what it is to be a man of Craigie from his father! My court, my people, lost a leader, and I lost my husband, and you expect us to accept this? Without so much as a genuine apology?" She did not care that she was shouting. "You expect the entire continent to accept this slaughter without punishment? To stand for these war crimes without due consequence?"

"Silence! We do expect these things, as will you. If it is compensation you need, then name the amount of coin you desire, and our coffers will find it." Lord Thillian said dismissively. "But if it is vengeance you want, young lady, then more death will befall your people. King Andrius cares not for the North, and his late wife, my sister, hails from our lands, and his son is of our blood. I know he would not mind seeing the North fall. And you will fall if you rise against us."

Lord Thillian stared down the standing Lady of Craigie. Despite losing position, Lady Kathilla did not blink or breathe an inch. Lord Thillian quickly grew tired of their staring game and threw a waving hand in the air, dismissing her anger as he continued.

"No one will speak of the truth of Broken Tower again. My soldiers involved in the battle will be informed to retain their silence, or else they will lose more than their lives. Lady Edgel, I suggest you tell your warriors, the few who survived, the same."

Lady Kathilla, heir to the Stone Throne, Lady of Craigie, daughter of the line that birthed the Great Civil War, would not go quietly. She shook her head and rested her hand on her belly, her voice just above a whisper.

"So, you kill my husband, the Lord of Craigie, and now the truth of his slaughter is to be a secret, and we are to be silenced about what occurred. Tell me, my lords, how is this just leadership?"

"Lady Kathilla, you are young, barely twenty. You do not yet know the intricacies of leadership and the dangers we must fight each day. If this were to get out, if the truth were to be known," Lord Daveed shook his head, attempting to aid Lord Thillian in getting her to understand, "it would be a danger to our alliances and the posterity of our courts."

"So what? Shall we tell everyone that my husband had it coming? That he deserved death?" she argued again, finding her anger amongst her pain.

"We shall keep our records short and brief: a battle of the border occurred and ended with intervention, and many were lost, including Lord Edgel." Lord Thillian said. "That is truly all the history books will care about anyway. Besides, all throughout this kingdom know quite well your husband's attitude and how he was often relentless in his battles and stubborn in his ways. Everyone will make their own decisions on how to feel about what occurred."

"He surrendered! He knew the fight was over and agreed to return home." She shouted and slammed her hands on the table as she screamed at Captain Theodus, "He surrendered, and you murdered him! You murdered them all!"

"Lady Edgel, will you please stop shouting!" Lord Thillian shouted and pressed his fingers to the bridge of his nose.

Lady Kathilla's eyes bulged, and she took several deep inhales as her body shook. She glared down at Lady Catherin sitting dutifully and quietly beside her husband.

"Sister, you shall allow this to happen without a word? Will you let them ruin your brother's name all for the reputation of this court? You will be silent while these men..."

Lady Kathilla's words were lost as she choked on tears that angered her more as they formed—a new determination formed as she raised her hardened face to the room of betrayal and met the silent face of the woman she once called a sister, a friend.

"If this is how it is to be, then fine. But know this: if war, famine, or any pain ever knocks on your doors, despite any aid, comfort, or care the North could bring, we will happily stand by and watch you all burn. And when you all die, Craigie will dance and piss on your sullied graves."

And with that, Lady Kathilla stormed for the door.

"Sister, wait!" Finally, Lady Catherin stood and spoke.

Lady Kathilla stopped at the threshold. She peered over her shoulder for only a moment as she mumbled a reply. "You are no sister of mine and no true daughter of Craigie."

Later that moon phase, in the gardens of Middleton Landing, Ayeshire

Lady Belva Vegaria wrote quickly, the quill in her hand cutting the air with each quick stroke she made in her book. The birds sang their praises around her, congratulating the future Lady of Ayeshire on her academic prowess. The clicking of a cane on the stone pavement did not distract her from her writing as it grew closer. Lord Daveed Vegaria approached with a fond smile; his steps slowed by the weight of years.

"Excuse me, young lady, but have you seen my daughter? The future Lady of the Landing? She is much younger than you, still a little girl, in fact." Lord Daveed Vegaria chuckled as he sat beside her.

Lady Belva laughed softly, glancing up from her writing to meet her father's gaze. "Father, I am fifteen, nearly an adult by law. Your 'little girl' has long since outgrown her childhood."

"Bah!" he exclaimed as he wrestled with the hard stone of the bench beneath him, "Nonsense! Because if you are my daughter and almost an adult, that makes me an old, old man."

She set her hand on his forearm, "Never, father, you are as young as the chickens that hatched this spring."

Lord Daveed laughed and rested his hand on top of hers, giving it a loving squeeze. He let out a long-held breath and nodded as he looked around. His lips were a thin line, and his brow furrowed.

The sudden shift in his demeanor caught Lady Belva off guard. She knew he had come bearing news or a burden that weighed heavily on him. Her brow furrowed in concern as she sensed whether the weight he held would be given to her entirely or shared between the two.

"Belva."

"Yes, father?"

"You remember the lesson I taught you girls when you were young? How, at times, I cannot be your father, and I must instead be your lord?"

She swallowed and stiffened her posture. She took her hand back and closed the book in her lap, resting her hands on the cover. "Yes, I do, my lord."

Lord Daveed's expression grew somber as he broached the delicate topic. "Theodus Montarian is coming to live here." The pause he held was only for a breath, but it felt like an eon for both, "and you will marry him."

"I will what?" she gasped, pure disbelief overtaking her.

Her father's features softened as he reached out to steady her trembling hands. "You need not marry him immediately," he reassured her, his voice gentle but firm. "But after your seventeenth name day, you will become his wife, and he your husband."

She rapidly shook her head. "No. No, I will not."

"Belva."

"No," she shot up, the book falling to the ground with a thud at her feet. She shoved away the trembles that threatened her voice. "No, you told me that I would choose my husband. That I would have a prominent say in the matter of who becomes my lord husband. So no, I reject this proposal."

She stood straight, firming her back and squaring her jaw as if she were in her father's courtroom, addressing the Lord's Council- her future Council- and holding her rightful place.

"There is no proposal for you to accept; this deal is done, and you will marry." Lord Daveed did not bother matching her firmness or posture. He sat with his back still hunched and his posture lazy. His voice had lost its understanding and sympathy and grew into quick irritation.

"What does mother say? Hm? Have you asked her?" she threw her hand toward the noble chamber hall across the garden. "If there is some duty owed to his family, why must it be me who marries him? Why not one of my sisters? Or a cousin?"

"Quit throwing a fit, child." He hissed at her and slammed his cane on the stone. "Do not disappoint—" he huffed and calmed his tone. "Please, Belva, you must understand that sacrifice is a part of our duty and positions. Besides, I thought that you would be happy with this, or at least content, since you have carried feelings for Theodus since you first knew him, have you not?"

She scoffed and threw her hands up. "A schoolgirl crush at times, yes, but I never put any thought into marrying the man!" She noted the distant voices of garden strollers and lowered her own as she crossed her arms and returned to her seat beside him. "Especially not after what occurred at Broken Tower. You told me the truth about what occurred- that Lord Edgel surrendered, but Captain Montarian would not accept that surrender and continued killing them while their weapons lay on the ground. You said I needed to know as your heir to protect that secret alongside our allies. Why would I wish to marry that?"

His hands drummed on top of his cane in front of him. "Theodus is a good man, Belva. He made a horrible mistake, as young men can do. He needs someone to guide and help him learn about leadership and control."

Her mouth fell open, and her brows rose. "And that is to be my job? To lead our country and raise a grown man? To fix him? To cover up his crimes and errors? Oh," she scoffed, "and bear his children for him, too."

He slammed his cane down harder. "This is what ruling is, Belva—making damned decisions in the worst of circumstances and knowing that no matter what you do, it is the best and worst option. Theodus will be a good and loyal husband to you, which you need, and his family, while stripped of their titles in Sebern, come bearing gold and coin that our coffers can live from for quite some time. He will be loyal to you and our family because we have saved him from total disgrace and given him a new life. He will be good to you because he is strong where your knowledge is weak, which is on the battlefield. You will be each other's strengths and beacons. Do you understand?"

Lady Belva sat in silence. Her hardened anger changed into reluctant agreement. She could not get out of this; she did not have a say. No shouting and anger would get her father to hear her.

"You will marry him, Belva. You will make heirs with him. You will rule with him." The Lord of Ayeshire glared at her trembling face. "And you will not disappoint me or disgrace our House's name."

Chapter 1

Autumnia 27, 690AC

"The Fool's Moon burns bright above, and here I stand beneath its mocking light- a trepid fool being called a queen," Lady Belva spoke to herself as she stared out the window of her receiving room. She had been standing in the same place for too long, an attempt to gather herself before she was to stand in front of her Council. Her hands trembled as they wrapped around one another, and her breath shook alongside her throbbing head.

A tear threatened to fall down her cheek, but she quickly brushed it away. She squeezed her eyes shut and bowed her head. "I was so sure the king would avoid a war. That we could raise our banners in secret and, when faced with the choice of war or trial and confession of what all he and his men have done..." she shook her head, "Now I see the folly of not only my optimism but my belief."

A gentle night breeze caressed her face, like a comforting hand brushing her cheek, but she craved no comfort tonight.

In her solace, she needed to break, to release her unsteady thoughts and uncertainties without the prodding comments and peering eyes of those who relied on her stoicism.

Lady Belva took a deep breath, trying to steady her hands and racing thoughts. The peaceful sound of nature outside her window felt like a cruel mockery of the calm she sought.

"A damn fool."

She returned her gaze to the star-studded sky, seeking answers among the guiding constellations. The Journeyman's Hammer and Nail flickered highest overhead, and the Hunter's Wolf and Bow moved higher each night, aiming to dominate the sky's central point when the impending new moon brought its time forth.

The Autumn Equalius had come and gone the knot prior without celebration or grandiose feasting. Instead, her family and the court had been gathered at Sandhill House in preparation for a new battle, and the only gift received had been two heads sent by the king, along with a chilling warning.

Like a dagger to her heart, forcing out a gasping breath, the memory of the king's words fell from her lips, "Peace will only come from your deaths. We hope your bird will sing for us as much as she sang for you."

Lady Belva spoke to the stars above her, hoping one would listen to her hurt and worry. "I have spent my entire life carefully treading and plotting among monsters disguised as men, overthinking and considering every single outcome that could occur with every ruling and every smile I gave, and yet that careful work has led us here. I thought too kindly of the king, of those around me. I thought too highly of others' desire for peace over power and lust for war." She shook her head, "But most of all, I have thought too highly of myself and my influence, and in doing so, I have shamed my House and been granted a title I deserve not."

Despite her confessions, the stars held their glimmer and winked at her where they rested, reflecting their light to her downturned eyes, "Why do the stars reward me so?"

Ancient words whispered in her mind. The Psalms of Fire and Fury played out in her mind's eye, tracing a secret long held, a revelation that would change history once widely known. These words had arrived, hidden in the trunk sent to her at Sandhill House with the traitor's heads and the king's threatening message—the royal line's secret and the prophecy that bound the kingdom in its endless, secret cycle.

The prophecy the king had tried so desperately to hide. The lies that upheld the throne and the Church.

"When the eye of the world has dimmed, and stars have fallen as if made of rain,

Of solid gold and stardust rulers shall remain,

forevermore until burned in fury and in flame

And the world of men shall be made to begin again."

Lady Belva dared not ponder what the king would do to Sister Ora once he learned she had shared such dangerous words with her homeland. Neither could she imagine the horrors unleashed once King Ivan discovered that Lady Belva had spread those words to her allies and the non-allied and silent Houses within the kingdom's walls—to all but His Majesty's pawns.

Her insecurity about her actions and anxiety about the future increased each time those prophetic words came across her mind. The king and those before him had kept the prophecy alive and in the dark—a prophecy that stated the world would end if the golden throne held no ruler. Lady Belva had begun a war to take down the tyrannical king, to put an end to his reign, and to aid in the beginning of a newer, kinder, more equitable rule.

For what she believed was justice, Lady Montarian had begun a war that could end the world.

"A damn stupid fool," she shook her fist and berated herself again.

A knock stole her attention away from her contemplation. Her Council had gathered and now awaited their lady–no, their queen– to call for justice, revenge, blood, or whatever else she wished upon King Ivan and his allies.

Lady Belva left her private room behind and held her head high as she stepped into her Council chambers. Father Robb had been brought in as she had ordered, not as her advisor as he had always been, but as a man of the church to be interrogated. As she looked at him, she used every ounce of energy left within her not to tighten her jaw so hard it cracked, not to shout and shed tears and scream accusations and anger at him.

She had left him behind when she sailed for Sandhill House, where her sister and Lord Bromlyn held sovereignty over a vital part of the southern kingdom. She left him with her son, Lord Taylian, to aid him in leading their people at home while she, her husband, and her oldest son and heir, Lord Digarius, went to war to find allies for what was to come.

And now he sat in front of her, a man who had spent so much of his life and her reign standing in her family's halls advising and teaching the Ayeshire nobles. A man who had dedicated his life to the Church, who hailed from the king's country, who may have been hiding his own secrets all this time.

While Lady Belva knew nothing about *the Psalms*, Father Robb, her High Scholar, must have known, must have betrayed her, and kept this secret.

He must have known that every word he preached and dedicated himself to had been a lie. He held one of the highest positions in the Church throughout the entire kingdom. First, Scholars such as him reported directly to the Head of the Church, Father Figgins, in Isilria, the kingdom's capital. Surely, the Church shared such secrets among those meant to continue its messaging.

She banished the rest of her thoughts as she sat at the head of her table. She refused to wonder if Father Robb knew; did his second, Sister Ora, know this entire time? Did other Scholars know, too? Were they all involved in a secret plot that–

No, we will not become paranoid about everyone around us. We must rule with logic and thought, not fear and paranoia.

Lady Belva improperly rested her elbows on the table and let her face fall into her hands. Her palms rubbed on her cheeks before coming together in front of her face. She crossed her fingers and looked over them at Father Robb, her eyes sharp and unyielding.

Father Robb looked back with broken pain and lost faith in his eyes.

Lady Belva knew that look well; she had worn it on her face these past days, too.

"How much did you know of these, Father?" she finally asked. While not raised or weary, her voice cut through the tense silence, demanding a reply. "How many secrets have you helped the Church keep from us?"

Father Robb stared at the crinkled papers in his shaking hands. His throat clogged, and sweat began to bead on his forehead. Lady Belva watched as he began to break and crack. She let him sit in his pain and panic. She had convinced herself that he must know of these secrets, but she still hoped that he did not.

But how could he not?

"Father Robb. What do you know about the Psalms of Fire and Fury?" Lord Theodus' deep tone and brutal candor reverberated in the quiet space even though he barely raised his voice.

Father Robb stayed quiet, the only noise being his hushed whispers as he flipped through the scrolls and shook his head as he scanned each word. He, like the allies of Ayeshire, received copies days before Lady Belva returned to Middleton Landing.

But this moment was his first time seeing the originals that Lady Belva had been given.

The Lady of Ayeshire let her hands fall and her arms cross on the table. Her voice was still assertive, but she offered a hint of kindness, "Father, please tell us what you know. For the good of the kingdom and our people, what did you know?"

"It really has been all a lie," The First Scholar of Ayeshire mumbled and choked out, his voice barely audible to the angry room. He trembled as he put the parchments down. His glistening eyes met the hardened ones of Lady Belva. "All a lie."

She dropped her chin, her eyes narrowing, but her voice stayed calm. "A lie you knew of?"

Father Robb swallowed and raised his hand to his balding head as he shook it, "This cannot be. It cannot be. How could—"

"Dammit, Father Robb! What do you know?" Lord Theodus slammed his words out as he slammed his fist on the table, making the room jolt.

Lady Belva Montarian shot her glare at her husband, "Lord Montarian, that is enough."

They glared at one another. Lord Theodus' anger came forward at how Lady Belva addressed him, not by name or the like, but as his official title and surname. She knew he hated it when she did that to him, but in this moment, she did not care how little it made him feel.

"Apologies, my lady," Lord Theodus replied curtly, his voice dripping with restrained fury.

The Lady of Ayeshire turned back to Father Robb, ignoring the rest of the Council and guards around her. "Father Robb, I do not wish to fall to darkness with you over this, but I will if I must. I will ask once more in kindness for the truth, but no more than that. Did you know of these? Did you know of this prophecy and the lies that the Church, your Church, have preached around it?"

Father Robb's resolve and demeanor broke into fifty thousand shards, the pain visible through his reddening eyes. His voice cracked and wavered as he confessed.

"I have spent every moment since I sailed here as a young man in oath to this country, your family, and you, my lady. I have spent my entire life dedicated to the true words of The One True, to the god I believed would save us all. And now, at this moment, I have learned that the foundation of my life, of my meaning, is a lie, so please excuse the moments it has taken me to say that I knew nothing of this. I knew nothing..."

The Council held a moment of silent contemplation, waiting for their Lady, their reluctant Queen, to speak- to be the one to breathe the first sigh of relief or to show her disbelief in his words.

She could believe him, yes, or she could find more ways to snuff out lies and the truth if that is not what he had spoken. Father Robb could be truly interrogated, tortured, bent to her will to confess anything that she wished, so she could ensure there were no lies between them. Who knows how many other betrayers stood in her advisory and needed cruelty to come out?

But would she be any better than His Majesty if she did terrible things in the name of what she said was right?

She was tired. Her soul, her body, and her heart had all become so quickly exhausted since the king had come to her home and pushed their alliance apart in the spring with a proposal that doomed so many.

"Very well, then, Father." Lady Belva Montarian let out a breath and nodded once. "You say you did not know, so this Council chooses to believe your confession. But, if I find your words untruthful or your loyalty swaying away from my title, your torn-apart body will be thrown into the pig pens just as Sir Rainey's was after his lies were uncovered. Even in your death, your dishonor will follow you, and you will find no arms of god or ancestors to fall into after this life ends. Do you understand?"

Father Robb nodded, "Yes, Your Majesty."

Lady Belva swallowed at the new title – Hells, how had she not seen it coming? – but she stood with firm resolve. She kept her chin high as she straightened her shoulders and heard the chairs around her move as her Council stood alongside her. "I hope to be merciful, as I have always been. I hope to be caring, as I was taught to be. But I will not be made a fool nor betrayed twice." She scanned the room, her gaze icy and unyielding. "And I will not offer forgiveness when fortune does not favor mercy."

"Yes, Your Majesty," was spoken around the table, and each member bowed their heads at her without hesitation.

Father Robb swallowed from where he still sat, shivering with sadness, his voice cracking again, "They will kill her over this."

The room did not need him to speak a name to know who he meant.

Lady Belva let her jaw shake momentarily before locking away her pain. She firmed her face, her voice a cold steel once again. She loathed how her demeanor kept cracking apart and reforming. "If the king dares to harm Sister Ora, we shall not let her sacrifice be in vain. We raised our banners not in hopes of war, but in warning, in worry over what we believed the king was beginning."

The world must know who truly brought their kingdom to war. She must ensure all knew who bore the real responsibility for her raised banners and declarations and who was truly to blame for the kingdom's current fall.

The history books must remember that the king's mistakes, not hers, caused this war.

"He is the one who began this; he is the one who did not offer us a chance to speak and to stop this path. He is the one who began this war, not I. King Ivan began this war, and I will end it. Let it be known that if he causes more loss, more pain, then I will rain down a vengeance upon him that will make the heavens tremble, and the stars shatter."

CHAPTER 2

Lord Shaital Pathis was not amused, that much his husband and daughter could quickly tell.

"I would very much like to punch him," Lord Shaital mumbled to his husband, Lord Nesima Mete. His tone was flat and bored, matching how he felt waiting for their ship to sail from Ryanar's docks.

"Lord Sebastian is the guild lord here, my love; punching him would be quite uncouth of you." Lord Nesima quietly replied, trying to hide his amusement at his husband's impatience.

Lord Shaital shrugged, his voice still nonchalant and lax. "It would only be uncouth if you deemed it such. You are the Lord of Odessin, and I, your lord husband. Perhaps you could quickly deem violence against annoyances proper acts of court."

Lady Silu Pathis snorted beside her father. "Careful, father, if you allow yourself to be any more riled up, you may fall victim to a failure of the heart."

"My dear," Lord Nesima released a fake worried gasp at Lady Silu's words, "Is this another vision of yours?" He turned back to his husband, sarcasm coating every word he said, "Darling, you must change your path. If you do not, I fear I may lose you to this anger."

Lord Shaital closed his eyes and inhaled deeply, shaking his head slowly. "My own husband and blood daughter, allying themselves against me. I feel as if we were back home many moons ago when you both bore me less wrinkles," he said, but Lord Nesima saw how he did not stop the smile that came across his face.

Lord Shaital was tall and slim, his skin a fawn-colored beige, and his hair kept in short caramel waves—the twin to his daughter's shoulder-length curls. His silk tunic was gold-tinted white and stitched with bright white swirls. Golden square buttons glimmered from his neck to below his torso, where the same fabric made straight-lined pants. Golden slippers adorned his feet, the toe of each shoe coming to a thick point. Diamond-shaped cuts ran along the edges of the boots and down the center.

Everything about how Lord Shaital presented himself was delicately selected and intentionally presented. He liked it that way, and Lord Nesima also liked it that way.

Lord Nesima chuckled and turned away from admiring his husband's very well-fitted clothing. He took in the port around them that they rested upon. Their large caravel bore the face of the dragon on its front, the sigil of Odessin, and sails the shape of dragon wings. Being the lord's ship, extra care had been taken to carve the wood of the hull into scales.

His crew sat on the boat, some playing card games, others leisurely smoking and chatting away as the sun continued falling down the horizon as the late summer afternoon began to wrap up. He tapped his foot on the dock, his brown fabric shoes playing a rhythm of annoyance. The slipper stitching came to a fine point that he wished he could kick Lord Sebastian with.

The Guild Lord was a pompous man and was very much pushing the limits of the power Lord Nesima allowed him to have. As the Guild Lord, Lord Sebastian held much control over the ports and comings and goings of the area, just as much as a real lord when it came down to the brass tacks of it. And Lord Sebastian knew that and enjoyed reminding others of it.

Lord Nesima's thick black hair had subtle streaks of silver throughout, catching the light each time he turned his head to watch the people of the dock. His umber-toned skin matched the deep brown of his round eyes.

Eyes that could only see what was in front of him, unlike his husband and his adopted daughter. The blood of the dragon ran differently through Lord Nesima's bloodline than it did through his husband's. He had been born a dragonblood fighter and strategist, not a dragonblood born with secrets whispering in his mind.

The tattoos peeking out from under his deep, rich orange robe served as a reminder to his people that he had earned his place on the battlefield long before he swore to lead the country. He wore his Dragon warrior belt—a dark leather strap with three gold coin strands hanging off it. White tassels decorated the ends of the metallic strings, brushing against his side each time he moved. The coins a reminder of the victories, the battles, the blood, the sacrifice from his time as a Dragon earning his honor and respect.

The dock was packed with irritable sailors and traders, especially those whose ships bore sigils of the Royal House Scott. After the shipping incident in the early spring, where a departing king's boat sailed into jagged rocks off Dead Man's Walk and fell into pieces into the waters, Lord Sebastian had grown tired of seeing ships from the king's city in his ports and raised inspection fees and port costs on all His Majesty's ships.

Lord Sebastian's anger that spring was not due to the loss of a ship that was not his own, but to what the king refused to do when Lord Sebastian's goods were lost to the waters. To this day, King Ivan still refuses to pay for the goods on his destroyed ship thanks to a ridiculous clause on the trade agreement that one of Lord Sebastian's men had missed.

That man now missed his eyes.

Lord Sebastian claimed that since the man who signed the contract was clearly already blind, he had no need for eyes because even with them, he could not see something as important as a payment clause that cost them countless king's coins.

"Silu, you need not wait here with us. It seems Lord Sebastian is taking his time with his inspections today. You have a long journey ahead of you back to the Dragon's Tower." Lord Nesima said as he looked down the dock, his patience now as thin as his husband's. He grumbled as Lord Sebastian slowly walked with his men towards their ship. "Perhaps I did give him too much power in this city."

"I promised to see you off, fathers," she replied. "Besides, my seers and I would like to collect the seawater, especially that which comes from the shore of Dead Man's Walk." She turned to the south as if she could see the shores of the thin strip of desert land that no soul would ever cross if it wished to make it to the bay. "It carries the spirits of the dead who felled upon the shores, and nothing holds more power than death."

"Let us quit this talk of Seeing. We do not know who may hear," said Lord Shaital firmly.

Lady Silu shrugged and casually replied, "It is not as if His Majesty truly cares for forbidden talk, Father. The lion knows nothing of what the waters will not forget."

"We have not spent generations working in the dark, daughter, to be found out so easily due to a lack of care and open talk of what we See." Lord Shaital whispered as Lord Sebastian finally made his way to their ship.

Queen Onetta crumpled the paper, her fist clenching it for a moment before tossing it to the side, hoping the parchment's sender would feel the pressure.

"Mother? Are you alright?" Princess Arminda queried from her seat. Her perfect posture did not falter for a moment as she loomed over the book in front of her- a catalog of court heraldry through the ages. The late-afternoon sun bathed the garden in a warm glow, casting intricate patterns through the leafy canopy under which they sat while taking their afternoon tea.

"Yes, I am fine." Queen Onetta's tone was clipped as she smoothed the creases of the book she had left open in front of her. "That letter was simply a waste of parchment."

"Did grandfather say anything about the comings and goings of his court as of late?" Princess Arminda casually asked as she turned the page of her book.

The queen's head cocked up at her daughter. Princess Arminda did not look up from her book as she turned to another page and replied. "The parchment from the Isles is redder than most; the wood of the Koa tree has more color than the ones our Scribes use to make their papers." She flicked her eyes up at her mother, her tone suggesting she was merely noting an observation, "and every time he writes, you scowl."

Queen Onetta smirked, not with deviousness or ego but with pride and an impression of her daughter's assessment. "You have always been so observant, haven't you, my darling?"

Princess Arminda's eyes flicked back to her book, her face and tone still deadpan and ungiving. "One must be aware of all nuances if they are to navigate the webs of court. You taught me that."

Queen Onetta nodded approvingly and leaned back in her chair, adjusting the folds of her regal gown. "Your grandfather writes yet another complaint about the succession issue and other drabbles I refused to read."

"Percy is meant to take the title in Thelimor, was he not?" her daughter asked with an air of innocence betrayed by the curiosity and hunger in her eyes. The queen knew her daughter craved more than what her allotment had given her—a future of being a bargaining chip to some random noble who had something the royal family needed.

Just like the queen's future had once been, when what she desired had been taken so cruelly from her by the men who raised her and held rule over her. Becoming queen was a consolation prize, she had decided, when her home, her lover, and her life were disposed of over a chest of gold and a handshake deal between two noblemen who needed allies.

"Yes, that was the plan," said Queen Onetta. "As my second son, it was logical to offer him the title before considering you or another bloodline, as Aisharian custom allows me to do."

"And if he does not wish to take the title?" the princess asked—again, so casually and carefree.

Ever so eager for answers, Arminda.

Queen Onetta smirked in amusement and let out a short breath. "Your brothers' loud quarrel last season made it abundantly clear that you would be next in line if Percy refused the title. I would not overlook you for someone with none of my blood."

Though her eyes remained severe and sharp, a soft smile curved Princess Arminda's lips, a familiar intensity to the queen. "I merely wanted to confirm that this is still your intention, Mother."

Queen Onetta's head tilted, her eyes moved up and down her daughter's silhouette. "It has been so long since you and I have spoken with one another without the prying ears of others and have been able to be brash, honest, and clear on our needs and desires." The queen joined her hands together in front of her, her elbows resting on the arms of her chair. "What is it that you truly want, Arminda?"

Her daughter's face shifted from the youthful innocence she carried at court to an eerie facsimile of the queen's own regalness, before the princess blinked and softened her eyes and jaw again, "I want what is best for our family, for this court, mother. As I always have."

Prince Arminda and Queen Onetta smiled at one another, but neither of their smiles showed their teeth or reached their eyes. As their eyes held one another, Queen Onetta's smile fell into its resting thin line. She let out a sigh as memories of her own past overcame her. Her eyes flicked down and then away from her daughter.

She took in the vast gardens she held domain over—her personal project as queen, the same as the royal women before her. It had become one of the only spaces in the kingdom and near the throne where she had no one to question her or answer to.

She turned back to her daughter, "These gardens have always been my favorite place within these walls. When I first came here at nineteen, betrothed to your father, I fired countless garden keepers because they refused me the one thing I wished—a small house, even just a room, in the center of these gardens and built only for me. I wanted it made of the same stone that my home was forged from on the Isles. If he could have, King Andrius would have had my head for even asking for that, let alone using my title to hold power over some of his staff.

"Your father," the queen struggled with a fond smile that jumped onto her face, "Your father defended me firmly against him."

"Father has his flaws, as we all do, but he has always tried with us." Princess Arminda's face fell. "Well, he did once."

"Yes, he did." Queen Onetta replied. "Darling, when I come to you and tell you how you may best serve this kingdom and our family, I only ask that you find something pleasant within it as I have. Find your garden."

"Yes, Mother." Princess Arminda replied too obediently, too calmly.

"Find some way to make true power for yourself."

"Yes, Mother."

The queen's teeth ground back and forth, "And find a way to understand, and someday forgive, whatever decisions the crown must make for you."

"Mother," Princess Arminda leaned forward slightly- a hair's breadth of movement, "is this a warning of something to come, or is this simply advice over tea?"

Queen Onetta refreshed her cup of tea, "What is advice but a warning given in kindness?"

CHAPTER 3

King Ivan stood near the open balcony doorway of his chambers, letting the cool afternoon breeze and warm sun run over him as he fastened the hook-and-eye finishes on his red doublet. He ran his fingers along the collar around his neck to ensure it lay smoothly and covered the dry red patches crawling up his neck. He checked the cuffs on his wrists, fidgeting awkwardly with the hooks at the ends, again pulling and adjusting the fabric to cover the marks on his skin.

After ensuring everything was in place, he picked up a dark bundle of fabric folded neatly on the table nearby- a pashmina shawl of charcoal black with a paisley pattern embossed in glimmering gold- and folded the long fabric over his left shoulder, wrapped it under his right arm and back over his left shoulder- grunting and grumbling as he worked the fabric, trying to recall how it was meant to be draped.

The king never did pay much mind when his valet dressed him.

He fidgeted a moment more with the pashmina before running his fingers along the embroidered collar of the doublet for a third time. Needlework of greenery and lions stitched in the same color as the red fabric added texture to his touch as he caressed down the center, continuing to the bottom hem.

He grunted again, this time his aggravation directed at his tremoring fingers. "Stop it, dammit," he whispered to his hands. "I said stop."

He clenched his fists, "My own body refuses to listen to the commands of its king."

He shook his hands out, pushed his overgrown hair back off his forehead, and set his crown atop it. The crown's jewels and metal shimmered amongst his fading hair; the short, hammered gold peaks were decorated with various cuts of red garnet, orange citrine, and clear diamonds. He fidgeted even more with the crown than he had with his clothing, struggling to place it properly on his head.

How in the Hells did all of this gilded wrapping stay on him?

"What happened to your valet?" Prince Percy inquired from the open bed-chamber door.

King Ivan jerked his head towards the door, surprised that he did not hear his son's entry. He grumbled before responding, "He has been growing increasingly irritating lately, so I sent him off."

Prince Percy strolled into the room, squinting at his father's sunken eyes, puffy face, and hair messily laid under the crown atop his head. Prince Percy's clothing stood in stark contrast to his father's bold fabrics. He wore an unpretentious, dark grey doublet with a swirling pattern of brushed bronze stitched into it and plain black trousers. Around his waist lay a simple, thick, brown belt, and his curls, which were recently trimmed, were neatly pushed back off his face.

He treaded slowly on his words. "It seems many servants and people have been irritating you lately."

"Yes, well, apparently, we have more imbeciles than competent individuals in our kingdom these days." As the king spoke, he grabbed a glass of amber liquid on the table and brought it to his lips.

"Do you really need to be drinking so early in the day?" Prince Percy now stood alongside his father, his hands clasped behind his back.

So arrogant. So aggravating.

Stop it.

"You do not get to query me, Percy," the king gritted out without thought or care behind his words. He gripped the crystal glass tighter, the tension making it shake in his hand. "I should not need to remind you of your place."

The words came out too quickly to be stopped.

"No, you need not do that, father. I know my place. I am but a backup plan should the unthinkable happen to Elion and be a placeholder while he is away. I have been taught that my entire life, so I know my place quite well." Prince Percy found courage that his father didn't know he was capable of: "But I am also your son, and I have a right to be concerned about my father." While his tone was hard and sharp, his eyes were filled with hurt and pain.

Upon noticing the hurt, King Ivan broke his look at Prince Percy. But he still swigged back the entire glass of his drink.

Stop it. King Ivan told his temper while he still held a sense of control over it. *Stop it, dammit.*

"We are late for the Council meeting you have called. Shall we go now, or would you like me to inform the others that the meeting will be delayed?" his son asked.

"No. Let us go." the king replied flatly.

Prince Percy held his hand out to pause his father at the doorway, shaking his head and pursing his lips, "You really must make amends with your valet," he said as he took the shawl off his father's shoulder and laid it on the dresser before turning for the door. "Quite tacky."

The two walked silently, their King's Guards surrounding them as they walked through the halls towards the King's Council chambers. The drunken calm lurked at the edges of the king's mind; the voices that whispered and shouted to him began to still- the haze muffling their words.

They were easier to quiet and ignore in the daylight.

Down the hall they walked, and a door slammed shut. Young laughter rang out as pairs of tiny footsteps raced across the stone. King Ivan looked up in the direction of the noise. The ghosts of a young Prince Elion, Prince Percy, and Princess Arminda raced down the hallway, giggling and shouting as they ran.

"Papa! You can't get us!" the phantom of Princess Arminda shouted as she disappeared into the wall behind her brothers. "You've lost us!"

King Ivan jerked to a halt and gasped. He snapped his head toward Prince Percy beside him—his young boy, now fully grown, who looked at him with worry and pain.

"Father?" Prince Percy asked. "Are you alright?"

The panicking king swallowed and blinked several times, turning his eyes back and forth between his son and where he saw the ghosts.

"Yes, I'm... Percy, I owe you an apology. Some days, I forget myself, and it seems today has been one of them." King Ivan's voice took on as much sincerity as he would allow it to. "It has been hard these days to be the king."

King Ivan did his best to ignore the long, inspecting stare that Prince Percy gave him. "Father, I worry not only about this realm but of you." The prince stepped closer to him, "Ever since Lord Orville passed, and even times before then—"

The midday bells echoed through the hall, cutting off the prince and jostling the king's momentary peace.

"Father, perhaps we can undo what has been done and make things right in the kingdom," Prince Percy harshly whispered and grabbed his arm.

The fading bells continued to ring, Prince Percy's breath spat at His Majesty, and a familiar fog reached out and wrapped its claws around the king's mind, choking his senses.

"Make what right?" King Ivan snapped; his voice hushed. "I have done what I must, done what needs to be done to control the kingdom."

"We do not need to control it; we need to save it, father."

"I am!" The king shouted. King Ivan rubbed his face and turned away from his son and the onlooking King's Guards. He looked up at the wall to see his father looking down at him.

No. No. No. No. No.

King Andrius's face stood out against the sharp, black-painted canvas. Glaring down at King Ivan were two deep brown eyes, sunken into a cold face with full cheeks. Between his glaring, emotionless eyes, a long, skinny nose ran down towards his thin lips. His peachy-white face was surrounded by wrinkles of old age, short grey hair, and a full beard that reached his collarbone.

Atop his head sat a crown much like King Ivan's current crown, but with more gaudy stones and gold. King Andrius wielded a sword with a gold hilt and intricate filigree grip- a blade of kings and conquerors.

The Conqueror's Sword had been passed down from monarch to monarch and now sat on display in the gallery beside the throne room. Looking at the painting, one would think the man in it was in his late nineties, not barely seventy, when he died and the painting was commissioned.

There was no emotion, no love or softness in the brush-stroked canvas. Out of everything the painter got exact, that was the most accurate.

"It has been eight epochs, and I can still feel that bastard's anger and malevolence everywhere- and on days such as this, I find myself much like him." King Ivan grumbled- the shock of seeing his father's eyes pushed back the fog that clouded and warped his mind.

"He never was one for emotions outside of his anger." Prince Percy scoffed and stepped beside him, "I still recall the lashings each time one of us attempted to call him grandfather instead of Your Royal Highness or any of his other titles."

"He was nothing but an unforgiving and brutal king in his life, even in his final moments. Almost as horrendous as his father before him." King Ivan angrily mumbled as he glared at his father's painting.

Did the crowns they all wore taint them with their gilding? Or did the men who wore them tarnish the gold until it faded?

Next to King Andrius's painting hung another. This one was warm, soft, and kind. The painting was of King Ivan's late mother, Earla Torrin, who was not even eighteen when she died from a complicated pregnancy with her and King Andrius' third child. She had long, soft chestnut hair that fell in full waves around her, a freckled button nose, bright, rosy cheeks, and equally bright eyes of ocean blue. While her body had been worn and tired from her young years of motherhood, her face still held the glow of youth and innocence that King Andrius could never take from her, no matter how much he tried.

Many believed she would have made a beautiful and kind queen- almost as loved as Queen Oriana was before the thievery of her throne during the Royal Civil War- had Earla only had the chance to live long enough to be crowned.

King Ivan softened as he remembered her embrace. Her love.

"I'm glad the aides found her painting." King Ivan mumbled, his voice far away and melancholy. "I'm glad they didn't throw it away as my father demanded and instead hid it from him until his death. For once, I am thankful our people disobeyed the crown."

"Father," Prince Percy swallowed, his tone timid and nervous, "I may have never known her, but I know what she was like from the stories passed down." He let out an anxious breath, "I do not believe she would be happy with the road we have walked."

How dare he? How dare he say that, Your Majesty?

The voices.

No, not now. Please, leave me be.

King Ivan heard his son's words, but his mind twisted them into accusations and malice again. The haze finished taking over his mind, but between the waves of fog, he felt a pull. At one time, that pull had been a cry for help, but in this moment, it was a pull to drown more in the numbing liquor, to not be cognizant of what he would say or do next. To not know.

King Ivan turned; his pace set back in their direction to the King's Council chambers. "You do not get to speak of her."

Brother,

It has been more than three phases, a whole season, since you put on your armor and left for battle. With all that has occurred here, it feels like much more than that. I do not understand how one kingdom can fit so much treachery and pain into such a small span of time.

Then again, it seems we are all capable of much more than we have let on during our times of peace and quiet.

She betrayed me. She betrayed our family. And yet, I still find my heart pauses and skips when I think of her.

You were right when we fought. Love can be a folly, a weakness. Care can be as well. I have learned that, to the detriment of my heart and our family. I have become nothing more than a man stitched together by his mistakes, and I wish for them to be undone.

Much more, I wish for our childhood to return to us, or even our adulthood before too much of our titling and inheritances had begun to divide us from one another and fold and bend us into the men the kingdom wished for us to become. Men forged to uphold what fallacies and structures exist and allow us to continue on this way.

I know what they did was treason, but Father Penn and Lord Orville kept the kingdom from falling into itself for so long. Lord Orville did so much for our city- he fed the poor and made sure we taxed those who hoarded too much- made sure they gave back to those whose labor filled the richest man's coffers. He spent his time ensuring you would stand alongside the people you would one day rule. He reminded both of us that we were meant to stand with, not above, the people we would lead.

And Father Penn always kept my head in the stars.

And in my books.

What if they were the last good men left? What if we are not as good as they taught us to be?

We have upheld so many lies. How can we claim to be good simply because we occasionally speak against lies behind closed doors where no one else can hear us? When we only lend our aid to those in need when we know it will be seen? How can we claim to have any goodness in us when we hold our loyalty to blood that spills so much of it for their gain?

Prince Elion rolled up the letter from Prince Percy without finishing it. The letter had been dated two knots earlier on the 16th of Autumnia.

The Heir to the Throne burned the letter by candlelight, holding the parchment until it became ash against his calloused and dirt-stained fingertips. His brother spoke words of treason—words that would have a man hanged—but the crown prince did not let a soul know of it.

Prince Elion exited his tent. He did not wish to read more letters from the castle, words from his father, or the King's Council shouting at him and demanding a successful siege of Ravenhall by the season's end. Prince Elion stifled back the feelings that came over him: the feeling of his shoulders sitting softer on his body and his mind more at ease the longer he stayed on the battlefields and slept in war tents, not the Crown Prince's eccentric chambers.

Here, he let himself think again. *The rules of leadership are much simpler. Here, I do not have to earn respect through sleuthing and politicking.*

While he genuinely did not hope to be a prince left forever in a battle nor a king over a crumbling kingdom, the Crown Prince did not miss the days he spent in long meetings with conniving men. He did not miss his father's scowling face, which looked too much like his grandfather's, the longer the crown sat atop King Ivan's head.

The prince made his way through the main center of the war camp that still sat upon the lands surrounding Lake Lahere. The weather had been muggy, and he did not wish to sweat and feel misery under the weight of armor or the fanciful tunics he had to wear often. He wore his simple linen undershirt and dark pants, blending in well with the sweating soldiers around him.

The sounds of a fresh cask of ale being opened called to him as he approached a lounging and laughing group of foot soldiers enjoying their drink and gambling.

"Lots of new armor fresh from training has joined us. Did you see some of them?" a female soldier gruffed to her comrades, "They're in for a hell of a surprise when we get on the field."

Another laughed, "Seems like they're willing to put any able-bodied into war these days. If you fit into some armor well enough, they'll send you off to join us."

The prince did not interrupt the conversation he came upon, and his presence was not seen among the crowd of relaxing men and women. His ears picked up another conversation beside him.

"Here's my thing. I don't want to die dumb. When I die on that field, I want it to take at least four men to kill me."

Prince Elion's thoughts caught hard on the soldier's phrasing.

When I die.

The prince turned from the keg of ale he had taken a pour from. "What happened to fighting to win? To the confidence of victory?" he asked.

"Hah!" the older fighter, his beard short and white, laughed as he turned, "That died when our scouts counted their men."

The fighter's face paled to match his aging whiskers, "My lor— my prince," he cleared his throat, "My apologies."

Prince Elion shook his head and waved his hand, gently dismissing the apology, "Are you apologizing for speaking lies, or did you mean what you said and are only sorry I heard you?"

The soldier looked to his full cup for the answer and gave none to the prince. Prince Elion noted that the crowd around them had silenced, and that worry had threaded itself through each of those gathered.

"No matter the size of the army, any battle is lost if you walk onto the field preparing to lose, preparing for your death. We may lose, yes, but we will not fight for a defeat; we will fight for a victory. We fight with our swords, arrows, and shields, but we fight most with our minds and hearts." The prince scanned the group of foot soldiers again, "When our greatest weapons are broken before the sound of the horns, our battle is already lost. Do not willingly break your hearts and minds because you are afraid and unsure."

Uneasy glances were exchanged among the crowd, and uncertainty hung in the air; unspoken fear and worry clung to each body beside the prince. Prince Elion would be a liar if he admitted to his army that he did not feel uncertainty or worry about being outnumbered so heavily by their enemies. But he would be a fool of a future king if he told them how scared he had been since he went from practicing his swordsmanship in the safety of the castle to leading an army in a war that became much too real, much too quickly.

"I understand your doubts, your worries," Prince Elion began again, steadying his voice and making an effort to speak less like a prince and more like a commander. "I know what it is like to leave behind those you love, to worry you will never see them again. But I leave behind no great love, no children- and many of you do. I will not pretend I stand here feeling the same pain and sorrow as you all, but I will stand here and ask that you remember what it is you have left waiting for you at home. We did not begin this war; our enemies did. We did not ask you to leave behind your families out of a passion for more power, but out of love for those you left behind. I do not ask you to fight only for my father's crown; I ask you to fight for them."

The Crown Prince raised his chalice, "For them," he chanted.

"For them," the crowd chanted back.

The prince did not linger long after that. He made his way through the camp, weaving between the tents and fires, his mind still heavy with the words of his brother's letter. Even in the moment of unity, Prince Elion could not escape the doubts that gnawed at him, the shadows of his brother's words.

What if they were the last good men left? What if we are not as good as they taught us to be?

Prince Elion clenched his fists as his eyes met the closed flaps of his tent. He pushed himself inside and let himself take a deep breath that ached to escape.

I was taught to be this. Our laws and our lies are for the good of the realm.

Everything I do is for the good of our people.

I am a good man.

Prince Elion spent the rest of his night tossing and turning in his bed, reminding himself of all the good deeds he had done. Each time a terrible memory fell across his mind, he countered it with conviction of its necessity for the greater realm.

As he finally drifted off into a fit of sleep, final fighting thoughts whispered to him.

I am the Heir to the Throne and I am a good man.

Aren't I?

CHAPTER 4

R*un.*

Sir Loren mouthed a single word to her as their eyes locked for the last time.

Run.

So, she did.

Sister Ora, with chains around her wrists, pulled free and fled from the platform. She had stood in horror beside the indifferent royal family, who didn't care about her disappearance, as her lover and friend were both beheaded before a crowd of fear-filled onlookers. She ran from Prince Percy, who stood beside her flat-faced and sure-footed; no acknowledgment came from him as she was put in chains. She ran from the queen, who smiled at her as she shrieked and stumbled away from her cold-clawed grip, the chains rattling as Sister Ora ran.

But she did not run far.

Sir Marion stepped into her path, once leaning casually against a stone pillar, awaiting her retreat from the execution he aided in orchestrating.

She fought, she clawed, she screamed.

He laughed as he threw her to the ground.

His dark eyes bore into her being; she saw her reflection thrashing in his terrifying glare. She saw the glimmer of the High Scholar pin she still wore to her chest. The pin that meant nothing anymore, a symbol of who she once was but would not be again.

"Stop fighting." He snarled as he grappled her thighs while she pushed herself out from under him. Sister Ora threw her torso upward, swinging her arm wide as she did, slashing the sharp blade of the Scholar's lapel pin into his face, the fabric from her dress clung to it from where she tore it off.

He swung back, a heavy fist thrown with all its might into her face while blood ran down his cheek. Her vision went black, and her body was dragged across the ground.

Sister Ora bolted up in bed, sweat covering her, the scream that escaped her as hoarse as the last one.

"Shut up!" a shout came from the other side of the chamber door, followed by a loud kick on the wood frame.

She shot out rapid thoughts.

Breathe. Breathe. Breathe. She told herself.

Between shaking breaths, she heard a strange rattling of metal on her lap. Her breathing steadied as her mind returned to the land of the living. Her eyes fell on the small pitcher of water on the bedside table, her raw throat begging for a drink to soothe the pain. She moved to sit up and retrieve it, but her body stopped halfway as the cold metal cuffs around her wrists prevented her from moving off the bed.

And then she remembered.

She rubbed her wrists, the pain from the fresh scars filling in the gaps that her haunted memories made her forget so she could survive. The cold chain attached to the cuff dropped flakes of rust on the single pillow she had. The bed, which felt more like a cot with all the amenities now removed, did not hold a single shred of luxurious comfort it once did.

How much time had passed since she was thrown in here?

She was not in prison, but she was trapped all the same. Her head fell back on the sweat-stained pillow; a forceful choking cry tried to break through her shallow breathing as she closed her eyes and blocked out the darkness covering her night-fallen room.

As quickly as her eyes closed, they opened to bright light and soft knocking at her door.

"Miss, it is time to wake." The soft, timid voice of her lady's maid, Kaylah, came through the grains of the door's wood. Her lady's maid creaked the door open and timidly walked to her bed, sitting beside her.

"Do you wish to wake today?" Kaylah asked, her voice soft and kind as it always was.

Sister Ora moaned and pushed her face farther into the pillow.

She did not deserve kindness.

A soft, sad breath escaped Kaylah. "At least eat something today, miss, please. If you don't eat or drink something... they will make me send him in."

Sister Ora heard Kaylah delicately set a small plate of food on the table beside Sister Ora's silent body. Kaylah sighed and stood up.

"I will be back tomorrow, miss, as I have been every morn since that cursed day."

"How many da'es has it been?" Sister Ora asked, defeat and misery hung on every word.

"Six."

Sister Ora closed her eyes again and curled into herself as she listened to Kaylah retreat and the door close behind her. The cold metal of the chains brushed against her fragile skin, chilling her to the bones once well hidden under soft curves, now closer to the surface, threatening to burst through in a short time.

It had been six days since she last ate, last saw the light, last knew some semblance of freedom.

Last felt hope.

Or anything.

Let them pierce my skin and bleed me dry. Let them take me to find my Loren in death. She thought as she groaned to cover the noises of her empty stomach.

Let me starve and die and rid them of this pawn that I am.

She forced her eyes closed until blackness overtook her mind again, and she fell into another fitful slumber.

Let me go.

Let me choose one last thing.

Let me die.

Chapter 5

"… and may the light of the Vahar bless your soul as it crosses from our plane to theirs." Lady Kathilla Edgel knelt on the marshy ground, her head resting against the pommel of her sword that she had staked into the earth. With her right hand centered on her chest, she finished her prayer, releasing her hand in an arch before her.

The field was a gruesome sight, still littered with the bodies of fallen desert fighters draped in golden orange silk and brute warriors in dark fur cloaks. The air was thick with muggy heat and the acrid scent of iron. Lady Kathilla had yet to clean the blood from her body, leaving her clothes stained red like the holy lands they fought upon. The blood of her fallen fighters and enemies pooled in the streams, joining the waters of their ancestors.

The Queen of the North rose from the small pile of bodies before her and bowed her head in reverence, honoring her fallen people one last time before moving on.

She was too tired from the lengthy battle to feel proud or boastful about the successful border camp raid. Upon the surrender of the border camp, the Odessians once again lay defeated in mixed pools of blood or had been sent away by the victorious Craigie warriors.

Even in her anger, Lady Kathilla would never kill a man who dropped his weapon and surrendered his battle. Even in her anger, she still had honor.

That was what the North was born upon.

The ache in her chest grew heavier as she felt the familiar breezes of the Land of a Thousand Rivers. Their next camp raid would occur where Lord Frasier Edgel, her late husband, had lost his final battle just outside the shadows of Broken Tower.

And then the lands would finally be theirs.

He would be home. She would make his soul's resting place part of the North, and he would be home.

Lord Fraser Edgel should have returned alive from that shadowed land to lament his failed pillaging efforts to his pregnant wife. Instead, Lady Kathilla felt his soul still wandering these lands alongside her ancestors who had fought valiantly for their freedom in the Great Civil War.

He had surrendered, just as many of their ancestors had ages ago, and yet he did not get to return home as they did.

Instead, the prior Lords of Sebern and Ayeshire had rewarded the man who led the slaughter of her surrendered soldiers. Instead, Commander Theodus Montarian was sent south to become a lord, and her people were encouraged, no, forced, to be silent lest the North fall.

She spit on the ground.

One day, her people would be numerous enough to speak out about what happened and find the strength to seek revenge or justice.

Justice and revenge were the same when the answer to the crime was blood. Lady Kathilla did not care what they would call. History would change the words anyway.

Every tyrannical leader in their history, in their ledgers and in the lies of their legends, had once been a young fighter, hopeful that righteousness would triumph. But power breeds darkness, and its shadows always claw at justice until the shredded remains transform into vengeance.

As Lady Kathilla began to ascend the hill, a group of her men tossed aside a golden-wrapped Odessian soldier with half-hearted attention and no care. She stopped her tired ascent and firmly addressed them.

"No, we will still respect them, especially on these holy lands. Leave their bodies for their people to collect and complete their own funeral rites. We only touch ours." She continued uphill, a limp in her walk that she overcompensated to avoid showing. The knife wound was not that deep; she had recovered from far worse.

"Mother, you are hurt," Barron murmured as his mother met with his stride.

"Do not worry. Thirdall will not claim me yet. She is not as stubborn as I; it is just a small wound."

Thirdall was the goddess of life, birth, and death to those who worshiped the Vahar, gods and goddesses who created man before they created the earth.

The Vahar were forbidden to worship, but in the North, they cared not for the laws of men, only those of their gods. If the king found their beliefs disturbing, he could ride north, tell the northerners to their faces, and silence them with armies.

But no king would.

Since the Great Civil War, no king bothered with the North; they were not worth the crown's important time.

"You should still have a Healer look at it," her son said.

She grunted as they moved, the pain increasing as the incline pushed her more. "And I will, but we have much work to do first."

Her daughter and heir stood atop the hill, watching the skies for the messenger hawk she had sent west.

"Hello, mother, brother," Gladys greeted, her eyes still glued to the clouds. "Mother, you are hurt."

Lady Kathilla grimaced as Barron chuckled.

The shadow of a hawk broke the sky of clouds and scavenger birds, swooping down as Gladys extended her leather-wrapped arm. The dark bird landed on the leather sleeve decorated with claw marks and indents, shuffling its feathers as it settled. Gladys untied the parchment tied to its claw, uncoiling it with her free hand.

Barron moved beside her, taking a small piece of meat and feeding it to the hawk impatiently waiting for its reward. The hawk crawled up her leather sleeve and perched on her shoulder, his claws carefully avoiding clamping onto her thick red curls and braids.

"What news does the West bear for us?" Lady Kathilla asked. She watched her daughter's expression as she read the letter, her eyes and expression twin to Lady Kathilla's icy blue eyes and firm, pale features.

"Madam Fury is coming east to fight." Gladys paused, "She must have ignored the call of her Lords to head south to the king's war and instead turned her Dragons around to come for us. How unexpected."

"Or perhaps she sent others south in her stead?" Barron asked, petting the hawk.

Lady Kathilla had naively hoped to avoid crossing paths with Madam Fury and her Dragons, though deep down, she knew their clash over scimitar and battle axe was inevitable. Their countries had been fighting for generations. The two women were fated to hate one another long before Lin Furia was titled Madam Fury and made commander of Odessin's Dragon Army and before Lady Kathilla ascended the Stone Throne of Craigie. Had the two women's spirits met before they formed in their mother's wombs, they would indeed have fought then, too.

While Odessin, before the land was titled or its people freed from their chains, did aid Craigie in fighting the king during the Great Civil War, the northern lands that were split apart and divided between Craigie and Odessin became the turning point in what could have been a solid alliance leading to long-term peace.

Odessin gained their freedom and own lands after the war ended, but that land had been stolen from Craigie. And those in Odessin were too bull-headed and selfish to realize the lands outside of the shadows of their desert mountains were not theirs to claim or be gifted.

Lady Kathilla's strategic patience in waiting to seize the Odessin border camps until Madam Fury was summoned away had borne fruit this past season, with many of the western Odessian camps taken with little battle and much ease. Only basic soldiers and guards had been close enough to the border to aid in fighting when news broke out of the attacks. No Dragons had been brought in to slaughter her people with their fire weapons and brutal attacks.

If their final fight was swift, Craigie might be able to seize the rest of the border before Madam Fury's Dragons arrived to drive them away. If that occurred, then the Dragons would have nothing left to fight for. Her warrior blood pulsed with the thought of facing Madam Fury in battle, to take on an enemy genuinely worth her time.

Any worry over a fated battle between her adversary and herself was extinguished as Lady Kathilla tasted victory on her teeth. She smiled; memories fell over her. "It has been a while since I have seen her. Battle will make for a wonderful reunion."

Gladys crumpled the parchment and set the hawk free to join the other birds soaring above the battlefield, searching for a meal to scavenge. Around the family, more forbidden prayers were said over the fallen, more bodies were laid to be burned with honors, and more vengeance and fury were lit aflame.

The sun was unforgiving in its heat, its rays burning down from where Soluar watched in the sky as if the old god was filled with the same heated vitriol as those gathered in the room of the Odessian border camp.

Lin Furia held back her rage, but only because the man crawling in front of her did not deserve the quick death that her released temper would grant him.

He deserved to suffer.

He deserved a punishment far worse than what the Seven Hells would grant his soul when she delivered the shredded remains of it to the Hell Keeper.

Madam Fury's chest rose and fell in measured breaths below her golden tunic, a shade brighter than the Dragons of Odessin she led, the color indicating her position as their leader. Like the tremendous golden dragon Vinicarius, who led the conquest of the continent seven hundred eons ago, Madam Fury incited deadly fear when her gold silhouette appeared on the horizon of a battlefield.

She rolled a bronze Dragon pin between her fingers. Encircled in a ring of carved metal was a roaring, scaled dragon head, its eyes made of tiny, glinting rubies and its teeth sharp and menacing- sharp enough that the pin itself could cause damage if wielded in a fight. The dragon's scales were meticulously detailed; the forgers had taken great care to create the piece.

This pin was not merely an ornament like the pins of noble Houses or guilds; it symbolized honor, duty, and unparalleled strength. The right to wear one was highly sought after, and a prestigious recognition granted only to those who had demonstrated the highest valor and prowess.

Runes and swirls ran over the back of Madam Fury's hand and along her fingers. The markings revealed more hidden paintings beneath her attire, the dark lines flexing on her hand as her muscles tensed. Her fingers twitched as they felt the curves of the pin.

The Dragon pin would be added to the existing pile of pins taken from others. Her soldiers had promptly ripped the pin from the pathetic man's chest when they dragged him into the hall.

Monsters like him were not worthy of calling themselves Dragons.

"So you admit to doing this?" Her voice was smooth, unbothered, and untempered, more terrifying in its calmness than if she were to shout.

"As I had said, Madam Fury, I was drunk and, and, and angry. I took it out on her without thinking," he turned towards his wife, surrounded by soldiers and wearing her black eye without shame, only anger. "I told you I was sorry."

"Speaking to her is a privilege. You do not. Have. Privileges." Madam Fury snarled, almost leaping from her seat as she stood. The gold of her eyes flared as she made for him. Her sleek, long black hair was held in thick braids running down her back that swished as she moved. Like a crown atop her head, four crescent moon-shaped blades were woven into the braids, the last blade falling at the nape of her neck, all within easy reach to pull out of her strands and wield if needed.

The guard holding the man's arm shoved his face forward to meet Madam Fury's glare. "I apologize, Madam. Please forgive me for my sin."

Her voice returned to its cold, calm tone. "You do not get to ask that of me, nor anyone else. We do not grant forgiveness to men like you. But we will ensure that you will never raise a hand to her, or any other, again." She bent over, now a hair's breadth away from his shaking frame. She leaned in, her golden eyes turning black.

"And do you know why?" she sneered.

He shook his head, his whole body trembling.

"Because dead men cannot beat their wives."

The man looked around the room in shock, only to be met with venom-filled glares. His fellow soldiers, war healers, and advisors offered no kindness to him, having already cemented their support of any punishment long before he was dragged inside.

"Madam Fury, please, I am—"

She stood straight and addressed the room, loud enough for all gathered outside its canvas walls to hear, "— an abuser, a lowlife, dishonorable and unworthy of serving alongside me or any soldier in my army."

She lowered her tone to address him directly again, "You are barely worthy of being the meal for our war hounds, but," she cocked her head, the sun catching on her teeth and the glimmer of the blades in her hair, "- they are quite hungry and in desperate need of a good meal."

As his cries of protest rang out, she walked back to the head of the room, shouting over her shoulder at the soldiers, "Take him to the hound pit and slit his ankles so he cannot run."

"Yes, Madam." The guards replied over his shrieking. They had already begun dragging his thrashing body out of the tent when she gave the order.

"What an embarrassment." Madam Fury mumbled as he begged and cried for mercy before spitting vitriol at her.

The room stood silent, not in disappointment, disagreement, or anything of the like, but in obedient satisfaction over their leader's decision. A laughing voice rang out outside the tent flaps as vicious barks and growls rose.

"Who's hungry for a good meal?!" the guards shouted, laughing.

The last sound heard of the abuser was his screams as the ring of an unsheathed blade sliced the air, followed by the sounds of slitting flesh.

Madam Fury threw the man's Dragon pin into a metal bowl filled with the other remnants of past soldiers who committed sins that could not be forgiven.

During the formative seasons of Odessin, when dangerous men ruled the lands of prisoners and "undesirables," calling oneself a Dragon did not hold as much honor as it now did. In the past, when their people were so desperate for their freedom and so fragile in their newfound stability, Odessin did not care much for honor among their warriors; all they desired was aid from those who craved blood and held no issue in spilling it in the name of freedom.

Her ancestors had quickly become fools for giving weapons to men who murdered for fun and who had voices in their heads telling them to inflict pain. It took far too long for Odessin to rid themselves of the monsters that lurked among all of the innocents who did not deserve a life spent in prison chains and stained cells.

Her lip twitched, and her brows creased, muddying the black ink swirls on her face that formed into a dragon.

Monsters did not get to become Dragons.

Not again.

Chapter 6

"My lady." Sgt. Emaline Kingery stood in the open doorway of Lady Belva Montarian's office. "May I speak to you?"

"Yes, yes, of course. Come in." Lady Belva replied from her desk, setting down the parchments and quill in her hand. "What is it?"

Emaline closed the door behind her, the click of the latch sounding unnaturally loud in the quiet room. She walked slowly to the desk, her movements hesitant. Her feet shifted back and forth as if she couldn't decide whether to advance or retreat. Her fingers were busy rubbing her mother's coin in her pocket, a nervous habit she couldn't control.

"Emaline, is everything all right?" Lady Belva's brow crumpled in concern; she tilted her head as she took in the sergeant's agitation.

"No, no, my lady," Emaline said, her voice barely above a whisper, her hands fidgeting at her sides. She paused, struggling to find the right words, then asked, "May I speak freely? I fear that if I must maintain my decorum, I will not be able to say what needs to be spoken."

"Of course." Lady Belva shrugged; her own hands joined on her desk. "You may always do so if needed."

Emaline inhaled deeply as if preparing to plunge into ice water or a battle. She looked straight at her lady. "Why have you done nothing to get Ora back?"

Lady Belva's face broke into angered shock.

"She was sent there because of His Majesty and you. You did not fight against his wishes of her engagement because of court politics, and now..." Emaline shook her head rapidly, her hand flexing on her sword's pommel. She now avoided looking at the Lady of Ayeshire, her words spilling out in a rush. "I was forced to leave her side and return home, but you were not forced to send her away. It is only a matter of time before the king..."

She huffed, shaking out her hands as if trying to dispel the tension coiled there. She kept waiting to be cut off and shouted at. "He took those men's heads and delivered them to your doorstep. He threatened much worse to her in his letter. Why is there no effort being made to save her? It is as if—" Emaline shook her head again, cutting off her words.

"No, Sergeant, please finish." Lady Belva said firmly.

Emaline finally raised her eyes, her gaze locking onto Lady Belva. "It is as if you do not care about her."

"This is a delicate situation. It is complicated." Lady Belva attempted to reassure her, but Emaline heard the anger in the accusations, despite knowing they were right. No one cared but Emaline. No one.

"It is delicate because you sent her there!" Emaline snapped, shocked by her own outburst, and calmed her tone. "You gave her up. You sent her away as a pawn in your politics. You sacrificed her."

"Sergeant, I may have given you leave to speak freely, but do remember that you are speaking to your Lady." Lady Belva threatened as she slowly stood up, her posture rigid. "You will show me—"

"I know exactly who I am speaking to." Emaline cut in, jabbing a finger at Lady Belva. She fought back her tears as she continued to dig into her soul for the courage she needed to be brave. "This was not fair. This was not justice. Not for her. When she came to be your ward and live here, you took her under your wing like a daughter. You knew of her past, how her real mother treated her." Emaline shook her head for what felt like the hundredth time. "And you treated her just the same."

"Do not dare say such things to me. I love her as my own flesh and blood!" Lady Belva leaned over her desk, her palms pressing down hard on the wood where she slammed them.

"Then do something, dammit!" Emaline screamed.

The doors slammed open behind Emaline, and guards rushed inside. "My lady, we heard shouting. Are you all right?"

The two women stepped back from one another, their chests rising and falling with heavy breath.

"Yes, I am fine. It's just a bit of a passionate discussion, is all," Lady Belva said, regaining her composure. "You are dismissed."

The guards exchanged uncertain glances but excused themselves and left.

Emaline could not stop the tears that began to fall. "Dammit," she whispered, wiping them away furiously. She worked tirelessly in her life to avoid giving in to her anger, it always ended in tears and embarrassment. "She is my sister, my lady, not by blood, but by choice. And I can do nothing for her. They took that away from me, but you still can do something. You have power." Emaline croaked out, her voice breaking.

Lady Belva looked down, rubbing her hand over her face before beginning to pace. "I have lain awake every night since sending her away, praying for her safety, waiting for some plan to form to allow her to return to us." She began to sniffle, the sound betraying her composure. "Hells, I even wondered if ending this war would bring her back, but the truth is that I cannot sacrifice so much for one person." Lady Belva took a shaking breath, holding her stomach to steady herself. "And I hate that truth so deeply."

Emaline let out a hard breath. "She is not just one person. This war would likely be lost if it weren't for her and the secrets she found, the risks she took for us- for you. You owe it to her to try to rescue her. This country owes her."

"It is not that simple. I must do what is best for our country, for the realm. I have to make hard and terrible choices, including this one. That is what leadership is, Emaline." Replied Lady Belva, each word heavy and lined with pain.

Emaline bit her tongue and nodded her head. "My apologies, I just thought leadership was quite different to the Queen of the People."

Emaline turned on her heel and marched out, ripping open the door and storming out before getting permission to leave.

Lady Belva stifled a huffed breath, waiting for Emaline's storming footsteps to fade before she made her own exit. "I will be at the chapel," she snapped at her guards, who hurried to keep pace with her resolute strides. They followed close behind her as she marched through the halls, her skirts whipping on the stone with every sure step and quick turn.

"My lady!" A parishioner turned from her conversation to greet Lady Montarian as she stepped inside the crowded chapel. "I mean, my queen. Apologies!" The woman stuttered and curtsied, setting off a ripple of similar gestures among the gathered crowd.

"No, it is quite all right; you do not need to address me in such a way." Lady Montarian replied

"But that is your title, Your Highness. You are the Queen of the People." The lady said, her head tilted to the side with the same confusion she held in her tone.

Lady Belva tried not to let her face show how that title made her cringe and grimace with guilt and worry. Queen of the People—a title that felt more like a shackle than a crown. The memory of Emaline's pointed words cut through her like a knife.

"It is just... apologies. Will you excuse me?" Lady Belva dismissed herself from the gathering group and went to the front of the chapel in an attempt to find Father Robb.

Lady Belva was perplexed by the crowd within the holy building. There was no service today. She glanced about to find the head of her church.

Everywhere her eyes fell, so did tears.

The chapel was a symphony of grief—quiet sobs mingled with loud weeping. Parishioners clasped their hands on the backs of pews, lost in their sorrow, while robed Scholars moved among them, attempting to soothe their anguish and confusion.

"But what is His Will, if not the Divine Houses and our paths? I have spent my entire life dedicated to this path He had laid for me, and now I am told it is a lie?" an elderly man snapped out. While his tone was full of anger, Lady Belva felt the grief underlying it all.

A young female Scholar, her hair as pale and bright as her white gown, bowed her head in grief with him, "I do not know, sir, I do not know."

His anger broke as she began to sob, and he let his tears fall, too.

Another conversation caught her ear.

"But what words are we to believe, Father? If these were a lie, what else is?" a young woman asked, her legs covered in clinging children. She held her youngest in her arms and squeezed the girl, "Does this mean I do not have to send her away when she is older? That my daughter will stay with me and not be sent away to the Citadel?"

Father Robb's face was that of a ghost, a phantom left wandering purgatory through mist and hollowed walkways. His eyes watched the woman, but they saw nothing and showed no life behind them.

"Father, please," the mother pleaded, "you are the Head of the Church. If you do not have the answers, what are we to do?"

Father Robb shrugged and shook his head. The mother shot her eyes over Father Robb's shoulder and caught Lady Belva's glance.

"My lady, what does this all mean? What do we do?"

Lady Belva began to stutter, but the woman gave her no room to be flawed in her speaking. She stepped toward Lady Belva, the child still on her hip, and others by her side. Lady Belva's guards tensed at her angered face and harsh steps, but they did not stop her from approaching.

"You were the one who set these words free," the woman continued, stepping closer with the child still clinging to her. So tell us, what scriptures can we still cling to?"

There was no peace, no knowing, no joy, no faith in this stone-laid building of worship and congregation. There was only community, but they had not come together in faith, but in fear and mourning.

"What have I done?" Lady Belva whispered to herself. Realization washed over her as if she were among the water being drowned at sea, not surrounded by waves of grief and emotion, drowning her all the same.

In her fury, Lady Belva, the Queen of the People, had taken more than just life from her people. She had taken away everything they believed in.

In her desire to turn the world against the king, she had turned her people against their god.

"My lady," the woman asked again. "Are we to have any faith left at all?"

The crowd did not hide their obvious eavesdropping and curiosity. They all looked to her, even those of the church, for guidance. She had taken away the faith of a god-fearing nation and given them nothing to turn to but an imperfect woman standing before them who did not wish to be looked upon nor granted titles of grandeur.

In her path, she had given her people darkness.

Instead of answering her people with words, Lady Belva walked towards the sanctuary candles and began lighting them. She lit one for each of her sons, her husband, and another for her country. When she was done, she blew out the long matchstick and sat in an empty pew to begin her prayers. She turned to her people, her hands in her lap.

"Would any of you care to join me?" she asked as she bowed her head to pray.

CHAPTER 7

Madam Fury's gaze swept over the landscape before her. Earth scorched beyond life, and ever-shifting yellow sands met beneath her horse's feet. To the south, the Black Fingers' blackened lands lay, and to the east of the stone pillars of the Black Fingers, the twisted remnants of the Old Forest echoed with an empty hollowness.

Madam Fury felt the pull of her homeland calling her to head south, not northeast to fight Craigie again. She had grown up surrounded by blackened death, burnt things, empty lands, and hollow places. But it had not bothered her to be enveloped by that all her life, nor to be raised to fight and kill, not in the same way it had impacted others- those too weak or soft-hearted to do what was needed for their country and cause.

For the winged beasts she wished to serve if they ever returned.

Not *if*.

When.

Deep inside her bones- which were much stronger than her heart- she knew that dragons had once been real, would return, and rise again.

Once we meager humans deserved their return. She growled internally.

Humans had become too eager for power, cruelty, and control, too full of desire to make themselves monsters to get what they wanted. And the tremendous four-legged and winged beasts, the serpents of the sea, wyrms of the land, and their wyvern cousins, all left humanity behind in disgust and horror at what they saw from the race they once allied with and lived alongside.

Or so many believed, especially those with Dragonblood pumping in their veins.

One day, Madam Fury thought, *one day, I will not only fight alongside my Dragon warriors but on the back of a true dragon.*

Like many who still believed in the myths and legends of magic and mythical beasts, Madam Fury had been deemed a zealot and a fanatic for believing so deeply in the return of the dragons, but she knew they would return.

Humanity just had to prove they deserved it first.

Madam Fury dedicated her life to preparing for their return, to learning to fight and wield her own power to take down those who craved too much.

Like Lady Kathilla Edgel.

The "Queen" of the North.

That brute bitch was one of the many reasons why humanity was not ready for the return of things more magical than the mundane bullshit that surrounded them. Lady Kathilla's thirst for power was one of the blights Madam Fury sought to purge from the world, though she knew it alone would not be enough to bring back the dragons.

And the king...

Madam Fury only hoped that the mess in the south that had begun would end before she had to get involved. She did not want to stain her hands with blood and ally herself with a man unworthy of her fighters– of the dragons. To fight alongside them, to soar on the back of a true dragon—it was her purpose, her calling.

Although her lords did demand her aid in the king's war, she had found her own way to prevent her assistance– for now. She would occupy herself in the north for as long as she could, fighting Craigie as they stole more land from Odessin, setting things right and balanced, and then, when that excuse ran dry, and the lands found quiet again, she would find another to forgo lending her aid to the king's wasted war.

Or, she hoped that her scheming and conniving lords would find a way out of the war. Lord Nesima Mete and Lord Shaital Pathis had always found ways to pull the strings of the kingdom around them, and they, too, believed in things greater than fighting for crowns and simple gold.

The land groaned under the weight of men like the king and women like Lady Kathilla. It would be Madam Fury who reminded them all that this world belonged to dragons, not kings, not queens, not monsters.

Madam Fury kicked her horse, urging the sand mare onward. She would balance the lands and right men's wrongs, and then, her gods would return.

"Ah, gentlemen! There you are. Welcome back to The King's Keep at long last!" Father Figgins greeted as he strolled into the glorious throne room where the Lords of Odessin, Lord Nesima Mete and Lord Shaital Pathis, stood admiring the intricate paintings embellishing the walls.

Father Figgins, along with several King's Guards, approached both Odessian men, who casually and quite slowly turned their attention away from the art to the approaching group.

The Hand of the King bowed to the two men. "I see you are admiring the masterpieces our finest members of the House of Craft created, depicting our triumph and history. If I recall correctly, you both are great art admirers, yes?"

"We admire many great things in Odessin, art being one of them, and truth and honesty being another. Neither of which this piece depicts." Lord Shaital Pathis said, his voice plain in tone and his cadence slow and deliberate. His posture was as firm as the finest forged sword, and his attire was well-kept and finely tailored. "While the artist's technique is admirable, this piece is rather... incongruous."

The painting depicted the end of the Great Civil War: a grateful kingdom on its knees for the First King, shackled and chained Odessians crying tears of gratitude to their new king, whose power melted and broke the chains that bound them, and Northern brutes depicted with blood on their hands and jagged teeth.

The corner of the painting depicting the Odessin lord's ancestors on their knees drew attention the most. Odessians had never volunteered to fall at the feet of a man holding himself above them. Even when the Alvarian conquerors came to the Continent, Odessians did not kneel to those they believed rode winged gods and were perhaps gods themselves. They did not fall in their surrender but instead welcomed the Alvarians with open arms.

Odessin was founded by its people's blood and sacrifice. Before it was a free country, it was a prison; its people held in chains and disposed of by the rest of the continent to labor the rest of their short and miserable days. It had been a land of "undesirables," and prisoners turned into freedom fighters, allying themselves with the North, then quickly changed their course when freedom meant forgiving the monarchy that encouraged their imprisonment in the first place.

Father Figgins's enthusiasm dropped from his face, and his eyes darted to Lord Nesima Mete, whose bloodline had borne the title of Lord and Lady for generations. Lord Nesima's face came to life with a proud smirk as he turned to The Hand of the King. "Father Figgins, thank you for receiving us today. Although after such a long journey made with such urgency, we were quite disappointed not to be greeted by the king himself or even Her Majesty."

"I understand. My most sincere apologies, Your Graces; unfortunately, the king is quite tied up at the moment. And Her- "

"Yes, yes, busy, I presume. I quite understand both of their schedules being full, given the news that made its way to us on our long journey regarding how His Majesty has not only lost control of his people, but of the temper he inherited from his father." Lord Nesima took a breath as Father Figgins began a retort that was cut off by more of Lord Nesima's words. "I do say, the spiked heads adorning the town walls add a new touch to the city, one our ancestors were quite familiar with seeing. Although, as His Majesty knows, it had once been our heads mounted by the crown as if they were trophies."

Father Figgins refused to be bested or undermined.

"Our history has been quite complicated, my lord, that we all can agree upon. It is why His Majesty betrothed the now Princess Easter to the Crown Prince, to right the wrongs of our pasts and to unite our families. We are all allies in His Majesty's throne room." Father Figgins asserted his point by admiring the golden throne at the head of the grand hall.

Forged of golden crowns of leaders who surrendered or were killed during the Great Civil War and melted with the dust of stars that fell on the Longest Night, the Throne of Stars glittered in sun and moonlight. A beacon and calling to many. A warning to others.

Many still believed that the restless spirits of those who once wore the crowns that formed the throne haunted the hall, whispering to anyone who listened or dared to sit upon it.

Father Figgins continued, his lip curling on one side into a smirk. "Princess Easter will look magnificent next to the future king up there, won't she?"

Lord Shaital chortled and stepped beside Father Figgins. He smiled and looked about the blended room of servants from both the king's halls and the citadels of Odessin. The Lord turned and stood over Father Figgins, then dropped his head by Father Figgins' ear to whisper.

A chill dared to slither up Father Figgins' crooked spine.

"You are not the only snake in the garden, Father. I advise you to be careful of whom you try to bite." Lord Shaital hissed.

The tension quickly turned taut, a bowstring ready to snap and ruin everything Father Figgins had been planning.

"Apologies for our curtness, Father. It has been many moon phases since His Majesty called us here to aid in battle, and the journey has made us weary and our tempers perhaps too short." Lord Nesima began, his voice smooth and controlled. "It seems we have much to discuss now that we are here. But perhaps we can do so in a more private setting?" he dropped his volume. "Where we may be more frank and less coded in ways we must speak, yes?"

Father Figgins maintained his composure despite the clear challenge and nodded. "Of course, my lords. Follow me, if you will."

Lord Shaital glanced at his husband, a silent communication passed between them that Father Figgins did not miss as they followed him through the halls, their blended set of guards following several paces behind.

Father Figgins led them to the King's Council chambers. A large table dominated the room, surrounded by high-backed chairs. As they took their seats, a servant appeared with a tray of wine and goblets, distributing them silently before retreating into the shadows.

"Before we discuss our business, may we toast to your new position, Father Figgins. Hand of the King after such a short time at His Majesty's side. Quite impressive how you managed to climb so high so quickly." Lord Shaital said over his raised goblet, his eyebrow raised as he spoke, but his tone a veneer of courtly etiquette.

Father Figgins nodded. "Yes, I am fortunate for this path that The One True has placed me on, and each day, I pray for peace for the troubled soul of His Majesty's prior Hand, granted me such an honor so soon. May he rest in His loving embrace."

Father Figgins raised his goblet, toasting to the late and dishonored-at-death Lord Robert Orville, the Hand of the King who had stood beside King Ivan and his father before him. The Lords of Odessin raised their goblets, too.

Lord Robert Orville's betrayal of King Ivan in early spring had shocked the Council and the informed masses throughout the kingdom. His capital punishment and execution had become the final catalyst for civil war as disgruntled citizens, after several seasons of unrest, attempted to fight against the king and his iron fist. Many questioned his right to rule, quickly driving Lady Montarian of Ayeshire to end the generations-long allyship between the two families and demand answers through swords and battles.

If the noble, compassionate Hand of the King had indeed betrayed the king, then many had wondered if perhaps the king needed to be betrayed for the kingdom. And if he hadn't betrayed the king but instead had fallen victim to a grander scheme of betrayal, then a war to dethrone the king was the proper path of justice in the eyes of many traitors.

Father Figgins took a sip of his wine and then placed the goblet down with a deliberate motion. "I understand your frustrations, you spoke of earlier, lords. But you must see that the king is doing everything within his power to maintain peace and order, even if doing so means reminding our people of what power the throne and its allies have. Those things sometimes come at a cost."

Lord Nesima leaned forward, his gaze piercing. "Peace and order, Father? Is that what you call the sight of heads on spikes and the screams of citizens?"

Father Figgins joined his hands on the table. He leaned forward, too. "We will call it what we must if this means the war will be won."

"Oh, we will?" Lord Shaital's lip curled at the corner, and his brow rose. He raised his goblet and slowly sipped as his eyes wandered curiously up and down at Father Figgins.

"Your daughter," Father Figgins scoffed and turned to look at Lord Nesima instead of Lord Shaital, "I mean, your daughter, is set to be queen- so long as this war is won, that is. If her husband's line is usurped, then what does she become? You will support His Majesty's war and lend your aid. You must."

"My my, Father. Your leash has been loosened, and now you speak so freely one might mistake your head for the one that bears the crown." Lord Nesima said.

"Your people know quite a lot about leashes and chains, don't they?" Father Figgins snarked back.

Lord Shaital kissed his teeth, "Yes, and we know how to break them and those who dare think they can put them back on us."

"Is that a threat?"

"No. This is a conversation. We would never dare make a threat, Father." Lord Shaital said. "A threat gives one's intentions away, and we do love to keep others guessing."

Chapter 8

The sun set and the moon rose as the twins of the sky said their greetings and farewells to the kingdom twice more since Sister Ora last spoke to another. The scuttling of a rat on her bedside table woke her, and she watched the furry thief take her spoiled meal, which had barely a bite taken from it. Sister Ora looked to the moon glimmering through the wind-swept curtains; the stars stayed where they belonged that night, and Sister Ora obeyed their whim and did not move either, even when the sun rose again, and the castle woke around her.

Nine days. Only a few more before her body could no longer sustain living like this.

The door creaked open, bringing in noises of the castle and her maid attempting again to ready her for the day. Soft footsteps found themselves beside her bed as a gentle touch reached for her arms to unlock the chains.

Sister Ora pulled her hands back into her. Exhaustion and nausea fell over her again as she spoke, "No. Leave me."

The color was drained from her hollowed face, her cheeks as pale as her dark complexion would allow.

"Miss, I'm afraid I cannot. And if you do not cooperate with me," Kaylah held a terrified pause, "they'll make me send him in to wake you. I told you this. They said that this is your last warning."

Sister Ora cocked her head up, regretting it immediately as it began to ache again, and the pain shot through her body. She took several short and pained breaths, wiping away the pain in her bones and bile in her throat before firing back a reply. "Let them. I do not care."

Kaylah had always been soft and kind to Sister Ora, a lady's maid quietly in the background of her life since Sister Ora was brought to the king's city. Her voice never rose, and her smile only ever faded into a stern line when she found herself deep in her work. In the days following Sir Loren's killing and the start of Sister Ora's torturous imprisonment, Kaylah continued in her soft kindness, letting her wallow in her pity and pain.

This made it all the more surprising when Kaylah's soft face turned to cold anger, and her soft touch became a death grip on Sister Ora's arm.

"I have had enough of this, Miss Ora. If you wish to die, then do it some other way- get it over with. Throw yourself from the window while I draw your bath, choke yourself with your chains, or something." Sister Ora tried to pull away from her grip, her eyes wide in shock and every muscle in her body tense, but Kaylah held on. She grabbed Sister Ora's face to hold her eyes on her, "But this must stop. This self-pity, this whining, this patheticness you are displaying. The world is falling apart, and you are doing nothing. Either die or live. I do not care which, but choose one."

Kaylah pulled herself away from Sister Ora, throwing the key to her chains on her chest. She walked away to the dressing chest to pull out clothes.

Sister Ora slowly sat up in bed, throwing the key at Kaylah's turned back and tried not to throw up from the nausea that accompanied the movement.

"I am so sorry that my misery frustrates you. I am sorry that I am suffering and hurting, and it brings inconveniences to your day," she snarked, her voice hoarse and dry.

Kaylah snapped around, throwing Sister Ora's dress on the ground and storming for her. "We have all lost many things as of late and over the course of our entire lives. This kingdom has brought us all to our knees, but some of us chose to get up from where we were forced to kneel. I do not wish to belittle your loss, but you are allowing it to consume you, to eat at your flesh, to starve you as you now choose to starve yourself."

Both women's eyes scanned Sister Ora's weakened body hidden under a crumbled day gown, dirty from her days spent in it, the front and underarms stained with sweat and tiny specks of blood from her capture.

Kaylah's eyes shifted to the door briefly, then moved back to Sister Ora in front of her. She whispered, "Miss Ora, you have strength that you have let them squander. You have abilities that could change the kingdom. You are letting them win, and your own self-pity is causing our cause to lose."

"Wha- What?" Sister Ora cleared her throat and rustled upright on the bed. "What did you say?"

"Do you wish to bathe and eat today?" Kaylah asked, her tone firm as she crossed her arms and stood straight.

Sister Ora's shoulders slumped, and she turned her gaze to her fingers covered in red. Her nailbeds were torn to pieces, and nails were ripped from her, picking and biting. In the silence of her contemplation, Sister Ora felt the pit inside of her open more, beckoning her to fall back inside. The darkness was a warm hug, a familiar feeling of numb emptiness, a cozy blanket, the feeling of a friendly embrace.

It felt better to fall back inside where her demons could bat away the pain of the light, where she felt the calling for her to lie back down and sleep, to stop fighting.

"No," she said and fell back into her darkness.

Chapter 9

"She hasn't seen battle since the dust of The Conquest settled. It is such a shame," Lord Shaital Pathis said. He clenched his fingers behind himself, holding back the desperate urge to reach out and grasp the displayed weapon.

The Conqueror's Sword was a sight to behold, with its heavy blade resting on a sturdy metal stand specially crafted to hold its great weight. The blade itself was relatively simple; the intricacies and fine workmanship were reserved for the guard and grip of the weapon. The full guard of the sword looped and swirled, flourishing in intricately forged art that began at the basic counter guards and arm branches. The guard was so detailed in its design that it looked as if leafy vines had sprouted from the blade and grew into branches that would perfectly wrap around the bearer's hand, providing both protection and intimidating beauty.

The grip was crafted from tough leather carved with matching vines. It had been perfectly contoured to fit the hand of its original wielder, Glenolyn the Great, ensuring the sword could be held tightly and securely during all her battles—indents from her fingers were still on the leather. The Conqueror's

Sword was a masterpiece of craftsmanship carved from a continent left behind by the Alvarian conquerors. Both beautiful and deadly, it was meant to transcend time and conquests, kings, and empires.

A worn phrase that Scholars fought over regarding meaning and pronunciation was etched underneath the crown-shaped pommel. It was in a language not currently known in the Six Kingdoms (likely long lost from the First King's burning), and no records remained, if any existed to begin with, to transcribe the meaning from the language that came from the Alvarian conqueror's abandoned kingdom.

Quai'i Dei Exelind'ar

The only known word from the phrase was the last.

Not a word, but a place, a name, a kingdom.

Exelind'ar.

Known now in history books as the Forgotten Kingdom, the days it would take to sail to the lost lands were too vast to learn if it still existed or if it truly had died in raging dragon fire and tsunamis brought on by sea serpents seeking revenge on the cruel king that once ruled it and forced the Alvarian siblings to leave their home and find another.

"Reduced down to a ceremonial sword to sit in a ruler's hand as they make false oaths to our kingdom." Lord Shaital sneered as he shook his head.

"My light, let us watch our words within these walls we do not know." Lord Nesima Mete replied. His husband turned his eyes to meet his knowing stare. Lord Nesima lifted a brow and cocked his head to urge Lord Shaital to move on. The two lords casually strolled down the little-visited artifacts hall, biding their time before the King's Council meeting.

"All these relics, yet we have learned nothing from their times." Lord Shaital said, quieter now, "and His Majesty sits on the largest one."

Lord Nesima asked. "What do you mean we have learned nothing?"

Lord Shaital nodded at a stone-carved map of the kingdom hanging on the wall, where mountains were raised from stone, and hills were carved like waves. Lakes and rivers were dug out of the stone, the sculptor's talent so vast that the oceans and currents appeared as moving water.

"It is hard to see the smaller cracks in the kingdom when we sit so far in our mountains, but now that we are here, it is easier to see how we are falling into dark times again. His Majesty seems... off, at best. Our sources were right that something is happening to him. And the stars continue to fall. Our kingdoms are in another war, and if what our spies tell us is true of the news Lady Montarian has spread, we will crumble and fall into another Great War before the first frost forms."

He paused, "We will be at the end of times. Again."

"The wheel of history turns, and we are but a spoke in that wheel." Lord Nesima replied.

Lord Shaital nodded, "If enough spokes break, does the wheel collapse in on itself or continue its turn?"

"We both know what that will lead to." Lord Nesima said. He glanced about the empty room. "Are we sure that this fall is the true one? Do you See the path forging rightfully?"

Lord Shaital nodded slowly as he moved his eyes around the hall, looking for listening ears. Thankfully, he found none that did not belong to their loyal aides. "We came here for knowledge. To know what we must do in this war and to find who else crawls beneath this kingdom's surface, only then can I know what I do See. Have you connived much from our allies yet?"

Lord Shaital stopped walking and stepped forward, taking his husband's hand in his and resting it on his chest. He rubbed his thumb over Lord Nesima's and leaned in to whisper, a moment in time that looked like nothing more than two lovers sharing a sweet moment.

Lord Nesima whispered to him, "I believe the second prince may be interesting to watch more than we have before. There is a shadow over him, one we may be able to contort and reshape. I recommend we keep our eyes there while Easter finds her way to her future king's army and handles battles in the way she knows best."

He lifted Lord Shaital's hand and kissed his palm, then moved their joined hands to their sides, holding them as they continued their walk.

They stopped in front of a painting of Carishna the Unforgiving and Glenolyn the Great soaring over the open seas, swooping down at mighty Kraken, both shouting their war cries as other dragon riders flew in the distance. Dragon fire in all its forms shot out of the flying beasts: flames of frost and ice came from the ice dragons, gas clouds of poison from the iridescent dragons of night, bolts of lightning formed from the jaws of storm dragons, and fire burned from golden dragons while crackles of pure heat popped from sand dragons.

In the forefront, Carishna's sand dragon, Riomiar, screamed in pain as a tentacle shot from the waves and wrapped itself around her long, thin neck. Her tan scales were broken up by cracks of orange and bloodied cuts from battle. The tentacle squeezed and contorted her neck as more came from the waves, forcing her under the depths of the ocean.

Carishna's own face screamed in vengeance as her sword, the Dark Dragon, swung down upon the Kraken's grasp. Her raven black hair flew out of control, and her gold eyes lit up as Riomiar shot heat from her nostrils.

Above her, her sister, Glenolyn, screamed for Carishna to leap from the back of her beast and ride away on Vinicarius together. The same golden eyes that Carishna had looked down on her in terror and anger. Glenolyn's blonde braid flew above her as Vinicarius dove down to Riomiar, blood dripping from the jaws of the massive golden dragon. Vinicarius's head spines formed a sharp circlet much like the crown atop Glenolyn's head.

While the painting only captured a brief second, the artist's attention to detail showed the anger and the worry on Glenoyln's face as her sister stubbornly held onto her falling dragon.

Historians from the Isles and the mainland argued for ages over the painting, whether it depicted a moment of glory or one of darkness and defeat. It was titled The Last Stand, a catalyst in time that secured the Isles of Aishar's freedom from the conquerors.

In front of the painting were statues dedicated to the great beasts that once dominated the lands and skies, most prominently a dark great sword that angered the lords so deeply to see in the king's hall.

The scabbard that held the Dark Dragon did not hide the sheen of the silver blade but accentuated it. The sheath was forged into two dragons, the tails of the beasts artistically wrapped around the blade, their claws almost touching on either side of the sword tucked between them. The monsters of the sky appeared as if they were gracefully climbing up the great sword's length, fighting to climb atop it.

The wings of the dragons were wide and broad, so wide one would not need back armor when wearing the sword. The heads of the dark dragons opened in a magnificent roar as if they were shouting at one another in front of the cross guard that rested behind them. A large dragon bloodstone sat on the oil-rubbed bronze cross guard between their teeth.

"The Dark Dragon should be in our tower. In our home with our people." Lord Shaital snarled quietly. "We should not have agreed to give it to His Majesty's collection during the marriage negotiations. He is not of dragon blood. He does not deserve it."

"It is not His Majesty's collection, but the king and queen of Victarius' collection- the throne's collection. Once Prince Elion is crowned, it will belong to our daughter and him. When Easter is crowned, it will belong to the blood of the dragon once again." Lord Nesima smirked, "We were quite careful in our wording of the agreement, my love. If not for His Majesty's ego distracting him, he may have noticed our chosen words."

"Yes, but it still should belong to you until she is ready to inherit her right."

"In due time, it will. I know it hurts to see it here, wasted in a hall and gathering dust, but it is all a part of the path."

The bells gonged within the halls, reminding the lords of the time and cutting their cunning moment short.

Prince Percy walked with heavy steps through the lit halls of the castle, his shoulders slumped and his face etched with lines of despair. He moved with the shadows brought in by the beams of sunlight casting through overhead arches and flickering torches, becoming a shadow himself, a shell of who he once was.

As he made his way towards the Council chambers, he passed by the hallway leading to the Hall of Archives—the grand library that had once been his sanctuary and home. He reminisced about the scent of leather-bound books and old parchment- the cologne of his youth.

His face fell even further, loss and longing gnawing at him. He missed the days when he was merely a Scholar, where his only duty was to advise and teach, not to lead and lie alongside his father's Council. Those days seemed like a lifetime ago, but it had only been a short season since his life had been turned upside down, and he had turned the kingdom upside down in response.

The rest of the grandiose spaces he had spent his life walking through passed him by with little acknowledgment from the prince.

Except for the glimmer of gold calling from the open throne room.

Prince Percy paused at the threshold and stared at the empty symbol of power that his father and monarchs sat upon before him. It was the symbol many ached to hold as their own, a symbol of unquestionable rule and power, an image of premonition to those who knew the secrets it bore and the path it forged for the kingdom when it was made.

Prince Percy stepped through the threshold of the throne room and held himself in the quiet. He walked down the carpeted aisle and stopped beside the grand golden throne. His hand stroked the arm of the metal warmed by the sun of high noon. His fingers tingled as they moved over the carved constellations and imagery; the foliage of all six kingdoms adorned the intricate piece alongside the wildlife that made up the crest of noble families, all the animals frolicking as allies and friends despite the bear and lion being beasts eager to eat ravens, stags, and other docile creatures.

"What will happen to you now after what I have done?" Prince Percy whispered as his hand came to the top of the chair's arch, "Will you burn as the prophecy states, or were those words merely metaphorical?"

The tower bells clanged to life in the air, snatching him back into the present moment. He shook his head and cleared his throat before hastily escaping the throne room to make his way to the Council room.

Sir Marion's fingers traced the jagged edge of the half-healed gash on his cheek, feeling the parts still sensitive to touch. The smell of the healing herbs he had rubbed on it each morning was no longer picked up by his nose; he had grown accustomed to the pungent stench burning his nostrils.

He snarled as the sting of the wound made his cheek twitch, causing his memory to jolt back to the moment that created it.

He wrestled Sister Ora to the ground; her attempt to flee had failed. He caught up to her with ease, having given her a head start to let her believe she had a chance before he found her. He grabbed her and clutched her body against his, throwing her onto the hard ground as she kicked, shrieked, and flailed.

"Stop fighting." He hissed between dodging her clawed strikes. Her knee met his groin as she continued to fight beneath him, crawling out from his tight grasp.

He recovered his stolen breath and growled as he stumbled to his feet, then fell back to his knees to grab her from where she still lay; his decision cemented to drag her down the hall if he must- the king's orders to be careful be damned. No one would know the harm he caused her if his fists left no marks, or his anger drew no blood.

As he reached down for her throat, her hand swung, ripping his face open with the sharp pin from the broach she had ripped from her dress. His blood trickled onto her petrified face as he took his turn, shouting in agony.

His vision blackened alongside his rage, creating the last memory of those moments before he slipped into the monster he released in moments like this.

"Who knew a little girl was such a glorious fighter? She almost took down one of Aishar's greatest." Lord Tyrrian laughed as he looked across the table at Sir Marion.

Despite the monster brewing inside him alongside his shame, Sir Marion maintained his composure. "It was only by His Majesty's order that I not harm her and be gentle. If I did not have to hold back my abilities, that little bitch would not have been able to do this."

Sir Marion had whipped himself for his failure. For letting her make him bleed. His thighs were still sensitive to movement from where he gave himself his lashings.

Father Figgins sipped his tea, watching the conversation over his cup. "His Majesty requested your gentle hand because she may be of great use to us in the future. Our little pawn needs to stay alive- we could negotiate with her life, use her as a bartering chip when needed."

"And how is it she will be played in the coming season?" Lord Tyrrian asked.

Prince Percy mumbled from across the table, "She is still a person- a human being."

The prince sat slouched in his chair, his shirt half-buttoned. His once well-trimmed curly hair was now a dull mess of black. The bags under his eyes and tired demeanor gave his once bright face a concave, shadowed appearance.

Sir Marion snickered, lazily lifting his crystal glass and swirling the liquor as he spoke. "Yes, a person who was betrothed to you and fucking another man." He took a swig and swallowed. "-a man you chose to guard her life. A man who aided her in manipulating you for information."

"A man wearing your King's Guard cloak," smarted Prince Percy.

"Tell me, prince, what did she give you in exchange for all that you gave her? Did you even get to feel her mouth on your– "

"Enough." Father Figgins ordered, then looked to Prince Percy. "We have quarreled enough on this. Yes, your betrothed may have learned too much since you do not recall all that you told her as she whispered lies and sweetness into your ear. Yes, the man she had her affair with was one of Sir Marion's. That is true. But now, we must change our strategy and assume she told our enemies everything she heard from you, or from Sir Loren. That is why we are gathered here today, to fix this mess."

The table looked to the king, who sat in silence. The king's eyes moved around the grains on the table. His skin had paled more in the prior days, and more dry flakes and redness had appeared around his mouth. His Majesty quietly smacked his lips together and swallowed repeatedly as if there were bits of sand causing roughness in his dry throat.

Sir Marion cocked his eyebrows as he watched the king.

Lord Nesima Mete cleared his throat, "I do believe it wise to rethink our strategy. We do not know what the Montarians and Torrins know, and I will not send my Dragons into a trap to be easily slaughtered."

"My fleet of ships have already arrived, and those aboard are eager to fight. We can only change so much before all we have done is wasted time and resources." Lord Tyrrian retorted, a blade-sharp edge to his voice.

"Your ships?" King Ivan asked in confusion, finally looking up at the meeting taking place.

Prince Percy leaned towards his father, his tone low and calm. "Yes, father. The ships from Aishar that we were waiting for. The ships to take the Ina Gulf."

King Ivan's brow crinkled. He avoided eye contact as he pulled on the sleeves of his shirt to hide the flaking patches of red skin that the room had already seen. Clearing his throat, he spoke sharply: "Yes, yes, I knew that. You do not need to explain things to me as if I were a simpleton."

His Majesty leaned back in his chair, resting an elbow on the arm and rubbing his mouth with his hand. "Go on, continue," the king ordered.

Prince Percy's eyes moved to the empty drink in front of his father, his face growing somber, "So what shall we do, if not take the Landing via battleship we have been preparing to do?"

Sir Marion rested his chin on his closed fist, his elbow on the table. Through his narrowed eyes, he watched the prince closely, noting every flick of his eyes and twitch of his brow. Listening for lies or disloyalty. Trickery or thieving. The young prince still had a soft heart, and that made him dangerous. Sir Marion was a man of shadows and often found what others tried to hide in theirs.

Father Figgins grunted, "No, let them think our plans have not changed; let them prepare for a siege they believe is coming."

"So we continue forward with the plan as we plotted it, a plan the enemy may already know in detail?" the naive prince questioned.

Sir Marion's expression hardened. "For all your books and studies, Prince Percy, you grasp little of the intricacies of warfare." His words dripped with condescension.

Prince Percy shared a heated glare with Sir Marion. Sir Marion flicked his memory away from the current moment, wondering to himself when he began to carry such irritation of the second prince. Was it when he first sailed across the sea to work his way through the rankings of the King's Guards to find a young prince enjoying his youth with a father who was present and caring? Was it when his envy shot out at the softness the prince got to enjoy while Sir Marion continued his path of rigid oaths and blood?

He did not know, nor did he care to learn. Diving too deeply into one's mind did nothing to heal the scars of war; that is what ale, whores, and medicine were meant for.

"Battle," Sir Marion said with a hint of cruel satisfaction, "is not merely made of swords and blood. War is also won in the mind. The enemy knows we plan to attack by sea, but they also know we have learned of their spying songbird." His lips curled into a dark smile. "We will let them stew in their own paranoia, doubting every move we make. Let them waste their resources and their wits on feints and deceptions."

He leaned forward, his eyes gleaming with a predatory light. "We will let them puzzle over our intentions, making them question their assumptions. Meanwhile, we strike in a key moment of the night, take them not by surprise but by force from all sides, not just the one they see." His voice dropped to a low, menacing whisper. "They'll be so consumed by their fears and confusion that they won't see us coming until it's too late."

CHAPTER 10

Lord Taylian Montarian stood beside a cadre of seasoned army officers, listening intently to their animated conversations of old war stories and strategic debates. The officers showed no hesitancy in answering the young lord's questions, nor did they bat an eye or roll a single one at his occasional naivety.

Several paces away, Lord Digarius watched his younger brother with a soft smile playing on his lips, pride glimmering in his eyes. He observed how his brother interacted confidently with the men and women he would one day fight alongside and, perhaps, command if he kept up his rapid pace of training. The more he watched, the more he was filled with admiration for his brother.

Despite his noble title and the ease with which he could have slipped into higher ranks upon enlisting, young Lord Taylian had informed his family that he wished to earn his positions in the army, not have them gifted to him as other noble soldiers did. He longed to fight in the pits and the mud, experiencing the harsh realities of warfare and lowly foot soldier life before knowing the cleanliness of high officer tents and their associated luxuries.

As Lord Digarius pondered these thoughts, he wondered whether he had ever told Lord Taylian how proud he was of his declaration, or whether watching his younger brother fight each day for his talents and victories had inspired the future lord to strive harder for his own achievements.

Lord Taylian looked up from his conversation and met Lord Digarius's eyes across the open space. The future Lord of Ayeshire cocked his head at his younger brother, motioning with a flick of his head for him to come over. Lord Taylian joined him at an unhurried pace, standing beside him as Lord Digarius shoved off the stone fence and began walking.

"I heard good things from Father Robb about how you handled yourself while we were away," Lord Digarius said, his tone filled with a mixture of pride and curiosity.

"Thank you, brother." Lord Taylian flattened his lips into a thin line and looked to the ground, a shadow crossing his features as he did so. "Although it did not feel good. Doing all of that. It was harder than I thought it would be."

Lord Digarius chuckled in understanding. "Well, yes, it is lordship. It is never meant to be simple."

"Yes, I just... how do you and mother make it look so easy while I..." Lord Taylian cut his words with a frustrated sigh. "I thought maybe I would have a better knack for the diplomatic side of our family duties, of the day-to-day requirements, but I don't."

"That is because you are a soldier, Tay, not a man destined to be a diplomat," Lord Digarius spared another glance at him, his eyes filled with a mixture of affection and concern. "Your destiny is not to live and die by papers and laws but by swords and battle."

Lord Taylian grunted. "Perhaps, yes."

"Why do you want to be so good at lordship? I thought you wished to lead on the field, not find your way into a smaller stewardship when you came of age," Lord Digarius pressed gently.

His brother shrugged, his expression pensive. "It is not as if I would spend every day with a sword in my hand. I need to learn more, do more, be better."

"Be better for what?"

Lord Taylian hesitated, his mouth opening and closing as he struggled to find the words. He stopped their pace and mustered up the courage for honesty. "I... it's just that... I see you and Father, and how you both handle everything with such ease. The way you command respect, how people look up to you, and how well you fight and lead. I want..."

Lord Digarius raised an eyebrow, encouraging him to continue but holding his silence.

His brother sighed deeply, running a hand on top of his locks in frustration. "You're really going to make me say it, aren't you? I want to be like you, Dig. And like father. I want to have that same strength, that same presence. The command that I cannot grip."

Lord Digarius placed a hand on his brother's shoulder, squeezing it reassuringly. "Our path is not yours. Your path is not about being like us; it is about being you, Tay." He shook his head and dropped his hand, "And trust me, you do not wish to be like father."

"What?" Lord Taylian cocked his head and stepped closer. "Why?"

Lord Digarius shook his head and swallowed, looking up the hill towards the Landing's fortress and the line of citizens signing up to take up arms against the king or waiting to speak with their new queen, who stood waiting.

Lord Taylian furrowed his brow and shifted his body again, moving himself into his brother's line of sight, "Did father do something? What happened at Ravenhall? Or was it Sandhill?"

"Son!" Lord Theodus called for Lord Digarius from where he stood beside Lady Montarian and several officers in front of a line of awaiting citizens.

"Nothing. I have to go," Lord Digarius sighed to his brother, his shoulders slumping. "It's complicated, Tay. Father is- I am- Focus on your path, on what is meant for you. Do not mirror your path after ours."

"Dig what are you—"

"Son!" Lord Theodus Montarian called again after Lord Digarius.

"I have to go, Tay, just," Lord Digarius rubbed the back of his head and left to stand with his parents at the front of the assembly. He stopped and turned back to his brother, "I just want what is best for you, and I want to see you grow up to become who you are, not who I am, nor father or mother. We will finish this talk later."

The streets of Middleton Landing were littered with preparations for war. Empty eyes and downturned lips filled the spaces where bright-eyed smiles had once been. Burnt-out souls that had once grumbled over the mundaneness of their lives ached so deeply for afternoon banter with bread makers and butchers over rising prices and for the simplicity that had so quickly become a memory. Now, those whose lives and labor built the Landing were preparing to watch it burn and try to save it from the flames.

Closer to the fortress doors, waiting lines grew thicker and more emotional. Lord and Lady Montarian and armored soldiers stood at the head of the line. Ayeshire banners framed them, and a table stood covered with quills and parchment. Seated at the table was a Scribe quickly writing oaths and mumbling incoherent words to those standing in front of the line. The scribe tapped the parchment at the bottom, encouraging the woman standing at the table to sign.

She scrawled on the paper and set the quill aside, nodding to the Lord and Lady before taking a metal pin from the basket on the table. She pinned it to her chest, moving along to allow the next in line to take her place. The soldier's insignia stood out against the downtrodden clothing she wore. The smooth curves of the metal rubbed against the well-worn cloth of her blouse that held the pin crookedly to her chest.

Behind her, painful words broke the routine process taking place as another person stepped forward to the table.

"Please, my queen, please do not take my son. Do not let him fight in this war. Undo his oath, rip it up. Please, you must." A weeping mother in mourning black begged Lady Montarian.

The noble mother could not allow herself to break, not here, not now. While many societal rules had crumbled since the war began, the Queen of the People could not waver on her own rules and protocol.

The legitimacy of the Divine Houses had been ripped to shreds upon the reveal of the Psalms of Fire and Fury, and many of the people of Ayeshire timidly accepted their freedom of change to pursue what was needed of them, not divinely bestowed upon them by a false church. Most did not walk away from their faith with joy; many did it as a snub to the king, not the beliefs they still tried to hold.

The Lady of Ayeshire asked for all to use their now untied hands to aid in their fight for freedom, no matter what pin they wore on their chest or guild they studied under. It did not take much favor for her citizens to take up their arms and ask what they could do for their country.

For their queen.

But she still stiffened at the title granted to her.

Lady Belva gently took the woman's hand, her soft grasp an attempt to soothe the shaking in her bones. "I am sorry, but he took the oath freely, and I must honor that." She spoke sternly, hoping the mourning in her own words would translate through with the soothing strokes of her hands on hers.

"Please. Please do not take him from me. He is my only child, my sweet, sweet boy." She choked on her words and pulled their hands to touch her forehead as she bowed to Lady Belva. "He is the only memory I have left of his father."

She parted their hands and pulled out an aged and worn coin, the sigil of a fallen soldier given to families upon delivery of the news of the sacrifice made.

Lady Belva's chin quivered, her firm resolution beginning to break. She swallowed and straightened her posture. "And his oath will continue the legacy your husband left behind."

The broken mother's shoulders fell, her head bowed again, and her heart shattered. She no longer spoke; she only wept as the guards beside her gently turned her away and aided her in her leave.

A noble messenger stood beside Lord Montarian, awaiting her return from her conversation. He held out a rolled parchment, the knot still tied, keeping the contents secret.

"My Lady, My Lord," he whispered, handing over the message.

Lady Belva unrolled the scroll, gesturing with a sideways glance at Lord Theodus and Lord Digarius to follow her as she stepped away from the crowd. With a tired and heavy sigh, she re-rolled the scroll, then flicked it towards her husband to read.

"More news bearing nothing."

Lord Theodus let out his own exasperation. "Simply confirming what our prior birds have sent from news outside the king's city. His Majesty has banned messenger birds that are not his own from entering or leaving the city, so we must continue to rely on information passed by whispers through the city gates and birds from the surrounding villages, and he has enacted curfews and gate inspections."

Lord Digarius read the note and crumpled the paper. "No news in. No news out. At least by wing. And no sneaking in, either."

Citizens paused their labors while the three walked by, bowing more reverently than before and greeting Lady Belva with her new title. She hid her grimace from her people but not from the two men who knew her best.

"The title suits you well, my queen, despite your distaste for such an honor." Lord Theodus said.

She ignored his words. "What true benefit would this offer His Majesty? If anything, he risks hearing less about what is occurring around the kingdom or in the war. A sane man would have hired loyalists to review all correspondence coming and going and paid off the bird keepers, messengers, or something of the like. All he has done is slow down his own network."

"Yes, a sane man." Lord Theodus grumbled, "Something he no longer is, it seems."

"Perhaps he aimed to prevent his people from learning the truth of what is occurring. All news will now be filtered through his channels or through those who manage to make it in and out of the city in secret." Lord Digarius retorted. "Which means our messages regarding the truth of the Psalms will take even longer to arrive in his city, lengthening the time it would take to turn those at his front door against him."

The trio reached the military section of the village where Armor-born trained their fellow citizens in the art of the great sword. Skill assessments were quickly done, and there was little time to thoroughly train those without experience. Citizen soldiers, young and old, learned the basic maneuvers of swordplay; others stretched back bowstrings and felt the flick of corrective fingers against their crooked arms; hand-to-hand combat broke out in corners; others learned the skill of field dressing wounds.

"Is it wrong that I found comfort in learning what the king had been hiding? That I felt... true vindication for this war when the Psalms were brought to us? I knew His Majesty was up to tyranny, but I had no idea it was as dark as what was revealed." She nervously rubbed her hands together, the rings of silver and gold catching on one another. She kept her eyes fixed on the horizon, observing the consequences of her actions as her city prepared for the war she had begun.

No, no. That the king had begun.

"Not at all," Lord Theodus answered. "I feel it as well. You knew he was up to something treacherous, and you meant to prevent a war, not begin one. And now we have more proof to back our prior actions."

"If you did not have the Psalms, would you feel any guilt over this, mother?" Lord Digarius asked.

She swallowed hard, "Come, let us break for lunch."

Lord Digarius watched his parents leave. His eyes traced their stature as they left. He recalled his father's confession of what he had done at Broken Tower—the crimes he committed, the horrid actions he covered up, how he slaughtered surrendering men to make a point and feed his own ego, and how the world rewarded him with a lordship that they feigned as a punishment.

His mind wandered to memories of Sir Rainey, as it often did whenever he stared at his father or a weapon for too long.

Both of the men who made him had turned out to be monsters in their own ways.

He watched his parents share a comforting moment between themselves, knowing the family secret they held onto and the fight they had in front of them. Lord Digarius stared at his feet, wondering which path he was meant to walk and if he were destined to tread his own or find a scrap of honor in following theirs.

"My lord." Emaline greeted as she stepped up beside Lord Digarius. "May I walk with you?"

"Of course," he replied, turning to begin a walk in the opposite direction of his parents.

"Did you wish to speak while we walked, Emaline?" Lord Digarius questioned after several paces were walked in silence. Oftentimes, the two would find themselves near one another in the fortress walls, Emaline walking to see Sister Ora after being dismissed from her duties, Lord Digarius wandering to find his parents or attend more training, and even finding themselves sparring in fighting rings during training.

None of the men wanted to risk ever hurting their future lord.

Emaline did not care and held back no punches or swings.

Lord Digarius was used to Emaline sometimes wanting silence, only to interrupt it with a random fact or thought before quieting herself again and occupying her mind with thoughts she rarely shared. It was a nice comfort for the heir to have a friend who was simply there at times- no expectations, favors to ask, needs to meet.

After several more beats of silence, Emaline asked, "I am just uncertain of how to state this."

He shrugged. "Just say it, Emaline, I always have appreciated your lack of care for democratic propriety."

She sighed, "Did your mother tell you of our conversation a few da'es prior?"

Lord Digarius inhaled deeply and exhaled, "Yes, she did. From what I heard, it was an exciting conversation. I admit I am shocked that you spoke to her in such a way, although I do understand your passion and concern and do not blame you."

In fact, if he were being honest, Lord Digarius respected her more for it.

Emaline's cadence took on the awkward pacing and pausing that Lord Digarius had become familiar with when she became uncomfortable, "What were your thoughts on our talk? Not on how I spoke to her, but on what was said?"

"Your questions risk putting me in a hard place, Emaline. Lady Montarian is not only our Lady but my mother, and you are someone I would like to call a friend."

"You're right, my lord; I should have considered that before coming to you with my troubles." Lord Digarius noted her fingers twitching and her face turning farther away from him as they continued walking. "I apologize."

"No, no. I find myself in this hard place regardless of this conversation, actually." his eyes wandered around the town as they continued their stroll. "I have begun to find myself searching for ways to disagree with them, even mentally picking apart their word choices and the subtle flicks of my mother's eyes and movement of my father's face in meetings."

"Is there concern to be had of this, Your Grace? A rippling in the family?"

Lord Digarius subtly shook his head and pursed his lips, "No. I should have said nothing; you came to me to speak of your troubles, not hear my grumbling. Forgive me."

"No forgiveness needed, Your Grace. You know I prefer honesty," she huffed. "My lord, I understand this war is delicate, but so is Ora, and your mother- Her Grace- has seemingly given up on caring or doing anything to aid her. She says she cares and wishes she could help get Ora back, but she is not willing to risk saving her, and I doubt she would hear any true conversation on how we could get her back." Emaline halted and turned to him, stepping closer so others would not hear her. "We must do something, Your Grace."

A darkness fell over Lord Digarius' face; this was a dangerous and treasonous territory and, despite his frustrations with his parents, a territory he was not prepared to walk the border of. He would not break oaths and commit treason, especially against his family, so easily.

"While I disagree with our lady and lord at times, much so more now than in the past, what you speak of is treason, Emaline. Going against my mother's orders, even considering it aloud, is treason. I am frustrated at choices they have made, yes, but until I am the sovereign over this country, it is my mother's word that is rule and law."

"But my lord-"

"No." his harsh hisses turned into spits of vitriol. "Enough, Emaline. You swore your sword to my family. Remember that."

Emaline's throat bobbed up and down, and she looked away with shame in her eyes. "I also swore my sword to Ora," her voice shook. "I'm just afraid for her, my lord. It is not right just letting her rot there."

"No. It isn't."

His voice softened. Lord Digarius understood her worry; he truly did, but he also understood his place in the kingdom.

"I'm afraid, too, Emaline. I'll talk to my mother and see if I can convince her of anything. We won't forget Ora, I promise you. And I promise you, whenever we win this war, she will be safe; whenever our feet march on their city stones, she will be rescued."

"Is that next, then, sir? Taking their city when they are done destroying ours?" Emaline's voice dropped to a whisper, and she leaned in.

"I cannot say, but my mother has ideas and plans that have been plotted since the beginning." He paused, "If we ever march upon the city, I will personally stand beside you while we cut them all down to get to her."

"You swear it?" she asked.

Something came over him. A pull and a yank to do more than speak words that could be twisted later or unsworn.

Lord Digarius found his right hand swiping the knife from his belt and felt the sting of the blade in the palm of his hand before he even realized he had cut it open. Emaline's eyes widened, and she gasped.

"My lord?" she swallowed and stepped back.

Lord Digarius let his palm bleed and met Emaline's eyes. "Emaline Kingery, I swear upon my life, my ancestors, my descendants, and my eternal soul; if we do not get her back, my life is yours to end."

Chapter 11

"I have found myself on a path that I cannot change or return from, yet I do not know if this is the path I should continue down. What if this was all a mistake?"

The private chapel room, reserved for the royal family to seek guidance in and take private confessions, echoed back Prince Percy's whispered words, but nothing more. The second prince cast his closed eyes upward to the domed ceiling and opened them to look upon the paintings adorning the panels. Many interpretations of The One True god looked down upon him as he sat on his knees in front of the altar, his knees denting the upholstered cushions laid out before it.

Prince Percy did not wait for the silence to grow or be interrupted with revelation; he began to ramble quickly, his tone an attempt at convincing his worry that what he had done was not reprehensible but respectable. "Father always told us that when it came to the throne, there was no line too far to cross, that anything and everything must be done for the throne. But what about for the kingdom? For our people? Should we not go to such extremes for those causes, as well? For what we believe to be true and right in our hearts? I betrayed my own blood for the kingdom, gave our enemies our biggest secret, and unveiled what we have hidden for ages, and– and…"

He sighed, his words catching in his throat as he struggled to speak. His shoulders sagged under the crushing weight of countless mistakes.

In the past many days, the prince had often found himself in this room, haunted by the memory of hiding the parchments containing the Psalms of Fire and Fury and other court secrets in the lid of a shipping trunk. He could never forget the moment he watched as the heads of his betrothed's lover and her helper were thrown into the trunk destined for Lady Montarian. The pain of his actions gnawed at him, a constant reminder of the irreversible choices he had made. Of his betrayal of his own flesh and blood. Of his choices to forgo familial duty and oaths for what he believed was fair and honest.

Despite knowing his actions were pure and light, ever since his betrayal, his feelings of sickness had not waned as he had hoped. The prince held his hands in front of him in silent prayer, hoping for a reply to his questions.

Once again, no words came.

Every time he spoke to god, He was silent.

Even in his most dutiful days and faithful times, god has never deemed the prince worthy enough to reply to.

Why?

"Is this my penance? In my quest to bring light to the lies made in your name, did I anger you, too?" He glared at the visage of The One True, the god looking down his nose at the prince. The One True's arms were outspread, ready to receive and give light and love. But along his grand robes of golden brightness lay hidden lines of darkness. The One True promised all darkness would fall away in His name if only devout loyalty was given to Him.

But as Prince Percy looked to his god, his knees as weary as his soul, he felt the world's darkness sneaking into the private chapel.

God had not held back the evil He promised to banish.

Instead, it seemed, He gave it life, so long as it was in His holy name.

"I have been so devout, so dutiful, so obedient- to you and to my family my entire life," he swallowed, "Despite my curiosities in other studies, I have been true to what has been asked of me to honor and know. I have forgone temptation. I have done everything I was made to do and only strayed when I knew what was asked was not of the tenants you speak to us about, or so I thought. Were those words also a lie preached in your name?"

Prince Percy looked away from the stained-glass imagery. He rose from his knees and removed a wooden box from the hidden drawers of the small altar. Inside were tools used for divination and communication, and different offerings to provide The One True to appease Him and ask for His guidance.

Or another god.

"And yet, despite all of this, I cannot recall the last time you spoke to me."

Prince Percy pulled out a black stick of incense; the scent of amber wood and myrrh gently wafted in the space as the prince lit it on one of the candles illuminating the room. He set it on the altar, letting the smoke cleanse the air and his mind.

He produced a cloth bag from the wooden box, holding inside a deck of red and gold striped and swirled cards. He loosened his shaking breath, flicking his eyes over the altar offerings for The One True. Despite their abundance, none had been good enough to earn the prince His words.

"If you will not speak to me, perhaps another will." He mumbled as he lazily shuffled the old, dust-covered, and worn deck, an old method for communicating with forbidden and legal deities. Each card bore imagery and words that spoke intent and messaging, meant for those who could not hear gods as clearly as others or wished for more answers than what was divinely given to them. Often, worshippers pulled from the deck to learn what god hoped for them to do or to tell the reader what their path held for them.

Prince Percy flipped the top card over, revealing an image of balancing scales.

A blinded-robed woman stood beside the scales, pouring coins and wheat on the unbalanced side, working diligently to even the scales. Her robe was spotless and pure white, an image of ethereal goodness. The other scale outweighed hers, its side packed heavily with more coins and offerings. A faceless creature hunched beside the scale, leaning on a sword used as a cane, its robe pure black, shadowing the space in the darkness, threatening to overtake the woman's pure light. But still, she dutifully worked to balance the scales.

Justice.

Truth.

Fairness.

Righted wrongs.

Prince Percy closed his eyes and nodded before inhaling deeply, the incense smoke curved its trail toward him. As he let the breath go, another card fell from the bottom of the deck, his loose grip allowing it to tumble. The card's image stared up at him: a hanging man dressed in the finest wares. The man bore no sadness over his fate and wore a halo of light around his face, his expression of calming acceptance of his death.

Trials.

Surrender.

Sacrifice.

The prince picked up the card, returned it to the deck, and returned the deck to its bag.

He stood and snuffed out the candles in contemplative silence. He wondered what it would feel like to have a rope around his neck or a sword butchering through it. He wondered if it would be worth it- if justice would be worth his life if it came to it.

Justice.

Truth.

Surrender.

Sacrifice.

As his head bowed one last time at the altar, a shadow quietly shuffled back into the darkness.

Sister Ora woke to the sound of muffled feminine shouts and the grip of a calloused hand wrapped around her neck.

She managed to let out a choking scream as she blindly swung her chained arms. More strange hands reached to wrap around her arms and hold her still. She thrashed more frantically, her panicked eyes meeting Sir Marion's, who hovered over her, his hand the one that gripped her neck. Two ladies maids held her arms down as she jerked and thrashed and hoarsely screamed. Sister Ora saw as much fear and pain in their eyes as she felt in that moment.

Sir Marion moved his hand to hold her jaw, pinching his grip and forcing his fingers into her mouth to pry it open. She bit down on his fingers, earning a hard smack across her face from his other hand.

Sir Marion forced her mouth open again and shouted at the maids beside him, "Now!"

Kaylah rushed forward with a drinking flask. Her tears glistened as she approached. "I'm sorry, miss," she said as she poured the ice-cold water down Sister Ora's throat. She did not stop pouring, forcing Sister Ora to spit and cough until she swallowed the drink. "But you must drink something."

The flask emptied as Sister Ora gave in to the forced feeding. Her face ran with tears and chilled water as she glared at the man, finding joy in the violence.

"Don't even consider it," he snarled.

She ignored his warning and spat in his face. Sir Marion fell back and pulled his fist back to hit her. "I do not believe His Majesty or your betrothed will care anymore about me leaving marks."

She snarled back, thrashing, a viscous and wild dog ready to rip and tear until she drew blood.

Armored steps entered the room. "Sir, there are women of sensitive disposition present. Though it be rightful, perhaps you should quell your anger."

Sir Marion turned to stare at the King's Guard standing next to the shaking and crying Kaylah. He turned back to Sister Ora, now sitting up in bed, her body ravaged and hair a mess, her teeth bared, and her body heaving. Her once-soft and tame demeanor was replaced by the fires of a woman broken and burned.

"You just lost bathing privileges," he snipped at her as he turned and left. "And you will live off of grime and gruel for all I care. But you will eat, bitch."

He slammed the door behind him, the rattling echo breaking through the space.

"I told you they would bring him in if you didn't let me help you," Kaylah whispered as she approached. "They said you could be free of the chains if you behaved. That if you acted like a lady, you could have some freedom. I told you."

Sister Ora's jaw trembled, her teeth still bared tight, feeling more to her like fangs belonging to a beast than the teeth of a tame woman. The water dripped down her face and saturated her hair. Where water would turn a normal fire into smoldering ashes, the trickles on her body sizzled in the flames, awakening within her cold corpse.

That man.

These men.

These monsters in human form.

Sister Ora recalled the sneering smiles of satisfaction the queen held when the shackles were put on Sister Ora at the execution. She remembered the smirks and smugness of Sir Marion when he captured her and threw her in here. The same satisfaction that returned just moments ago when he threw himself atop her to cause more pain and suffering.

She remembered how much joy this entire court seemed to draw from her pain. She felt the cocoon she wrapped herself in after Sir Loren's death crack open. She felt the fear she wore as a blanket through the coldness of the castle fall away as she sat up in bed and heaved heavier breaths.

The serpent she kept locked in her chest slithered and stretched awake. It shook its scales and moved around in her chest, waiting for her permission to be set free, to harden her heart and resolve again.

I will not let myself suffer by their hands.

They do not get to win.

They do not get to kill me.

They do not get the satisfaction.

She snapped her head to Kaylah, her words shooting out in sharp, firm sentences. The words of a true lady of the court, the tone and candor she learned from Her Majesty herself. "Draw me a bath. Tell the kitchen to prepare me a meal fit for the king himself and call the other ladies' maids in. Now."

Sister Ora threw her body off the bed, her chains clinking beside her. She forced her dizziness and nausea at her starved stomach and tired misery to dissipate, "And get me the key to these fucking chains."

Kaylah hid her smile as she bowed and began her work.

CHAPTER 12

Ephraim jostled as the passenger cart rocked over the stony path, maneuvering around the walking travelers and pack mules.

The small villages surrounding Iron Bay were almost identical replicas of the large port city known for its black stone buildings and smoky atmosphere that hung low in the sky. The village of Nesshine- Ephraim's hometown- was crowded with high energy and families of all definitions, each person going about their daily business with purpose. Aisharians walked among the fair-skinned villagers who hailed from inland Ayeshire towns; their voices rising with different accents and inflections, creating a beautiful symphony of sound.

Over the crowds shouting, long-necked white birds flapped above, traveling from lakeside to shoreside of the Ina Gulf, looking for their next meal.

The reaches of Iron Bay existed long before the Alvarian Conquest. They were founded by hardy Aisharians and sea-loving inlanders, both of whom made the most of the city's natural harbor and turned it into a thriving center of trade for the south. The air smelt of sea salt and smoke, most prominent during this time of day when factory workers were busy coating themselves in soot and sweat. Despite the king's ban on his allies trading with Ayeshire, the inner city still managed to busy itself with the effects of the lively port capital just outside of the reach of the king's shadow.

As the passenger carriage came to a halt, Ephraim jumped down and helped others off while those waiting impatiently formed a queue to board the carriage. Charcoal fires marked the sky, and the smell of smelted iron filled their senses. Ephraim took a deep breath and looked around at the familiar sights of their home village.

"Ah. The smell of home." They chuckled as they made their way towards the outlying streets of the city, where their childhood home sat nestled between gardens and cabins of farming families and livestock.

Their walk was short, aided in part by their fast pace, and before they could reach the threshold of their family's property, let alone open the garden gate, their mother's voice rang out over the buzz of bees and the sounds of the trees rustling in the wind.

"Ephraim! Oh, my sweet child!" Ephraim's mother hiked her skirts up and hobbled through her perfectly manicured garden beds, tackling her child into a hug that took the breath from Ephraim's lungs.

"Mother." Ephraim smiled into her hair as they returned her embrace. "How I have missed you."

She pulled back and held her hands on their biceps, taking in every hair of overgrown scruff on their face and every tired wrinkle lining their smile.

"What is wrong?" she asked, her eyes squinting as she continued her inspection, her smile now faded.

"Mother..." Ephraim sighed.

Not even a moment into their return, and their mother had already begun her questioning.

"I know you; you and I share the same face, darling, and you did not write ahead to tell us of your visit. So, what is it that is wrong that brings you back to this place?" She turned and linked their arms together and walked them through the aisles of her garden, the greenery taking up as much space as possible on their small piece of property, feeding the bees that would provide the honey for her tinctures and healing drinks. The cottage house was covered in vines with flowers coloring spots on the stone and logs and twisting themselves around the shop sign that hung in the front.

Aber Apothecary

Elixirs, Tonics, Tinctures by Miss Meliandre Aber.

Below the sign dangled two short chain links that once held an addendum to the sign but had swung freely since Ephraim was young and sharing a bedroom with their siblings. A flood of broken memories fell over Ephraim as they remembered the day the addendum was ripped apart and used as a weapon on their mother. The late King Andrius had not been kind to those who still believed in the power of potions and dared to believe themselves more than simple Healers and scientists.

Who dared to still believe the earth could grant one magic.

Ephraim looked to their mother, happily walking them towards the back door of the home; the same green eyes that Ephraim was known for glimmered on her face, and her dark, wavy hair fell down her body and framed her high cheekbones and soft cheeks. Ephraim's eyes fell to the shadow of a scar on her cheek, healed with time and tonics. But her hobbling limp never quite healed. No matter the therapy and work she and other Healers did on her body, her hip still ached when it stormed and throbbed when she felt a liar in her midst.

According to His Majesty's cronies, letting her live had been a merciful punishment after destroying her potions and her bones.

"Your father and brothers are at the factory. They all took extra shifts this day but promised they would be home for dinner. I had a feeling this morn that a large roast with root vegetables would be best for dinner, and now I see why. Oh, what a lovely surprise they will all have when they see you at our table again," she said and rubbed Ephraim's arm.

Ephraim smiled and nodded but remained silent.

Meliandre squeezed her youngest child's arm and stopped their walking. "It is the war, isn't it? You wish to help and be a part of it like your friends, but it pains you to reflect on how your abilities would best aid in the war."

The familiar pain of reflection came over Ephraim again. They still regretted the lashings of anger they threw at Gerald when he was tasked with asking Ephraim to use their abilities and knowledge to create weapons of warfare.

To create Hellfire.

A chemical weapon so dangerous and volatile that its blue flames would incinerate an enemy and everything around them in a single blink. Most days, Ephraim's innate ability to heal and create was a welcome blessing. Still, as they recalled their apprentice times in the citadels of Odessin with other highly talented Herbalists, where unspeakable experiments haunted their waking hours, their talents felt less a blessing and more a burden.

The things they were made to do, the experiments they had a terrifying talent for, and the screams they still heard were all the reasons why Ephraim swore their life to the Healer guild the moment their apprentice tour was over. An oath that made them promise never to take another life again.

They could not burden the sky with more souls.

Ephraim let out an exasperated sigh. "Mother. I still do not know how you do that."

She smiled brightly, and her eyes crinkled. "The same way you do. I have told you of our ancestors. They saw and sensed many things no other could; they were one with the earth, just as you and I are."

Ephraim shook their head, and she retorted, "My darling, whether you believe it or not, there are things, magical things, beyond any understanding that still linger in our lands. Dragons were formed from the elements of this world; terrifying beasts who retreated into an eternal slumber and held more power than any of our man-made weapons could dream of. Our people once knew their true power. Your ancestors once talked to them."

"Mother, stop. If the wrong person hears..." Ephraim swallowed hard. Their eyes darted around, fearing a king's loyalist would hop out of a rosebush and cause their family more pain.

Meliandre rolled her eyes and led them into the house to sit at the kitchen table. She covered Ephraim's hands with her own. "They want you to forget this so that the earth's magic gives up on you one day, just as you have of it." She paused, and her face softened. "They cannot beat the magic out of you, just as they could not beat it out of me."

"But they could kill you or me, as they have threatened before." Ephraim began to shake. They pushed away the memories of the old king's soldiers busting into their home in the night while Ephraim stood with their mother in the kitchen, brewing up salves and spelling them with desires and incanted words.

Ephraim was barely knee-high when it happened, and they first felt the iron fist of the throne strike them and force them into behaving. But it was worse watching their mother be beaten and seeing their father, a true beast of a man, be held back by several men while he thrashed and threatened to kill them all if they dared touch his wife. While he could do nothing to protect his wife from those men's hands.

Obedience and silence were safe. They guaranteed Ephraim's family would not know the claws of the lion again. Staying out of the war meant that the crown might grant their family mercy if the war were lost.

"Yes, they could kill anyone the king wishes, no matter what we do. The king kills whoever he wishes, as it is, Ephraim. All monarchies do. Yet that fear has not stopped your father or brothers from aiding the factory in creating more barricades, weapons, and tools to fight against the throne. Nor has that fear stopped me from training new Healers and creating more tinctures for soldiers to take with them into the field. Why does it still stop you? You have been frozen since you were a child; when will you allow yourself to move?"

Ephraim rubbed their forehead, their mother's words hitting the same parts of their soul that they always had. "Mother, I do not know what to do. Every option is the wrong path to take. I know how to create such terrible things and cause such destruction, but I also know how to stop it. I have watched terrible men, prisoners who did not deserve to live for their crimes, burn to death and suffer until their last breath while we took notes and calculated refinements to our toxins and experiments in the Citadel."

They loosened their breath. "I have watched children be born from mothers who may not have lived had we not intervened. I have... I have done everything, yet nothing. I swore an oath to uphold life, not take it. To heal, not harm. And now I have been asked to cause harm, to aid in killing— no, not aid— to do it myself. It is all wrong, and yet, how can I be a good person if I watch others die while I can stop it? But how can I be decent if I aid in ending lives to save another?"

Their voice trailed off as tears overtook their vision, and they shook them away. Their mother rubbed their arm, reassuring them through her touch. Meliandre waited for her child's tears to lessen before speaking again.

"Do you remember Alisia's husband? The one who beat and bruised her? And how she would not leave him or go to the city guards to stop him?" she asked.

"Yes. He died in his sleep, didn't he?"

"Yes, he did. It was quite odd how his heart failed him so young, wasn't it." She turned her eyes to the open back door where a small patch of bell-shaped blooms blossomed in a pot. A wire cage covered the flowers so no creature could taste the poisonous buds. "The foxglove flowers were so lush that year, weren't they?"

Ephraim met her stare. Meliandre's eyes lacked any shame, fear, or regret at her hinted confession. Instead, on her face was firm resolution, content with her path. Her eyes shot to the ceiling covered in drying herbs, and she closed them.

After a brief moment, she took a breath and looked Ephraim in the eyes again.

"Terrible people do terrible things, Ephraim, and sometimes, even the kindest soul must fall a bit to set the world right. I will not tell you how to answer the questions in your own head, but what I do see is that no matter what decision you make, there will be death at your feet. Whether that death is at your own hand or your inability to save those taken by another, I do not know, but it will be there." She held Ephraim's hands and squeezed them together on the table. "You must ask yourself, how much death do you wish to see before it is too much to simply watch?"

Ephraim's eyes darted back and forth between their mother's eyes and their own hands. "But, mother..."

She squeezed their hand again. "Ephraim, you hold so much power in these hands, no matter what you do with it, so long as you believe it right and do it in the name of justice, it is right. Whether you stay your hand or you move it, that is your choice, your destiny, your burden, and your legacy."

They swallowed the hard lump, choking the words stuck in their throat. "But what if I do, or do not, do something in the name of justice and righteousness and it turns out to cause more harm, to hurt more people? What if I do something and it breaks me?"

"Then you work to make things right again. And again. And again. That is life, dear. At least, that is what life should be."

Father Robb held the scripts close to his eyes, his weary stare long since burned holes in the words on the page. His heavy sighing and shuffling of papers broke the empty air of the study around him. Father Robb had stopped bothering to ask his Scholars and apprentices to report for work. There was no longer a purpose to what they did.

Their faith was but a lie—his life of teaching nothing more than a fallacy to uphold evil men.

He set down the parchments and pinched the bridge of his nose.

Perhaps they were not evil, but men in power too afraid of their people to remove the boots from their necks and instead pressed them down harder. While using god and faith to justify their tyranny and harm.

Calling those men evil was too simple and kind of a word.

Father Robb had found himself once again surrounded by piles of books and texts. Parchment and paper of various creams and aged yellows stuck out from the bindings and rolls, but his research gave him no comfort, and he found no reasoning for the Psalms beyond hunger for power. After they came to light, Father Robb slept in the study, as did many of the Scholars under his wing. Together, they searched for records high and low, old journals of Scholars' past, and teachings and theories of young and old.

They searched for some crumble of honor in the lies they unknowingly upheld. Some inkling that creating the holy Houses and placing citizens in tiny boxes was a divine ask, not the means of men desiring control.

But their endless nights turned up empty. And now their studies and chapels stood empty as well.

"Father," a soft voice carried delicately from the doorway and over the stacks of books he and his hunched back hid behind. "There is another who asks for counsel. Shall I send them in or turn them away again?"

Father Robb let out a breath and shook his head. "I have no counsel to give. Please send them home."

The Scholar's aide hesitantly stepped inside; her head bowed in respect as she approached him. "Perhaps I could provide some counsel? As part of my training? She seems to need simple comfort from the church, Father, a conversation with a person of god."

He snipped out a reply, "The church has no comfort it can provide." His eyes shot to her, and he tried not to cry again. "I am no longer certain what He can do for lost or weary souls. Or what parts of Him gave any guidance to begin with."

She sighed and nodded. "Yes, Father." She turned and left, leaving the door open behind her.

Soft murmurs came from the hall; quiet tears and sniffles followed the Scholar's apologies. Father Robb saw the shadow of a widowed woman, adorning a black veil, pause in front of his door. Under her veil, he saw her wet eyes glimmering and felt the sting of tears threaten his own. They shared a momentary, somber look.

"If you do not have faith, Father, where does that leave the rest of us lost souls?" he did not reply, and she asked again, "What are we to believe in?"

Father Robb turned his eyes to the rosary he had thrown on his desk many moons ago.

"I do not know."

CHAPTER 13

"It is your duty to protect these lands and our people, Augusta. Especially from those thieves and beasts in the North that have been stealing Odessin land for centuries." The Lord Dowager of Broken Tower, Ferrik Lisarian, argued. He leaned onto his cane, where both hands rested, avoiding the glaring eyes of his new daughter-in-law, Lady Reval Lisarian, a daughter of Craigie.

"The blood of those thieves and beasts runs through my veins, your sons, and the late Lady of the Tower." Lady Reval Lisarian firmly corrected the slander thrown out about her home country. "And it is not our people who stole the land- it is yours."

She tossed a hand in the air against the dowager lord before turning and pacing the length of the table, running a hand through her fire-red hair.

Lord Augusta Lisarian sat with his chair pushed out from the table, separating the two adversaries from one another. He leaned his elbow onto the chair arm and, in a full display of his tired frustration of the two, set his forehead in his palm. Lord Augusta was a tall and broad young man of twenty-three, his traits a thorough mix of his Odessin and Craigie blood. His skin was a sun-kissed cream, with light freckles dotting his nose and cheeks, and strawberry red running through his dark brown hair. The same dark hair his father used to wear in a short crop cut before the balding grey overtook his once-thick locks.

"Enough fighting, you two." He mumbled, then sat up straight and spoke sternly, remembering his place as the lord of the land. "We will do as our House has always done, end the fighting where it stands, remain neutral, and move onward."

The Lord Dowager and Lady Reval exchanged a look of deep-rooted conflict, their silent communication a testament to the tension between their opposing bloodlines, before turning their gazes to Lord Augusta.

"It is too late for that." Lord Ferrik mumbled.

"What do you mean, father?"

"I mean... it is too late to stop anything already done." The Lord Dowager said, his voice teetering between sharp confidence and timidness.

Lord Augusta slowly stood, his father avoiding eye contact. Lord Augusta's deep baritone rumbled as he glared down at his father. "What did you do?"

"I did what must be done," Lord Ferrik said, his voice shaking with age, not emotion or terror. "Lady Edgel has gone too far this time, and you know it, Your Grace."

Lord Augusta inhaled deeply as his back straightened. His stance was as angry and firm as his wife, who now stood alongside him. "I ask again, what did you do?"

Lord Ferrik uncomfortably adjusted himself on his cane, try-ing to stand up tall; the frail bones in his back prevented such pride from winning. "I did what you, nor your mother- god rest her soul- ever would. I declared that we would end this border squabbling once and for all. Lord and Lady Torrin received their birds, as I am certain both Odessin and Craigie have as well. And, from what I have gathered, Madam Fury is on her way back up the border to clean up the Northern scum."

Lord Augusta's eyes grew wide as his square face sat rigid. "You no longer have such authority. When mother passed, her title came to me," he stood closer to his new wife. "- to us. You lost your right to do such things once I took my oath." He darted his eyes at his noble Scholar, who conveniently remained quiet and avoided eye contact during the discussion. "And you also hold no right to coerce other advisors on my council to aid you in your ambition, as I am certain you did not write those letters yourself."

Lord Augusta only gained his title in early summer when his mother succumbed to her spring fever. As autumn fell around them, his father struggled to accept that his son now ruled the marshy lands of Broken Tower. But mostly that his son now held power over him.

"Something must be done, child. You know it, the king's war in the south will soon rise to our lands, and we cannot fight on both–"

"Enough," Lady Reval's voice cut through the air like a blade. Her alabaster skin tinted pink as her anger boiled. Her face carried delicate and thin traits- a long, straight nose, a small smile, and soft almond eyes. But beneath the delicate surface was a woman to fear, respect, and never cross. "As your child- the Lord of Broken Tower- stated, it is not your place. It is our duty to choose what side we will take and what we will do, not yours, not any longer."

Her body threatened to storm for him, to show how hot Craigie's blood boiled when enraged. If it were possible, her soft blonde hair would turn into flame from the heat inside of her.

Lord Augusta shook his head, fixing his body between his wife and father. "Born from many, now as one. Those are our House words, and we must stand by them. It is not our place to take sides—since the day Sir Oryst accepted his title over these lands generations ago, our blood was sworn to honor our oaths and nothing else. Not power, not praise, not ambition." He eyed both his father and his wife.

A fearsome knight and man well known for the oaths he held tightly to, Sir Oryst Lisarian led the siege of Broken Tower during the Royal Civil War- known then simply as The Tower, after the ruling family swore fealty to Queen Oriana and not the man Sir Oryst had sworn his fealty to- the Usurper King, who ultimately won the crown and the kingdom.

"It is our place to keep peace and remain neutral. Our line was born from both Craigie and Odessian blood, wed together each generation in the name of peace. Our marriage, and all before and after ours, are crafted in the name of upholding that peace and maintaining neutrality between Craigie and Odessin. We take no sides—" Lord Augusta's head jerked as his father cut him off.

"Neutrality is a side. And it has gotten this House no great glory."

"Aye." Lady Reval nodded in agreement.

Lord Ferrik's eyes twitched in surprise at her agreement with his words. She returned his expression with the glares she so often gave him.

"Not all in this kingdom seek glory. That is how we have fallen so far and why our continent is killing itself." Lord Augusta turned to his Scholar. "You will rescind the birds sent across the lands, correct what the dowager lord has stated, and confirm our House's neutrality."

He turned back to his father. "And you will not overstep again. Or you will be had for treason."

The lord nodded to all gathered in the room and saw himself out, Lady Reval close behind in quick step.

"Your grace, I hate having an agreement with the dowager lord," she shouted at her husband's back.

Lord Augusta continued walking, answering with a shrug. "Then simply choose not to agree. You both so often find ways to argue, even over the chicken we eat for dinner, you must feud."

She huffed, "Yes, well, unlike your father, I prefer my chicken seasoned and cooked rather than salted and burnt black like the lands he hails from."

Lord Augusta sighed, "What is it you need to speak to me about?"

She grabbed his arm and stopped his steps. "The ink has well dried on our joining, yet I know so little of our House and our future. What is it you seek? For your name? Your House? If not glory, then what?"

Lord Augusta thought for a moment, mulling over his words. "I seek what I must: the law, my oath, our House words."

"So I truly have married into a House of no ambition, no glory." She stared up at him, her body as close to his as it had been only at their wedding altar and on drunken nights since.

"If choosing what I believe is right, my oath over ambition and all else, does not put my name into history or even gain me recognition in rooms at court, then so be it. I hold no issue with being forgotten."

She crossed her arms and put distance between them. "Even an oath keeper must break his words if the right cause comes calling."

Lord Augusta nodded. "Yes, but that day has yet to come. And until it does, I will be the ever boring, unglorified, forgettable Lord Oathkeeper."

He raised a brow and the corner of his lip as he said the nickname and descriptors given to him, in private jesting comments not made for his ears, by his new wife's ladies during their quick season of courting and marriage negotiations. She pretended not to recall the words nor to look back on the prior season when she felt like livestock sent to show to capture the attention above all others, prancing about in the ring.

She scoffed and rolled her eyes. "And you expect your new wife to do the same, yes?"

He stepped towards her, closing the little distance between them and glaring down at her.

"I expect my wife, and all under my House, to do the same, yes."

She shook her head and thinned her lips into a small line, turning away from him. He gently tucked a finger under her chin and returned her face to his.

"Born of many, now as one. We are one now, my lady. It is not just my oath, but yours as well."

Lady Catherin Torrin turned the crisp page of the children's book, pointing to the painting of the three-tailed green dragon flying over barren lands and dry rivers, "And so Baethorn flew for ages, circling the southern lands, once barren and brown, finding his perfect spot to rest. Like his rider, Baethorn was wise and took much time to decide.

"Finally, he nestled his nose into the hills and lakes of the southern lands, smashing his tail about the land and creating rivers for him to drink from and to cool his scales. From his back sprouted grasses and trees as green and shimmering as he."

She turned the page, side-eying her son's closed eyes and quietly deciding to turn to the final page of the tale. "And thus is the tale of how Baethorn and Patrius the Wise saved the southern kingdom and brought to it a lush life from its dried and plain lands."

She ran her hand along the portrait of Baethorn, the ancient green dragon sleeping on the ground. His body formed hills and valleys while trees and grass sprouted along his back. Baethorn was a fit dragon of pure muscles and razor-sharp scales, his body lankier and thinner than his siblings. His back carried ridges and bumps, like hills in a landscape, and spikes ran down his three tails, each ending in spikes.

"Are the dragons coming back, mum?" Ennis sleepily asked, leaning against her side and pulling his blankets up higher to tuck under his chin.

"Oh, my sweet boy, I do not know." She laughed. "I can only hope that if they do, we will be the riders on their backs instead of those in front of their fangs."

Ennis opened his eyes that sparkled with hope. His sleepiness faded, his excitement taking over for a moment: "Do you think I could ride a dragon, Mum?"

Lady Catherin closed the book and set it on the table beside his bed, then moved to fix his pillows and bring up a warmer blanket on top of the quilt he held against his chin. "If the dragons do ever wake, my love, then I will tame and ride them alongside you."

Ennis closed his eyes much harder than necessary, his face squinting in concentration.

"Ennis, what are you doing?" she asked, giggling as she spoke.

He peeled open one eye, "Praying for the dragons to come back. And if they do, to bring father and brothers back with them, too, so we can all ride one together."

She rested her hand on top of his little fingers, clenching the edges of his quilt. "I shall also pray for that."

Lady Catherin rubbed his hair and kissed his forehead before leaving, "Goodnight, my love."

Her walk to her chambers was quick despite her belly's extra weight hindering her typically fast-paced walking. She rubbed her stomach absent-mindedly with each step, a small huff escaping her as she paused in front of her bedroom door.

She pushed it open, not paying any mind to its being left ajar, and was surprised by the presence of her son, Lord Lyall, standing by the writing desk.

"Oh, goodness, Lyall, you startled me," she said as she entered the room.

"Sorry, mother. I—hold on." He cut himself off as he quickly moved to pull out a chair for her and assisted her in sitting.

"What is that in your hand?" she asked, noticing the parchment he held.

"A letter from the North," he said as he handed it to her.

She sighed in exhaustion, her mind already burdened with the weight of the unknown troubles the North could bring them, "What has Lady Edgel gotten herself into now?"

He shrugged and rubbed the back of his head, jerking his head around to find a chair. "Well, quite a bit, it seems. What shall we do about it?"

Lady Catherin read over the scrawl, the poor handwriting forcing her to take pause with each word.

Lady Edgel intends to battle at our doorstep before the season ends. We will not allow her violence to continue on our holy lands. In keeping with our sworn oath, House Lisarian and all of Broken Tower will rise to defend the borders.

Lady Catherin shrugged, not in a lack of care, but in defeat over the repeated anger and aggravation from the borders, "Nothing at all, Lyall. It is not our place to interfere. This is but a courtesy warning from the new Lord Lisarian, nothing more."

Lord Lyall awkwardly ticked his pointer finger, trying not to interrupt his mother, "Um, sorry. There is more."

He pointed down to where the paper was still curled. Lady Catherin unrolled the parchment further.

Craigie's thirst for blood and power will end on this day once and for all. Permanently.

Lady Catherin heaved another sigh, "If Lady Edgel's head ends on a spike in favor of Madam Fury and Odessin, Lady Lisarian will kill her own husband and wage war on her own House."

On paper and by contract, that neutrality played out for generations.

Lord Lyall nodded his head back and forth, "And if Madam Fury's head is taken instead, half of Lord Lisarian's family will kill him- including his father."

She pinched her brow, "The new Lord Lisarian is a neutral, honorable man, just as his mother before him. The few times I have met him, he had always been steadfast and held tightly to his oaths of neutrality. This does not feel right."

Lord Lyall drummed his fingers on his lap, "But the dowager lord, he was always a bit..." he shrugged, "You know."

She rested against the back of her chair. "Yes, he always made shared holidays with our home unbearable. I still do not understand how, or why, the late Lady Lisarian was paired with him out of all the other noble families of Odessin."

"Their ways are odd, that family." Lord Lyall added.

She nodded while her hand slowly rubbing her sore stomach. "Their ways are as old as time and meant to keep the peace of the lands, Lyall."

Lord Lyall scoffed and kicked his foot across the stone floor, "Fine job they're doing of that."

"Aye," she mumbled, then let out a sigh, her brow pinched in thought.

"So, what shall we do, mother?"

She shook her head. "Nothing, Lyall. The dowager lord has no true power and cannot command an army. If this letter is the dowager lord's doing, there truly is nothing to worry about;

Lord Lisarian will correct his father's behavior, and this will simply be noted as family dramatics. But if it is Lord Lisarian who writes this threat –" the baby kicked in her stomach, prompting a gruff from her and a heavy breath that forced her to pause.

The greenery outside the castle had already begun changing with the autumn chill. When the snow finally fell this winter, she would no longer feel the kicks in her stomach that kept her up at night. She gingerly rubbed her stomach again, "If this letter is from the true Lord Lisarian, then we must wait and see what such vagueness truly means. Those are his lands to protect and keep the peace in. As the House above his, we are only to step in if he breaks his oaths or we deem his actions intolerable, and even then, we must be careful."

She paused again, recalling that last significant moment in time when House Torrin stepped into the mess of the north and fought against those scuffling outside of Broken Tower. Her belly had been just as large all those ages ago as had Lady Kathilla's. She had hoped to raise their boys together as much as they could, but their lands were not the only distance placed between them upon the death of Lady Catherin's brother and the slaughter at the borders. She mumbled, "I do not want to repeat the dark history that curses that land."

Chapter 14

Lord Cossius dramatically sighed, throwing his head back as he lounged beside the campfire, his legs extended out in front of him and his ankles crossed. "Father, you did not warn us that holding lands from a siege could be so... boring."

Lord Rener's eyes lifted from the pages of his book and landed on his brother's face, dripping with impatience. The silence hung heavy as Lord Cossius awaited a response from their father and ignored his brother's staring. Lord Cossius had always been eager to take action, and the monotony of awaiting orders and guarding land did not suit his restless spirit.

He needed to fight- to take down those who awaited them west of Ravenhall. He needed to do something.

Lord Cossius continued, now looking straight at his father. "Why must we continue to sit in agony, waiting for them to strike us? It has nearly been two moon phases since we last drew blood."

And gods, forbidden and legal, he needed to draw blood or at least strike his sword at more than straw-stuffed dummies in the practice fields.

"Wrong." Lord Rener mumbled before looking up and closing his book. "Our outermost defenses have seen a few skirmishes since our battle at Lake Lahere; minor tussles meant to test our resolve and lines. Seized land requires armies to guard it, and that is what was asked of us to do. We protect this land and keep its banners from turning back to the kings."

Lord Cossius ignored his brother's correction. He was the heir, not Lord Rener. He knew more about what decisions a lord must make in peace and war. "Father, we are not the stewards of this land. We have protected it well, and it is now sworn to our queen—why don't we leave a few thousand men behind and take on the prince again? We do not need an entire army to sit by and guard here. Our army will be between the princes and these lands, and to our backs lie our borders- not the king's. The north holds mountains and desert, and the south holds our allies."

Lord Cossius had given deep thought to his argument against holding. While he was often impulsive, in his eyes, following his intuition to move on their enemy was the right tactic. He knew they needed to battle, not sit and only respond to attacks.

Lord William Torrin blew into his mug of hot drink. Finally, he shot his eyes at his eldest. "No," he said simply with firm- ness.

"But we are a fit match for his army at this moment. He camps only a few da'es away from our lines, yet we sit here, outnumbering his and letting him mock us by holding onto lands he snatched from our allies before. And with the news that came from Lady Montarian of the revelation regarding the Psalms, many of the king's men will turn against him in due time." he worked to keep his anger and frustration in check, to argue his point with the calm resolve that his brother often had- the brother that was listened to more than him so often.

"There are many ifs that we must consider with your argument, brother; if the prince's army has not grown, if the king's men received word of the Psalms, and if they believed it. If the truth mattered to them and they were willing to risk their own lives for it." Lord Rener mumbled. "And we do not even know if Lady Montarian sent word the way of the king's men." His head cocked, and his eyes creased in contemplation. "In fact, it would have been smart of her to ensure His Majesty and his army knew nothing of what has been revealed. To let them be shocked by any turn in our favor."

"Exactly!" Lord Cossius exclaimed, "We should strike while the tide is turning more in our favor; use the king's lies more to our advantage."

Their father sighed. His hot morning tea grew cold.

"We were a fit match in number, yes. That is, until the rest of their army makes it to their camps- the new army the king has enlisted from other Houses and any allies from the Isles of Odessin." Lord William's tone was even, flat, factual. "Our birds are silent in their news, not even coming back here to where we lie in wait. Our scouts have yet to return, and we do not know how well the reception of the Psalms has gone. Cossius, I am as eager as you are to end this bloody mess and return to peace, but we do not know what awaits us the moment we cross these hills. We cannot battle in blindness– we must wait for updates."

This waiting is a mistake. He kept thinking. I've thought it over. I know I am right.

"Then send me." Lord Cossius confidently said with a jerk of his chin. "Send me to scout. I will find our scouts that have yet to return and find the information we need to continue onward. Send me."

Lord William glared, aggravated at his heir's irresponsible suggestion. "No."

"Father, I—"

"—No."

Watchful eyes observed the argument, and side glances were shared among the soldiers and healers nearby in the camp. The lord stood up; a small grunt of soreness accompanied his movement as he bent to the fire to check the water kettle.

"We will move, Cossius. We will fight, but we will not do so carelessly. A war is not won in a single battle. Each battle in this war has turned the tides in different favors." he turned his eyes to scan the crowd watching them. "We will not risk being the tide that favors the king."

"Then what shall we do?" Lord Cossius' tone still held its edge, but even the advantageous heir knew when to pause his pressing.

Lord William returned to the tree log turned sitting stool. He took a sip of his tea, which he had refreshed with more hot water. "We wait for orders. We are fighting this war under Lady Montarian's cause, not our own personal gain. We move as one under her banners, under her direction."

Lord Rener nodded in agreement, then returned his nose to his book. Lord Cossius sat down on his stump across the fire. He felt a familiar tug and pull inside of him, one that felt like hard scales dragging on his skin. The sensation reminded him of the feeling of dragon scales that he had never felt but often dreamed of sitting upon with the wind in his hair and fields of ice below.

His mother's family often joked that Cossius was Balnar the Brutal reincarnated. His demeanor and silhouette were reminiscent of the long-dead Alvarian prince, and his cries at his birth sounded less like those of a babe and more of a fierce battle cry. But that was nothing more than a foolish joke. Reincarnation was not possible. The church had always preached that once a soul was sent to judgment and rested in the seven hells or the stars above, it would never return to the earth.

But, his mother's ancestors believed many different things than Lord Cossius was made to accept.

And even as the heir to his beloved country, Lord Cossius had always been made to accept many things: that his brother's eloquent words were more apt than his, that his duty would be keeping peace and not truly ruling, that while he had his own mind, he would always have to follow others' oaths and orders.

The sharpening stone sang across the blade.

Prince Elion's hand moved with steady precision, honing the edge of his sword, his expression as sharp as the blade. His officers watched him in silence, the weight of their predicament settling heavily on their shoulders as they stayed gathered in their war camp one hundred miles west of Ravenhall. Only a few more days of travel, and they would be at Ravenhall's fortress walls.

Lieutenant Jeffrey Swift broke the silence first, his voice a low rumble. "My scouts report that Sebern's army has held strong in their size, double our own as of late. Every village outlying Ravenhall that we thought barren or neutral has turned out more men, with several families leaving for shelter in Sebern, and the ghost towns leaving us nothing to pillage or use against them."

"And where does their army lie?" the Crown Prince asked, slicing another song on the blade.

"They're still camped in the hills around Ravenhall and inside the walls, waiting like wolves." Lieutenant Jeffrey replied.

Prince Elion finally looked up, his eyes calculating as they swept over the gathered officers. "And our allies?" he asked, his voice calm, almost detached.

"Still many da'es away, Your Highness," Sergeant Valen, a blonde-haired and heavily shouldered woman, replied. "But they're coming. If we wait, we'll have a fighting chance to take back Ravenhall with their help and ensure lessened losses on our end. We can meet them just outside the enemies' lines and set up the siege together."

The prince nodded, setting the sword aside with a final, deliberate motion. "Then we wait and move to meet them," he said. To the prince, the choice was clear— rushing into battle without their full strength would only lead to unnecessary loss of life. They had already fought and torn down their enemies' men in the height of summer and pushed them back closer to their own lands. They could not risk losing what they held, especially when the aid they needed was only a few moon rises away.

"But we could attack now, Your Highness, pack up toda'e and attack just before Odessin arrives. We could successfully take the fortress lands back without them." Sergeant Valen timidly offered.

Prince Elion left his elbows resting on his knees and intertwined his fingers. He cocked his head up at her, knowing what it is that she suggested. "We will not take Ravenhall by the north. I have already said this."

Corporal Caden, a thin-bodied and equally thin in his patience man of fair skin and dark hair, cautiously argued, "I know you did not favor it before, but if we wait much longer, Sebern will come for us instead. We could rush them from the northwest villages, catch their stronghold off guard, push them back towards Tower Bridge, and take back the fortress. We would be able to overtake Ravenhall before they even knew what was happening."

Prince Elion's gaze hardened, his voice cutting through the tension like steel. "The answer is still no," he said firmly. "The attack from the north would result in too much loss of life for our men and those who live north of the fortress walls. I will not risk innocents when other options are available. We uphold the rules of war. We do not violate them for the sake of victory and desire."

Commander Blackley stepped forward, his grizzled face lit by the flickering flames. "The ethical rules of war are important laws, yes, but laws that hold us back at this moment," he said, his tone measured. "Are you certain you want to hold to them so rigidly? The northwest approach would work."

"The price of that victory is not one I am willing to pay," Prince Elion replied, his voice resolute. "Proportionality demands that we use only the force necessary to achieve our objectives. If we storm Ravenhall from the northwest, we risk too many civilian lives—innocents who have nothing to do with this conflict and risk destroying and fighting upon their farmlands- lands my father holds very close to his heart, given what the Three Sisters' fertile soul offers our country."

Prince Elion did not continue explaining his lack of desire for this plan; they had all heard it many times. Attacking through the Three Sisters and villages north of the fortress of Ravenhall would result in catastrophic damage to the area and destroy essential fertile land that grew much of Britia's green vegetables, wheat, and fruit. While the lands around Isilria did produce agriculture, the clay soil in the area caused a lack of diversity in what could be grown in the west, and the king's city relied heavily on other areas of the continent to feed his city.

The officers were silent. Commander Blackley's eyes narrowed as he studied the young prince, the man he had trained and mentored for years. "Sebern wouldn't hesitate to use such a tactic," he pointed out, his voice low. "They'll see our adherence to these rules as a weakness and exploit it."

The Crown Prince met the older man's gaze, unflinching. "Our fate is our duty, and our duty is our faith. Our faith requires that we adhere to the laws set forth by His Will and the will of the throne. Negating to follow the rules of war is a violation of everything my House, and our faith, stand for."

Should stand for, the grating voice in his head corrected.

A tense silence followed, and then a voice, rough and tinged with anger, cut through the quiet. Lieutenant Jeffrey hesitantly spoke to his lover, "With respect, Your Highness, we have all heard the tales around the campfire of what His Majesty has been doing in Isilria- the things he has ordered and done to those who have spoken out against him. And he is sending other armies to Middleton Landing to seize it and destroy it- a command far worse than the plan we offer you regarding Ravenhall. If the king doesn't adhere to the rules of conduct, why should we?"

The air around the fire grew thick with tension, the other officers exchanging uneasy glances. Commander Blackley's eyes flicked to The Heir to the Throne and met his, gauging the prince's reaction.

Prince Elion's expression darkened instantly, his eyes narrowing as he fixed the lieutenant with a piercing stare. "You would do well to watch your tongue," he said, his voice low and dangerous. "The king's actions are not for you to question. My duty is to uphold the law and to ensure that we fight with honor."

Lieutenant Jeffrey Swift opened his mouth to respond, but the lion prince cut him off, his voice rising. "The laws of war exist for a reason—to protect the innocent, to maintain order. Order we will all follow. If you or anyone else thinks otherwise, you're free to leave—though I will have your tongue first for committing such treason. No one is above the law."

Except the throne.

He shook the thoughts away. When had that voice begun to speak to him? It sounded too much like his conscience, too close in tone and cadence to be anything other than a sibling to the moral guide tied to his soul.

The fire crackled in the silence that followed, and the officers stared at the prince, some in shock, others in grim understanding. Commander Blackley stepped in smoothly, diffusing the situation with a calm but firm tone. "The prince is right—our duty is to the law and the honor of this army. We fight for the Crown; we do not raise questions against it."

Lieutenant Jeffrey, visibly chastened and scorned, nodded stiffly. "Apologies, Your Highness. I spoke out of turn."

Prince Elion's gaze remained icy, but he gave a curt nod. "See that it doesn't happen again," he said, his voice tight with lingering anger. He picked up his sword and sharpening stone again, slicing the air with more song.

Chapter 15

Gerald pushed open the tavern door, the warmth of laughter, fire, and comfort came over him as he stepped inside the familiar space. He craved nothing more than a quiet corner of his neighborhood tavern and a bottle, or perhaps a whole gallon, of heavy ale to wash away his exhaustion.

He smiled in polite greeting at the familiar faces of his neighbors and drinking mates and made his way to the end of the bar—his preferred spot to sit and take in the space and patrons. He nodded to the barkeep, a familiar lover Gerald had taken home after many long nights, and tapped his fingers twice on the bar top, signaling for a stein.

"You looking for anything else tonight?" the barkeep asked as he set down the full tankard before Gerald.

Gerald shook his head and passed over the coins, "Not tonight. Just a drink and a meal."

The barkeep nodded and left to fetch Gerald his food.

"Hey there, you look like you could use some company," a feminine voice crooned behind Gerald's shoulder. He sighed and set down his tankard. It had barely been pressed to his lips before the woman spoke. He turned to bid her goodnight, only to see her attention directed to the table behind him and a woman sitting with her eyes downturned at her hands, toying with a coin and flicking it back and forth between her fingers.

"I'm fine," Emaline muttered to the woman leaning against her table.

But the flirting woman did not move, her smile widening as she very clearly misinterpreted Emaline's discomfort. "You sure? You've got a pretty face—looks like it could use a little cheering up."

Gerald watched as Emaline looked up; her eyes flickered up and down the woman's body before looking away as the woman leaned in more.

"She's fine. Leave her be," Gerald said, his voice firm as he stood up and slid into the seat across from Emaline. The flirting woman glared at him but walked away, muttering under her breath.

"Didn't seem like you wanted company," he said.

Emaline barely glanced up, her eyes darting away as soon as they met his. "No, I didn't."

"She was cute, though."

Emaline nodded in agreement.

Gerald studied her closely. He could see the tension in her rigid posture, the way her hands fidgeted, and the slight tremor in her voice.

"This is not your normal watering hole," he said as he sipped his ale.

"I wanted to go somewhere different, away from the rest of the guards and soldiers that only wish to speak about this fucking war." She flicked the coin on the table too hard, and her eyes bulged as it rolled away from her. Gerald stopped it from rolling off the table's edge and returned it to her. She mumbled, "I don't want to talk about the war."

"I know," he nodded, then shrugged, "Me either."

She looked up at him. Gerald saw emotion flicker across her eyes for a moment—lonely sadness and pain. Two aches he had become close friends with over his life.

"I miss her, too. We all do." Gerald began, trying to keep his tone calm and measured.

Emaline mumbled incoherently.

"We don't have to talk about it, but not talking about it may be worse than actually talking about it." Gerald cocked his head to the side, confused by his own stumbling of words. He shook his head and took a swig. "You know what I mean."

Emaline kept flicking the coin.

Flick. Spin. Fall. Clatter. Flick. Spin. Fall. Clatter. Flick. Spin. Fall. Clatter.

Each flick grew more aggravated and aggressive. Gerald sighed, "But I'm sure it would be nice to have someone to take your frustrations out on. Someone who enjoyed annoying you into speaking about what is angering you."

Emaline flicked her eyes up at him, then back down to her coin.

Flick. Spin. Fall. Clatter. She smacked her hand over the coin and stopped the clattering. "I made a promise to Ora. I swore an oath, and I can't just sit here and do nothing. That is all everyone keeps asking me to do – nothing to her."

There it was.

Gerald knew Emaline needed to be annoyed, pushed, and gently shoved with every force in one's bones to talk through things and express her emotions. Since they had met and he, in her words, forced his friendship upon her, he had always enjoyed being the one in their friend group to aggravate the emotions out of her.

He tried his best to never let Emaline or Sister Ora know how their natural familial ease bothered him, how they fell so quickly into a deep and meaningful friendship while Gerald still felt a struggle to deeply connect with Emaline, despite him knowing Emaline longer than Sister Ora.

"You're not doing nothing, Em. You're fighting in this battle, one of the many that will lead us to victory. There will be no Ora to save if we lose this war."

She kept her eyes on the worn coin in her hands. Her thumb absent-mindedly rubbed its surface.

"You trust Lord Digarius, don't you?" he pressed gently. "He's become your friend, too. And I am certain he is doing everything possible to ensure we win this war and get Ora back safely. We need to trust and work with him, not against him. And to work alongside Lady Montarian as she leads our people and usurps the king. The Montarian family are good people, you know this."

Emaline's shoulders slumped. "Then why– I just hate feeling powerless," she admitted, her voice softer now, tinged with frustration. "Ora's my friend, my sister by bond and by love. I don't want to lose her… I can't lose more of my family."

Gerald felt a pang of sympathy. He reached out, hesitating only momentarily before placing his hand over hers. He ignored the twitch in Emaline's arm at the physical touch. "We won't lose her, Emaline. But we need to be smart about this. We need to fight together, not let our emotions drive us apart. We win the war; we get her back, and all will be right again."

Emaline didn't move, didn't speak.

Gerald squeezed her hand gently before letting go. "We'll get her back, Emaline. But we need to trust each other and stick together. That's the only way we win."

Emaline nodded and murmured. "I just… I can't stand it, Gerald. It's all wrong."

"I know," Gerald said softly. "But we'll make it right. I promise."

Emaline sighed and focused on the worn coin she held between her fidgeting fingers while Gerald took several sips of his ale. "How many of us do you think will die?" she asked.

"Hells, Emaline," Gerald replied to her bluntness that broke the momentary silence between them.

"What? You cannot tell me you have not wondered it yourself. Somehow, all of us, our entire little family of friends, have gotten dragged front and center into this thing- Sedrick, Ora, and Leaf are not even soldiers, nor blacksmiths, or even war horse handlers, and they're involved now- it is only logical to wonder which of us will make it out."

"I don't," Gerald shook his head. "I can't think about that. I don't wish to wonder."

Gerald felt Emaline's eyes on him as he shook his head and looked at his beer stein. He did not wish to wonder which good-byes would be his final words to his friends, which embraces he did not hold onto long enough, which smiles he did not spend enough time memorizing.

Emaline shifted in her seat in front of him and sat up straight. She drummed her fingers on the table. "Gerald. Talking about feelings is hard for me, and I know it can be frustrating for everyone to try, but" her fingers tapped in anxiety and frustration. "I am here for you to talk about anything. I'm working on being... better about understanding other people."

Gerald leaned back in his chair, "Emaline, you don't have to."

"I know that, but I want to. You were my first real friend here, but we never really talked about things deeply, and that is not fair. I know you and Leaf have... something going on, or wanting to go on, between you two. Even I can see it, and now they left to go home to 'think about some things' and visit their family, and they barely said goodbye to you. Ever since then, you've been, well, a grump."

"I'm not a grump." Gerald grumped.

Emaline tilted her head and simply stared at him.

"Fine. I may be a little upset. I just wish they had understood where I was coming from instead of reacting so rashly and angrily about being asked to try to recreate Hellfire for the war. It is not as if it was my idea or my order, I was the one who was just sent to talk to them!" Gerald found himself beginning to shout, and he shot an apologetic look at the tavern and Emaline's scrunched face. "What is it?"

"Ephraim may not be like me, with my different thinking and all that, but they do have a code of honor and oath they take very seriously, like I take mine. You asked, and you pushed them to throw it away because their skills might give us an advantage in this fight."

"I didn't push," Gerald grumbled, then took another swig of his beer.

"You pushed."

"Fine. Fine, maybe I did, but you must admit that I had valid points. You just said it yourself in different words. This is becoming everyone's war. It has affected us all, and Leaf is no exception, just because of the oaths they took when they were younger."

"So they should throw their oaths aside so easily? Let go of what they hold onto so dearly and what guides them each da'e?"

"Sometimes we have to bend ourselves so we don't break."

"Then maybe you should throw away the ones you swore to the Montarian family and to Lord Digarius himself, just in case those become an inconvenience to 'the cause'. Hells, why don't we all do what Sir Rainey did and betray everyone and our oaths? After all, they're just words and our duties are just jobs, right?" Emaline now sat back in her chair, her arms across her muscled chest, and her jaw hardened.

Gerald narrowed his eyes at her. "Not everyone will go down the path that Sir Rainey did. Why would you– Why are you being so extreme about this, Emaline?"

Emaline slammed her hands on the table and jumped up. "Why are you not?! Why is everyone in this Hells-damned kingdom so tolerant of breaking their oaths and promises?!"

Before Gerald could finish standing to calm her, she was already out the door.

It was best not to let them see you break. Not your enemies. Not your allies. Not your friends. Not your foes.

Emaline stormed out of the tavern on a wave of overwhelming fury and panic.

Promises. Promises. Promises.

Everyone made them, but no one would keep them. Why was she the only one who kept her promises and oaths no matter what?

Her mother promised to be there for her, then she left and got herself killed in a battle before Emaline could memorize her face. Her father promised to love her and care for her, and then he dumped her at an orphanage without a note or a name to chase after. The orphanage promised to take care of her and protect her, but then the other children grew up and pushed her around for being slow, odd, *different*.

They told her she must not be human, must be a changeling child, with how she acted so differently. "Bet her father dumped her off here because he knew she wasn't a real girl or a real kid. Left her to be our problem now," one of the girls had jested. That same girl glared Emaline down when the Scholar running the orphanage got the switch and beat her bottom red. That same girl and her friends found their own revenge when the Scholars were not looking that night.

Then the army promised so much to her. A new life. A calling. A duty. A destiny forged by god Himself. And god promised her so much if she just obeyed His Will.

But the wheel of betrayal kept turning as she fought to survive a childhood in war camps and leaky barracks.

The king promised to justly rule the kingdom.

Sir Rainey promised his loyalty to the Montarian House.

God promised her His Eternal Love.

Lady Montarian promised Sister Ora's safety.

And the lies just kept coming.

The promises kept being broken.

The oaths spoken with crossed fingers hidden behind backs.

Emaline heaved heavy breaths as she leaned against the back wall of the tavern. She lucked out tonight when she stormed down the alley, and everyone disappeared to leave her in her haunting solace.

"She is the only one who kept her promises to me." Emaline gritted out between clenched teeth and burning tears that blurred her vision. "And I betrayed her by not keeping mine."

She finally let the tears come out in their loud entirety. She bit her arm as she shrieked in internal pain.

I promised Ora I'd protect her life with my own, and they sent me away.

It wasn't my fault.

I should've fought them more.

It wasn't my fault.

I should've refused to leave.

It wasn't my fault.

I should've gone back.

It wasn't my fault.

It was my oath. My promise.

It wasn't my fault.

She is my sister. My closest friend.

If she dies, it is because of me.

If she dies, it is all my fault.

... Why couldn't I keep my promise?

Chapter 16

Queen Onetta stood by the tall, arched window of her receiving room; her gaze fixed on the horizon of the city that lay below. The incoming light cast long shadows across the room, illuminating Father Figgins standing behind her. He stood quietly, his hands clasped together in front of him. Queen Onetta had left him standing there while she worked to grasp the power in the air and take the upper hand for herself.

He was always such a tricky man to deal with.

Queen Onetta began, her voice cool and even, "I trust there's no need to remind you that there is no room for error regarding the wedding between Percy and that woman. I am not to be made a fool by her."

Father Figgins offered a slight, almost mocking bow. "Yes, Your Majesty," he paused as he straightened his spine, "But if I may speak so plainly, I have been left to wonder if the prince will cooperate as fully as we need him to and if your plan will truly aid our cause."

Does my husband allow such open questions on his decisions and plans?

Queen Onetta's gaze shifted from the window to the old man before her. "Percy has always had a bit too much of his father's softness in him- a charm and a curse."

"And a dangerous trait in times like these." Father Figgins stepped forward with a wry grin. "His softness may be endearing to the public eye, but without his full cooperation, Sister Ora might start thinking she has some leverage- that she has a chance of happiness. She could use him again in new ways..."

Queen Onetta's smile faded, her tone sharpening. "I know he still harbors foolish feelings for her despite his promises that he does not. But his feelings will be squandered before they cause us more problems. I will ensure it."

Father Figgins let out a small breath, "Your Majesty, with all due respect, how do you plan to keep her in line if Prince Percy refuses to be the iron hand we need to control her?" he tilted his head, a sly look in his eyes. "We can only do so much if he does not stand with us and our desires."

The queen's eyes were cold. "She will be given the chance to cooperate. I saw the weakness in her when we first met in her homeland. She can be tamed and caged. We continue to keep her isolated and under constant watch, only brought out when she obeys and is needed for some matter of the state. We remind her what happens when she acts out of line. Percy's kindness may shield her from the worst of what we wish, but she'll soon learn that kindness is a fleeting and useless thing. And Percy will soon give in on it when he sees that kindness is pointless."

Father Figgins chuckled, the sound low and dark. "A gilded cage for the future bride then."

"Precisely."

"I must bring up another delicate matter before the wedding planning continues. The reason I came here today is to speak to you in private. We all know about her little... indiscretion with that guard of hers. The affair and the possible consequence that festers within her."

Queen Onetta raised her chin. "You suspect she's with child."

"Not just suspect," Father Figgins said, stepping closer, his voice a conspiratorial whisper. "Given the timing of their tryst, it's highly likely she is carrying his bastard. I have asked about it, and while it is still early, the maids informed my birds that she has not bled and is two knots late."

"Perhaps it is her misery and grief preventing her bleed?" she queried.

"Perhaps, but would you wish to risk it?"

Her lips pressed into a thin line. "That little whore has always been intent on ruining everything, hasn't she?"

Father Figgins' sneer widened, his tone slick as lamp oil. He produced a large vial from his billowing sleeves. "I already took the liberty of having a tea prepared for her... unexpected development."

Queen Onetta raised an eyebrow at him and took the vial. "You are always so many steps ahead, Father Figgins."

The Hand of the King bowed, and his eyes gleamed with dark satisfaction that the queen recognized well. "You and I know quite well that one does not rise to such a stature as ours by happenstance and luck."

Sister Ora's body sank deeper into the warm bath, enveloping herself in the soothing embrace of the milk-clouded water. Her eyes fluttered shut for a moment, and she let out a contented sigh as her mouth fell just below the surface. She lay there in her boredom, idly blowing bubbles in the water with her breath, watching them break the surface and disappear.

Beside the tub, an empty vial that once contained goat milk sat, its remnants dripping on the side of the glass. The sweet scent of lavender wafted through the air, and petals of the soothing floral floated on the surface of the water. The steam rising from the relaxing bath created a fragrant mist that filled the room and gave Sister Ora a single, simple moment of peace.

She ran her hands down her arms, letting them caress her chest and stomach, the rag in her hand gently wiping away the morning. The rag brushed against her breast, and she grimaced at how sensitive it felt.

Kaylah hummed to herself as she set out Sister Ora's clothing for the day. The sun brightened the space and their moods as it approached its morning height, beckoning both women to hurry about their morning of leisure so that they could break their fast.

For a moment, Sister Ora's gilded cage glimmered.

Between calming breaths, the bed chamber doors burst open, startling the two women. Both yelped and jumped at the intrusion, their hearts skipping a beat.

A swarm of ladies' maids flooded into the room, not acknowledging the presence of the two, and marched straight towards Sister Ora's bed. They quickly began tossing about the disheveled sheets left over from her previous night's slumber.

"Excuse me?! But what in the hells are you doing?!" she shouted. Sister Ora jolted up in the bath, her arm covering her exposed torso, and shared a confused look with Kaylah.

The women did not reply as they finished stripping her bed and inspecting the sheets and each layer they removed.

"Excuse me!" Sister Ora shouted again.

Slow, deliberate steps clicked into the room. Sister Ora turned to see the queen smiling at her at the threshold of the open doorway. She felt more exposed than she had before, not just at the queen's intrusion but also at the door being held wide open, allowing any curious eyes to look inside at her indecent state.

"No blood, Your Majesty," one of the queen's ladies said to the queen as she tossed the sheets back onto the bed in a lump.

Sister Ora felt a chill run through her bones at the declaration, at what their inspection and intrusion meant. Sister Ora had given herself no time to wonder or worry over the possibility of her affair with Sir Loren producing a child. Her time since his death had been spent in too much stress and agony to wonder when her next cycle would appear.

She had not even bothered to continue to track the moon and her cycles as she once had; she had no energy in her grieving to bother with anything but sleeping away the depressing fatigue, the nausea, the misery.

Her hand dipped below the water, and she touched her stomach. She had never had a flat stomach; she had found comfort and love in her curves, but perhaps...

Her mouth parted in a small breath.

Maybe I didn't lose all of him. She thought as she held onto her belly and begged for a flicker of life to kick at her, yet fearing for it all the same.

She corrected her tone to be obedient and proper, playing the role of an innocent child. "Your Majesty, may I ask why your lady's maids are stripping and inspecting my bed?"

"According to the moon and what my ladies have told me of your cycles, you are well past due for your bleed. Yet you haven't for two knots."

The queen slowly made her way to the tub where Sister Ora still sat. "Since you do not bleed, I must assume you to be carrying your dead lover's seed." She kneeled in front of Sister Ora, her voice still calm and slow, "And if that is true, then I will cut it out of you myself if I must. You will not marry my son with a bastard's babe in your body."

Sister Ora's brows flickered, her innocent demeanor flickering away with the movement, and her anger jumping out, "So you shall cut me open on the assumption and let me die?" Her tone sharpened as she cut her teeth on standing up against the queen, "If you wish me dead, why not just drown me here? It is not as if any of your ladies would step in to stop you."

The queen rested her palm on Sister Ora's cheek. When she jolted away from the queen's grip, Queen Onetta grimaced and dug her nails into the back of Sister Ora's neck to hold her. "We are one of the richest families in this kingdom, little bird. We have access to more science and medicine than you know. I would not let you die. You do not deserve that peace."

She jerked her hand away from Sister Ora, returning to her tall stature, and turned to leave.

Sister Ora rubbed her neck and sat up more. "I demand answers!" she shouted despite herself. When the queen did not turn, she threw the glass bottle of goat's milk at the queen's feet. "Why do you keep me alive? What is the point of this? What is the use of forcing me to marry your son?"

Queen Onetta did not turn to reply, "Death can be a mercy. Ending your misery would be kind, and I do not wish ever to be such a weak thing."

"So you gift your own child a life of misery, too. Why bring him into my punishment?"

The queen paused, her chin lifted in the air, and her shoulders rolled back.

"The world is a cruel place and I am its queen." Queen Onetta said, then flicked her hand, prompting her lady's maids to leave as she stepped out of the room.

Sister Ora let out several breaths as the doors clanged closed. The tightness in her body calmed as she inhaled and exhaled. "What in the Hells?"

Kaylah ran to the tub with a towel, holding it up for Sister Ora as she stepped out. Shaking from the chill and adrenaline still pumping in her veins, Sister Ora dabbed herself dry and shook her head in disbelief.

"Are you okay, my lady?" Kaylah asked.

"Yes. I believe so." Sister Ora breathily replied. She held her towel around her body and walked to her dressing area. She turned her head over her shoulder. "Did you know of this? That Her Majesty was tracking my cycles?"

Kaylah followed close behind and laid out Sister Ora's under-clothing. "No. Although it does not surprise me that she would. Servants talk, the scullery and washing maids were likely asked to report any bleeding to her. And I– well, I knew you were late, but we had much more to worry about than if that lateness was due to your love of Sir Loren or your pain at his loss."

Kaylah held out Sister Ora's chemise. She swallowed a breath and huffed out a worried new one. "My lady, if I may, you are past due to bleed, and" she took another breath, "you did lie many times with Sir Loren after your last cycle."

Sister Ora shook her head again and refused to listen. Her towel lay loose around her body, and she quickly snatched her chemise from her hands and began to dress herself.

'The world is a cruel place, and I am its queen.' Sister Ora ran over the queen's last words again. *A queen full of dramatics and venom holds the key or the noose to my future.*

"At least it would be on your terms, my lady." Kaylah continued, cutting off Sister Ora's thoughts, as she stepped behind Sister Ora and began lacing her chemise.

Sister Ora's jaw shook as she set her hand on her belly. It had grown no bigger since she last felt Sir Loren's touch, but there were other signs- her nausea, fatigue, mood swings of mostly anger- that one could attribute to pregnancy or a physical manifestation of her depression.

Sister Ora did not reply, nor did she hush Kaylah's talking.

"There is a tea that ladies maids make quite often for noble women who enjoy the beds of their lovers or wish not to carry more heirs. If you take the tea and are with child, then you could say goodbye on your own and not on a medical bed, drunk on the poppy, surrounded by Healers and covered in blood while she watches... While she wins."

"No." Sister Ora managed to mumble.

"Miss-"

"No! I will not allow them to take anything else of mine." She choked out. Her hand found her stomach again, both hands now wrapped around it in protection. She prayed for a flutter, a sign of Sir Loren, a memory of what they had that she had hoped was love. On the dresser beside her box of jewels lay a simple grass rope, braided by large, firm hands that caressed hers in another lifetime. She stared at it with such intensity that she swore her mind rippled through time and into the past.

She watched their short love story play out again: their first forbidden glances, her first blush and surprise at a joke he surprised her by making, the moment they shared on a bridge overlooking the sea when she swore he spoke of her beauty, not that of the waves. The moments where they shared her bed and he would hold her like she was a delicate, breakable thing after he spent the night shattering her body into pieces and putting it back together again with his touch.

Her stupid desire to feel an inkling of love, to understand what genuinely being wanted felt like, had murdered a man.

She would never be so careless with her heart again. Following it never amounted to anything, and feeling anything within it only sent pangs of pain throughout her body and destroyed people around her.

After all this time, she was still the naive little girl who wanted childish and trite things like love and laughter. She wished for fairytales, heroic knights, true love, and happy endings.

But this world was not made for such dreams. It may contain castles, but the men inside were not heroes of tales.

"Why do you even care, Kaylah?" Sister Ora sniffled, her pain lessening the punch of her hard words.

Kaylah shrugged, "The world may be cruel, but this court is crueler. And the way I see it, I can either stay loyal to the coin that feeds me, or I can help where I can to rid this place of its horrors."

Sister Ora shook her head. "And possibly lose your job, or your head, in the end? For what? Hope?"

"Yes."

Sister Ora looked at her in disbelief. But still, she understood, even if it was only somewhat.

Kaylah reached out and squeezed her hand, "If someone like me, who has had the king's boot on my neck my entire life, does not fight, then who will? Those who sit in his comforts?" She shook her head. "It will take too many generations for them to truly stand, but now, seeing what the Queen of the People has to offer, I can finally see a guided path for our dissonance and disgust to follow."

Sister Ora scoffed. "And you see how well following that path has gotten me."

Kayla dropped her hand and took a breath. She grabbed Sister Ora's clothing to aid her in dressing for the day. "If you wish to fight, as the anger in your eyes has shown you to wish to, then you must be prepared for loss, for pain, for sacrifice and lies."

Sister Ora sat on her bed and tilted her head at Kaylah. She recognized her shaking as Kaylah grabbed a chemise and gown from the wardrobe. She recognized the trembling jaw.

"Who did you lose?"

Kaylah sniffed again and held a pause before whispering. "Alicent. Her name was Alicent, and we loved each other so deeply since we were girls. We could have married, but servants don't get to marry those born in Divine Houses above them. She was a Scholar and taught me how to read. We were going to move out to a smaller village where she would teach, and I would serve. We were going to adopt three children."

"What happened to her?"

"She was sent away for more schooling, and when she returned, we asked for permission to leave and marry. When we were told no because of our stations and because the Church needed more women like her in their leadership dedicated to God and no one else. She couldn't take it. She drowned herself."

"Kaylah I am so—"

"Don't. Just... don't, my lady."

Sister Ora swallowed the lump in her throat and closed her eyes. No matter what, the kingdom would take her joy, her unborn baby, and more from her. But if she made the right sacrifices, alliances, decisions, she could take more from them. Sister Ora stayed silent the rest of the morning and throughout the day.

But that evening, she called Kaylah for her tea.

The next morning, she awoke to blood on her sheets and shooting pain in her stomach.

She cried all day. From mourning or relief, she did not know.

CHAPTER 17

Lord Nesima Mete lifted the golden sifter from the iron kettle and placed it in a small bowl beside it. The sifted tamarind fruit dripped its precious juices on the table as it was separated from the steaming kettle of tea. The lord slowly stirred the drink, adding his preferred amount of sugar cubes as he did so.

"What are your thoughts on the boy now?" he asked his husband.

Lord Shaital Pathis took a deep, slow inhale and joined his hands behind him as he walked back from the open balcony.

"I am... concerned. I fear that continuing with our discussions of his future, of allowing the second prince inside our citadel–" Lord Shaital shot his eyes at his husband as he stopped in front of him. "- inside our true citadel– as a teacher and Scholar may not be as wise as I had once believed."

Lord Nesima poured them both a cup of tamarind tea and guided them to the seating area. His forearms peeked out from the short, loose sleeves of his robe, exposing his warrior band tattoos to the light as he set their cups on the short table between their floor cushions.

The middle band on each wrist was shaded with imagery. On his right wrist, a long, thin dragon flew around his wrist, with its mouth almost biting its tail. The dragon was detailed with scales, and its wings were spread, making it look as if it were in motion. On his left wrist, there was a band of marsh skullcap flowers. The flowers were beautifully detailed, with each petal inked with great care, and the band wrapped fully around his wrist.

"Is this new concern due to his betrothed's betrayal or another reason?" Lord Nesima asked.

Lord Shaital sipped before responding. "Both, yet neither. She betrayed his people, yes, but she did so for her people; a courageous act we cannot turn into such a simple thing, an act we can find empathy with and understand, given our own history and our futures. But the young prince's carelessness in divulging such sensitive information to her before he knew if she was trustworthy is where my concern lies."

"Then you worry as I do, that he may so carelessly let slip things we wish to continue to keep from His Majesty."

Lord Shaital took another slow sip. He closed his eyes and savored the sweet taste as Lord Nesima watched his mind ponder through his thoughts. His husband's face always bore the same thoughtful expression when deep in thought. Lord Shaital furrowed his brow, and his lip occasionally twitched.

Lord Shaital set his cup down on the short-legged table before his plush sitting pillow. "We know many things His Majesty does not, and unlike the throne, our ancestors learned quickly that knowledge is the most powerful weapon- it does not dull throughout a war like a blade does."

He paused to let out a laugh. "His Majesty does not even know that the Psalms have been spread throughout his own lands, and if he were not so stupid as to kill all the birds in his city and terrify his own people into hiding in their homes, perhaps he would know what is happening under his nose in this very city full of angry and hungry people."

Lord Nesima nodded slowly. He sat cross-legged on his ornate pillow, his casual indoor robe loosely folding around him. He rested his elbows on his knees, with his cup held in both hands in front of him. "I worry the second prince is either too tied to the loyalty of his family and may feel inclined to share everything with them, but I also see a boy who is shaken by his father's actions, and that makes me wonder if his betrothed is not the only one capable of betrayal."

Lord Shaital cocked a brow at him, a silent request for him to continue his theory.

"There are very few who likely knew of the existence of such a prophecy. Our own citadel that lay hidden under our mountains bore no such documentation, despite the resources those before us hid and remade after the great burning of the First King, so we must assume such a secret was known by only those closest to the throne, dating back to the time of dragons and conquerors."

"But could it not have been his Hand? Father Figgins does believe himself the most vicious viper." Lord Shaital jokingly countered, mocking the man of the cloth and gaining a satisfied laugh from his husband.

"We have befriended garden snakes more dangerous than that man." Lord Nesima continued, "It is but a theory, founded on simple deduction of suspects, but I believe it wise to assume this theory true of the second prince, which could make him a man too dangerous to know what lies beneath our mountains, of the records and books burned and reforged by our ancestors who saw what was coming for them and protected and rebuilt it all. This act shows he is willing to let the longest secrets into the light."

Lord Shaital nodded in agreement. "But, perhaps we can still make an ally of the young prince, a tool, or a weapon. If not of him, then of his betrothed. We still need another in with the royal family. While we do have Easter, her husband will not be one to divulge secrets or to be easily manipulated. Prince Elion is too tightly tied to his laws and his neutrality on the morals of his father's ruling."

"I sense another one of your plans hatching. Your eyes always glimmer when you are scheming." Lord Nesima smirked at his husband and drained the rest of his cup, the contents now cool enough to quickly drink.

"My eyes always glimmer." Lord Shaital did the same with his drink.

"Yes, I know," he chuckled. "So when shall this plan come to fruition?"

"You know me better than that, my love. It has already begun."

Chapter 18

The queen felt his presence before she heard his steps.

"Walk with me, my lord," she said, sparing the smallest glance over her shoulder at Lord Tyrrian Priscius. She swallowed hard as a heavy emotion came over her. She could not place it, but it felt so much like guilt.

He sauntered to her with a crooked smirk on his devilish face. "I knew I would find you here," he said.

"And why is that?" she replied, casually strolling down the garden path with him now at her side. She walked slower today, her body not wishing to rush any movement.

"Because if you are not in my bed, or yours, then you are here, in the gardens, plotting and planning and overthinking every step you take." He looked at her chest as it rose and fell beneath the low-cut bodice of her gown. Every cut of her dress was as sharp as she was; harsh angles cut the bell sleeves; the deep-V of the neckline was stitched in gold filigree trim accented with the same wine red of the dress's plush fabric. The dress tied shut with perfectly laced golden threads and matching buttons and latches running up the front and back of her torso.

She loosened a long breath, not letting it hitch or shake as her body warned her of another incoming pain in her stomach. "Do you ever think of anything else besides what lies between my legs, my lord?"

The devil smirked again, and his bedroom eyes darkened as he leaned in. "On occasion, I think about what lies between mine and how I wish it were your hand or mouth wrapped around it."

Queen Onetta composed herself, the faults in her foundation firming again as she straightened her spine and joined her hands softly in front of her. Her shock a feign to hide how she needed to hold her stomach, the insides still feeling as if they were being ripped apart. For once, her fingers lay bare of stones and jewels—all except for her excessively large wedding band that she twisted back and forth.

"He knows," she said firmly.

"Hmm?"

"My husband. His Majesty knows of us. He knows this never truly ended and has started again. We had a... creative discussion earlier this knot about it between his fits of whatever it is that ails him."

Lord Tyrrian shrugged as they descended a set of stone steps in the garden. Queen Onetta grimaced as she struggled down the steps.

"I would worry for the fate of his rule if he were so clueless about what we do. He knew of our past and what our families took from us to set the kingdom on 'the right path.' Only a fool would not know what burns between you and I."

Queen Onetta chortled, "My lord, is that a compliment to His Majesty?"

Lord Tyrrian chuffed, "I would never."

The queen nervously adjusted her intertwined fingers. Lord Tyrrian stopped walking, prompting her to do so as well. She hid her relief at their paused movements. The tea that was meant for Sister Ora had not treated the queen's body well.

His eyes crinkled in anger and worry, the same emotions that coated his words, "Has he threatened you about it? Stepped over the line? I will take care of this, of him, if he did."

She held up a softened hand to rest on his chest but found herself, and retracted it back. "No, there were no threats, and if there were, it would be up to me to control my husband and correct his behavior."

He took a deep inhale and huffed out a hot breath.

Queen Onetta turned her stare away from him, taking in the gardens and the castle framing the paths of greenery. Her eyes wandered down the many paths her feet had worn over her time living within The King's Keep's walls. In the beginning, she and King Ivan tried to form something between them. But their garden walks and private dinners did not last long.

The king and queen accepted their intertwined fates and only truly vowed to one another one promise: they would never grow to hate one another, as both sets of their parents did.

Whether it was their time spent in each other's beds or all their time spent forgetting the other existed, over time, that vow became easy to uphold as the space grew between them. But even the queen felt the coldness creep in each night she spent alone, and each conversation with her husband felt more like a formal business conversation than one between husband and wife. And the resentment for what she lost and could have had grew with each passing day.

"Have you ever wondered what it would have been like for us to rule the Isles together like we had hoped to do so when we were so young and naive?" she asked, her voice almost a whisper. Her hard facade softened in a rare moment of vulnerability, but her eyes stayed far away from his, and she dared not touch her empty and aching belly.

His hand gently reached for her, and his fingertips brushed up and down her bicep. "Every day, my queen," he whispered.

She felt it again- the pain, the longing, the desire for softness. She cut it off at its edge before it cut through her.

"My father wrote to me. He grows even more impatient in his old age, pressuring and pushing me to name my heir so they can begin to take his place." She turned to Lord Tyrrian, her face stone again. "He intends to name a new heir from another bloodline if I do not name one to replace me."

They returned to their walk with the encouragement of the various eyes they now noticed around them.

"Why have you not told him that you have named an heir? Is this part of another one of the power games you two have played for your entire life?" Lord Tyrrian asked.

"Everything about power is a game," she replied.

"And how do you intend to play? I assumed that Prince Percy was to be the Thelimor heir."

"Yes, but Arminda shows much promise as she grows. I sense much of me within her. She plays the role of an innocent princess quite well, but I know the facade she paints on in court. That could be quite helpful in a place so viperous as Thelimor."

"So you shall name the princess, then?"

She shook her head slowly. "If Percy cannot make a decision, then he and Arminda can fight over it- prove their ambition and ability to successfully lead in such a place as Thelimor. I had hoped that by telling them both that the title is Percy's, should he choose it, it would cause some sort of... competition between the two. I hoped that Arminda would not disappoint me by being so accepting of her brother gaining it over her and putting up no fight for it."

Lord Tyrrian stopped again, and his brows crumpled in confusion. "Why would the princess fight about this? Birth order is a well-known determining factor in titling. Why is there an expectation that she would go out of her way to argue against your wishes and rulings?"

Because I did when you were taken from me and became my sister's husband.

When the future I wanted was ripped away from me.

The queen huffed. "Because she should learn to fight for what she desires, as should Percy when his rights are threatened by another. My children have been given everything and have fought for nothing."

"And they know nothing of this, I assume? They have no clue that you desire them to fight one another and somehow prove their worthiness of such an inheritance?"

The corner of her mouth twitched up. Satisfaction at her scheming crawled under her skin, a comforting blanket she enjoyed holding onto, "No."

"This ridiculous game you are forcing them into is simply an extension of your constant fighting with your father."

"Excuse me?" she whirled on him in a snap of fury.

Lord Tyrrian's words hurried out, his aggravation surprising them both. "Why do you bring the children into these games? Why must they get involved in this ego fight between you two?"

Her jaw firmed, and her anger rushed to meet his; she did not care for calm and proper decorum now. "Because they must fight for this, earn their futures, as I have fought and earned everything given and forced upon me. Simply giving them a better future will not help them. If I had to fight, then so must they."

The queen saw the internal debate in his eyes as he thought out his next words. "Why do you do this to the girl, Prince Percy's betrothed? Why must she marry your son? If you hate her so much, get rid of her."

"No. She does not get to escape her treason so easily," Queen Onetta said firmly.

He crossed his arms, "So giving her a prince's hand is punishment? Really, Onetta, I thought you were better, smarter than that," he chuffed.

"Do not insult me," she gritted out. "Why do you fight me and aggravate me, Tyrrian?"

A smirk crawled across his lips. Queen Onetta frowned as she stood beside him. "You have no idea what to do, do you?" he said, "Sister Ora's scheming behind your back was not something you foresaw, and you are livid about that."

Queen Onetta's face tightened in fury.

I know what I am doing. I have a plan. I always have a plan. She threw a curve in it, yes, but she is nothing to me. She is just a dumb country girl.

I am the queen.

Lord Tyrrian laughed again. "You did not have time to plot and scheme as you normally do, quietly and carefully, always biding your time, and you are simply guessing at what is right to do to her, about how she will play into your hand and your game of power. You locked her up in her chamber because you needed time to mold back into your plans."

She shot her words at him between gritted teeth and a clenched jaw. "I am your queen. You will not patronize me in such a way."

She shook from the inside. Her anger began to rise out of control. She loathed it, not because she did not find her fury a great tool, but because of how weak her emotions always made her look, make her think. Angry tears teased the corners of her eyes, knowing how much she hated it when they appeared.

How dare he say such things? How dare another man in power try to laugh at my pain, my power, my plans?

I am the queen of this empire.

I am in control.

Lord Tyrrian took a deep breath and let his satisfaction slowly melt off his face. "My apologies, my queen."

The queen glared at him with more anger. She damned the wetness in her eyes, "You have no idea what I must do each and every day. You have no idea what it is I have been forced to do to survive here."

She again refused to touch her stomach, to feel herself acknowledge another sacrifice she had to make to survive her role.

Lord Tyrrian seemed not to care for the gardeners around them as he reached up and planted a soft hand on her cheek, his thumb caressing her soft skin. She melted at his touch.

"So tell me, my love." He stepped forward, and a heated breath warmed her face and body as he spoke, "Invite me in."

But she couldn't, not truly. Not all the way.

Chapter 19

Lady Belva sat in the candlelight, focusing on calming her mind before she fell into another restless slumber. Her mind was wide awake, racing with worry and anxiety. The pillow beside her remained empty, as it would for several more hours. She knew that Lord Theodus would likely not come to bed until close to first light, slipping into the sheets beside her only briefly before rising early to continue his duties of preparing the army and awaiting the birds from the Sebern army.

The book in her hands remained on the same page it had been for the past hour and for the past several nights when she had tried to read it for simple pleasure. Her head fell back on the headboard, a soft thud amongst the muffled noises of the night. She tried her breathing exercises, hoping to relieve the tension in her mind and body.

Mind stilling, Sister Ora had called it when Lady Belva caught her doing it several seasons ago. To release tension and calm the mind.

Guilt wrapped itself around the words in her mind, reminding her of all she had done since taking up her father's title. The endless lives she had to protect, the control she could not let go, the calmness she did not have the luxury of feeling any longer.

The betrayal she felt for the grown girl she treated like a daughter, only to send her away to the king to be a spy and a tool to Lady Belva's needs. She tried to quiet her mind around the sadness, to push it away again, but each time she butted against it, Sister Ora's broken face stared back at her. She had known Sister Ora's history and how she had once been treated. Emaline had been right; Lady Belva had treated her precisely like Sister Ora's family once had.

But there was nothing Lady Belva could do now for her, and there was so much more that Lady Belva had to focus her mind on.

Her eyes remained closed as her chest rose higher with breath. She counted slowly on an inhale and focused only on the numbers as she spoke them internally. Her head relaxed to the side as she let her breath out for the same count.

Reminders of her task list for the next day barreled through her attempted clarity. She swiped them away only for new words to take their place: the words she so desperately wanted to say to the mother who had begged for her son to be taken out of the war, the empathy she had not offered because she could not give it in front of her people, the anger she did not get to shout when her orders were ignored in favor of others, the reminders her mother gave her of how she had to lead without being too much of anything for the men below her to swallow alongside their pride.

"Beautiful," her husband's voice crooned over the noises in her mind.

She opened her eyes and smiled at Lord Theodus as he leaned against the closed door. His dress coat was tucked under his arm, his blouse half-unbuttoned and a mess.

"How long have you been standing there?" she asked softly.

He smiled at her, shaking his head slowly. "Long enough."

He pushed off the door and slowly strode to her, gently placing his pointer and middle finger under her lips and lifting her chin to meet his face. "Every time I look upon your face, I am reminded that I am the luckiest man to have ever lived."

She let out a low laugh. "And why is that?"

"Because I am the only man to have ever married a goddess." He gently pressed his lips to hers, slowly savoring her returned kiss.

"Mmm," she crooned. "I bet you say that to all your wives."

He kissed her again, moving his hand to cup her face and draw her up, shaking his head as he kept kissing her. "Just my favorite one."

He gently took the book from her lap and set it on the bedside table, tossing aside the coat he carried as well. His face was still pressed against hers. "I have missed you, my love. You have been right here, but I have missed you."

Lady Belva recognized the hitch and hunger in his heated voice. She felt the heat, too.

The need.

The want for distraction and release.

She moved farther into the bed, her hands on his face, pulling him forward with her.

"Then be with me," she breathed as she moved to lie down below him, the nightgown she wore already shifting itself down her arms and chest as she moved. "But I do not wish to think, to give orders, to make commands. Command me, Theo."

Lord Theodus found himself starving as she moved his hand to her bare breast and squeezed her hand atop his before moving to rip his shirt open.

"As you wish," he growled, rubbing his thumb over her hardened nipple and grinding his hips into her, shoving her nightgown up to expose her bare waist.

She let out a low moan, feeding his hunger for her as her claws found the edge of his shirt and pulled it down his arms. He released his grip from her breast only long enough to remove her clothing, then returned to his stroking. He moved his face down to meet his hand, replacing his thumb with his lips and licking her nipple, drawing circles around it and flicking it to draw out a shudder from her core. His hands found her back and pulled her up against him, allowing him to pull her nightgown off her body entirely.

He threw it off the side and pulled her legs around his waist with a feverish hunger and force.

"I am hungry for you, Belva, for every inch of you," he breathed into her as his tongue slowly drew a path down her naked body. "I'm fucking starving."

She whimpered at his words, her body already flushed with deep heat with every one of his growls and whispers. Her hands ran across his shoulders, trying to encourage him to hurry his pacing as her body ground beneath him, impatient for his touch, any touch, that he would give her.

He shook his head as his mouth hovered over her throbbing center, his breath hot where she was spread and waiting for him. "Only on my command."

Fuck his command.

She had not been touched in so long and needed him to uncoil every tight thread throbbing inside of her. She bucked her hips up and reached her hands down to control him. He looked up at her through his eyelashes, then shifted himself upward to pin her wrists to her sides. "Only on my command," he growled.

And he did not let go until she agreed to obey him.

His mouth found her clit, and he kissed her with such passion she felt she would erupt in seconds. Lord Theodus calmed his hunger despite the need she knew he had for every part of her to shiver and tremor all night.

His tongue teased at the spot above her clit, slowly rubbing it in a small circle and feeling her legs begin to tremble. He pulled back as her stomach twitched, smiling at the frustrated groan she let out.

"Not yet," he whispered as she felt him sink two fingers into her, stroking back and forth slowly- much too slowly for her. "It is always so much better when I make you wait, isn't it?"

She panted and nodded her head as her chest kept moving in the short breaths her body allowed. The half-moon in the sky moved higher as Lord Theodus continued to bring her to the edge to draw back again endlessly. Only when her entire body was coated in sweat, and he feared he would come undone in his own pants, did he finally allow his fingers to stroke inside of her and his tongue to flick and circle the way her climax needed him to.

"Cum for me," he commanded as his fingers quickened their pace inside her.

And she did.

Her back arched as she cried out, throbbing lightly around his fingers that he did not still, coaxing her to an orgasm that kept escaping her. Tears welled behind her eyelids, but she did not allow them to fall. Lord Theodus felt the tension still left in her body; he knew every part of her so well that he knew when she did not give him every piece of her.

She watched her husband turn primal as he moved off her and took off his pants, his strained shaft coming free for only a second before she found him on top of her and fully thrust inside of her. He threw her hands above her head, holding them there with one hand while the other lifted her lower back up against his body. His strokes were fast and careless but accurate with each groan.

She tightened around him, and his body stuttered for a moment before picking up its pace again. He shoved his face into hers, and his tongue forced itself into her mouth, "Cum for me again. I know you need to."

Lady Belva's body shifted beneath him, and her closed eyes scrunched in concentration as she gripped the sheets bunched at her hands. His hand found her clit as he rubbed in circles that matched his thrusts. "Let go for me. Let go of control. I've got you."

Her breathing shortened and hitched as her body moved, and her mouth moaned with his strokes. He felt her tighten around him, and he did not falter in his movements, but continued. Her body loosened underneath him as her high escaped her again.

This time, Lord Theodus did not demand it; he pleaded for her to allow this. "Let me give you what you need."

As the final words fell from his lips, he could no longer contain himself for her, and he came undone inside of her.

"Fuck." he grunted in frustration and ecstasy. He gasped and shuddered as his orgasm finished. He panted and looked at her beneath him, rubbing a hand over her face to move her hair from where it stuck to her sweating forehead.

"I'm sorry, Theo," she breathed out. "I'm sorry."

"You can let go sometimes, my love," he said, stroking her cheek. He kissed her gently. "You can let go."

Chapter 20

Sister Ora's breath came and went in sharp exhales as she walked tirelessly up the endless sets of steep stairs. Her guards had taken a wrong turn, forcing them to double back down the highest set of stairs in the castle and back up another.

She dared not express her accusations of their "accidental" misdirection. Father Figgins had called for her that morning for mid-day tea and conversation. Even if she had been allowed to deny his offer, she would not have. She missed the air of the castle, the ability to roam and see what activity her prison was bustling with. But she did not miss the thousands of stairs and all the painful walking.

She clutched the stair railing as she took her first steps on the landing. The blood inside her abdomen rushed down to the padding she wore between her legs, and she bit her lip to stifle a cry, the pain shooting through her body in a bolt.

"Hurry up; the Hand of the King does not like to be kept waiting," one of her guards gruffed at her.

Sister Ora gritted her fangs and snapped at him, "Give me a fucking moment."

The guard chuffed, "So weak she can't even walk without having to stop and cry about it."

Before she knew it, her hand was clenched in a fist at her side, aching to swing.

Weak.

Weak.

Weak.

That is what he wants, she reminded herself. *That is what they all want.*

Do not let them win.

She loosened her fist, took a long breath, and brushed past her guards. She swallowed her pain and lifted her chin, "Let us not keep him waiting. Hurry up."

Father Figgins' dining room was as ostentatious and demanding of attention as the man himself.

Every available surface was crowded with ornate candelabras, jeweled objects, and vases overflowing with aromatic flowers, their scent cloying and heavy in the confined air. The stone walls were hidden and suffocating behind heavy, ornate tapestries and large gilded frames. Though small for the room, the long, narrow table was weighed down by an overabundance of gold and silver accents and a plethora of food to feed much more than two.

"Come! Sit, sit, please." Father Figgins smiled too widely and brightly for Sister Ora's taste. He pulled out a chair at the dining table for her, and she mentally groaned at the hard seat of the wooden chair that looked up at her.

She nodded apprehensively and gently sat down, gritting her teeth at the ache that pulsed through her again.

Father Figgins snapped his fingers, demanding the attention of the aides floating about the space. One stepped to Sister Ora's right, blocking her view of Father Figgins sitting at the head of the table. The aide wore a cloth cap and coif on her head and pale cream robes, much like those of the most devout order of Scholars- the Silent Order- who gave up their lives and took vows of silence. But they were not servants of people, but of the church.

The woman opened a wooden box and quietly displayed the contents for Sister Ora. Inside were blends of herbs and dried fruits nestled inside glass jars.

Sister Ora's stomach revolted and shot in pain at the thought of drinking tea again after what the last cup had done to her. She cast her eyes up at the aide, who looked straight forward while Sister Ora shook her head no. The aide nodded once, winced in pain as her neck bobbed down, closed the box, and left.

Father Figgins poured from the steaming kettle that had already been on the table in front of him. "I thought you enjoyed tea?"

She did not miss the slight upward twitch of his lip as he spoke.

Of course, he was involved in what the queen pushed me to do. Of course, he would know.

"I do. I am just not thirsty at this time. I apologize," she said.

He snapped his fingers again, twice, and wagged his fingers at the table of pastries, treats, and small sandwiches in front of them. The silent aides stepped forward and awaited an order; their posture emulated perfection, their chins held high under their coifs, and their shoulders rolled back.

"Tell them what you would like, and they will plate it for you, Sister," he said without looking up from his cup of tea. He spooned several lumps of sugar into the fruity-scented steaming cup. Sister Ora looked at the aides more closely.

She noted that not a single aide truly looked at her or Father Figgins, nor had any dared a sniffle since she entered the room. And they did not so much as smile, grunt, or sigh. The women's faces bore no cosmetics to color their pale cheeks, and the male aides did not have a single hair on their faces. Just like the Silent Order was commanded to appear- cosmetic-free and without hair to style and maintain.

But the Silent Order was not meant to be simple aides serving scones and tea.

"Are your aides of the Silent Order?" she asked.

"My usual," he said to an aide beside him. The aides worked in tandem, plating one of each of the most sugared sweets on the table alongside a hefty serving of cured meats.

Sister Ora could not help but furrow her brow at the oddity of the food choices.

"Yes, the Order serves the Church in many ways; this is one of them," Father Figgins replied matter-of-factly.

"I thought— isn't the Order meant to take their vows of poverty, chastity, and silence, to ascend closer to god and work in His holy name? Not... silently serve pastries?"

His voice nipped at her like a parent scolding a child who would not listen, "As I said, the Order serves the Church in many ways."

Sister Ora blinked several times and turned away from Father Figgins as he tore apart a rolled pastry filled with cinnamon and sugar and stacked a slice of cured bacon on top before eating it.

"Please, help yourself," he said between bites.

"I am not hungry. My apologies." Sister Ora said as politely as she could muster. While it was a lie, her worry colored her decision. What if the pastries were poisoned? Contained some ingredients to cause her more pain? "I ate too large a breakfast before the invitation was sent to me to join you today."

Father Figgins' kindness left the air as if a window had been opened and a gust blew it all away. His face turned to stone.

"Bring her the plate," said Father Figgins to no one in particular, ignoring Sister Ora's words. "She clearly needs it."

An aide carried a silver cloche-covered plate to Sister Ora and set it in front of her. She did not miss the slight shaking of the aide's hand as they lifted the cloche from the plate and walked away.

Sister Ora raised her eyes from what lay before her and scanned the room. Her eyes widened as she looked about. Suddenly, the perfect posture and careful movement of those in the Silent Order made sense. These aides could not look at her nor nod without pain, not because of an inner turmoil or obedience they felt, but because of what lay hidden under their coifs.

Sister Ora stared down at the plate. It contained no food but a collar with a double-ended fork in the middle.

A Heretic's Fork.

A device used by the Church during the time of the First King and then again during the reign of the Usurper King to force silence and repentance upon those who spoke blasphemy against the Church or State.

Her jaw trembled.

"Put it on." Father Figgins cooly said, taking another bite and licking the sugar off his fingers.

Her mouth slowly fell open as she turned wide-eyed to him.

"Try it on for size," he said, folding his hands on the table. His eyes glared at her in ice-cold anger. "I need you to understand what happens to heretics and traitors who do not know when to quiet their tongues or listen to commands."

Sister Ora did not move.

Father Figgins slowly leaned forward and licked his lips, crumbs of sugar disappearing as he did. "I offer you this option in kindness, but Sir Marion eagerly awaits your impudence so he may place it on your neck himself."

The door behind Father Figgins opened, and Sir Marion strolled inside. He casually leaned against the back wall, one leg propped up, and his arms crossed.

Her hands shook as she raised them from her lap and hovered them over the torture device. She held them there for what felt like ages. She felt the presence of Sir Marion looming near her, his body pulsing with a desire to inflict the pain upon her himself.

She would not give him the chance.

Weak.

Weak.

Weak.

The words echoed in her mind again, and her body reminded her of the bloodied pain that still coursed throughout her abdomen. Pain these men played a significant role in inflicting on her.

Her anger egged her to fight him.

But how could she fight when her enemies watched her so carefully?

How can she rebel when she could not even speak without risk?

How could she fight when she also had to behave?

Sister Ora unbuckled the collar and lifted her chin. She placed it on her neck and focused her mind on counting the shallow breaths she took. She only swallowed once after putting the collar on, the points of the fork pinching the skin under her chin and on her collarbone, and reminding her not to move.

One of the Silent Order aides stepped beside her with a plate full of food that she could only see from the corner of her eyes.

"Now," Father Figgins said, "let's eat."

He looked at her, "And you will eat."

Chapter 21

Water rippled with each movement; the quiet flow of the marshy river offered no noise cover for intruders. A single splash or hushed command would echo over the stillness and betray the Craigie warriors stealthing across the water.

A full surprise attack held little promise; the Odessian camp stood at consistent alert, fully aware that Lady Kathilla and her warriors were poised for a deadly assault on the camp any day, yet recklessly rushing in would ensure a deadly disaster.

Like many Odessian border camps, this one offered no true coverage for intruders, an intentional defense by its keepers. Over time, boulders were crushed into small rocks and used to build the camp, trees were cut for fire and building, and the camp dwellers took turns tending the lands, keeping the foliage short and useless for hiding.

Odessin soldiers were trained masters of long-distance combat, their arsenal designed to defeat enemies from afar before they ever had a chance to know the faces of their kill. The Craigie warriors had to close the gap swiftly, creeping as close as their stealth would allow before their presence was noticed.

Clumps of mud and moss slowly moved with the ripples, large bundles tangled together to form a cover for those hidden underneath. The Craigie warriors held their breath and came up for air only when necessary as they walked across the shallow river bottom.

Underfoot, Lady Kathilla felt the ground of the salt marsh amid the slick tangle of roots and wet debris. Her foot wedged into the oncoming shore, her traction slow but growing more sure as she continued moving, knowing her soldiers were behind and alongside her. Her eyes and nose broke the surface as she peered out under the cover of marsh clinging to her red hair. The cordgrass on the shore would offer enough covering for them to quietly crawl and gather together before sprinting to attack the camp that sat in the shadows that Broken Tower cast.

She quietly huffed and plunged below the water again, drawing her weapon underneath the muffling water barrier before breaking the surface and making her way onto shore. Her eyes weaved between the line of cordgrass, blocking their view of the camp up the hill.

Lady Kathilla moved her vision to the quiet rustling nearby. The sounds of her warriors breaking the water's surface and crawling ashore attracted her attention. She watched those beside her take their place behind the grass, hiding behind the green waves, awaiting their orders. The breeze caught the grass as if they were asking for her attention to be turned forward back to them.

She ignored their waving, preparing her breath to give the call to attack, when the whistle of an arrow informed her that their cover had offered them nothing.

The arrow embedded itself beside her arm- a warning shot, a welcome into battle.

"Go!" Lady Kathilla shouted as she lunged to her feet. She used her anger at being found to fuel her movement.

They broke through the thick, perfectly maintained, too-tall grass and were met with a sea of orange and gold. Bows armed with glimmering arrowheads greeted them first, with lines of ranseur spears and shotel swords in heavy hands directly behind.

"I am disappointed in you, Lady Edgel." A familiar voice to Lady Kathilla broke through the line of soldiers as Madam Fury sauntered her way to the front. "We made this trap so obvious," she waved her hand across the line of grass on the shore, "I was hoping you would not have fallen for it, but I admit, it was quite entertaining watching you crawl on your hands and knees into the waters and make your way onto shore."

Down the line, Lady Kathilla heard an arrow knock onto a bow. She snapped her head in its direction, keeping the corner of her eye on Madam Fury. "Do not draw that bow, warrior."

Madam Fury smirked. "I see you still keep your hounds well in line."

Lady Kathilla's hand twitched on her battle axe. "Did you come here to fight us or to play with us?"

"Oh, you know how I like to play." Madam Fury slowly crooned, her lip curving on one side as she continued to stare down Lady Kathilla. She reached for the metal dragon curving over her shoulder and unsheathed her sword, the scales of the grip finding their place in her grasp, the head of the dragon wrapping around her wrist. She flipped the sword in her hand and took a leisurely fighting stance. "You and I have spent ages ending up at the end of one another's weapons. Might we finally end it here and put this to bed? Just the two of us?"

Lady Kathilla's face heated in more anger—anger at herself for arrogantly missing the trap that was laid for her and anger at being so close to victory and knowing it was now simply a moment in this endless cat-and-mouse game between the two countries.

Barron stepped forward beside his mother, spitting on the ground in the direction of the Odessians. "We shall end it here and now with your heads on spikes."

Madam Fury cackled.

"And here I was, believing that-" she lifted her sword to point at Lady Kathilla, "I was speaking to the Queen of the North, the one who does not bend or bow. Perhaps I was mistaken about who the true leader of your lands is."

"Step. Back. That is an order from your queen." Lady Kathilla gritted out at her son between bared teeth. He hesitated, the pause in his obedience noted by eyes onlooking from both sides of the field.

"Long may she reign." Madam Fury said, twirling her sword again, preparing to strike, while Lady Kathilla glared at her son.

Lady Kathilla shoved Baron back with her free hand and lunged forward, preparing to parry Madam Fury's impending strike. Lady Kathilla's forceful steps and heavy swings were met with finely tuned finesse and swordsmanship ingrained in the pulse of Madam Fury. Battle was like a dance to the finest Odessian fighters, light and swift footwork essential to staying alive against those they opposed, who often bore heavier weapons and larger frames.

Madam Fury swung her left arm forward, her small shield hidden in the hand she had hidden behind her back, and slammed Lady Kathilla's battle axe away. Lady Kathilla grunted and swung again as their steps met, swinging for her legs. The clang of the metal shield easily deflected her.

Madam Fury lunged forward, thrusting her sword straight for Lady Kathilla's unprotected neck just as she raised her axe and used the handle as if it were a sword to deflect the multiple blows Madam Fury sliced at her. Their dance moved them in a circle, with their back facing enemies that dared not move without order from either woman.

Their bodies lunged for one another, and Lady Kathilla swung down again, a shout erupting from her as she threw her whole body into the motion. She aimed for Madam Fury's arm to cut it where it met her sword. Madam Fury twisted her arm, the curve of the dragon wrapping around her wrist bearing the brunt of the blow, and only a small nick drawing blood from her arm.

As blood came to the surface and drips fell to the ground, Madam Fury's eyes shifted to her allies behind her enemy, now readying their weapons to respond to the strike that drew first blood. Madam Fury pulled herself back, breath heaving as she ordered her people behind her. "The first fighter to move will lose their head."

She lunged for Lady Kathilla again, sword and shield at the ready, and adrenaline allowing her to forget the slight sting in her arm. The battle axe carved through the air towards her knees, the only portion of her lower body left unarmored by scales or leather. Her shield met the strike, echoing the clang of metal through the hushed valley.

She jumped forward as Lady Kathilla withdrew, swinging her sword from above to strike across Kathilla's body, missing her strike as she had to move her torso out of the way of the incoming axe. Lady Kathilla's axe drew wide as she took a lunge position to swing with more force, the wind of the movement the only force that brushed along Madam Fury's body.

Lady Kathilla continued the arc of her swing, standing up as the axe cut across and bringing it in an arc above her head to slam it down upon Madam Fury, whose quick dodge and turn was so swift that Lady Kathilla blinked and jerked her head in surprise.

Flames now burned in Madam Fury's eyes; it had been mere seconds since the fight had begun, and yet it was too long for her to go without drawing blood. She marched forward to shove Lady Kathilla against the solid sea of orange and gold. Like a vicious animal cornered by a predator, Lady Kathilla struck out, her axe again being met by the heavily dented shield nearing the end of its life.

Madam Fury squatted her body under her shield and struck in a straight line across the air as her momentum carried her forward. Lady Kathilla's torso felt the sting of the blade through her leathers, the only sign of the strike being the shock on her face and the grunt that escaped her mouth as she stepped back and around Madam Fury.

As Lady Kathilla found her back to her fur and leather-clad warriors, she felt pain shooting from her leg; the old wound she had let herself forget now stung in pain as she put all her weight on it in her stepping. She stumbled, and before she could recover, she heard a gritted movement behind her as Barron growled.

An axe flew forward, not for Madam Fury- whose eyes were still deadlocked on Lady Kathilla- but for a fighter directly across from where Barron held his line. The axe met the Odessian soldier's head, splitting it with a crack and thud.

Lady Kathilla swung her body to where Barron stood, his arm shaking hard and his veins popping to the surface as he gripped his other axe to strike. His gaze intentionally avoided where she stood.

Before the dead fighter's knees hit the ground, both lines descended into chaos.

"Fuck!" Lady Kathilla screamed, shaking her head as she moved forward to join the brawl.

There was not a moment to be strategic about strikes or movement. The heavy cluster of metal and raging bodies only allowed instinct and adrenaline to take the reins and make deadly choices. Lady Kathilla thrashed and threw herself through the broken lines.

She shouted over the shoulder of a hacked Odessian, "You fuckin' fool, Barron!"

Barron broke his grapple with his foe, his crazed battle eyes and hard, steel jaw aiming for his mother. "Someone must lead," he growled as he pulled a great sword from the body beside him and swung near his mother.

Lady Kathilla's eyes bulged at his swinging arm, and she moved her battle axe to her other hand to parry his blow. His sword swung wide and met its target behind her. In her rage and in the chaos, Lady Kathilla did not hear the Odessian moving in for the kill. She glared at Barron.

"Then ensure our warriors leave her for me," she growled, returning to the chaos to find Madam Fury and ripping apart anyone who stood in her way.

Thundering hooves broke through the clashing, drawing attention away from opponents and forcing enemies to disengage and separate as armored horses stormed through the makeshift battlefield. Those who were not quick enough with their movement or chose to stay within their path met the ground and had their bones shattered by the war horses' movements.

The incoming party broke the sea of fur and fine silk, parting them from one another and circling them, closing off any escape paths and herding them. Lord and Lady Lisarian sat side-by-side on their steeds, both faces grim and firm. Heavy grey banners bearing their house sigil framed them as their presence demanded silence and complete attention.

"Lady Edgel, Madam Fury," Lord Augusta Lisarian addressed, "must we meet again so soon? It was my hope that we would not need to do this so quickly after my titling ceremony."

Both women heaved heavy breaths as they pushed through their enemies and allies to stand before the noble couple.

Neither woman bowed.

"Reval," Kathilla stepped forward, her limp more noticeable and her brow covered in blood and dirt. "I see your new position is treatin' you well."

Her eyes fell across Lady Reval Lisarian's attire. The woman, once clad in leather, furs, and heavy fabrics of the North, now bore a charcoal dress with wide sleeves trimmed in white and black rabbit fur, her hands covered with black leather gloves.

Lady Reval held her chin high, looking down at Lady Kathilla. Unlike Lady Kathilla's words, Lady Reval spoke hers with a heavy tint of malice, "It suits me as well as it was forced to... cousin."

Her jaw trembled at her last word, and Lady Kathilla watched as Lady Reval's eyes traced along the crowded lines of her former people, her former warriors who wore no delicate dresses and garments but a uniform fit for fighting. A uniform the new Lady of Broken Tower used to don with pride on and off the battlefield, an outfit no longer fit for her new station.

"Lord and Lady Lisarian, Odessin welcomes you to our camp. As you can see, we were here defending what was rightfully ours, and we thank you for your aid." Madam Fury said.

The ego of this woman. Lady Kathilla growled internally.

Lord Augusta's horse impatiently stomped as he firmed his grip on the reins. "We offer no aid to either of your sides; neutrality has always been our oath. We are here to end this in favor of neither House. Lady Edgel, under our eye, you may take your dead from where they were slain and go home."

Madam Fury smirked and let out a satisfied scoff.

Lord Augusta's head jerked in her direction. "As can you, Madam Fury."

"My Lord, need I remind you—"

"You need not remind me of anything," he shot at her. "Do you not have a war in the South you are due for? You were to leave these holy lands many moons ago, were you not?"

His eyes met Lady Kathilla's. "As you might expect, as it has always been in this tug of war, the rest of my Lisarian banners are now at the camps you overtook, returning them under Odessin stewardship and sending your people home as we would if Madam Fury performed this same maneuver against you."

Before she could retort, he raised his voice to address the angry crowd, "Go home, all of you—enough with this petty squabbling. Do your people and this kingdom a favor and stop this senseless fighting. No one will win, and these holy lands truly should not belong to any one country and hidden behind any one border. Find peace in your lands. Find peace at home."

He kicked his horse and turned it about, jerking his head for his wife to do the same and for his bannermen to follow. The mounted Broken Tower soldiers remained, parting ways to allow those remaining on the field to move, retrieve their dead and their weapons, and return to what had always been between the two countries—forgotten promises, lost history, old alliances left behind for blood-shedding.

Lady Kathilla threw her stein across the hall, the carved horn crashing and skittering across the stone floor, leaving behind a trail of shattered fragments and splatters of ale. Nobody dared to move. Defeated and embarrassed warriors hung their heads and let their pride fall alongside their gaze. They lined the room and obediently took their lashings, Barron most of all.

"You made a fool of us, of me, Barron," she seethed as her chest heaved beneath her fur cloak. She jerked her pointed finger at him with each stab of words. "You were told to stand down, and you refused. You disobeyed me. You made a fool of me."

"You were cut, and you were stumblin'. You could have failed," his large finger pointed right back at her. "And then what?"

"I lost my footin', yes, I admit, but I was nowhere near death nor failure." She scanned the room, her head shaking. Her words forced the warriors to raise their stares and meet her anger. "You do not fight without my command! I am your leader—I am your queen! You do not bleed nor make others do so without my order!"

"We could have won; they were not strikin', and we had the advantage to attack, but you would not let me lead or let our people fight because your ego refused to stand aside. You wished to fight for yourself, not for our honor," he shouted, retaking her attention.

"My ego? You speak as if you were not the one viciously waitin' to show yourself and take over where I stood every step of the way. I am your queen. You do not disobey my order," she growled her final words.

He growled back, "You are no queen."

The air in the room stopped moving, eyes shot between the two, and bodies around them moved nervously. Lady Kathilla stilled her hand but not the twitch in her lip or the anger on her face.

He continued, "You could be, but you will not do what needs to be done. There is a war in the south that we could use to take over all of these lands. To honor Sir Nealson and fix the wrongs that have happened, but you distract us with petty squabbles here, while the south could become ours. While our bloodline could lead the entire empire."

Lady Kathilla's eyes darted around at the faces lining the room, trusted warriors and council members shifting their focus between mother and son and one another. Her chest stung as faces bore expressions of agreement with Barron.

"Reclaimin' our land, our holy land, is not some petty squabble. It is a battle our ancestors fought for as well as—"

But her son was not finished yet. "Our ancestors fought for this land, for everything beyond our borders, and you sit here and-"

"They fought for freedom! Not domination!" she shouted, storming for him, her fist ready to strike.

"And what freedom is that?!" He met her steps with his own as they stood face-to-face. "Despite your promises and your words, freedom is nothin' more to our people than a war cry before defeat."

"Watch. Your. Tongue. Boy." Each word was spat at him; anger ripped her apart as she no longer saw her son in front of her but an enemy. Barron had pushed before, but never so hard, never so much in front of their people.

From any other, she would have taken his head several sentences ago.

"Or what?" he towered over his mother. Both with shaking fists at their sides.

A sword unsheathed behind him and pushed into his spine.

"Or we both will cut you where you stand, little brother. I shall remind you that you are not her heir. I am. I shall remind you, if she is gone, I will only replace her." Gladys stepped closer behind him, the sword poking his skin as it broke through his leather vest, "Do not test us and make yourself a kinslayer. A dead kinslayer."

Behind him, warriors unsheathed their weapons as well, not in threat against his sister, but in alliance with her claims.

Barron turned to open the space between his mother and sister, his eyes shifting from one to the other. "A kingslayer? Then what would that make you, Gladdy?" he jutted his chin at her pointed blade.

"Satisfied." She smiled.

He relaxed his rigid form. His jaw softened enough for him to crack it open to speak. "I wish no harm to anyone here. I only want what is best for our country and our people. As you do, mother. As we all do..."

He looked to both women before turning and storming his way out of the room, past the gathered crowd, and out into the cold chill brought in by the nearby Falls of Glinton.

Lady Kathilla stepped beside her daughter. With a subtle nod of appreciation to her, they both lifted their heads, piercing the room with unwavering determination in their eyes.

"Everythin' I do, I do for the greatness of our people. Everythin'." She made sure, slow steps across the space, each echoing with purpose and power. "If any among you harbor anger, cast it aside now. If any question my queenship, speak your doubts and we will squash them."

She fixed her gaze on each individual, particularly those who had previously nodded in agreement with Barron's words. Her fury pierced them to their core, reminding them of the woman beneath the furs and behind the blades. No man or woman dared to clear their throat or flick their eyes away from her.

With a sharp movement of her chin, she sliced through the quiet, her resolve unyielding like the blades she carried. We move forward as one people. One purpose. One Craigie. We fight for freedom. For honor. For our ancestors. For each other."

The Queen of the North did not let her people see the flicker of worry in her mind at what her son's words and anger had threatened. She did not let them see the shudder that ran down her spine when Gladys unsheathed her sword. She did not let them see her wonder if Barron had been right in his accusations against her.

She only let them see a queen.

CHAPTER 22

Prince Percy knocked on Father Figgins' office door and silently sighed as the hinges creaked and the door opened.

"Father, your aide said you called for me?" the prince said as he stood in the threshold with no desire to cross into the room.

"Ahh, yes," Father Figgins replied, his face turned down at the parchment before him. He waved his hand in the air with the quill still in his hand, gesturing for the prince to enter. "Please, come in."

With reluctance, Prince Percy stepped inside, closing the door behind him, and approached Father Figgins' desk. The Hand of the King finally deigned a glance up from his parchments and nodded at the chair Prince Percy stood beside. At his gesture, the prince sat on the worn and ill-stuffed cushion of the visitor's chair.

Prince Percy gave a polite nod to the Scholar who stood in the room.

While the prince's chair was plain and functional, the rest of the room was adorned with luxurious, elegant furnishings that exuded opulence and grandeur. Father Figgins' chair- another new addition to Lord Orville's more saturated and subtle furnishings from his time as Hand- looked like a miniature version of a throne, with ornate carvings and intricate details that mimicked the Golden Throne and carvings found in the grand pillars of the church. The bookcases lining the walls were equally impressive, with brackets that added an extra layer of grandeur to the already lavish surroundings.

Father Figgins scratched out several sentences on the parchment he reviewed, added adjusted phrasing and notes, then flicked the paper up to his timid Scribe, who stood silently beside his chair.

"Make these corrections immediately and have this on my desk before dawn." Father Figgins said to the Scribe, dismissing her without a glance or expression of gratitude in her direction. She stepped back with a bow to both men and quickly shuffled off, closing the door behind her and trapping the two inside.

"Prince Percy, I called you here to discuss your marriage contract and lay out your terms of arrangement."

"Isn't that done with both betrotheds present and their chosen advisors?" A line appeared between Prince Percy's brows, and he shuffled in his seat.

"Typically, yes, but your bride is still forcing herself to be... indisposed and," Father Figgins reached in his desk drawer and pulled out a pile of parchment, "it is not as if she is in any position to have a voice anyway."

Father Figgins chuffed.

Prince Percy did not.

"As a representative of the Crown, I took the liberty of appointing myself your advisor and drawing up the terms of your contract." He flicked his gaze at Prince Percy, a warning laced in his eyes. "Your father approved of my advisement and heavily agreed to my influence on these terms."

The prince adjusted in his seat again, the discomfort of the chair having no influence on his uneasiness and agitation. His words snapped out, "So now your role as the Hand extends to defining the terms of my marriage?"

Father Figgins folded his hands in front of him and leaned forward. The metal pin on his chest flickered in the sunbeams and candlelight, its shimmering metal blending well into the gaudy golden-brown cloth he adorned himself in. The gold on his fingers clicked together as his hands tightened their grasp on one another.

"My role extends as far as it needs to, Your Highness. Wherever my influence is needed to secure the kingdom's future, I will be there. Whenever the Church or the Crown are in turmoil or threatened, I will step in." His hands came undone, and he tapped a finger on the papers in front of him, "Even if that makes you uncomfortable, even if that means your marriage has terms that you and your bride must meet to satiate the kingdom."

"And what terms have your influence on it? All of them?" Prince Percy sharply asked. He felt an uncomfortable anger rising in him, but he did not quell it. "Such as when we fuck and how we do it?"

Father Figgins folded his hands in front of him again, ignoring the egging comment. "First, your vows will be exchanged when the harvest season ends- on the first of Pyria."

Prince Percy's eyes bulged, and his mouth opened to retort.

Father Figgins continued each statement with a stab. "You and your bride will stay here, under our watchful eye, until the war is done and her people are ruined. You will not go on a honeymoon tour. You will not have separate chambers. You will create your first heir within the winter season. She will have additional lady's maids attending to her day in and day out during each of her mandated pregnancies to ensure she does not kill the child out of spite- or herself. Once each babe is born, she will not have unsupervised time with the child. Nor will she be left unattended before or after the wedding."

Father Figgins paused. "She has a bad habit of going places she should not and running off," he dared to smile at the prince. "Lastly, she will not gain a title and, as with all royal children, the throne will be the true, legal guardian of all of your heirs."

"No." Prince Percy snarled between his gritted teeth, "You will not make her more of a prisoner than she already is. You will not treat her like this."

I may hate her, but even my anger has its limits.

Father Figgins sat back in his chair, his head cocked in curiosity. "And why do you care how the crown treats her? Your Highness, this woman betrayed you, your family, and the kingdom. Empathy for an enemy is a fault that will crack you."

Father Figgins let his mouth curl into a one-sided smile. "It already has once, and look where that got us. Look where it forced her to end up and what it has forced your father's Council to do. Your empathy for her is what put the chains on her wrists and spilled more blood in this war."

In another rare show of his father's anger, Prince Percy slammed his hands on the arms of his chair, the jolt of anger forcing him to stand. "I have no empathy for anyone who is my enemy, and I will not marry a woman who is stuck in chains and would be better off dead than betrothed to me!"

Prince Percy's fists shook.

Father Figgins dared another smirk at the angry prince, knowing he held the upper hand. "Something you must know, young prince, a lesson that your father has tried to teach you for many eons is that a great leader is willing to do anything for his kingdom. Anything."

Prince Percy's eyes narrowed into slits, his mouth twitched at the corner as a snarl threatened to break across his face, and his jaw hardened like chiseled marble. "Trust me, I know."

I know more than you ever will.

I know the taste of betrayal for the sake of the kingdom.

Prince Percy almost let his next thought slip and fall from his lips.

And you know nothing— not of His will, not of love, not of any-thing.

"Good. And are you willing to do anything for the kingdom?" Father Figgins leaned forward and pushed the marriage contract in front of the prince.

For far too long, Prince Percy had not let the dots and lies connect fully. He had not let himself put every piece together to realize the truth of the evil intertwined with the crown. His father's mania, his anger, and the tyranny he walked towards had not been a path chosen by his own will but by his Hand.

The true evil of this court was not on the throne but standing right beside it.

And he had to put an end to it. Now.

Prince Percy's jaw feathered and softened, and his breath caught. He snatched the papers from the table and shoved the chair out of his way. "You have no idea what I am willing to do for this kingdom."

The prince stormed out, his path a hard line for his mother's sitting room.

Prince Percy did not care to slow down his pace so that his King's Guards could catch up to him. His mother always took her afternoon tea in her sitting room, and as he passed by the beams of afternoon light, he knew her typical tea would just be beginning. His footsteps echoed through the grand halls lined with centuries-old tapestries, statues, and gold. He whipped around the corner and down the royal chamber halls, barely stopping to nod at the guards stationed outside her closed chamber doors.

"I need to speak with Her Majesty," Prince Percy said firmly, his voice brooking no argument.

"She is taking tea with a guest," one of her guards replied, his tone respectful yet unyielding.

"I don't care," the prince snapped, stepping forward with authority. He knocked quickly and pushed the door open despite the guard's insistence that he wait. "Mother, I must speak to you about— Lord Tyrrian."

Prince Percy halted, the parchment in his hand crumpled as his grip tightened.

"Your Highness," Lord Tyrrian greeted as he stood up from his chair that was angled much too close to the queen's chair. "A pleasant surprise to have you join us."

"Yes, my lord, a surprise for all of us." Prince Percy narrowed his eyes and flicked them back and forth between his still-seated mother and Lord Tyrrian. "May you please excuse my mother and I? I have an urgent matter we need to discuss."

"Of course, my prince." Lord Tyrrian bowed his head at the prince and queen, then gracefully exited the room.

"Percy, come, sit," Queen Onetta said, gesturing to the chair beside her, her expression composed and soft.

Prince Percy sat where Lord Tyrrian had been and handed his mother the he had taken from Father Figgins. "Have you seen this contract that Father Figgins drew up for my marriage?

These terms are... these are prison sentences, punishments, not terms of a relationship."

Queen Onetta did not open the parchment, but instead, she pushed it away. "A marriage can often feel like that, Percy."

He slowly cocked his head, more pieces falling into place, "You knew of these terms, didn't you?"

His mother's lips thinned into a line as she looked away, then over at him, "We must ensure she plays her role well."

"You helped write them. This was not only Father Figgins and father's doing, was it?"

The queen gave a single nod.

"Mother," he sighed. He shoved away what bubbled in his chest and instead reached for hope: " Why is this still happening?"

"A vow and promise was made on behalf of both of you to wed; we must keep that and not break it."

"Yes, I am very well aware of the oath and promise made," he snapped, then composed himself. His mother knew well the pain of being shuffled into vows with one you did not love; she had always been a logical woman. She could be persuaded to change her mind. "But why can't we simply forgo it? She is a traitor now, and her people have risen against our House. If we nulled the arrangement, our people would not see it as a broken oath or harmful change of heart."

Queen Onetta snapped back at him, her eyes flashing. "No. We are sworn to it because it is our duty to follow through. Fate. Duty. Faith. Those are your father's House words— are our

House words." She corrected herself, "Those are our obligations to hold onto regardless of how we feel."

"Mother, she has betrayed us; she has betrayed me. I can't- I can't even look at her." His voice cracked, and he looked away, his emotions overwhelming him, "It hurts to do so."

"Then you close your eyes when you fuck her."

"What?" he turned to her, his shock evident and plain to see.

As was his hurt as he realized that the cold nature of his mother did not stop at her children's doorstep.

Had she ever held me as a child? Or was the love I remember from my childhood that of a nursemaid with hair like hers?

The queen sat back in her chair. "Do you think I enjoyed what it took for your father and I to create you or your siblings?"

"Mother, I do not wish to think of that."

"Neither do I," she said, reaching for her cup of tea.

Prince Percy shook his head. "Perhaps father can undo this, then. There is no alliance to keep. If you wish not to make her a martyr, make her an aide, a lady-in-waiting, or something else until this war is done."

Please. He wanted to cry. *Please hear me. Please be a mother to me, not a queen.*

"Percy, stop your begging and pleading. Your father is not well, and you know it, and before this, he was never good at such decisions, even on his best days." Queen Onetta's eyes shifted, her fingers quickly tapping on her mug. "For now, you will still marry her. We must give the people something joyful to look forward to. A wedding in the face of such hardship will benefit our people's spirits."

Prince Percy watched her mannerisms. Her lips were pressed into a thin line; her eyes avoided him, and her fingers tapped quickly on her cup—mannerisms he often found himself and others doing in times of uncertainty and worry.

"Mother, please." He leaned forward, elbows on his thighs, turning to her. He hung his head and shook it. "I am trying so hard to do what is right, always what is right, no matter what it costs. I have lived in Elion's shadow since my birth. I have accepted that my duty and future will always be in the name of the realm—even when it comes to love. But this, please do not make me go through with it."

The weight of the realm bore down on Prince Percy. He let himself feel the envy and sorrow he had kept buried over being born as the spare heir. He let his frustrations boil over at the cruelty his family had wrought on the kingdom, and now on him.

"I hate her, but doing this to her is cruel. Doing this to me is cruel," he confessed. He looked up at the queen, letting her see the fullness of the pain and anger in his eyes. She had to understand what this would do to him and how it hurt. He knew her past. She had to empathize with this. "Please, I do not wish to live my life tied to another in misery."

His mother sighed; her demeanor softened.

"My darling," she rested her hand on his face, brushing her thumb softly on his cheek. "I envy your softness and fragility, I truly do, but this world does not care for second heirs—so you must make it care, as I have. You can use this to your—"

Prince Percy pushed her hand off his face and stood up, shaking his head. He made his way to the door. "I was never a son to you, nor to father. I was but a pawn. And I still am. I see it now, and I was a fool to believe you saw me as anything else. Anything deserving of love or care."

"Percy, stop." She walked to him, her anger matching his. "Your father and I have always had to do hard things in the name of the throne and the realm. We have done it all in the name of duty and love. Not just for the realm but for our children- for you."

"That is not the type of love a mother bestows upon her child." He whispered, then firmed his jaw. "Choose Arminda."

"What?"

"As your heir. Choose Arminda. Give her the seat in Thelimor; I do not wish to have it. I have another option: away from this court, away from you and Father. I do not wish to be tied to you nor this family in any more ways than I must."

She laughed, a cold, humorless sound. "Yes, an option to lord over books in a dusty tower in the desert? Percy, you are a prince of this mighty realm, not some lowly Scholar." She stepped forward again, reaching a hand out to him.

He jerked away from her grasp.

"After the wedding, after this war, we will leave this court, never to return. Never to speak to you again outside of what is required by law." He stepped to the threshold, "It is what is best for this realm."

As the spare prince stepped over the threshold of his mother's chambers, he left behind the last of the guilt that haunted him from his betrayal.

He left behind the duty he felt to his bloodline and the Crown.

And, most of all, he left behind the family he realized he never truly had.

Chapter 23

Emaline found herself standing among the pews again.

She had been here, in this cathedral, and many others throughout her life, countless times.

The pews, empty now, whispered memories of prayers and pleadings, some answered, many ignored. She faced the confessional booths, their dark wood looming like silent judges instead of places to lay down one's burdens and be free of them. The wood creaked and groaned around her, as if it too had heard too many broken promises and meaningless pleas.

She had tried to find her faith, many times, she did. She found things to believe in during her journey of enlightenment: people, causes, beliefs, stories, myths, lies.

But she could never find it with god.

Each time she felt a droplet of faith in Him, it slipped through her hands like water. Like the blood she could never wash from her calloused grip.

She anxiously awaited her turn for confessional, and it took no time for her to face the screened door and step inside. The confessional lines had once been arduous to stand through and wait in, but not anymore. Most still came out of fear of the

Psalms being false—a test of their faith from God, or because, regardless of the truth, they still held faith and fear in His love and wrath.

"Do you enjoy the killing? Many do, perhaps not the blood, but the power or something else," the church Scholar asked Emaline through the booth's privacy screen.

Emaline held her tongue, hesitant to confess. The pair had run through the standard confessional small talk, Emaline wary of diving too quickly into whatever it was, pulled her into the church. But, it seemed the Scholar was able to decipher her anxiety without much word spoken from Emaline.

"No. Even when it is just, even when I have no other choice, I hate it each time. When I had to execute Sir Rainey," she could not blink for fear of seeing it again. He had been the father who had not abandoned her in her girlhood and womanhood, and yet, his betrayal had been an abandonment, hadn't it?

She could still feel the weight of the sword as it cleaved his life from his body; the sound of his death echoed in her ears. She had killed him, but his betrayal had killed her first.

"When I had to execute him, I still threw up afterward. I still shook and panicked."

The Scholar's voice pressed on. "Did you pray for his soul? For all the souls you've taken?"

The question was a sword in her chest. Emaline let out a shaky breath, her chest tight. "No."

"Is that not part of your sworn duty as a sword? As a child of the House of Armor, is it not your duty to pray for each soul you take to ascend to heaven to lie among the stars or to fall to the Hells to atone for their sins?"

Emaline sighed, "I can't do it."

"Why not?"

"God has never listened to me. He has never heard my prayers before, so why must I waste my breath? If he does not listen..." she let herself lose the words, knowing the Scholar would be able to understand what she could not speak.

"What would you do if you met God?" The question seemed innocent enough, but the answer to it was not.

"You wish I speak true?" Emaline asked.

"Of course."

"I would spit in His face."

"That desire is a sin you would be cast aside for even thinking!" the Scholar gasped.

"As if He did not already cast me aside the moment I took my first breath," she scoffed and shook her head. She watched her hands in her lap, fidgeting and fiddling with the coin– her mother's coin– that she had held onto her entire life. "As if He wasn't the one who turned His back on me first."

"The One True does not cast aside His children, even those who do not have faith in him. He patiently waits for them to right their paths, to fall into the arms of his love—"

"If God is so loving and kind, then why would he give us so much pain and sorrow? Why would a creator who loves us not do everything in His power to prevent this?" her voice cracked, "to prevent this pain, this hole so many of us carry."

Emaline saw the shadows of the Scholar's shape. The Scholar shook her head in disappointment at her, a silent reprimand that hung heavy in the air. Emaline did not care and confessed the rest of her sins and anger.

"The One True asks us for unwavering faith at all times; meanwhile, he has done little to strike down cruel men who, for eons, have preached words in His name we now know as false. He asks us to pray to Him when He created a world that takes the voice of many into account. He asks us to listen, but only speaks to a few. Where was He when I begged for help—when I screamed for Him to save me from the fighting pits, from the war camps, from my own mind? When I begged for death, and He left me to rot?"

The silence between them stretched, thick and suffocating, before the Scholar spoke again, their voice quiet and somber. "Did you ever try, my lady?"

"Try what?" she snapped out.

"To die?"

Emaline swallowed, then mumbled a reply, "Yes."

"And you were never successful."

"Obviously."

Emaline heard the smile in the Scholar's words, "That was because of His love. His strength empowered you to stop."

Emaline snapped and slammed a hand on the grate between her and the Scholar.

"It was not His strength that stopped me, but my own." She snarled, then threw the door of the confessional booth open and stormed out.

"Then perhaps you should stop with your quest for faith," the Scholar shouted at her back, their anger echoing alongside the remains of Emaline's rage. "Perhaps you are far too lost for Him to find you."

Emaline did not turn back.

"Father Robb," Emaline called out as her footsteps rushed down the paved path. She caught up to the elder with ease, his slow shuffling no match for her broad stride. "I tried to find you in the Scholars Hall or church, but had no luck."

"Have you considered that this old man wishes not to be found in those places? Or at all?" he grunted out.

She crunched her brow, "Well, no."

He huffed as he continued his walk, "If it is counsel you seek, then I have none to give."

He waved his hand at her, an attempt to dismiss her as he had all the others who sought him out as of late.

"Why not?" she asked, undeterred by his moving hand.

"Because I am old. I am tired." he huffed between each statement, his age made him grow quickly tired on walks, especially when he had to exhaust himself with talking. He used to enjoy being sought out for counsel and sage advice. He had once spent countless endless nights in pews, taverns, and homes, aiding those in need without once wishing for the person in pain to shut up or let him leave. But now, he felt like a liar and a fraud, and what kind of man would know he was those things and still believe he had a good counsel to give?

He continued, speaking truth to his feelings, "And I have been preaching lies my entire life, it seems. Would you really wish to be advised by a liar?"

Emaline shrugged, "You didn't know they were lies. You believed them to be the truth, so you taught them. That didn't make you a liar." She shrugged again, "It just made you wrong."

Father Robb left out a chuff of laughter, "Always so brash with the truth, my dear."

"As you have always been," she swallowed and looked down at her moving feet, "As Ora had always been."

"Had? You speak as if she is dead," he huffed and puffed as he continued to walk. He wished for a spring of youth to return so he could run off and escape this conversation. He did not want to remember what had escalated these past two seasons.

"She may be. We don't know if she is dead or alive or somewhere in between. Father, I need someone to talk to. I have tried speaking to Lady Montarian and Lord Digarius, even Gerald attempted to comfort me, but," she stepped in front of him and caused him to halt. "Ora was— *is* — like a daughter to you, and she is a sister to me. If anyone in these lands feels the deepest pain of her being gone, it is us... No one will let me just talk."

She swallowed again and attempted not to choke on her words or the tears glistening in her eyes, "Please. I need some-one."

Father Robb knew Emaline's story as well as her strength. Seeing her allow tears to even begin to form broke something in him. The war camps that had raised her had preached about not breaking, not bending, not crying—it was all a weakness that an enemy would exploit.

And soldiers had no need for emotions, only strength.

A lesson Father Robb and his Scholars tried to brush up against each time they would travel around the country to bless and preach to the newest soldiers graduating from the camps. Each time he sat across from a broken soldier who had lost everything in the field and wished to carry on no longer.

He knew Emaline had locked her heart in a dark box and left the key to it behind in her youth. Her tears showed him now that, perhaps, she had lessened the hold on keeping the lid shut tight.

Father Robb sighed, his shoulders slumped. "Come," he said as he walked off the town path and silently led Emaline to a bundling of trees atop a small hill. Carved benches sat among the foliage but were left unused on the slightly chilled autumn afternoon. Father Robb sat on his favorite bench underneath the smallest oak in the gathering and patted the stool for Ema-line to sit beside him.

"Now, tell this old man what aches your soul." He softly smiled at Emaline and patted her hands, which she held together tightly on her lap.

But instead of speaking, Emaline hung her head and cried.

Her chest heaved as the tears fell in heavy streams down her face and left stains on her clothing. She wore no armor today; her sword hung from a looped dark brown belt wrapped around her waist twice, holding up her deep gray trousers that matched her stitched vest.

"I hate it all. I hate all of it," she gasped in aching breaths.

Father Robb let her weep and softly asked, "Hate what?"

She lifted her head and shook it, roughly wiping the tears off her face, "Everything... my life. I hate it so much, Father."

Father Robb choked on his breath. He had heard those words before from soldiers like Emaline. Many of those soldiers had been laid to rest not long after their confessions, their ask for help coming too late to lessen the burden in their bones.

"Oh no..." he softly said, "Emaline, my dear, please do not say that."

She snapped her head at him, sniffling as she spoke, "Why not? It is true. I wasn't– my family didn't even want me. My mother died, and my father gave me up. If the one who brought me into this world did not wish to have me, why should I wish to– to..."

"To live?" Father Robb finished her sentence for her.

She nodded in shame.

"How long have you felt this pain, Emaline?" he inquired. A ripple of shame and anger coursed through Father Robb. Not at Emaline, but at himself. In his selfish pity and pain, he had almost sent away a woman on the edge of being lost forever.

How could I do such a thing?

His conscience spoke to him again: *how many others have I turned away in my own grief that is perhaps now gone?*

She began to pick at the dirt under her nails and kept her head hung, "I do not know a day without it. Even as a girl, there were days I wondered what it would be like to stumble in the fighting ring and let a sword cut me deeply. I go into every battle fighting as if it were my last, pushing the boundaries of what one can survive without care if I do."

She shook her head and held her silence, waiting for Father Robb to speak.

But instead, he let her sit with her words.

"I did not wish for this life. I hate the fighting, the sounds of battle, the constant need to be around people. The killing. I hate it all. I became good at fighting because I had no choice but to, and now I must spend the rest of my life doing it. And for what?"

Father Robb had no answer to her question, so he asked another, "What kind of life do you wish for if you could have it?"

She took a long, deep breath and let the silence hang for several moments, thinking, "When Sedrick would read me his poetry, and Ora would recite old stories, it felt nice. I felt... hopeful to hear these tales of myth and made-up people full of love, emotions, and dreams."

"Ahh, hope, that pesky little thing that keeps us breathing."

"What?" she asked.

He tossed aside the holy verses on finding strength in His arms, any parts of their truth stained with lies, and instead spoke of what he knew to be true above all else.

"Hope is what keeps us living when we know only hell. Whether you like it or not, hope has kept you from letting an enemy gut you in the field or your thoughts drown you in their depths." He nodded as he watched the oncoming sunset, just now realizing how long they had let the pausing silences go on for between words, "That is what you live for. You live for the hope of it all. For the light you desire to see in a world missing it in the darkness. You live to create something grand and beautiful when all you are given is ugliness. You live because you can. And if that is not enough, then you live to spite those who wish you dead."

"But how do I find that hope? Where do I look?" she asked, her cracking and breaking voice tearing apart Father Penn's own heart. She had hidden her pain so well it was as if it did not exist to anyone outside her own head until now.

Father Penn pulled out a small book from his satchel and handed it to Emaline. He always carried several books with him to occupy his mind during times of boredom. "Read it to me. The words you know, and I will help you learn the rest."

She timidly held the book in her lap and looked Father Robb in the eye, uncertainty and confusion covering her swollen and tear-stained face.

"You want hope, Emaline?" Father Robb tapped the book cover. "It is right here in front of you."

Chapter 24

Lord Digarius nodded at the busy cooks prepping for dinner at the Landing. The aroma of fresh herbs, hearty game, and bread wafted around the kitchen and followed his path as he made his way through and out the back door of the lower kitchen.

He descended down the outdoor steps, leaving the fortress behind, and excused himself into the underground cooling room beside the back gardens. He stepped inside the creaking door that protruded from the man-made hill and walked down the cold, creaking steps; lanterns on the wall guided him down the worn treads and past the aisles of cold storage.

"Your aide told me that I may find you down here." Lord Digarius greeted as he turned the brick-arched corner and called out to his father sitting among dwindling barrels of beer and ales. The scent of the alcohol mixed harshly with the damp air of the room, a beer barrel lay empty on its side on the floor beside Lord Theodus.

Great, Lord Digarius thought, he truly is drunk.

"It seems, despite there being no Harvest Close festival this season, you are still drinking to your desire," Lord Digarius attempted to joke.

Lord Theodus let out a half-hearted chuckle as he took a swig. "Well, someone has to drink all this ale. Otherwise, we would dishonor our brewmasters. Come. Sit."

Lord Digarius hesitated at his father's slightly slurred words.

His father looked up, furrowing his brow. He swayed slightly where he sat, the effects of the ale evident in his glossy eyes and his slowly spoken words. "Or perhaps you sought me out for a conversation that requires standing?"

Lord Digarius shuffled back and forth before sitting and accepting a fresh ale poured from a newly opened barrel. He watched the foam in his stein swish and settle as he steadied his hands before him. He remembered many beer-laced nights with his father spent jesting and joking, talking and reminiscing. Building a bond he never realized could so quickly be broken.

Lord Theodus made plenty of room for the silence in the dark room as Lord Digarius ruminated. His father had never been one for emotions, but he did enjoy his words. His father's silence pushed Lord Digarius to fill it.

"This war, this path, it will define me as a man." Lord Digarius said to his stein. He did not drink; instead, he shifted it back and forth between both hands.

"Yes, it will," his father replied. No question, no emotion, simply a spoken fact.

Lord Digarius swallowed a large chug of ale, his throat dry and hoarse even after the drink. He hoped to swallow his concerns and drown them in drink, lose his courage, and let the buzz clear his mind of his feelings.

He took two more swigs to no avail.

"Just like your battle did when you were about my age," he said, sparing a sorrowful glance at his father.

"You speak of Broken Tower," the lord gruffed.

Another swig.

"Yes." Lord Digarius drank again.

"I told you we do not speak of that battle," his father said, his voice gruff and frustrated. Lord Theodus grunted and glugged his beer.

"When Sir Rainey was closer to Taylian's age than mine, he swore loyalty to our House," Lord Digarius took another large gulp, "then he broke it, but not before he taught me all he knew of battle and swordsmanship. His oath did not define him. His words meant nothing in the end."

"Correct." The word was harsh on Lord Theodus' tongue.

Lord Digarius let the brew decide his next words. His stomach had been empty of everything but anxiety that day, and the alcohol worked quickly to loosen his words.

"How can I make myself a good man when both the men who shaped me were liars when honor mattered most?" He slowly lifted his eyes to watch the jagged lines and cuts of his father's face turn to stone. He felt the heated heartbeat coming from his father, but for a moment, no words accompanied the aura of anger, just hard silence.

"That was different." Lord Theodus finally gritted out between his teeth.

"How?" the alcohol asked.

"We had people to protect, a potential war to prevent." Lord Theodus's voice boomed. Beer-stained spit flew out with his anger.

"Is that not what the king told himself each day when he carried on the lies his ancestors fed him?" Lord Digarius raised his voice and stood, looking his father in the eyes for the first time since they spoke of the Battle of Broken Tower in their war camp many moons ago. How his father did not yield when Lord Edgel and his men did, how his father let his ego and pride swing his sword, how Lord Digarius' family upheld the lies to cover his father's tracks.

Lord Theodus' lip curled into a snarl, and the shadows on his face deepened. He jolted to his feet, and only a slight stumble accompanied his movement; his anger sobered him quickly. "Don't you fucking speak to me like that."

"You lied to protect yourself, and others aided in your mistruth, and you were rewarded for it. That was no different than what His Majesty has done, that very thing that we fight against. The scale was simply smaller."

"What I did, what our families did, was different."

"How?" Lord Digarius asked and took another step toward his father. "How," he again said. It was not a question but a demand, an order for the truth.

An order to try to understand and justify what his father had done. To get something from him so Lord Digarius could lower the wall he had raised between them.

Lord Theodus held his son's eyes and chugged from his stein. He had no reply.

That hurt him more than another lie.

Lord Digarius gently set his stein down and shook his head in agony and disappointment at his father. He stepped away but paused at the corner, his voice low as he turned over his shoulder at his father. "How can I trust who I am becoming when what I am becoming is you?"

Lord Theodus' anger cracked, and his face broke apart. He swallowed and his hurt carried into his voice, "Son."

Lord Digarius turned back to face him. "What if I do the same thing? What if, in my quest, I commit another sin such as Broken Tower?"

Lord Theodus vigorously shook his head. "You won't."

"But how do you know?"

Silence mingled with the anger and ale around them.

"Because you are so much better than I. So much better than I have ever been."

"Father, I –"

"No, listen to me, Dig," Lord Theodus stumbled over his words and walked to him, setting his hand on Lord Digarius' shoulder, "I push you because I want you to do better, be better than I was, than I am. I push you because... because I do not want my past to be your legacy."

And just as well as everything had broken between them, everything had begun to repair.

Chapter 25

"We could kill them, Your Highness." Corporal Caden, coated in sweat and dirt from a long ride, said.

"No. We can't." Prince Elion corrected, his voice aggravated and on the edge, "The execution of prisoners of war is a war crime, you all know this. It is against the very Code of Arms that my ancestors put in place generations ago!"

The Crown Prince pinched his brow and worked to quell his anger. "Had you killed them on the field, that would have been a lawful kill in this war," he glared at Corporal Caden. "But you instead captured them and brought them here, and now they are to become either our prisoners or set free to go back with as much information as they desire to give to our enemies."

Four scouts of the Sebern army stood in chains and ropes before them, caught in the act of spying despite their disguises as villagers and travelers. Bruises covered many of their faces, clothes turned rags hung off their bodies, and, despite the prince not knowing what they normally looked like, one could easily tell they did not enjoy much food or kindness on their journey here.

"Son of a bitch." Commander Blackley mumbled as he walked up to the scene.

Prince Elion was tired of reminding his soldiers of the rules of war and the codes they must uphold, no matter how they felt about each rule. Why did they continue to present ideas and situations to him when they knew their desires went against their codes?

He wondered more as he looked at them: *did they hope to break the prince's resolve? Tear him down until his oaths meant nothing, and they could do as they wished and win the war at any cost?*

"Forgive us, my prince." Lieutenant Jeffrey Swift carefully sauntered towards the prince, stepping around the prisoners that he had aided in bringing in. He bowed his head at the scowling prince, "We were eager and hopeful to gain more information from our enemy so that we captured them with the intent to bring them to you for questioning."

"Right," the prince said and shook his head, looking away from Lieutenant Jeffrey. His lover had begun to grow too bold in his words around other men.

Aggravation coursed through him. Jeffrey had pushed before, but his confidence and comfort in publicly questioning and irritating the prince had grown in days past. It incensed him more that his lover would grow so bold in front of men who knew what they did in the night.

Prince Elion knew what they implied when they said they brought the prisoners in for questioning.

Not questioning or interrogation, but torture.

His ancestors may have won wars or fought to gain their crowns through such means, but the Crown Prince would not stoop so low. He couldn't.

He had already committed too many sins to protect the kingdom from itself and kept too many secrets.

"Prisoner," Prince Elion shot his voice at the large male in front of him. " Were you treated with dignity upon your capture?"

The prisoners shared side glances, their looks uncertain and contemplative. The man turned his face back to the prince, shut his mouth, and then hardened his glare.

Prince Elion scoffed, then looked at the prisoner beside the man and said, "And will you stay silent as well?"

She also held her tongue.

The Crown Prince laughed in befuddled amusement, "Prisoners brought to me for questioning when they act as if they are mutes." he tilted his head at Lieutenant Jeffrey, "How helpful. And judging by their appearance, they do not fully look as if they were treated according to the Codes, either."

His men looked away in shame as the prince continued, "Prisoners are to be treated with dignity and respect, not tortured or manipulated, enslaved, harmed, or killed." he took a breath, finding the only solution that would not steal their resources or cost them information, "But they may be made useful and put to labor as if they were one of our own. They cannot go back; they have already seen too much. We are short on camp aids, so we put them to work and place them in guarded tents when their labors are done."

"Yes, Your Highness." Corporal Caden replied.

"Lieutenant Swift, come with me now," the prince ordered as he turned to make his way to his tent without confirming if Jeffrey followed. "Everyone else, dismissed."

The prince stormed into his tent, Jeffrey coming in behind him. Prince Elion paced around the tent while Jeffrey calmly walked into the center and stood awaiting his prince's words.

Prince Elion stepped for his infuriating lover, "You are infuriating, Jeffrey. You push your limits with me every day. And you push me to go past my own morals and rules."

"You need to be pushed, my prince." Jeffrey stood his ground beside the bed. "The games of war require strategies and sacrifice that you must be willing to make."

"You push me too far in front of men who know who we are to each other. Do you know how that makes me look? How it make *us* look?" Prince Elion stepped for him again and shoved a hand between the two. "To have my own lover question me and push me in public is... they will talk."

The prince turned around and rubbed the back of his neck as he paced again. The embarrassment fell over his face before he could fully turn away.

"So let them."

Prince Elion jerked around and glared at Jeffrey. He shook his head, "It is not your head that will wear the crown; that will have to worry about the questioning glances and the souls growing too bold in their desire to tear you down."

Jeffrey casually walked towards the angry prince. He let a hand fall on his face and through the prince's hair, "The crown is not even on your head yet, and you worry every second about the weight. I try my best to help with that, all of us in your command do, which is why we push you now. When you are our king, it will be your hand that must do what your father, grandfather, and all the men before have done. Do you truly believe you can rule a kingdom without sacrificing a part of your soul?"

The prince shook his head, "I will sacrifice much for victory, but I will not sacrifice everything. The things you and other officers have attempted to push me to break are the laws that I am sworn to uphold and the laws that I must obey when I wear the crown of the king."

"But your own father-"

"I am not him," the prince breathed and pulled out of his comforting touch.

"You are right. You are a good man, my prince." Jeffrey whispered as he stepped forward and ran his hands up and down the prince's chest. Better than many

Prince Elion did his best not to shrink at the kind words. He did not want to feel what those words did to him; what they made him think and worry about. So instead, he stepped around Jeffrey and stood between his lover and the bed. The crown prince sat down and leaned back on his elbows, "Then show me how good a man you believe I am."

Jeffrey smiled like a devil and slowly went to his knees between the prince's legs, pulling on the prince's pants as he did, "Yes, my prince."

Chapter 26

"While Lady Nilkimm did extend her support and confirm her alliance to our banners, evacuating the remaining families to the lands around Iron Bay may not be a welcome or wise solution." Lady Belva Montarian said.

Due to a mixture of exhaustion and a newfound lack of care for decorum in such moments, Lady Belva physically and mentally relaxed as the meeting took shape, sitting lazily in her chair at the head of the table. She continued, "And the king's armies will sail past Iron Bay from the west. There is no telling if that would turn into a war zone as well, simply for the sake of the king wishing to fire off cannons and cause destruction. We must send any who wish to leave south and east."

"But Your Majesty, the cities that remain to the south and east-" Father Robb began.

Lady Belva snapped her head to him and squared her posture. "It is Your Grace or My Lady; do not bestow me such a title."

The room shared hesitant glances.

Father Robb's voice took on a grave timbre, each word weighed with caution as he addressed her once more. "Lady Montarian, we have found ourselves in an unparalleled time in our history— a period woven by your guidance and actions these past seasons. In their loyalty to your House- to you- your people have fought without hesitation or questioning and honored you with a title they deemed worthy of. It would be a disservice to their trust and devotion to hastily cast aside what they have bestowed upon you."

Lady Belva sighed and rested her elbows on the table. Her head fell into her hands, the shifting of weight offering no reprieve from all the aches she carried on her shoulders. "This was not meant to be a war to usurp a king to take his place," she mumbled into her hands. She shook her head and sat straight again. "Of all of the plans and potential outcomes I accounted for, our people naming me their queen was not one of them I truly thought would occur."

She finally let her worry show. Her mask fell as she granted each advisor in the room a solemn glance.

"If I may, Your Maj— Your Grace, what was your plan after the war was won?" Sgt. Pell asked. "If not queen, then what?"

"My hope was not to have a war at all. I wanted our banners raised in preparation in case the king would not answer for all the rumors, whispers, and known truths about what he had been doing. I wanted an investigation, and I had hoped that, if needed, we could... form an interim leadership council, crown a new king or queen, either from his bloodline or another," she said.

Of all of the plans her mind had mulled over, that was the most realistic and preferred option she could contrive in the privacy of her studies and self-reflection. "But I did not walk into this war hoping that mine would be the head that wears that ugly crown when this all ends."

Lord Digarius grumbled a reply, his frustration well on display, "It should hardly be a revelation that our people deemed you fit to be the new queen, given how you have led them in this charge, Mother. Our history is rife with tales of those who spearhead rebellions, earning the highest titles."

Lady Belva's eyes shot up and down at her son's rigid posture at the edge of the room; her brow creased at the unexpected intensity of his words. She opened her mouth to rebuke his rudeness, sharp words readily poised on her tongue, but she held them back. He was right, after all.

"Regardless of what history has shown us or how our people may feel, the outcome of this war is far in our future, I fear. We should focus our efforts and our minds not on that, but on what is right in front of us- an attack we know is imminent." Lady Belva said.

"I must ask this question again." Lord Digarius pulled himself away from the wall. He moved to the table and placed his hands on the top to lean on. "How do we know this attack is still coming at all? The king knew that Sister Ora was gleaning information from them, as Sir Rainey was from us. How do we know they are not moving to attack elsewhere while we are distracted here?"

"Lord Torrin and those who lie in wait holding Ravenhall can adequately hold the land if this turns out to be a diversion. That is why we split our forces earlier this season." Lord Theodus gruffed, "I do not believe our efforts would be wasted either way. We are focusing on protecting our people from the worst that the king has to offer. Even if this attack does not meet our doorstep for some time, preparing now is the right plan."

He shared a look with Lord Digarius. There was kindness there that Lady Belva noted, one that had been missing between the two for a time. "I would agree with looking into a strategy change if we did not have the Sebern army at our side.

"In due time, when we see ships sailing down the Gulf- because one day, they will come- we are completely prepared for an attack. We must trust in that." Sgt. Pell added with a firm and confident nod toward Lord Digarius, who still hesitated.

"And trust in one another." Lady Belva said. She held a knowing tone, her cadence telling her son that she fully felt his distrust and frustration.

Lord Digarius' jaw tightened, and his lips pursed. He did not relax his shoulders, but he finally took his seat. He sat with his hands on the table and turned his chin to his mother. His voice dropped into a half-whisper of worry: "But what if this is all another trap?"

Lady Belva leaned forward to her son. "Then we fall in it together as one united front."

"And then the war is lost and our people dead," he replied. Sgt. Pell and Father Robb both grumbled in agreement.

She raised her chin to the room, the sparks of fire and resilience lighting her eyes. Each syllable a hard declaration of her resolve and determination. The Lady of Ayeshire, the reluctant Queen of the People, commanded the room and made her power and purpose known.

"This war has begun quickly; this kingdom had grown restless long before I called for the fall of His Majesty. If we are not careful, we shall fall, too. I mean to win this war. But I cannot do it alone, nor with a Council of anxiety and fear- fear that will only hold us back."

This meeting, this moment, felt too familiar to her. Like it kept repeating in her life, and she kept failing to properly quell any worries or hesitation. As if the anxiety just kept choosing a new person in her Council to manifest in so that she could be questioned for every thought and idea.

Lady Belva was tired of inspirational quotes and speeches and men questioning her too much.

"This war is ours to win. This kingdom ours to save. You will stand with me, or not at all."

Chapter 27

E phraim held the shopping list in their hand and studied it intently as they strolled down the dirt causeway leading back to the town center. The shopping list had a variety of ingredients that would likely take them to every corner of Nesshine to find. Like many children, they knew that their mother always had a secret plan when she asked for their help during a visit- it was never a simple ask for aid, running errands, or making dinner.

Mothers always had secret plans.

Despite knowing this, Ephraim had yet to decipher what her plans were for the ingredients on her shopping list or Ephraim's trip into town on her behalf. They looked down at the scrawled list again:

Seven large iron nails- rusty preferred

Salt- coarse, not finely ground

Gardening gloves

Mustard seeds- only if the imported spice supply is not running low from Odessin

Ephraim moved with the rising of the sun, unable to sleep well in their childhood bed chamber, especially when their family woke as dawn began anyway, just like the rest of the town. The villagers of Nesshine woke early to begin their farm and factory work, long before the heat of the sun became unbearable, and the sounds of chickens clucking and cows mooing would quickly fill the air, alongside boots trodding down the paths, while many throughout the country still rested in their beds. Like Ephraim would when they were back in the city of Middleton Landing.

As Ephraim arrived at the main causeways, they were greeted by the bustling townspeople moving to and fro. The streets were lined with vendors selling fresh produce, baked goods, and various meats. The sweet aroma of freshly baked bread and pastries, mingled with the savory scent of sizzling meats, filled the air, making Ephraim's stomach growl. Bakeries and cafes held their doors open to entice the early risers to come inside and enjoy a moment of peace before their workday began.

As they weaved their way through the lines of people waiting for their morning meals, Ephraim's eyes scanned the area. Nostalgia nestled in their heart as they passed by familiar shops and vendors that had shaped their youth and young adulthood.

The hearty and greasy scent of gravy and sausages caught their attention the most, leading them to Gillian's Tavern, a favorite place to dine before and after a long shift in the fields or factory. Gillian's meals were not the most nutritious the town had to offer, but when one would work off three times as much food as they could eat, grease and fat were a favorite way to begin the workday.

Ephraim's face lit up as they entered the tavern, causing them to put their mother's task on hold. In spite of the early hour, the tavern was teeming with liveliness. Barmaids carried hot steaming mugs of warm drinks, and cooks behind the bar served up large piles of gravy and meats atop plates of biscuits and breads.

"By the stars, it's the Aber's youngster." A gruff, larger man hunched over the bar, barely allowing himself to swallow his bite before speaking. "Get over here, Ephraim!"

As Ephraim made their way to the bar, patrons turned their heads and smiled kindly at their arrival- a politeness offered to all in the town. Ephraim eased through the crowded tables and pushed out chairs filled with hungry, waiting patrons. The heat of the bodies and the roaring fires behind the bar held a fog in the space; the heat was deterred by Ephraim's lighter ware. While citizens of Nesshine were too busy to care about one another's personal preferences for their appearance, Ephraim had always preferred to blend into the understated simplicity of the townspeople when visiting. They wore light linen breeches and a rolled-sleeved blue tunic, the blouse's V-neck cut left wide open and untied.

They pushed a hand through their curls, having yet to return to their regular buzz cut, and enjoyed the waves they inherited from their mother.

Creegan, a familiar farmer and respected community leader who had shouted at them when they arrived, greeted them and placed a heavy hand on their back as Ephraim took a seat.

Creegan joked, "Look at you, back to visit! So you're not too good for our little ole town, eh?"

Before Ephraim could reply, a hot mug of coffee appeared and was placed in front of them alongside a heavy pile of gravy-soaked meal placed in front of Creegan. Ephraim acknowledged Creegan's greeting and replied, "I'm just back for a bit of a visit. Needed to step away from the Landing for a moment."

Creegan responded, "Aye. I don't blame you. Have any news you can share with the likes of us about what is occurring?" The other patrons and workers around them tried to listen discreetly, but their obviousness was astounding and almost laughable.

Ephraim blew on their cup of coffee- a soon-to-be rare commodity that was imported from the Isles- and took a sip before replying, clinking their signet ring against the cup, the engraved bee shimmering in the changing light. "If I had news to share, I would have shouted it at the door."

The faces around them fell, taking Ephraim's words and tone as that of defeat.

The gruff-looking cook behind the bar beckoned, "Lady Nilkimm came through and told us what she could as well. She informed our soldiers they could take up arms for Her Grace if desired. We got our factories working overtime to produce more weapons and fortify our bay. How worried should we be?"

Gillian's head popped up from his workstation. He wiped his large and scarred hands clean and stepped around the kitchen worktables. "More importantly, what is Her Grace doing to protect us in this war she began?"

Gillian's body had been built for heavy lifting and hard work, a man perfect for heavy field or factory work, but the stars divinely determined he would be better suited serving others and using his natural strength to break up tavern brawls and lift wine casks.

Ephraim's head fell, and their appetite was lost. They felt Creegen's large hand on their shoulder again, this time in comfort. "Ephraim didn't leave for the country's capital to become a war general, Gillian, but to be of aid to Her Grace and the people of the Landing through their healing abilities."

Gillian continued, "Well, Her Grace has gotten us into a damn war that won't end well, I can tell you that much. Our ports are quickly running empty of ships filled with goods to trade. Did Her Grace think of that, or how the Aisharian fleet would stop our ships when we ran our regular trade routes up the coast?"

A ship captain sitting at the end of the bar added, "My crew and I have never had to bribe so many captains to allow passage in our lives. At this rate, we will lose more money than we could make on whatever those northerners decide to price-gouge us with."

"And what has she decided for all the jobs lost now? No trade. No work." Another asked.

Creegan's words cut through the air like a knife, sharp and precise, "Enough. Ephraim has nothing to do with Lady Montarian's decisions, and you all know what has come of His

Majesty's rule as well as I do. Nothing but higher taxes, more loss, and fucking lies passed through the crown. We all heard the words on the parchments Lady Montarian sent across the kingdom. We all know that His Majesty has kept up an empire made on lies."

His tone was measured, but there was an edge to it, a hint of disappointment and frustration that hung in the air alongside the muggy heat from the kitchen fires. As he spoke, the patrons in the room shifted uncomfortably in their seats, their eyes cast downward in shame at their prior shouting as if they were children being scolded by their disappointed father.

Everyone knew that Creegan was speaking from a place of genuine concern, that his words were meant to inspire change and understanding, not to shame those who spoke out.

"Her Grace is doing what many have been too terrified to do. Respect it, or shut the fuck up. You're spoiling my breakfast." Creegan eyed every man, woman, and child in the tavern, daring anyone to counter his words. Despite Creegan's hard and scolding tone, respect and understanding made their way through the room.

No replies came, only silent nods and the quiet clinking of silverware on plates, followed his declaration. While there was no official mayor or lord of Nesshine, everyone listened when Creegan spoke.

He turned back to his plate, glancing at Ephraim and leaning in. When others around them took up conversations again, he quietly said, "But you lot are doing everything you can to end this, right? To lessen the loss of life and help us smaller folk?"

Ephraim looked into Creegan's dark blue eyes, clouded with fear and concern. They observed the tavern slowly returning to its normal liveliness. Happy families shared a hot meal; barmaids smiled extra at the workers with pockets padded with coins. They watched the light from the sunrise break into the windows of the tavern, and the door swung open several times with more patrons bustling in and out.

When the king's ships came, the coasts of Iron Bay would be the first decimated. And if they came by land, Ephraim's home would be toppled on the army's path of destruction.

It would all be gone in fire and blood, and nothing would come from the end except more destruction and oppression. And no matter what, there would be blood on Ephraim's hands. Whether it came from soldiers they could not save or those whose lives Ephraim took to save others, it did not matter; blood was blood, and it could never be washed clean.

But their oaths still pounded in their head. Their fear and worry. There were other ways to win. Other people Lady Montarian could call upon, and others to answer the calls of war. Ephraim did not need to be the one to fight; they could stand down and let someone else be a hero.

A killer.

Ephraim nodded once in reply and left it hanging in shame: "Yes, yes, we are."

Chapter 28

Lord Rener Torrin rested against the thick trunk of a tree at the edge of camp. The sparks of fire and conversations were quiet background noise as he sat in the dark with his journal, attempting to scribble his thoughts with an ink-filled quill pen that was nearly empty. He squinted up at the stars before huffing and pulling out his viewing scope to see the closest constellations clearly.

As his vision focused, another star fell, bringing with it three others before they disappeared at the crest of the tree line. Lord Rener let out a worried sigh as other stars followed the falling path, joining in the descent. A noticeable hush fell over the camp several yards away as soldiers stood up and stared, pointing at the same sky in awe and worry.

"They do this so often, yet each time they fall, the world does not end." Lord Cossius Torrin said from the nearby tree that he stood against. He turned his chin to his brother on the ground. "Why do we continue to believe their fall signals our own?"

Lord Rener kept his eye on his scope, studying how they fell and the tails they formed, searching for patterns and meaning.

"Because they do not fall this often without cause, brother. It was believed that the Old Gods rode them like steeds, flying across the skies as they saw fit, and when they all would fall, it meant a war in the sky. Unhappy gods fighting among themselves or falling to our plane to express their displeasure," he casually mumbled as he took more notes on the star fall.

"The old gods are myths, Rener. I could cut out your tongue for even speaking of them."

Lord Rener shrugged, his voice light and half attentive, "You won't."

He paused as a larger group of stars fell. "Besides, everything is a myth to those who wish to replace ancient stories with their own."

Lord Cossius scoffed. "Well, if the old gods are coming to war with us, might you ask them to aid in our victory since you talk to the skies so often?"

"I do not talk to them, I listen." He shrugged, putting his scope away and closing his book. He rubbed his eyes that hurt from the strain of constant concentration. "Something you may learn to do one day yourself. If you remember your history lessons, you will recall why this brings much worry to me, to father, and to all of us. The last time the stars fell for this many nights, they all disappeared, painting our skies in a black ink that stained the lands with blood."

"The stars did not stain The Land of a Thousand Rivers with blood. Men did." Lord Cossius corrected. "Men like the ones who threaten our people. Men who we must put an end to."

Lord Rener pinched his brow and sighed, standing up as he spoke. "Those same men who are likely doing what I am now and making their decisions based upon the stars you ignore."

Lord Cossius shoved himself off the tree to walk with Lord Rener as they went back to camp. "It is ridiculous that they would do so."

"Maybe, but those ridiculous people are the ones who will put swords to our throats if they say that The One True deemed it necessary or that the stars wished for it." Lord Rener held up a hand before his brother could retort. "The world, despite what little we know of it, is much bigger than your beliefs, brother. You cannot rule our lands if you do not try to understand our enemies or our allies and what motivates and terrifies them." He peered at the stars, still blurry to his far-sighted eyes. "Or understand things much more ancient than our family line."

"A lord has advisors for such things. That is why you will be my trusted Hand." Lord Cossius corrected his brother. "Everyone listens to you anyway," he mumbled.

Lord Rener tried to ignore his brother's grumble.

"And you will have a Master of Currency for your spending, a Scholar for the church, a Master of Armor for battles, and an heir to learn their ways from you." Lord Rener stopped walking and turned to his older brother, "You, Cossius, no one else. You will lead, you will teach, you will decide the fate of our country once father is gone. And that fate is directly tied to those you find ridiculous in their beliefs and faulty in their faith."

Lord Cossius crossed his arms and glared. "The lecture is not necessary. I know what it is that I inherit."

Lord Rener shook his head, "When will you take your inheritance more seriously?"

"I do." A threat, not a statement.

"No. You take your swordplay seriously. You take your desire to puff your chest and fight seriously. You care of little else besides which woman you will coerce into your bed!" Lord Rener did not realize he had begun to shout. But he was tired of constantly having to right his brother and fix the problems he ignored.

Lord Rener knew that Lord Cossius was gifted in different ways than he was, but since they were children, Lord Rener had always had to make up for his older brother's lack of scholarly wit and help his brother pass his exams and recall important histories and texts.

Lord Cossius turned red, grabbed him by the cloth at Lord Rener's chest, and fisted the cloth tightly in both hands. "It is not your place to correct me, little brother."

His brother's quick anger did not surprise Lord Rener. He had always been easy to rile up.

Lord Rener slammed a hand onto one of his brother's flexing forearms. He did not show fear or blink, "Then whose is it?" he gritted out.

They had come to brotherly blows before. Perhaps they just needed to get a few swings out of their system as they had done before.

"Mine," their father's voice said from behind them. "And apparently, I must do it in front of our entire camp."

Lord Cossius unfisted his brother's shirt and shoved away from him, wiping a hand over his heated face. "Father."

"My tent. Now." Lord William ordered.

⚱

"In front of the whole camp. Really?" Lord William said. He paced back and forth in front of his sons. He stopped behind his desk and hit a pointed finger on the surface, "We leave for a battle soon to take on the prince's army, finally. Finally, we get to move after too much time awaiting orders, and you both pull this bullshit in front of those who are supposed to believe in our leadership- in our unity."

"Father, it was—" Lord Cossius began.

"Shut up," Lord William corrected, his finger jabbing at his eldest son. "I do not care who began it, but it is done. Now. You are brothers, but you are also leaders. You may squabble and fight, yes, but you do not do it in front of the men you lead. Is that understood?"

"Yes, sir," the brothers replied in unity.

"Good. Rener, you will aid your brother when his time comes, but you are to remember that above all else, he may be your brother, but he will be your lord and will hold your command." Lord William felt Lord Cossius' smirk before he saw it. He shot his attention at him again, "And Cossius. Your brother is right."

Lord William took a long, slow breath. "I will die someday, and you will take my place. It could be many seasons from now or in the throes of this battle, but I will die, and then you will lead and hold life and death in your hands." He shook his head and sighed, "I have let you enjoy the benefits of your inheritance for too long without putting my foot down on the duties you must learn. Perhaps I relied too much on Rener to make up where you fell short. That ends now."

"Excuse me?" Lord Cossius shifted on his feet. Even Lord Rener felt the pain from their father's comments, pitting the two brothers against one another.

"I've been too lax with your attendance in the mundane meetings and everyday duties you will one day do. Perhaps it is from remembering my own time at your age, bored to tears in my father's meetings, but no longer. Everywhere I go, you go. You sit beside me at every meeting I attend. Every decision I make, you witness. Every boring duty, every gripe I hear, every thought I must ponder, you will be there."

The Lord of Sebern straightened himself taller. "You are men now. And war makes men into many things. It is time I made you ready for what you both will become."

Chapter 29

The morning sun rose behind the king, the light illuminating his downtrodden figure as he sat at his desk. There were no piles of paperwork to sort, parchments to sign, or correspondence to review. His desk had been cleared of such trite things as the menial paperwork of the kingdom's day-to-day happenings.

King Ivan met with his Council so often that any news on his desk was often moot by the time he returned from his meetings. And with his current health, his odd tremors often would void his own signature, making it appear as a poor forgery of His Majesty's name. Under the advisement of the Healers and Council members who knew of his sickly state, King Ivan deferred paperwork to Father Figgins, allowing his signature and seal to replace his own requirement.

Queen Onetta sat across from the king and drank from her cup, savoring the warmth of the coffee it held.

The king sipped on a different form of dark liquid, his tired eyes shuttering closed as he sipped, wincing as the alcohol burned the sore on the edge of his mouth. He hissed and crunched his face as the sore burned. He pressed his thumb to the redness, the pressure slightly alleviating the pain.

"You know it must still occur, at least for now, for our own prestige. And besides, what shall we do with her otherwise? Send her home? Behead her?" Queen Onetta calmly said, obviously growing tired of this repeated conversation.

King Ivan grumbled and wiped the blood off his finger. "We should have taken her head the moment we learned of what she was doing. I wanted to take her head, but none of you would let me. Instead, we took her lover's."

His wife scoffed. "You still do not understand what would have happened had someone that close to our family been brought out as a traitor again, especially so soon after your own Hand was removed for the same acts. Our reputation would never have recovered. Our city would have turned into our graveyard, Ivan."

The king rubbed his jaw, the stubble grown out to hide the splotching redness on his face. The hair was rough on his aging hands. "Fine. So she lives, but she does not need to marry Percy. This marriage will not only punish her but him as well. He doesn't deserve to be drug down alongside her."

Queen Onetta set her cup down and rested her hands in her lap. Her back straightened as she took a breath. "There is nothing else this family knows better than sacrifice. We all have our roles to play in this kingdom. You and I know that very well. And Percy understands that sacrifice is needed. He was once a boy who dreamed of a quiet life with true love and without politics, but that life is gone for him now, largely in part due to what his betrothed and her home country have done. He will not be dragged down alongside her."

King Ivan's fuse had grown relatively short these days. "She stands to gain much from this marriage, and Percy does not know the role he must play yet. He is too naive. Too willing to still speak out against our wishes in the Council meetings. What if this marriage pushes him away from us?"

"Percy knows quite well his role, my dear." The queen corrected him. Her eyes flicked for an instant, and the king wished he knew his wife well enough to understand what that moment of emotion on her face meant. "We have discussed it recently. His opinions on the Council are only that, opinions, and they are temporary."

She sighed, "He means well, and we only have ourselves to thank for allowing those Scholars and their books to raise him for us."

Their eyes held for a moment, a softness appearing in both their gazes, as if there was a potential for them to regret their choices or feel sorrow for what they had done. The softness disappeared from the queen's eyes first, replaced with the coldness she was known quite well for showing.

She poured herself another cup, then reached to refill his as well, gently sliding it across the table with the tips of her fingers. The king nodded in gratitude before sipping and setting it down before him.

"He may have stumbled but has grown and learned," she said.

King Ivan held his breath. He sighed and set down his drink. He still held on to his sanity today, and he wished to make the most of his temporarily stable mind. "How do you believe we have done so far?"

"As king and queen, as husband and wife, or as a mother and father?"

"All of them," he softly said, his anger diminishing into sadness as he swirled his cup and watched the contents slosh.

"Our kingdom is falling apart, and we cannot stop it. We do not even look at one another except to snarl and feign niceties in court, and our children were only born for politics and duty, not of love or desire," she said.

King Ivan smirked, hiding his emotions. "So we have done quite exceptionally, then."

She snickered and rubbed the bridge of her nose before looking back up at him. "We have been faithful to our duty, and in that, we have succeeded."

"I still do not like that she must live," he said.

"And neither do I. But sometimes, living is more torturous than death. Sometimes losing your love of your own consequence is more painful than being sent to His embrace or to burn in the hells."

King Ivan sipped his drink again and watched his wife's face falter to the long-held pain that she wore when they first met. The poor, tortured queen who had been taken from her prior life of being the ex-lover turned mistress to Lord Tyrrain still sat in misery all these ages later.

Oh, the agony. To be the queen of an entire kingdom and wife to a husband who lets you do as you wish with whoever you wish in the bed his family paid for. He thought. What a terrible life.

"How is Lord Priscius this morning?" he asked, his anger returning.

She cocked her head and crumpled her brow, her tone sharp at the underlying accusation. "I do not know."

The king rolled his eyes and grumbled. "Must we continue this game with one another? We have fulfilled our duty as husband and wife as agreed upon. You have your whores, I have mine. Although I do a better job at keeping the few I bed discreet."

A half-truth, and they both knew it. The king had kept them discreet from himself because he could not remember which hired women of the night he had slept with by the time the morning came, and they were gone.

Queen Onetta firmed her jaw as she jutted her chin towards the drink he had raised to his lips. "Our Healers run dry of mugwort and pennyroyal teas because of your recent, discreet, and drunken adventures. You haven't fucked this many whores since I was last pregnant. Might I advise you to calm your cock for a moment—"

King Ivan's eyes shifted to behind the queen and quickly cut her off. "May we help you?"

"Yes, um, apologies, Your Majesties, but I have brought Sister Ora as requested," a shy, quiet feminine voice answered.

King Ivan shifted his annoyed look back to the queen, who set her cup down and returned his look.

She turned her head in acknowledgment. "I will be out in just a moment. Have her wait in the hall."

The maid bowed before exiting, properly ignoring the queen, who was reaching for another pastry and refilling her cup.

The king snorted at her gesture. "You were always best at this part of the game."

Queen Onetta smirked and slowly cut up her pastry into unnecessarily small bites, thoroughly patting her mouth with her napkin between each small nibble and slowly sipping from her cup.

Her ability to play these court games had always amused and intrigued the king. He watched on in continued amusement. "Do you remember the breakfast after our crowning? With your father and the other lords and ladies?"

Queen Onetta patted her mouth, removing the single crumb on her lip as she cocked her eyebrows and replied. "I do."

"I will never forget the redness on your father's face for what you did. Making his noble lordship wait until you had cleared every last crumb on your plate before he was allowed to leave." He laughed, "That breakfast lasted into lunch."

"It was a nice bout of revenge for what he forced me into," she said calmly, reaching for another bite.

King Ivan lost his momentary kindness again.

"It has not been that horrendous, has it?" He shifted his eyes up and down at her.

She sighed, not in regret or anything of the like, but in annoyance, that much the king could tell. "No, it has not. I have given god my gratitude each day that you are not like your father to your mother. And for that, it has not been as bad." With that, the queen set her napkin on the table and stood, exchanging pleasantries with her husband, before leaving for the hall.

The king eyed the collection of liquor he had displayed in the room. As her words sank deeper, he picked out the bottle he would have for lunch, and the second he would have for dinner. His one moment of sanity and clarity had passed, and the truths he heard made him wish to fall back into a stupor and forget it all.

Sister Ora stood with her back turned, staring much too intently at the single painting hanging in the hall.

Her eyes were fixed on the canvas, studying every detail of the artwork. The painting depicted a valiant knight on horseback waiting before a towering turret, lifting a red rose to the sky as a sign of his undying love for the dark-skinned princess in the tower above him. The knight's armor glistened in the light, and his face lay hidden beneath his helmet. With her long brown hair cascading down her back, the princess gazed down at the knight from her high perch, reaching down to pluck the rose from his extended hand.

The princess had hair, eyes, and a shape just like Sister Ora.

"Are you enjoying our newest addition to the hall?" the queen asked.

Sister Ora's jaw trembled in rage, still turned away from the queen and looking at the art piece. She quickly quieted her breath, blinked away the angry tears, and turned to dutifully bow at Her Majesty.

"Yes, Your Majesty. It is quite lovely," she flatly replied as her eyes glared at the ground, still composing herself. She stood up straight, tossing her hair behind her shoulders, exposing the rich silver stitching on the collarbone of her dress.

The queen's smile faded as she looked at what she wore.

The deep emerald green dress had a long cape, exposed collarbone, and long, exaggerated sleeves. Stitched in silver on Sister Ora's dress were freesia flowers, oak leaves, and several small stags dancing between the foliage. Around her neck was a diamond necklace adorned with emeralds that matched the ones in her ears.

The green banner of Ayeshire stared down the red lion queen.

"Come." Queen Onetta said as she turned down the hall.

Sister Ora followed, her nerves close behind, causing the slight smirk on her face to disappear. The queen slowed her pace for just one moment so that she and Sister Ora would walk side by side with the King's Guard close behind.

"Now that you have bled, I have finalized the date of your nuptials to my son. The first of Pyria shall be the day of your wedding," she said firmly, looking forward as they walked.

"Wha—"

The queen raised her hand to silence her. "You shall wed him; in your vows, you shall plead your allegiance to your new family, forgo your former house, and bear his children in prosperous amounts until he is satisfied with the number of heirs." She stopped walking and turned to look down at Sister Ora. "You shall be obedient, dutiful, and quiet."

"But that is less than a fortnight away!" Sister Ora stuttered.

"Oh, good, you do understand how a calendar works," the queen said flatly, then walked away.

Sister Ora's eyes narrowed into a sharp glare as she watched the queen's retreating back, her anger growing with every step the woman took. Her hands balled up into fists, and she felt the urge to shout, to stupidly fight back, or even turn and run for the gates. She struggled to control the wave of fury that threatened to overwhelm her.

"Tell me, my queen, will I be kept in chains on our wedding night for your son to fuck me, or shall I finally be free from my cage then?" Sister Ora shouted at her, raising her wrists out in front of her body, displaying the bruises her chains had left behind.

The queen glanced sideways at the servants whose eyes were wide at Sister Ora's outburst. The onlookers averted their gaze, knowing better than to meddle where Her Majesty was involved.

Queen Onetta stepped for Sister Ora. Slowly, perfectly, carefully.

"You should be thankful for your gilded cage, little bird." Queen Onetta snatched one of her wrists, squeezing hard on the bruises and cuts still fresh, but her voice showed no struggle or grit. "And if I have to hold you down each night to ensure your obedience, then I shall."

Sister Ora grunted and held back tears at the pain. She finally hissed, "I feel so sorry for you, Your Majesty."

Queen Onetta dropped her wrist, laughing, still standing too close to her. "You should not. There is no need."

"Yes, there is." Sister Ora firmed herself up, cocking her head as she glared into the darkness of the queen's eyes, her voice but a soft whisper. "I am so sorry that you were never actually loved and that it made you a monster."

The queen threw the back of her hand across Sister Ora's face, and the slap echoed through the hall. Sister Ora bent over, her hand clutching her cheek and touching the streak of blood falling out of the new rip in her skin. The queen reached down and jerked Sister Ora's head upward by her hair, then moved her claw to wrap around Sister Ora's throat, making sure to press onto the cuts Father Figgins' device had left behind.

Queen Onetta snarled into her face, her choking grip tightening. "You are perching yourself on the edge of a very dangerous precipice."

This is stupid.

I am stupid.

What am I doing?

Still, Sister Ora softly laughed between broken breaths. Queen Onetta responded with a tighter grip. Her hands smacked at the queen's arm, trying to break her grasp. Sister Ora heard the gasps of nearby aides and castle dwellers.

Let them see me weak. Let them see what the queen is capable of.

"Please. Stop," she choked out as she filled herself with fake fear and let lying tears fall down her cheeks. Her eyes darted around at the newly gathered and watching crowd of castle aides and visitors. As she met the eyes of those gathered around, Sister Ora made her doe eyes bigger, softer, and more innocent. She made her face plead for help.

Queen Onetta's intense glare broke when she heard the quiet whispers and hushed gasps of the crowd gathered across the walkway. Servants and castle inhabitants held their hands over their mouths in shock, several whispering to one another about the scene they witnessed.

Even the birds chirping a moment ago had gone silent as if they knew what had just happened.

The queen slowly dropped her hand, trying to compose herself, while Sister Ora hunched over, loudly and dramatically gasping for air. She delicately touched her neck where the queen's hand had left deep bruises. She didn't bother hiding the cocky smirk as she looked up at the queen.

"Well played." Queen Onetta whispered, straightening the rings on her hand while waiting for Sister Ora to compose herself.

She finally did, straightening her disheveled hair and neckline. Sister Ora cocked a brow at the queen and slowly stepped for her, the same calculated movement the queen had done just a moment prior.

"I will wear these bruises and this scar," she gestured to her bleeding cheek, her tone quiet and calm, "-like a badge of honor, Your Majesty. Now, if you will excuse me." She bowed to the queen and brushed past her, heading for the Royal Hall of Chambers.

Sister Ora stormed through the halls with fury and pounding adrenaline. Her new guards- whose names and voices she did not bother to learn- followed closely behind, their armor thumping loudly with each hurried step. The castle's labyrinth transformed into a clear path as she turned corners and rushed through the threshold of several halls.

The contours of her face were hardened by the streams of light coming from the open windows. Gone was the softness of her full cheeks that crinkled her eyes when she smiled. The cut on her cheek thrummed with each of her hard steps. She hoped it would scar.

Her mind was a chaos of emotions, and she needed some time alone to sort them out. She did not yet know what she would do with her anger, but she knew she needed solitude.

The bedchamber hall lay in front of her. Her eyes locked onto her chamber door, and she bore a hole into the wood as she shouted over her shoulder at her guards.

"Leave me. I will take my luncheon in my chamber and -"

Prince Percy casually stepped out of his chamber, mere steps from the storming fury that was his betrothed. Sister Ora halted her steps, her body jostling into a crooked bow at his presence.

"Your Highness," she greeted in shock.

Prince Percy nodded his own greeting. When his eyes met her face, they widened in shock and softened in worry. He scanned the dried blood on her face; then, his gaze drifted down to the newly forming bruises on her neck. He slowly moved his hand as if to brush her cheek, but clenched it into a fist and let it fall to his side.

"What happened to you?" he asked, his voice barely able to form into a whisper.

Sister Ora quickly debated curating a lie, but she held no quarrels with any punishment she may face for admitting what the queen did to her. It is not as if the prince did not know of her cruelty, and she knew how quickly the castle would talk about what they saw anyway.

"Your mother," she said as she straightened her face and set her jaw.

In a moment of quiet kindness, Prince Percy pulled out a kerchief from his pocket and gently rested his hand under her chin. He gently patted off the blood on her cheek, careful not to put too much pressure on her face. Prince Percy kept his eyes on her scar, and his throat bobbed up and down as he touched her.

Could I spend a lifetime with someone as kind as him? Even if I am surrounded by his cruel family?

And more importantly, could our betrothal be used for me to escape them all? Or to survive?

Sister Ora set her hand around his and softly smiled. "Thank you, Percy."

He looked at her hand on his and met her eyes. His throat bobbed up and down again. In a quick swipe, he ripped his hand away and stepped back from her.

"It is Your Royal Highness," he said coldly.

"I—my apologies, Your Royal Highness," she timidly replied, shocked at how cold his voice became.

Prince Percy eyed her guards and his own, who had been waiting outside his chamber door. "I will take her the rest of the way down the hall. Please pardon us."

And then he turned and walked without waiting for her.

Sister Ora shook her head and quickly met with his strides. Beside her, Prince Percy's hands wrung together behind his back, and his breath huffed deeply each time he exhaled. They walked in uncomfortable, painful silence. The handful of steps to her chamber doors took centuries to come to an end.

They stopped in front of her door, and Prince Percy took a deep breath, finally letting himself look at her again. "I presume mother spoke to you about our upcoming wedding and the date."

She nodded quietly.

"I have been thinking a lot about our impending marriage. Do you recall when we were first betrothed, when I promised you our marriage would, at least, be that of friendship?"

She smiled. "Yes, I do."

Yes. I could survive this family, she thought. I could get away from them with Percy by my side and fight them while we are stuck here.

His jaw hardened, forcing her smile away. "I am afraid I can no longer offer that promise."

Her mouth fell open, but no words came out.

He continued and tore his face away from hers. "I do not know if I could ever look at your face, one that I once believed to be the most beautiful, and not be filled with disgust and anger. I will never forgive you, not for Sir Loren, not for your lies, nor your manipulation of me. You will receive no love from me, but I will do my best not to loathe your existence," he returned his look to her. "That is what I can offer you after what you have done."

Tears wetted her eyes. She did not see Prince Percy in front of her. Instead, she saw Queen Onetta's dark hair, King Ivan's angry glare, and both of his parents' stern coldness.

"What happened to the kind prince I met all those moons ago?" she asked, stepping forward to try to offer her touch. "Percy, please look at me."

He jerked away. Sister Ora swore she saw tears in his eyes, too. "I may think of you fondly at times, or, who I believed you once were, I may even remember the kindness you offered between your lies. But I would cut off my hands before ever reaching for you again."

His throat choked, and dryness filled each breath he took.

She could not believe that his anger at her had grown so deep, had festered into this. She recoiled. "I thought you did not wish to be like your father or the men you plot and plan with."

"Yes, well," his voice was soft again. He swallowed hard and moved to leave her. "I have learned the lesson of what being soft means in this world."

She spoke to an empty hall as Prince Percy left her behind.

"You would have been easy to love, Percy." Sister Ora found herself saying as she turned to him. "In another life, another timeline where we were not on opposite sides of this war, where we both did not have to do foul things in the name of what we believed was right. In that life, I would have easily loved you."

His back remained to her, and he mumbled. His voice was soft enough to avoid their guards' eavesdropping ears but loud enough to crack her apart, "In that lifetime, would you still have fucked another man under my hospitality? Or would you have not been a whore?"

Her heart and voice shattered. "Percy..."

His head straightened as sharp as his spine as he left her behind. "It is Your Highness. I can never be Percy to you again."

Chapter 30

The butcher's table ran red with blood, the basket beside it filled with freshly skinned bodies, and the wet ground at the butcher's feet painted with feathers.

"Got another one for ya, boss." A red-caped archer greeted as they threw down a bird freshly shot from the sky, dropping it on the table with a simple acknowledgment before walking towards the fire and fresh ale nearby.

The butcher grunted and grabbed the bird, immediately getting to work, making an incision on the underside of the breast and pulling the skin and feathers off. He hummed a quiet tavern tune as he flipped the bird back over, cutting down both sides of its back and cutting through the ribs.

He paused, humming to grunt in frustration at the chunk of broken arrowhead carelessly left in the carcass. His fingers ran over the shard, tapping on it as he thought. He spared a cursory glance around the red-ordained war camp, then quietly pushed the arrowhead into the bird carcass more.

He quickly looked around the camp, meeting the eyes of the female Sebern scout he had been captured alongside, now tasked with dumping latrines and medical tent rubbish. Their glance was short and unnoticeable, barely a flick of their eyes.

Prisoners put to work were not supposed to acknowledge one another.

The butcher set aside the bird, placing it with intention with the others ready to be cooked. He set aside his tools, leaving them on the table uncleaned, and brought the birds over to the fire nearby to roast, keeping an ever-watchful eye on the bird with the shard inside it. He would be sure to lend a hand with serving the soldiers that night.

The crackling fire echoed the sounds of nighttime pleasures, merging with nearby conversations as the sun said its goodbyes and the stars awoke for the night.

Prince Elion's breath came in short and fast bursts, matching the pace of his thrusting body. His clawed grip tightened on Jeffrey's hips as he moved in and out of him, his body kneeling on the bed behind Jeffrey.

Jeffrey's hand wrapped around himself, keeping pace with Prince Elion's thrusts as his other hand clutched the bedsheets below his body. Jeffrey's knees shook, barely successful in keeping his body from collapsing as Prince Elion increased the intensity of his thrusting.

The Crown Prince let out another loud gasp, his movement faltering for one, two, three strokes until finally he could not move anymore, and his cock twitched inside of Jeffery, and he felt himself fill with Prince Elion.

The prince held himself over Jeffrey, gasping out as he came back down from his high. Underneath him, Jeffrey continued stroking his own throbbing cock.

Prince Elion leaned forward, kissing Jeffrey on the neck slowly, deeply, as he ran his hand down his moving arm and gently nudged Jeffrey's hand off of his length, the prince replacing it with his own and changing the once fast and hard stroking with his own deep, slow movement. The prince rubbed delicately around Jeffrey's tip, the swirling motion that always made Jeffrey tremble and shudder.

Jeffrey's cock twitched in the prince's hand as he came undone, the sheets below their bodies now covered in one another's sweat and orgasm. But the prince did not stop his stroking. He continued as Jeffrey's face twitched, tensed, then calmed in pleasure.

"That's my boy," Prince Elion whispered in his ear, "good boy."

They both shared a soft breath before untangling and finding their shared place at the head of the prince's bed, detangling themselves while they shared in wine. Prince Elion chugged greedily from his stein before sharing it.

Jeffrey watched Prince Elion's throat as he greedily chugged the wine, noticing the subtle movements as it bobbed up and down. Despite the prince's arm remaining casually draped around Jeffrey's shoulders, Jeffrey's eyes narrowed, and his lips tightened into a thin line of frustration. Just as he had the time prior, the prince avoided making direct eye contact with Jeffrey once they had finished their fucking, and just like the last few times they had been intimate, Prince Elion ensured that their eyes did not meet.

"Why do you no longer look at me, my prince? Why do you avoid looking me in my eyes while you fuck me?"

"Do not be so vulgar about it." Prince Elion replied as he shook his head and set the stein down.

"Vulgar?" Jeffrey jested, "After the words you say to me while we are inside one another, I do not believe you have the right to call me vulgar."

Prince Elion did not join in his boisterous tone or snickering. He remained silent and stern-faced. His harsh quiet continued to make Jeffrey uncomfortable.

But he tried not to let his worry and anxiety show. He moved, setting a gentle hand on his love's face. "Please talk to me. We have barely spoken to one another as of late. You used to confide in me and seek solace in my comfort, but now you do not even offer me love after we are done with one another's pleasures."

The prince turned his head away from him, causing Jeffrey's hand to fall from where it rested on his cheek.

"I am not a good man, Jeffrey." Prince Elion mumbled. He wiped the wine from his mouth and the sweat from his face. "And someday, I will have to be even worse than I already am."

Jeffrey shifted to sit up, leaning onto his side to face the prince he had known in so many ways for so much time.

"I do what must be done for the crown, my future crown. I have done horrendous, heartless things." The prince shook his head and turned his face farther away from his lover. "And as you have said before, I will have to do much worse things once I am the one wearing the crown."

"We all do horrendous things for power, for justice, my prince," Jeffrey replied, running his hand soothingly on Prince Elion's chest, a familiar gesture he did to comfort the prince during his times of turmoil. "It does not make us evil. And you have refused to do things of horror even if it would give you victory and power. You are a good, lawful man— and you will be that same kind of man as king."

"You know nothing." Prince Elion dropped his hand onto Jeffery's, pushing it off him.

Jeffrey recoiled in shock, sitting behind the prince, who now moved to the edge of the bed, his feet on the floor and his head bowed.

"That is a lie. I know who you are. I have known the dark within you alongside the light." Jeffrey shifted forward to try to get close to him again. "And I have loved each and every part of you all of this time."

Prince Elion turned his head, peering at Jeffrey over his shoulder. "You know nothing."

The prince stood up to dress, his movements slow and sullen.

Jeffrey sat glaring from the bed, throwing the blankets off himself and grabbing his clothes off the ground. He forcefully tied the laces closed on his pants, shaking his head as he looked over at the prince. He threw his shirt over his head, pulling and adjusting it as he shot his words at Prince Elion.

"I know that what you did earlier in this war to that woman disguised as a Healer placed a crack in your heart when your duty demanded her head. I know you sentencing those three villagers to their deaths cracked it even more, knowing you had to hang them for their treason. And any other man would have broken the law to torture those prisoners for information or strung them up to send a message. But you always do what needs to be done to abide by the law despite how it hurts you."

He stood beside Prince Elion. "And I know that you are placing your anger at your father and yourself onto me, where it does not belong."

Prince Elion quietly turned to face him, finishing rolling the cuffs on his sleeves and reaching for his jacket. The prince swallowed hard. "I do not believe it appropriate for us to see one another anymore. I am betrothed to another, and I must remain faithful to her and the oaths we have sworn for our future together."

Jeffrey stepped back. "You are a damn fool, Your Highness. A damn fool. And a fucking ass."

Jeffrey stormed to the tent's entrance, throwing it open and letting the camp's noises and scents inside. "And I know you mean nothing of what you have said to me this day," Jeffrey growled over his shoulder as he left.

Prince Elion fell back onto the bed, his elbows on his legs, and his body sank over. "Duty will be easier this way," the crowned and burdened prince convinced himself. Attaching himself to people only opened him up to their influence, their ideas, and their pain when he did have to let go of the man he was to be the king he had to be one day.

Jeffrey had been right the other day. One day, the prince would have to do terrible things like his father had been doing. The prince would have no choice but to become too much like his father. He would have to learn to be cruel, callous, and angry. He would someday have to learn how to bend the laws to his will in order to keep his power, to keep his kingdom in one piece.

"Your Highness, dinner is ready." A servant informed from the entrance of the tent. She stood timidly, uncertain in her movements as her hands intertwined and fidgeted, awaiting his reply. She cocked her head at his dining table. "Shall I bring in your plate?"

"No. I will dine among my soldiers this eve," he said to the floor beneath his feet before getting up and leaving.

The prince asked the soldiers to forgo formalities as he walked through the open dining area of the camp, shaking several hands and patting backs as he followed the scents of cooked meat, fresh bread, and stewing vegetables. He made his way to the line of soldiers awaiting their food, insisting on waiting among others instead of being served formally before them. The line grew hectic and long as impatient stomachs grumbled and the butchers and cooks brought out more food.

Music played from the bards gathered along the space, adding slow, calming notes to the air, encouraging those gathered to make peace with their impatience and converse with their neighbors.

A fresh plate of foul brought cheers from the line as each bird on the tray was quickly served, and claims from the line rang out over who would enjoy each slab of meat—the manner of their cooking uneven amongst the platters.

"Butcher, please, no, we shall serve it. Gather more from the fire if you wish to help," a kitchen aid corrected the quiet man who brought forth the fresh tray of birds. He hesitated in his retreat, shifting uncomfortably and in silence before obeying the aide's shove to remove him from the crowded space.

The prince and the remaining soldiers made their way through the line, all obediently sitting down for their first plate and hesitating to get up for seconds. Even among brutal fighters in the middle of a war, many knew their proper manners, especially so among their prince.

Prince Elion properly jested and spoke with the officers around him, keenly shifting away from the empty chair beside him that was always reserved for Jeffrey and keeping his glances away from the table where he heard his ex-lover's sweet tenor coming from.

The prince spoke of light-hearted plans, cutting into the potatoes and ripping apart the bread on his plate. He lazily cut into the blackened foul, continuing his words with his officers as he raised a large chunk to his mouth and chewed quickly. The scent of the dinner overwhelmed his common sense and made him eager to dine. He swallowed twice, the piece he took too big for a normal bite.

Then he choked.

And choked again.

"My prince, are you okay?" Officer Blackley began to stand in a panic next to him as the prince continued coughing and choking, hitting his chest with his fist.

Prince Elion shook his head and waved his hand towards the wine chalice in front of him, quickly chugging half its contents before taking a breath. The prince cleared his throat. "My apologies for the fright. I was always lectured and punished for not minding my proper dinner manners."

The air calmed at the excitement as the music began again, relaxing emotions and creating a jovial atmosphere. Prince Elion continued, much more careful now in his eating and engaging in jokes and banter with his soldiers as the moonlight shone down and its light overtook the space.

He smiled, he laughed. Even among the hurt, he put on the proper show he was meant to display.

And then he heard the gasps and shouts.

Then he saw a choking face that broke his heart and stole the air from his body.

Prince Elion slowly watched as Jeffrey— his Jeffrey— clutched his throat, and his head lurched forward repeatedly.

The prince could not take his eyes off his ex-lover as the blood began to fall from Jeffrey's lips.

"No. No. No!" Prince Elion watched on as the blood dripped down Jeffrey's face, and the men and women around him clamored for aid.

Prince Elion threw himself around the table, reaching for Jeffrey's fallen-over, hacking body.

"Healer!" he screamed, "Where are the Healers!"

Before the words finished escaping him, Healers were rushing from their tents and abandoning their posts, the crowd parting in obedient waves as they made their way to the falling and heaving man.

Prince Elion held himself back as the Healers gathered around, holding onto Jeffrey's face, feeling the movement in his neck, while others pulled out tools and herbs. While they busied themselves with different activities, they all exchanged knowing looks that the prince refused to believe meant his lover was already gone while he still gasped for air.

Their efforts were for the satisfaction of the prince; it was much too late to save Jeffrey.

Prince Elion knew that. But he could not believe it.

Jeffrey hacked and spit vomit on himself, then jerked his body over onto his hands and knees, throwing up one last heave of vomit and blood before falling into a limp mess on the ground.

In his last movement, Jeffrey had reached for the prince's hand.

Silence fell. Even the clamoring of the cooks did not echo. They knew it was better to let the food burn than to disrupt the moment.

A Healer dug his fingers through the pile of vomit and blood gathered around Jeffrey's head as the others moved to shift his limp body out of his own filth. The Healer lifted a metal shard, a fleck of an arrow singed and covered in remnants of meat. He held it up and turned to the prince. "Your Majesty."

Prince Elion ripped it from the Healer's hand, his hands shaking in rage and grief. He turned to the onlooking crowd, holding it up for them. "Who did this?!"

"Who did this?!" he shouted again. "Tell me now!"

The crowd stepped back from his rage. His soldiers were even fearful of his anger, and the servants and cooks responsible for the meal trembled behind their work tables and held one another.

Prince Elion threw the fleck of metal to the ground, immediately forcing his way towards the cooks' campfires and butcher's stations, shoving past the soldiers trying to hold him back.

Screams of different pitches and tenors broke out as the enraged prince kicked over and tore apart their stations, feeding the fires under the cauldrons as food, debris, and supplies rolled into them.

When the Crown Prince ran out of supplies to break, he turned his heaving body towards the prisoners he had put to labor in the camp, even the ones that did not work in the kitchens.

He put his hand on his sheathed sword and ignored the shouts and hands reaching for him, urging him to stop.

Metal unsheathed and rage unleashed as the prince found his revenge, and everywhere he looked, the Crown Prince created death.

Chapter 31

Madam Fury stood beside the open window and admired the damp green landscape in the distance. Broken Tower sat between two unnamed small lakes and a seemingly never-ending river that also bore no true name. All the streams and masses of water within the Land of a Thousand Rivers had never been officially titled by any sovereign, only given names by those on opposing sides of the borders who chose their own. Past kings had deemed such a small thing so trivial compared to their other duties.

But when your ancestors bled and died on those shores to free themselves from their chains, to only have land promised to them shrunk in nearly half, honoring their sacrifice by bequeathing their resting ground with a proper name was nothing small.

Not for Craigie.

Not for Odessin.

Madam Fury's ancestors did not balk at or fight against the great Alvarians and their winged gods when they came ashore. They joined them in their cause before the Conquest even began, knowing the Alvarian winged beasts and their power would bring more prosperity and riches than one continent could handle, knowing they would not bow or kneel to such conquerors, but stand alongside and gain much from the gods that men rode. Those who bled the blood of Craigie had been too stupid and stubborn to see what the Alvarians would do for their lands.

Odessin had been set to become a prosperous and promising land before it even had a border or a name. That was before the throne changed hands and their people became chained.

Madam Fury's homeland soon became the dumping ground for undesirables and criminals too horrendous to be held kindly in a regular prison, or for citizens deemed worthless to those around them. After their chains began to rust and the rumblings of a civil war began, any annoyances with their northern neighbor bore no more weight, and their people joined arms in war.

While the allied enemy's unity brought Madam Fury's people their freedom, it was not enough to extinguish the fires when the treaty from the Great Civil War redrew the lands and gave so much to the North. So much for the people who had not known imprisonment and pain as her people did.

The Odessians lost their chains and more than they thought they could. Their magic. Their bonds. Their faith. But not the fight built in their very being.

Hustled steps in the hallway dissolved her remaining reflections. Madam Fury hardened her face as she turned to the closed doorway. The sheen of her straight black hair was exaggerated by the sunbeams breaking through the clouds above and the open window behind her. She had her war braids removed as a sign of good faith that she was not here to fight.

She hoped she did not have to add more black marks to her skin today; for once, she did not feel like drawing blood and earning more tattooed marks that spoke of victories and kills.

"You lied," she greeted Lord Augusta Lisarian as his aide opened the door and he stepped inside. "Your letter stated you were coming to put an end to our skirmishes, that Lady Edgel had gone too far."

Lord Lisarian cleared his throat as he finished entering the room. He nodded in greeting and bowed at his neck. "Good afternoon to you as well, Madam Fury."

"Yes, good morning," she said flatly, then stepped forward. Madam Fury did not care for small talk or niceties. "I had received your letter and so stupidly assumed it to be true that House Lisarian would finally stand for something. I sent my best Dragons and myself to finally put an end to the Craigie grab for land, assuming your banners would fly beside ours. Yet, when you came, you offered no aid to us but sent us all home with our tails between our legs. Why?"

He sighed and mumbled as he walked around the table to sit, "Ah, yes, that letter."

"Yes, that letter," Her tone reeked of aggravation and emotion. She did not bother to put on her mental armor in this room. Lord Lisarian would use no weapons against her "—cousin."

"That letter was from a Lord Lisarian. It just so happened to be from the Dowager Lord, not I." He said as he leaned one elbow on the table, his chair turned outright to face her. "Your distant cousin, uncle," he waved his hand carelessly, "- relative has been up to his ways again."

The lines blurred long ago between many Craigie and Odessin families where the Lisarian clan was involved. Over the course of arranged marriages between the two countries, the children of the stewards of Broken Tower created many distant cousins, uncles, aunts, and more. Few bothered to keep accurate records of the intricate weaving of long-distance families. Cousin was often just a title to note lineage, not true relation.

He looked back up at her. "The Dowager Lord desired to strong-arm me into aiding you all, believing sending a letter on my behalf would put me in a precarious position with no choice. Either that or to order the aid himself and think I would not call it back."

"And you chose to keep your oath to the House and your lands."

"Yes," he said.

"And your father desired to undermine you and aid his people."

"Yes."

"So the House that is to hold us in peace is falling, too." She subtly cocked her head and smirked, "Interesting. Very interesting."

"Do you Odessians do anything besides plot and plan?" Lady Reval Lisarian snarked from the other side of the cracked-open door.

Madam Fury glanced at her as she stepped into the room. "We brood as well, although not quite as well as your people do."

Lady Reval entered the room and stood beside her husband. She crossed her arms. "What are you doing here, Madam Fury?"

Madam Fury smiled without her teeth. "I am sure you know exactly what I am doing here, seeing as you have been standing in the hall this entire time." She paused, "You brutes breathe too loudly not to be heard."

Lady Reval clenched her fists and let out a low growl. Lord Augusta moved his arm that he had rested on the table, gently holding an open hand out to his wife to pause any further commentary.

"As I was about to say, Madam Fury, our House has not and will not fall." He stood. "I offer my apologies for what has occurred and will rectify my father's transgressions in whatever way we deem appropriate. We are allies, Madam Fury. We should not forget that, especially during these times."

"Yes, we should not." Madam Fury nodded, then glanced behind Lord Augusta to Lady Reval. "Tell me, Lady Lisarian, how does it make you feel to know that we are allies now? That you are no longer allowed on the battlefield against my Dragons?"

"We are not –" Lady Reval began to snap. Her jaw tightened so hard it looked as if it would break. She gathered herself. "We may be allies on paper due to this marriage, but that means nothing to me."

Lord Augusta sharply turned to his wife. "You will not speak in such a way. Leave us. Now."

Lady Reval did not move.

Lord Augusta leaned forward and dropped his tone into a dangerously low register. "Do not embarrass yourself further by forcing me to call my guards in here to drag you."

As the door slammed behind Lady Reval, Madam Fury spoke again, her quippy remarks not yet running dry. "What was that you were saying, my lord, about your House not falling apart?"

He glared at her as he sat back down. "Madam Fury, please."

She scoffed and sat down as well. "I am done. I promise."

"Why else did you come here? It is not like you to ride so far out of your way for what a letter could answer."

She kept her eyes moving around the room. "Do you have any wine? Port, perhaps?"

"Yes," he said slowly, signaling to his aide to retrieve and pour each of them a glass.

"Great. Now, tell me, my lord, how are we to still be allies when the Houses we serve under are currently at odds?"

He grunted and growled. "Now I see why you asked for port and not tea."

Her smile widened as her senses picked up on Lady Reval still eavesdropping in the hall. "Now, what would you say to us making a deal?"

There was always more than one way to torture and defeat an enemy. Madam Fury ran her hand through her smooth hair, the ridges of a tiny hidden war braid bringing warmth to her dragon-scaled heart.

Chapter 32

"There once was a queen named Bee, humble and lovely was she…" Sister Ora rolled her eyes, "- you've got to be kidding me."

She sat well-guarded in a small library within the castle alongside her lady's maid, Kaylah. She had wished to be in the Grand Hall of Archives today, not the youngest princess's children's library, but the queen apparently did have a sense of humor, despite the fact that all she did was scowl.

Sister Ora had asked for permission to be among books again, to have her leash loosened slightly since she had learned to behave and be quiet since her tea with Father Figgins, barring her outburst with the queen. She touched her neck where the Heretic's Fork that Father Figgins had made her wear left marks under her chin. Proof that even when she obeyed, they found ways to hurt her.

No matter what she did, this court would harm her. She could not escape yet, but she could survive. She looked down at the painted parchment of the book; the fictional blonde queen beamed in the sunlight that bathed her in its light on the crinkled page. Sister Ora let out a tired breath.

After Prince Percy had confessed his disgust and hatred for her after her fight with his mother, Sister Ora had found no noble allies to shield or protect her, so she had to make new ones. She had known through private conversations with Kaylah, who enjoyed her gossip with the other aides, that the Odessian lords enjoyed art and literature among secrets and griping about the king.

Sister Ora had hoped to run into the lords in the Hall of Archives today by pure happenstance.

Planned happenstance, actually.

Queen Onetta granted permission for Sister Ora to be let out of her room for the afternoon after receiving a heartfelt apology for her behavior, followed later by a request to breathe some fresh air and enjoy some reading. Any hidden excitement Sister Ora had felt over being set free among books had dissipated when she entered the royal children's library.

She was certain Queen Onetta was somewhere sleuthing in the castle, laughing loudly at her joke.

Sister Ora closed the book and brushed her stomach before resting her hand on the hardcover. She forbade any illusions to dance across her mind, her belly swollen with a babe or visions of a young child sitting in her lap as she read the tale she had pulled from the shelves. Her jaw trembled, and her breath shook. She lifted her glistening gaze to the ceiling in an attempt to prevent the tears from fully forming while her hands clenched one another.

The anger rumbled awake inside her belly and heart again. Her breathing became intense, her jaw locked as her face heated, and she shook her head. The guard's unwavering gaze bore into Sister Ora's back, a constant reminder of her captivity. The scent of old books and polished wood filled her senses, a stark contrast to the suffocating tension in the air.

She heard her mother's voice scolding her: *Ladies, do not show such emotions... Quiet yourself... Be silent—it is better this way... Stop being so much!*

"My lady?" Kaylah's voice broke the ones shouting inside her head. Sister Ora jolted in her chair and cleared her throat. Kaylah sat across from her in an upholstered red chair before a bookshelf. Kaylah's stitching paused as she watched Sister Ora return to herself. "Everything alright, my lady?"

"Yes, yes, thank you. It seems I just got lost in my thoughts." Sister Ora rubbed and pulled on the long sleeves of her midnight blue dress while her mind desired to pull on her skin. She ran a hand over her forehead to brush her fallen hair away. "It is just that I—"

Kaylah scanned the room and quickly returned her glance to Sister Ora, a reminder that they were not alone.

"It is just that I would prefer a different book." Sister Ora got up and moved to the bookshelf beside Kaylah. As she casually scanned the shelves, feigning interest in titles well below her grade, she whispered so quietly she wondered if Kaylah could even hear, "Do you believe the queen learned of my intent to run into the lords in the Grand Hall? Or is this perhaps another one of her jabs at me?"

Kaylah pulled another stitch and murmured, "Mhmm."

Sister Ora pulled a book from the shelf and flipped through the pages. "Have you any more knowledge of their schedules? Or any others I may attempt allyship with?" she hissed as she raised her hand to her neck where the queen's fingers left marks, and the Heretic's Fork left dots of red.

"What're you two whispering about?" The sudden intrusion of the guard's voice across the room demanded their attention.

Sister Ora snapped her head around. "Nothing."

"Doesn't sound like nothing," he glared.

She snapped again, "Is it a crime for a lady to mumble to herself while she is sequestered to look about a room of books made for toddlers?"

The guard stepped forward, his voice laced with threat, "I don't know; perhaps I'll ask Her Majesty if she opposes it," he growled at her.

Sister Ora started to rudely retort when Kaylah shot out of her seat and held a hard hand on Sister Ora's arm. She spoke on her behalf. "Our apologies, good sir. My lady is tired and restless, it seems. We apologize for her outburst."

Kaylah pulled Sister Ora back down to sit. Sister Ora stared out the narrow paned windows behind Kaylah, each providing beams of sunlight between the bookshelves they broke up. She cocked her head as she looked at the ornate teapot and cups that sat at the table between the two women.

She may not have access to Council chambers and war rooms or access to much, but she did know the proper ways of the court: learn the titles, the faces, your place, and find your allies and aides. In her schooling, court politics and behaviors were a typical lesson, their teachers preparing all the future Scholars for potential roles among the most noble or royal. She learned early on how ladies and gentlemen of the court were to act, what was considered taboo among different courts, and the differences in their cultures.

Sister Ora sat up straight, "How could I have been so rude?" she scoffed. "The Lords of Odessin have been here for over a fortnight, and Prince Percy and I have yet to write them to treat with us. It is Odessian custom that guests host a tea as a thank you for being welcomed into one's home, but they only will do so when the host sends an invitation requesting it."

She tutted, "Terrible hosts, we are, we never sent one."

"Yes, how terribly rude, my lady." Kaylah set down her stitching. "And it would be quite rude on their behalf to deny you two their time. Even if they take offense to the delay, it is not Odessian nature to decline such an invitation."

Sister Ora smiled, "It would be quite uncouth and unlike the lords, from what I hear."

Her teachers and mother had taught her well what her place should be and how to stay in line. Sister Ora's posture changed. She could shove down and hide who she was and wished she could be. She could harden herself again. Maybe in the future, she could be kind, delicate, soft. The things she had begun to be before she was sent here.

But not now, now she had to don her many masks again.

As Prince Percy and Sister Ora made their way towards the grand suite where the Lords of Odessin awaited their arrival, a hard silence stayed between them. Not a single word was spoken between them as they reached the open doorway of the lord's guest chambers. Prince Percy gave a gentle nod to Sister Ora; his eyes turned away from her as he gestured for her to enter the guest quarters before him.

No servants or aides greeted them as they stepped inside; instead, Lord Shaital Pathis came strolling from the balcony, his hands extended and his smile wide in greeting.

"Sister Ora, it is lovely to meet you finally. I do hope you are well after such a long illness." Lord Shaital Pathis smiled as he wrapped her hands in his and nodded his head at her. "Your letter requesting tea with us was so kind, and I am grateful you are feeling much better now."

"Yes, my lord, I am feeling quite fit thanks to the aid the king and queen offered me." She nodded in return and smiled with her lips closed. Her soft eyes held his crinkled look as their hands parted.

"Ah! My prince." He then greeted Prince Percy in the same friendly and intimate way. "My husband is preparing our drinks now. Come in, come in, please."

Prince Percy returned to his quietness after exchanging his required pleasantries with the lord, choosing instead to silently take in the room as they were led to the seating area. Sister Ora chose to discuss the weather, the lord's travels to the castle, and the upcoming holidays with their host.

She was unusually chipper.

It must be the fresh air and freedom.

The guest quarters that once boasted traditional Britia decor had become an exotic oasis. The ostentatiously carved pillars and trim on the walls were still intact, but the heavy pillows and fabric that once adorned the room had been replaced with softer, more breathable materials brought in with the lord's caravan. The muted browns, purples, and rich reds that colored many of the spaces throughout the castle had been replaced with bright and vibrant hues; orange, yellow, and purple silk floor pillows and semi-sheer curtains were draped around the room, embellished with tasseled trim and detailed patterns, while incense burned beside the open windows, coating the air with serenity and calm.

Sandalwood and Oudh greeted the prince at the same time as the crown lord, Lord Nesima Mete, sat beside him. The Lord of Odessin rested on a bright orange cushioned pillow on the floor; a pile of other cushions surrounded a short-legged table. As Lord Nesima settled, Prince Percy took a moment to adjust himself to the comfortable yet unusual seating on the ground, uncertain if he should cross his legs, sit atop them, or let them sprawl out in front of him.

"My lords, you have decorated your quarters so beautifully, I feel as if I am in the lands of Odessin myself. Although I have never been there, only heard of its beauty." Sister Ora softly said as she sat with her legs folded beside her, her ankles crossed at her side, and her dress softly billowed around her, covering the cushion beneath her. "Did you do so because you believe your stay with us will be long?"

A muscle twitched in Lord Shaital's lip that turned into a one-sided smile. "We are unsure of how long we will stay, but regardless, my lady, our culture is important to us. We do not wish to lose who we are, even for a moment."

Lord Shaital nodded at her attire, a rich green dress with noticeable wear where stitching had once displayed detailed patterns, now replaced by new, simpler lines that attempted to cover up the indents where swirls and ornate filigree had once been.

"Something you may also understand." He whispered as he leaned closer to her and handed her a metal cup of drink.

Prince Percy creased his eyes and cocked his head at the comment not meant for him to hear. He watched his betrothed's face, not missing the slight curl of her lip, then to a knowing smirk before she cut it away.

"We were curious," Lord Nesima spoke up, "after you two are wed this coming season, will you tour the kingdom?"

Prince Percy and Sister Ora shot eyes back and forth at each other and the walls around them.

"Because we would love to host you in our city." Lord Nesima continued, more inquiry and curiosity in his tone. "And send letters to our friends and family to host you as well, if you wish."

Prince Percy replied in hurried and rushed words, "A honeymoon may not be appropriate at this time."

He did not wish to tell them that his mother forbade their honeymoon tour. Although she was the queen, he felt embarrassed being a grown man bossed around by his mother.

"But without a tour, where will you two decide to settle down and make your life? You have several paths available in front of you, Your Highness. Would it not be best for your bride to experience what you have seen so she can provide insight into which home would be preferred for you both?" Lord Shaital asked, his peripheral glued to Sister Ora's profile.

The prince did not miss how she watched him back, too.

"Whatever do they mean you have several paths available to you?" Her words shot out at the prince, even though she disguised them behind a higher-pitched tone and smile.

The prince swallowed the lump in his throat and looked down at the richly patterned rug beneath him. He had yet to tell her of the argument and anger between him and his mother, how he told her that after the war was won, they would leave the court and never return. Even before that decision, he had never told her of the options that had been placed before him:

Thelimor for a lordship crown or Odessin's Citadel for a quieter life among books.

He was sure Sister Ora would hold no anger against their leaving, but talking to her was painful.

In many ways.

Lord Nesima broke the quiet and cleared his throat, "How rude of us, Your Highness and My Lady. I do not believe you know of this drink we wish to share with you. This is apricot nectar and rose water, a drink we often enjoy during times of fasting or between meals. Please, enjoy."

"Thank you, my lords." Sister Ora mumbled and took a generous gulp. She licked a droplet of the nectar from her lips, then raised her chin to Lord Nesima. Prince Percy had to shake his head to avert his stare at her mouth.

"Would I be improper to assume that one of my betrothed's paths involves your lands?" she asked sternly, not letting go of the forgotten comments.

Lord Shaital replied, his expression covered by his raised cup. "Not improper at all, my lady, in fact, quite correct. That is, would the young prince be okay with us sharing this with you? We would hate to cause an issue between you two or speak when we should listen."

Prince Percy cleared his throat and fidgeted with his drink. He worked hard to keep his voice firm, but his posture and mannerisms gave away his anxiousness. "Before we met, I was offered a teaching position at the Citadel in Odessin, and I am considering taking the post."

He had yet to tell the lords that he had already made his decision.

He had once been eager and at ease to share information, but now he wished to hold all he knew within him.

"What a lovely offer, Your Highness." Sister Ora said to Prince Percy. While she smiled at him, irritation was evident on her face. "Tell me, my lords, if my betrothed were to take this position, would he and I both move from his court to yours?"

"Oh yes, yes, of course. That is, unless you two would prefer to be separated." Lord Nesima said. He let the silence sit at his final words while he leaned forward toward the snack tray sitting on the low table in the middle of the group. The lord broke a square biscuit containing green nuts in half and slowly enjoyed both halves while the group ruminated on his words. "However, I believe that you would enjoy our court, Sister Ora."

She poured herself more of the nectar juice and sipped it slowly. "How so, my lord?"

Prince Percy quickly recognized the back-and-forth, the tones used on both ends of the growing conversation.

What game is she playing? What game are they playing?

"While in all six kingdoms, one's gender is of no issue to those of us with a hint of intelligence, traditional roles and court rules that are common here are unheard of in our country. Our court is a bit more democratic, one could argue, like those of foreign lands that sail here when they dare cross the wide seas," the lord replied.

She sipped her drink again; every word was laced with piqued curiosity; Prince Percy could see cogs and wheels turning behind her hazel eyes, but knew nothing of what they worked towards. "And what would make you believe I would enjoy that more than where I am now?"

"In our court, you would have more of a voice than what you have been given here." Lord Shaital spoke and took a torturous pause, "And in Odessin, we don't believe in chains."

He shot a glare of fury so hard at Prince Percy that the prince felt the flames under his skin. Lord Shaital was obvious in his movement as he slowly turned his anger to Sister Ora's wrists, which she now rubbed and tucked into her sleeves.

"Our ancestors broke their chains ages ago, but not before our mountains were littered with their bones and haunted by their spirits." Lord Shaital reached for his own snack. "Our kingdom was built on the backs of the kingdom's 'undesirables' who were shackled in our lands and imprisoned in our mountains. Their blood fed our landscape, and now look where their blood finally rests."

Lord Nesima smiled with pride. "Next in line for the throne. Their blood, our blood, our daughter, to be queen of the kingdoms that once believed us unworthy of being a true country or equal people."

Prince Percy's shoulders fell. He had been so foolish to think that leaving this court would mean leaving behind the politics and posturing, the games and hidden promises.

And he was foolish to think for one moment that this afternoon tea was simply that.

Of course, his betrothed would not come here for simple tea and gossip. Just like the lords did not accept her invitation out of basic kindness.

And the prince, he realized, was the only one in the room in the dark on the plans being laid.

Sister Ora stopped Prince Percy outside her door, her voice a hushed and stern whisper. He had made her a fool during their tea with the Lords of Odessin by not telling her of his plans, of his potential position at the Citadel.

I need him to cooperate, to know his role if I am to survive, if we are to survive this cruel court. If I were to get any sort of revenge or freedom, I need him with me.

"Your Highness, I understand if your forgiveness will never be granted to me, but we are to be wed soon and will be beside one another until death or something worse occurs, and it would serve us to remember that."

He opened his mouth as if to speak, but she shot him a glare and continued. She found more power within her and stepped forward, cutting her chin up at him. "We do not have to tolerate one another, but we do have to speak. If we are linked to one another, we must have some alliance; otherwise, this kingdom will eat us alive no matter where we go. Even through your anger, you must see that. We must be a team."

"I cannot trust you." He replied in a mirrored, harsh whisper.

"Then don't. But imagine if we were in that room together, and those men wished to make us their pawns." She paused and huffed, "And for all we know, they were attempting that. We made ourselves look like easy prey; a house easy to divide because you kept your future- our future- from me. I may be a prisoner, but I am still to be your wife, I deserve to at least know in what ways you wish to control my life."

"You sound like my mother- plotting and planning and playing their court games." He shook his head and pinched his brow, stepping away to leave.

Sister Ora stepped closer and blocked his path. Her voice no longer a whisper, she spoke to him now not in anger, but in an attempt to convince him of how they must act, must be. "And look at how powerful she is."

His eyes scanned her stern face and fell to the lips she knew he had once dreamed about kissing. "You wish to speak? To be a team? Fine. When we wed, we will leave this court as soon as we are able to. We will stay away from these games and poisoned politics. We will move to the Citadel in Odessin and never come back to this country."

Another decision, another choice, ripped away from me before I even knew it was there.

Her eyes dared to glisten, making her look weak and sad. She hated that her anger always seemed to end in tears.

The prince offered her softness as he looked down upon her hardened face and quietness, "You won't be a prisoner there, Ora."

"Then what will I be?" she asked. She wiped away the feeling in her chest at seeing how he looked at her in that moment.

Pity.

It was pity he gave her. It was pity that made his eyes soften and scan her face and cock his head slightly as her lips parted in a shaking breath. Nothing more than pathetic pity.

He shook his head and shrugged, ice forming over his words and freezing out the softness he showed her a moment prior. "I don't know, and I don't need to know."

"Will I be the mother of your children? Your true wife and partner? Will I be held up in a room all my days, forbidden from living? If I still get no say in my life, even when my chains are taken from me, then tell me what I get to be."

She ignored the realization that burst across his face as her voice choked on her confessions.

"You get to be whatever you want to be. It does not matter to me."

She felt an arrow pierce her heart. She hated the wretched organ even more for the pain it threw into every part of her body. She was not supposed to be the one hurting in this conversation, not the one coming to more realizations about their future and feelings.

She needed to remind him of what his family had done to them both. She needed to remind him that this court is the poison—the enemy, not her.

"I know you hate me for what I have done, but it would serve your ego to remember who else was forced into this marriage, who was taken from her life and thrown into yours. It would serve our future family better for you to remember that you're not the only one suffering and in pain because of your family and the choices they made for us. Choices they made without our consideration or care."

The prince stared back at her, tight-lipped.

She shook her head and dropped her voice to show her pain. "If you cannot care for me, if you will never find joy in coming home to me, then at least do me the honor of tolerating me and being an ally. I may be a whore, a monster, a traitor, but I am still someone–"

She choked on her confession but knew she must speak it.

"– I am still someone who deserves some sort of countenance from the man she is to wed."

She turned and opened her chamber doors, glancing over her shoulder at him. She met his eyes, searching for any care he once held for her, anything she could grasp onto and use. She had done it before; she could use love as a weapon again.

It is not as if she would ever deserve to truly experience it, to have it, to hold it without its sharp edges cutting her open again. The pain that love had given her had shown that it was nothing more than a weapon to wield, and she would not walk through this world again unarmed.

Prince Percy's eyes softened again, and his shoulders fell. He swallowed a lump as she turned to look at him.

"Please, Percy. Please help me wish to live."

As she shut the door behind her, she felt her heart crack at the words she used against him. And she swore, as she heard his footsteps shuffle back and forth before retreating, she heard his crack a bit, too.

Chapter 33

Sir Marion opened the throne room door, allowing Father Figgins to enter first. By the time Father Figgins averted his attention from himself and looked towards the dais steps, Sir Marion's eyes had already locked on the throne, a salacious smile wide on his face at what he saw.

"Is this why you came here? To see how it feels?" Father Figgins asked as he stared down Lord Tyrrian Priscius.

The Lord of the Isles lounged on the king's golden throne. His long fingers idly rubbed up and down the intricate arms, feeling the ridges of the detailed carvings. His hands paused, and his fingertips drummed on the gold. He pursed his lips, then cocked his head at Father Figgins.

Sir Marion felt the power and ego thrumming in the room. For a moment, he let himself see the crowned lion on the banners replaced with the Aisharian kraken. How nice it would be to finally be done with his work here and go home.

"For a throne made of pure stardust and old rulers' golden crowns, it does leave one wanting for more." Lord Tyrrian crooned.

Father Figgins slowly walked down the aisle towards the throne. Sir Marion stayed posted at the door, his chin raised and his posture proud. He enjoyed seeing his lord on the gilded seat. The true blood of the Isles sitting where it always should have- not in a place below a crown, but at the top.

"You have always been advantageous, my lord. Your people have always wanted more, haven't they?" Father Figgins smirked and paused at Lord Tyrrian's feet. He did not nod or bow; instead, he moved to circle the throne.

It is in our blood to crave more. Sir Marion's jaw feathered at the thought.

"One could say the same of you, yes? I find it curious how quickly you became the Hand after only serving but a few short moments as the Master of Law. Other men have served the throne for much longer and yet were overlooked for such a position when Lord Orville was executed. Why you?" Lord Tyrrian asked. His lax and cool demeanor did not crack, even when his eyes met the heavy stare of Sir Marion- the hand that bled, the hand that killed.

"His Majesty chose his new Hand, not I, so you shall have to ask him." Father Figgins said, his voice now coming from behind the throne.

"Did he?" Lord Tyrrian replied, his chin turned towards his shoulder. He sat slouched to the side, his elbow resting on the arm of the throne, and his fingers rubbed against one another.

Father Figgins chuffed. His hands stayed gathered behind his back, a familiar position that left his posture broad and firm.

He now stood in front of the throne again. "I could have you hanged for daring to sit on His Majesty's throne," he said with arrogance.

"As if you have not sat here yourself, imagining a crown atop your head while you fist your own cock to the image." Lord Tyrrian leaned back and gestured to the three in the room with an open hand. "We all have, Father. This whole kingdom would if they could."

Father Figgins stood quietly.

"Pleasure. Power." Lord Tyrrian stroked the arm of the throne. "We men will always desire both. We need both to survive."

"As a man of God, I have forsaken such things as pleasure and power. Desiring... craving such things is a sin of a simple man. And I am no simple man, but a man of God and His divine light."

Lord Tyrrian laughed, then shook his head. "If you are afraid some little songbird sits in the shadows listening, you need not worry, Father. Your act of propriety can be dropped."

Father Figgins had always been terrible at playing the role of a true holy man. At least, it had always been easy to see through for Sir Marion. He recognized the hunger in the Father's eyes from the moment they met. Even more so, he recognized the wealth the Head of the Church had, the kingdom's coffers he had access to.

Lord Tyrrian stood and slowly moved down the dais steps to stand before the quiet Father Figgins. "But I admit, there is a problem with desiring power. A warning even your God has spoken of, the reason why it is a sin in your eyes, and something your Church preaches shame about. Power, like a good cunt," he took a deep inhale and closed his eyes, "once you taste it, you will always crave more."

The Lord of the Isles stepped beside Father Figgins, his head turned down towards him, his voice low and directed at his ear: "And I am wanting."

"Why did you ask me here, my lord?" Father Figgins asked as Lord Tyrrian walked away from him. "To speak words of tyranny to the Hand of the King? Or for something more?"

Lord Tyrrian cocked his head over his shoulder, "Tyranny? I would never, Father."

Sir Marion let out a small huff of laughter at the sarcasm and lies from his lord. He left his hands resting on the pommel of his sword and kept his shoulders lax.

"You sit on the king's throne and speak of the Church as if it is not your faith as well- not only a sin, but a crime. You speak of craving more power when the only true station above yours is the king's." Father Figgins sneered as he slithered towards Lord Tyrrian, "Sounds like tyranny to me, my lord. Now, what is it you want?"

"I want you to remember me on that throne. I want you to remember your station near, not on it. You reach high, Father Figgins, too high for your own good. I see you. You are helpful, yes, but your ambition," he paused and shook his head, "Your ambition will kill you. Well, someone will kill you because of it."

Sir Marion took note of the lord's behavior and demeanor and stepped beside Lord Tyrrian. Not to ask the lord to stand down, but to stand beside the man he had sworn his blood to.

Lord Tyrrian continued, "As it runs now, you risk remaining being nothing more than a minor footnote in history books, Father. But I will be immortal."

Chapter 34

King Ivan stood in silent solace in the tower, a refuge hidden from the clamors of the court. Standing by the window, he cast a gaze upon its weathered stone frame. The age-worn and weathered rock had borne witness to countless secret rendezvous and whispered confidences. His eyes traced the faint etchings of initials, worn with too much time and harshness of life.

I.S.

S.S.

Both sets of initials were faint memories from when the king and his brother carved them there as young boys.

"So the world will never forget us," Stephon had said.

Their father had never forgotten, and he beat them both bloody for desecrating such a sacred space in the castle.

On a stone three paces away, two more appeared, less worn with time.

P.S

E.S.

The king smiled and ran his fingers over his sons' initials, no doubt left when they were of the age he and Stephon had been when they carved their own. King Ivan never told his sons he had seen the initials, nor did he ever raise his fists in displeasure at them for acting like the young, innocent boys they once were.

The night's wind brought in a slight chill, reminding the king why he was in the tower alone. He brought his attention back to the skies being showered with moving stars.

...and stars have fallen as if made of rain

The Psalm's words were carried in the wind, an ethereal voice crooning the words instead of his father's angry bravado exclaiming them. His body tilted as it followed the breeze coming through the turret's many windows. His hands held themselves behind his back as he unsteadily leaned out of the tower to view more of the stars that called to him.

Lean more.

Come this way.

Just listen!

A ghostly voice he had never heard outside this tower beckoned him to lean out the window more. The cool air soothed the dried redness on his skin, and he lifted his hands, opened his jacket, and dropped it to the floor. The king rested his hands on the edge of the window, the tension in his body lessening as the cool stone chilled the heat and irritation on his skin.

His eyes closed as his head bobbed down, and the voices grew in number.

Haunt you.

Hunt you.

Betray you.

They know.

They all know.

They're after you.

Then, a cold silence.

JUMP.

He gripped the cold stones, fighting the voices as they grew from sweet whispers to angry shouts.

JUMP.

JUMP.

JUMP.

His fingernails tried to dig into the stone and hold him in place, his nails splitting in places where his constant itching and rubbing had already made them frail.

Join me.

Won't you join me?

It's so easy, darling.

Just jump, my sweet son.

Did you hear me?

The king leaned farther out the cold window, lifting a leg to stand atop the sill. As his knee brushed the wall's edge, a hand rested on his shoulder.

"Father."

The voices dissipated as his eyes shot open. The king jerked away from the hand holding him and faced a disgruntled, worried Prince Percy.

"Father, I asked if you would like to join me. I have had a hard day and could use some comfort."

King Ivan's eyes were still glazed over, his mind still finding its way into his body again.

"No, I cannot." He turned to the window, pointing at the falling stars. "They speak too much. I must stay and listen. They said... they told me things."

Prince Percy still held onto his father as his brows creased. "Who speaks too much?"

King Ivan jerked his head back to look at his son, his eyes wide. "Do you not hear them?" he laughed, "They do not speak to you, young Scholar?"

Prince Percy shook his head slowly, his mouth slightly agape in confusion. "Who do you speak of, father?"

King Ivan slammed a hand out the window, his finger pointing at the skies. "The stars. They speak. Just as the Scholars say they do."

Prince Percy's eyes did not follow where his father's hand pointed; he instead stepped closer to him, placing himself between the king and the window. "That is not a literal meaning, father. The stars may tell us many things, but they do not actually speak."

King Ivan maniacally laughed, "Not to you. My second son, they may not speak to you as you wish they would, but they do to me just as they have spoken to rulers for centuries. You just do not get to hear them."

Push, the voices said. *Push the non-believer.*

"What is wrong? What has happened to you?" Prince Percy shook his head and whispered as King Ivan fought the voices, pushing him away from the window. King Ivan continued to laugh, now mumbling chaotic words between fits of laughter.

No, no no, push him out.

"Father."

The king continued his mumblings, "No. No. Not him. No."

"Father!"

King Ivan still did not reply; he felt himself fly into his own world in the skies.

Prince Percy grabbed his laughing father's shoulders, turning him roughly to bring him back to this place. He gasped as he eyed his father's body, the rash and redness, the dried blood crusting on the flaky skin, his sunken eyes hidden in the concave shadows of his face, their blueness emanating from the shadows in madness.

King Ivan did not break from his wide-eyed insanity and grabbed Prince Percy's arm, attempting to shove his son away so he could be beside the window again. The prince pulled his father back, jostling him with the rough gesture and forcing the king to stumble against his body.

King Ivan wrinkled his brow and blinked several times, his pupils returning to normal size and hardness falling over his face as he stood up and looked up at his son. His head twitched as his gaze calmed and the shrieking voices faded. Awareness washed over the king at what Prince Percy bore witness to on his exposed skin.

King Ivan quickly pulled himself out of his son's grasp and picked his crumpled jacket off the floor. "It is nothing—a mere heat rash. The Healers say it is from stress and will calm once winter comes and this war ends. Do not worry."

He gave no room for Prince Percy to reply before turning for the entrance and beginning his descent down the turret stairs and back into the castle's main halls.

As the king led the way down the tower steps, Prince Percy paused at the stairway entrance and peered about the room, pausing to feel any magic or presence.

He stared at the window where he found his father, the shadows of his father's hunched-over figure replaced with a new one- one the prince's mind must have created from portraits of Mad King Jameston found in old parchments and art halls. The weathered phantom of the Mad King, often depicted wearing a crown of long thorns dripping in blood as it was now, stepped onto the window ledge, his heavy cape billowing in the wind.

The shadow turned, gaining more color the longer Percy stared. The hands that gripped the stone were covered in chunks of skin, dangling on pure white bone. The skeleton face of the Mad King, well eaten away with time and death, smiled at the prince before free-falling from the ledge.

Before the phantom disappeared, Prince Percy swore he heard it say: "You will never leave this castle."

CHAPTER 35

"You did not truly believe you could be in town for the Harvest Close and not come celebrate with us?" Mika, Ephraim's eldest brother, teased as he wrapped his arm around Ephraim's shoulders. Mika had the same dark hair that curled atop Ephraim's head, but was at least two heads taller than his younger sibling and twice their size, thanks to their father's lineage.

Petru, their father, stood in the doorway, chuckling at his grown children, "Mika, leave them alone. If Ephraim wishes to stay at home, they may. Although I find it a sad excuse to get out of our drinking games."

"Yeah, looks like Ephraim is forgetting that this is their chance to take back the Dablo title." Askla, Ephraim's other brother- only half a head taller but still built of hard muscle- joked.

Ephraim threw Mika's arm off their body and shook their head, "First of all, you all still play Dablo? A game of no strategy or skill, played only with hope for the right roll of the dice to take what is on the cloth?" Ephraim grunted as Mika attempted again to wrap them in a half-hug to drag them out the door.

"Secondly, how is it we are in the beginning of war, and all of the town is celebrating the close of harvest?"

Askla grabbed a handful of fresh-picked berries and popped several in his mouth, talking as the blue juices stained his teeth. "We still play Dablo because it's the only game that Mika the Slow can keep up with."

Askla's manners earned him a shoulder slap from their mother, Meliandre, and a glare from Mika.

"If we do not find joy or celebration, especially in times such as this, then the king has already won, and the war has already been lost." Meliandre calmly corrected, "And Mika is not slow, and no, I did not drop him on his head as a child, despite what your father likes to lie about and tease."

She giggled and poked her husband in the belly at the memory of the jesting story he had told all the children for years.

Ephraim couldn't help but smile at the familiar banter that filled the room. Despite the looming tension of war, there was a warmth that only family could provide. Petru, still chuckling, stepped forward and clapped Ephraim on the back. "Come, please. There's nothing quite like the Harvest Close to lift the spirits. Besides," he added with a mischievous glint in his eye, "you wouldn't want to miss the chance to see Creegan try to dance again, would you? It's been a highlight for ages."

Ephraim sighed, fake defeat carried in their voice, "All right, fine."

As the family stepped outside and into the sounds echoing from the festival grounds, Meliandre gently rested her hand around Ephraim's bicep as they walked. She leaned in and whispered.

"Nights like this are a reminder of what we're fighting for, what we risk to lose in the coming tides. That is why we celebrate."

The air was filled with the enticing aroma of roasted meats and spiced cider, mingling with the laughter of children and the music of lutes and drums. The once serene wheat field, now a vibrant celebration ground, was brought to life with color and sound; banners of harvest hues fluttered in the breeze, and the warm glow of torches and bonfires cast a magical aura over the open field.

It was a night of revelry, a night to dance, drink, and most importantly, honor the Reapers who had bestowed upon them the bounty of the season. This was a night to remember their roots, their strength, and their unwavering hope for the future seasons.

Long tables laden with roasted meats, fresh bread, and vibrant vegetables lay in straight lines. Tankards of ale and spiced cider were rolled into the dining area, and several more were brought over to the dancing area.

Mika, always the life of the party, spotted a group of old friends and pulled Ephraim along, introducing them to familiar faces from their childhood. The group wasted no time challenging each other to a few rounds of Dablo, and before long, the small group had grown into a crowd; trinkets and gold coins were tossed onto the square-covered cloth before being quickly snatched up as winners rolled the right dice to snatch the loot from the numbered boxes.

In such a short time, Ephraim found themselves caught up in the energy of the night, their earlier reluctance forgotten as they matched their brother's drink for drink and laughter for laughter.

The feast continued late into the night, and the townspeople showed no signs of slowing down. Musicians took turns playing lively tunes on their instruments while the bards wove tales of old heroes and forgotten battles, their voices carrying over the noise of the crowd. The joy was contagious, and soon, everyone was caught up in the spirit of the Harvest Close, dancing and singing as if the war was a distant memory.

Eventually, Askla drunkenly grabbed Ephraim by the arm, his eyes gleaming with excitement. "Come over here!"

He led them through the weaves of tables and crowds until they reached where a large bonfire blazed in the night. The flames licked the sky, casting long shadows over the faces of the gathered townsfolk. Around the fire, a group of dancers, their bodies moving in perfect rhythm to the loud, pounding drums, spun and twirled with wild abandon, masks covering their faces and costumes fluttering around them.

The dancers were a blur of color and movement, their feet kicking up dust as they stomped in time to the beat. Some wore traditional town garb, while others had adorned themselves with garlands of autumn leaves and wreaths of flowers.

Mika gave Ephraim a playful shove as he met up with his drunken siblings. "Let's get in there!"

Before Ephraim could protest, Askla had already joined the dancers, his muscular form moving surprisingly graceful for his size, and Mika strong-armed them into the dancing circle. Meliandre and Petru stood nearby, their arms around each other, swaying gently to the music as they watched their children with pride and glossy eyes from much wine.

The music took over, and they found themselves lost in the rhythm, their feet moving of their own accord as they joined the throng of dancers. Ephraim could feel the ground beneath them vibrating with the force of the movement and music, the energy of the crowd washing over them like a wave.

As the last song reached its climax, the dancers threw their heads back and sang, their voices rising in a powerful, joyous chorus that echoed through the night. Ephraim's voice joined the others, the sound of their laughter blending with the music, the worries of the world forgotten in that perfect, timeless moment.

When the music finally ended, and the last echoes of the song faded into the night, the dancers collapsed around the fire, their breaths coming in ragged gasps, faces flushed with exertion and happiness. The crowd cheered, their voices hoarse but filled with unbridled joy, and Ephraim found themselves grinning from ear to ear, their heart full.

Mika slumped down next to them, his chest heaving as he tried to catch his breath. "See? Wasn't that better than moping at home?"

Ephraim, still laughing, nodded. "Much better," they said as the siblings all took their last heaving breaths and made it over to their parents on the sidelines.

They watched the joy ring out at the display as new musicians took over and began a new chorus of song, this one more relaxed and smooth. Children leaped and giggled to the music, young heart-eyed lovers clasped hands, and the elders pointed at the sky and found their families in the stars.

Ephraim's throat became as hard as a stone as they tried to swallow the bile and pain that rose within them as they remembered the world they would wake to in the morning. The longer this war dragged on, the higher the chance there was that all of this could be gone.

All of this life.

All of this love.

They knew they had to act, or it would all be lost, and they would hold a share in the blame. Their bloody hands would soil every meal they took in and stain every moment they would be granted in the future if they did nothing, but also if they did anything more than what they were doing as a Healer. They held power that could transform the landscapes of the war, yet they held it hostage inside them.

Out of pride.

Stubbornness.

Fear they covered up with a code of honor.

Ephraim swallowed more bile, more pain, more fury, and worry.

The king would decimate their lives. He would hold no hostages, give no mercy, hold back no pride in his conquest to keep his throne and ruin the lives of his enemies' allies.

Of Ephraim's family.

Ephraim looked to their joy-filled brothers and father, remembering the work they were doing in their factory in town. Without pause, they took up the extra labor to forge weapons of war and tools of defense.

The king would find their names on a list and kill them without a single tear.

They are dead if we lose the war.

Ephraim's body ached with memory of what King Andrius' men did to their mother when they were children. Despite her fears and what happened to her, their mother did not stop her practice and did not stop believing in what she knew was right.

But Ephraim had.

Coward.

Ephraim scanned the festival crowd as the word repeated in their mind. They all feared the king just as Ephraim did, but they did not let the fear win and be a tool for their complicity in the king's system, not like Ephraim had.

Coward.

They are all dead if I do nothing.

Coward.

"I have to go. I have something I must do." Ephraim choked out to their mother.

Ephraim looked at her standing beside them, her eyes glistening with tears and knowing. Meliandre rested her hand on their face and rubbed her thumb on their stubble, "I will see you after the war."

Ephraim nodded and glanced at their brothers and father beside them, "I will see you after the war."

Chapter 36

Tember 29, 690AC

Lady Kathilla stood at the edge of the rushing water, but the crashing rapids did not drown out the screams.

She had not been there the day her husband had been slaughtered, nor had she even been a glint in her ancestor's eyes when The Darkest Night ended the Great Civil War on these bloodied lands. But still, she heard their screams.

The veil between the world of the living and dead had drawn thin as the days dragged on, and the late autumn chill made its return to the North. With that thinning veil came more phantom visits from ancestors, more visions and dreams, and more screams of death as Lady Kathilla moved to the edge of the holy lands that had cost her people so much. The cries were relentless, filling her with sorrow that seemed to seep from the very ground beneath her, intertwining with the roar of the river before her.

Traditional Last Fire offerings meant little to Lady Kathilla as the cries of her people clawed at her skull. Her ancestors deserved more than grains, livestock, and song. They deserved the honor she was meant to bestow upon them—the cause they fought and died for. Her ancestors deserved what they could never reach: freedom.

The blood and charcoal runes drawn on her body itched with power and calling. Her charcoal-covered eyes and forehead dripped with sweat while the bonfire behind her roared to richer life as the edges of the forest were thrown into it. The heat from the flames was intense, a fierce contrast to the biting cold that nipped at her exposed skin.

Her caravan of warriors had traveled far in their days, making camp where the Land of a Thousand Rivers reached its edge. The rivers formed into one long rush of water before cascading downward into the Falls of Glinton.

Her people had traveled far, but would break their steadfast journey home for a tradition such as this. While the Church had stolen the true holiday from her ancestors and turned it into the Harvest Close, the North worked tirelessly in the dark to practice the traditions bastardized by the church of the true autumn holiday: Des Mortem.

Where the mainlands would honor the end of harvest with freshly baked bread from the first cuts of wheat and praise the farmers for their labors, inviting them to dine like kings for the day, the North would do the same but honor their dead with sacrifice and flame and seek out ancestral and divine guidance through the veil between worlds.

Lady Kathilla implored the Vahar for silence from the screams, but her hidden gods offered her none. She turned from the waters, her breath shaky as she took deep inhales to steady her mind. The screams persisted, gnawing at her resolve as she walked towards the wall of man-made fire.

A small path lay in the center of the raging bonfire, just wide enough for one to walk through so long as they did not fear the licking of flames against their skin. Warriors dressed in fur-wrapped tunics and dark muslin stood gathered at the entrance to the flaming path. Priestesses painted sigils on their bodies as warriors stripped off their clothes and adorned their bodies with bone shards and animal skulls. Others spoke unheard prayers over skins of water before warriors doused their hair with it.

"As the veil thins into nothing more than a speck of ash in the air, we honor our ancestors by walkin' through the veil, by becomin' one with their wisdom and sacrifice and listenin' to their words." Lady Kathilla jutted her chin towards the path in the fire, "Tonight, we walk through the veil opened by our flames. If any of us are unworthy, may the flames take us— may we no longer walk this realm or any other."

Lady Kathilla poured the priestess-blessed water over her face, streaking lines into her runes and markings and dousing her thick red hair. The water was cool against her skin, a fleeting moment of relief before the trial ahead.

"I am the blood of Balnar," she whispered the words of a vow and a plea. Balnar the Brutal- the most furious and unforgiving of the four Alvarian siblings who conquered the lands- gave the people of Craigie their fierce passion for fighting.

In contrast, his ice dragon, Grerdort, had given the northern lands their permanent banks of snow when he shed his ice scales all along the north before slumbering eternally in the lands that became the mountains formed by his back.

His blood ran through her, as did Sir Wallace Nealson, the rebellious freedom fighter who ignited the Great Civil War to bring freedom to the lands. The man who sacrificed his life for his people when the war was lost and granted his people peace through his brutal execution- an execution that First King Lucarius demanded be done at the hands of Sir Wallace's own men.

"I am the blood of freedom."

Sir Wallace Nealson was sent to the capital city, where he was disemboweled, left in the public stocks to rot, and picked at by birds. After the king was satisfied with his rotting body, Sir Wallace was then hanged, beheaded, drawn, and quartered in front of citizens and many of his own family. His ruined remains were thrown into the sewers outside of The King's Keep, where many believed his phantom cursed kings and servants alike at his will.

Lady Kathilla was the child of freedom and rebellion. The Queen of the North would bow to no man nor king.

"My blood is that of salvation."

Lady Kathilla stripped her body of furs and muslin, baring her naked body and soul to the sacred flames, and walked through the path of fire.

Chapter 37

The lord's aide stoked the fire, breathing more life into the flame. While the early sparks of winter were another moon phase away, the chilling call of the upcoming season had already wafted its way into Broken Tower while many of the settlement's citizens begrudgingly paid their tithes and taxes as the recurring Node Da'e came to a close.

Lord Augusta Lisarian blew hot air into his cupped hands as he settled into his chair near the fireplace and rested his head on the back. He let out a long groan and slumped into his soft chair, "I always hate Node Da'e. Lines of citizens out the door paying the taxes that they can and bringing with their coin complaints I can often do nothing about. It is so tiresome."

"That is quite tough, my lord." The aide flatly said as they jabbed a log harder than it needed to be. They finished prodding the fire- the crackling logs sparking more flames and heat- and stood up, turning to Lord Lisarian and bowing before dismissing themselves.

Beside the lord's overstuffed chair was a round table covered with parchment pads and a heavy ledger book. Lord Augusta rolled his head to the side and looked down at the pile. He let out another sigh. The throbbing ache in his head increased as he considered sitting beside the fire throughout the night to rid himself of the chill and read more of the issues he had to resolve.

"And I still have all of our winter preparations to begin and winter festivities to finalize." He paused and closed his eyes, continuing his one-man conversation. The fire warmed him more as he rested his eyes and felt the blanket of the night beckon him to rest. "That is if we are to celebrate it at all."

He let out a long breath and a groan as he felt himself drift away. "That, however, will be a problem for me on the morrow."

He achingly stood up, the long day of sitting in his stiff chair in the receiving hall taking its toll on his back. He walked down the hall to the noble chamber space. A chill overcame him as he left behind the small fire and passed by the torches and candles lighting his path.

He rubbed his neck as he turned the corner and passed through the doors into the chamber room. Lady Reval Lisarian sat in her reading chair in the couple's shared common room, a private living space between their two-bed chambers. If she heard his entrance, she did not show it. She sat looking out at the night sky and along the darkened landscape of the north.

She always looked north.

"My lady." Lord Augusta politely greeted.

She subtly turned away from her window and nodded. "My lord."

She pulled her robe tighter around her to hide what her nightgown underneath did not cover, and turned back to the open window. The whisper of her words and the paleness of her attire, paired with the background of the night, made her appear ghostly.

The way she had chosen to disappear into herself since Madam Fury's visit only added to that.

"We missed you in the receiving hall today. Many of our people were eager to meet you. They all wished to give a welcome to their new lady from the North," he offered as a point of conversation between the two. He cleared his throat when she did not reply. "The winter chill has come a bit early this season. I thought perhaps we could begin our winter preparations soon- get them out of the way sooner."

"The cold does not bother me. I am used to it. It was much colder in my home village." Her tone was tired, and her words were spoken to the north, not to him.

"Yes, I know. But this tower is old and," he let out a small chortle in an attempt to lighten the mood and stepped forward, "-well, broken."

"Well, maybe you could fix it," she retorted to her window, the end of her words now carrying a hard snap. Her arms shuffled in her lap as she fought to cover herself more with her plush robe.

He shuffled on his feet. "Well, yes, I do intend to... I was just wondering if you could lend me your aid in something. This winter has the potential to be much harsher than the last, and with the South fighting amongst each other, our trading partners may not be able to fulfill our standard contracts. But, perhaps now that we are wed and since you are a lady of Craigie, we could open up trade negotiations with them."

She slowly turned to him, her eyes pinched in annoyance. "Craigie does not trade with other countries. We are self-sufficient and need not from others, especially those who choose the side of our enemies."

Her chin jutted and pointed harshly at him.

Lord Lisarian's casual stance became harsh as he moved forward, pointing a finger at his wife and then at himself. "We are not self-sufficient. We trade with other countries and other Houses. We have people that rely on us and demand much of us as their lord and lady. You are my wife, the Lady of Broken Tower, sent here to marry me as part of an agreement between many Houses, and sent here by the lady of your former country. The duty of our House is to—"

She gripped the arms of her chair and leaned forward, positioning herself as if she were a predator readying herself to leap. "We are done with this conversation."

"What has gotten into you? I am trying to—"

She stormed off around him, slamming her bedchamber door behind her with heavy force and loudly clicking the lock closed.

"I thought you would appreciate my offer!" he shouted at the door. "It was a chance to work more with your people, to bring more of who you are here."

He grimaced and mumbled at the silence that spoke back. Lord Augusta walked to her window and slammed it closed, a crack forming in the stained-glass facade. "It was a fucking olive branch."

Chapter 38

The Healer winced as they dabbed more salve onto the king's open wound. King Ivan hissed at the sensation, his back twitching against the medicine as he sat with his hands on his knees, hunched over in a hard chair.

"Your Majesty, I suggest you change your attire for some time. The stiff fabrics of the court have not helped your drying and scabbing skin. Something of softer and looser fabric would be best so as not to irritate the wounds," the Healer said.

"A king cannot go about ruling in cotton robes or loose tunics." King Ivan gruffed his reply, shooting his chin over his shoulder to where the Healer stood working. "I have a presentation to uphold."

The Healers sighed, stood straight, and reviewed their work on the king. "Have your visions gotten worse, Your Majesty?" they casually asked as they turned to their table of tinctures and medical gear, their back now to the king.

"Visions?" Queen Onetta, who had been standing quietly at the side, stepped forward. She jerked her head to King Ivan, who kept his head bowed and his shoulders slumped. Her voice was sharp and slightly panicked. "What visions?"

"My vision, Onetta. That is what the Healer means." King Ivan corrected. He kept his head down, avoiding her gaze. "My sight is not what it used to be."

Queen Onetta turned slowly to the Healer. She stared them down. She did not need to speak to scare the Healer or to clarify what she wished to have answered.

Is the king lying?

The Healer flashed their eyes away from the queen, saying nothing to her silent demand and mixing together another white cream with herbs. They rubbed the salve onto a more healed part of the king's flaking and drying skin.

"My king, this simple skin rash is much worse than you let on. You told us it was a heat rash, but the autumn winds have chilled the air and it still persists. Perhaps we should speak to the Odessin lords and ask for their insight. Their citadel holds the greatest healing minds; they may know more of what bothers you," Queen Onetta suggested with a mixture of concern and authority. She moved to rest a hand on his shoulder, then subtly flexed her fingers back and away from the scabbing red skin she wished not to touch.

"No," he sharply replied, lifting his eyes to meet hers. "They need not be bothered by this."

The queen did not care for his disagreeing opinion. He always found ways to disagree with her. Even on his kindest days, he always found ways to make her feel small.

"Healer," she jutted her chin at them, "What say you?"

The Healer's intentional pause frustrated her more.

"His Majesty is strong, both in mind and body." They wiped their hands on a towel. "I believe if he follows our treatments, holds back on the bottle, and stresses his mind less, he will heal in time. I did my studies at the Citadel, Your Majesty. I remember much of what they taught in those lands. Sometimes ailments take time to cure one's pain."

The Healer offered a soft, kind smile and nodded at her irritated face, then turned their gaze back to their work.

Queen Onetta's lips pressed into a thin line as she slowly walked to the table of medicine and herbs the Healer busied themself with. "What exactly is this treatment plan of yours that is taking so much time to work?"

"Onetta, please stop pestering," King Ivan said, his voice weary and tired, bordering on frustration and aggravation. He rubbed the bridge of his nose as he spoke.

She picked up a bottle of liquid, her eyes narrowing as she inspected it. "I am the queen of this realm; I deserve to know what is happening to the other half of the crown."

"The other half?" King Ivan scoffed and turned in his chair to look at her, "Once again, you think so highly of yourself."

"It would be foolish for one in such a high position to think lowly," she corrected, not allowing herself to snap as she wished to. She studied the dark red color in the glass bottle—a wormwood, garlic, leek, and red nettle mixture she knew quite well as a treatment for the most painful of headaches. The queen did not pick up the jar of leeches the Healer had brought with them; she grimaced at the thought of being treated in such a way.

Queen Onetta's eyes scanned all the tinctures left on the table and swallowed nervously at a white ceramic jar with blue lettering spelling out what it contained.

Theriac.

Her heart pounded so hard in her chest that it reminded her she still had one buried deep beneath her pain and anger.

"You have brought Theriac with you, Healer? You believe the king poisoned?" she worried. She moved quickly to stand beside His Majesty.

"My lady, I have brought with me many oils and aids for His Majesty. Theriac has been known to cure and aid with many problems- not just poisoning." The Healer gave her a soft, closed-mouth smile again. "Do not worry. It is simply a precaution."

"But do you believe poison could be what ails him?" she asked, her voice trembling but still demanding.

"Woman. Enough!" King Ivan shouted, his patience snapping. "Leave us. Now. You are of no help to my ailment."

"Ivan, I am simply—"

"Out!" he shouted again, his voice echoing in the chamber. He hunched back over in his chair and rubbed his head, groaning in pain or agitation, she did not know which.

Queen Onetta refused to move, huffing and hardening her jaw as she looked at her husband's blemished skin, paling features, and fading self. She knew that she had intruded with unwelcome acceptance into the king's appointment after hearing about him taking himself to the Healer's ward in the castle, where she stormed into the room mid-discussion.

Her lips pursed and thinned. She huffed and turned to leave. As she stalked out, she heard the Healer murmur, "We can increase your nightly dose of poppy if you wish. It can help silence the –"

Queen Onetta held onto the sides of her blood-red skirts as she forged her path through the castle. The gold-trimmed fabric was sure to wrinkle, so she gripped it so tightly. The hummingbirds stitched on either side of her chest fluttered their wings away from the irises stitched beside them as she heavily breathed and hastily moved.

She needed to find a way to channel her rage; the pulsing heat thrumming through her would cause her to make herself a fool again in public.

Lord Tyrrian's chamber doors and the balcony doors inside his chambers were wide open. She curtly nodded to her King's Guards as she crossed the threshold into his chamber, quickly closing the door behind her and leaving them outside.

"My queen." Lord Tyrrian crooned. "What a surprise."

He lay lazily on the bed, his feet bare and the buttons of his robe undone. The Lord closed the book he held and slowly sat up.

Queen Onetta said nothing, reached for the deep cut of her dress, and pulled her dress open, laying bare her chest. Lord Tyrrian's eyes bulged, as did the fabric at his waist.

"You have been walking about this castle all day with nothing beneath your dress?" He took a deep breath, and a primal groan escaped his throat as he loosened it.

She shuffled out of her dress and kicked the bulk of fabric behind her. Queen Onetta stood naked before him, her eyes blazing with a mixture of defiance and desperation, her chest heaving in lust and in anger.

Riding him until her body broke was one sure way to release all of her tension.

"Fuck me. Now," she commanded.

Lord Tyrrian crawled across the bed to her. "As my queen commands."

There was minimal conversation in Prince Elion's war camp as the workers finished loading wagons; only words of duty and critical need were spoken. Orders to quench the remaining fires were heard throughout the camp, the final signal to prepare to march east for those enjoying the warmth of the campsite one last time.

Standing along the treeline, two soldiers held themselves in contemplation.

"What do we do with them?" Private Jearn, a tall and well-built archer, said. His head cocked to the side as his eyes scanned up and down the swaying bodies in the tree.

"Leave 'em." His cohort, Private Lindst, replied, shrugging as he furrowed his face in disgust the longer he looked at the bodies. "I don't imagine His Highness would want us to waste energy bringin' 'em with or cuttin' 'em down. The predators here will 'ventually enjoy their dinner and clean up for us."

Private Jearn stared at the bodies' bare feet, covered in sores and open wounds that matched the ones growing in number on their faces and exposed skin. "Looks like they already have been," he mumbled in disgust.

"Aye! Quick gawking and get over here! " their squad officer. Both soldiers held their gaze for a moment longer, their throats bobbing in remembrance of how the bodies got there before joining their squad, ready to march.

Crows descended from the trees as the men dispersed from the area, pecking again at the dead skin. The butcher had been their favorite to rip apart; perhaps it had been the extra flesh on his bones or the extra stab wounds and slashes put on his body by the prince during his rage. Beside him hung the young cook who had plated the food that killed Prince Elion's lover despite her swears and promises that she had only been responsible for preparing the potatoes that evening. The prince had ignored her shrieking, telling him she was one of his own, not one of the prisoners they had turned to workers in their camp.

Down the line hung the rest of those who once flew green stag banners, all now punished for their potential involvement in the murder, all now left as symbols for what the prince was willing to do.

Prince Elion stood over the small water trough, water splashing around him as he threw his wet hands up at his face and rubbed the coldness over him. He still felt like absolute shit. Not for what he had done to those who killed- or assisted in the killing of- Jeffrey, but for the drinking bender he went on to forget how his soldiers looked at him after they ripped his thrashing body away from his slaughter.

Commander Blackley stepped beside him, speaking flatly, "Your army awaits you, Your Highness."

The prince grabbed a kerchief from his pocket, wiping his face off as he straightened himself. He ran his hands through his messy curls and nodded at the commander. "Thank you, Commander."

Commander Blackley held no eye contact and moved his gaze to the ground as he nodded and grunted in response.

Prince Elion stepped forward. "What is it? You may speak freely. I have always trusted your advisement, Commander."

Commander Blackley lifted his head and scanned the treeline of hanging bodies, shaking his head. "This is not you, Prince Elion."

Prince Elion's eyes followed the commander's frustrated gaze to the seven bodies strung up on trees. He scoffed before turning back and snipping, "Killing traitors, murderers, is not who I am?"

Commander Blackley looked at him, still slowly shaking his head and voicing a cold disappointment, "That is not what you did to those people, you slaughtered them in rage for what could have been an accident or the rebellious act of one man—that is not the prince that I have trained from his youth."

Prince Elion felt the rage building in him like a roaring fire as his jaw became steel and his gaze hardened. He stepped forward. "Then what am I? Since you know me so well?"

Commander Blackley stared at the prince and let out a deep sigh.

"I am your prince!" Prince Elion shouted in reply to the silence.

Around them, heads snapped in their direction, and what conversation remained in the camp came to a complete halt.

"Indeed, you are, Your Highness. And we heed your commands because of that. But..." Commander Blackley lost his words as sorrow overcame him. His eyes closed, and his head fell before he looked at the prince again.

The prince bristled at the implication of the words not yet spoken. His face contorted with scorn. His jaw trembled. His father's inherited anger overcame him. His pain rode its coattails and rushed out before he could stop either.

"I am the heir to the throne! I am your commander! That is who I am. That is why I am here." The prince shoved back the tears forming in his eyes, forced more rage to the surface, and firmed his booming voice. "That is my purpose, and you will honor that. All of you."

Commander Blackley bowed his head at the prince. "Yes, sir."

Prince Elion wiped the spit from his face and stormed towards his decorated steed and the crowd of onlooking troops.

"We ride now. We move east to meet with the incoming Dragons and then end Sebern's hold over Ravenhall lands. That is my command," the crown prince ordered. "He took a deep inhale. "And we slaughter anyone who does not kneel to our banners."

Chapter 39

Princess Arminda waved away her King's Guards as their path ended at the summit of the outdoor steps. Along the walkway, foliage planted in urns and green beds had transformed into autumnal hues of orange and red, a fitting backdrop to the princess's Aisharian-style dress. Its color was that of fresh blood, and the fabric so light and sheer that she felt almost entirely exposed. The dramatic slits and high cuts of the dress did little to remind her that she did not stand naked in front of a crowd of her people. A gold metal corset, etched with ocean waves and iris flowers, cinched hard against her hips as she started her descent down the steps.

But she paid no mind to the tinge of pain as she held her head high.

The trail of her dress cascaded down the stairs behind her while she took in the sight of her bloodline, her people she had never met, and her heritage, which she knew only a morsel of. She firmed her jaw harder and walked towards the large outdoor tent.

Between her breasts rested a golden clasp of a kraken, holding together the front of the metal corset and framing in the sweetheart neckline that allowed the cool breeze to raise the bumps on her exposed skin and arms.

Her hair flowed free beneath a simple metal headband she wore. The crest of the noble lion was stamped in the center and was surrounded by golden jewels. As heads turned to watch her take the final steps on the stairs, Lord Tyrrian swiftly moved from conversation and extended his arm for her to take.

"Your Grace," she nodded in greeting as her hand rested on her uncle's bicep.

"Princess." Lord Tyrrian nodded and bowed his shoulders. His eyes flickered up and down her clothing, noticing the meshing of both of her bloodlines. He smiled, a hint of pride perhaps hiding behind his teeth, as they began to walk. "Will your siblings be joining the ceremony today?"

"I do not believe so. Percy has no desire to partake despite this being part of his wedding festivities, and Kalia," she paused quickly to choose her words, "- is perhaps too young for such things."

"I attended my first vision ceremony when I was about her age." Lord Tyrrian said, "But then again, life is quite different on the Isles than it is here."

"So I have seen in large evidence since your visit began, uncle." Princess Arminda took in the people around her, dressed in exposed fashions often looked down upon or viewed as odd by people within the princess's social class. Healed scars adorned the exposed skin of many, and unashamed flirtations that bordered on brothel activities took place in the public space.

And the food...

Princess Arminda inhaled the smoky scent of the fare being passed around, and her stomach spoke of its desire.

Lord Tyrrian chuckled as they stopped outside the tent's closed opening. "The feast is here for those who are guides in the ceremony and those who have already taken part. You must not eat right before. Your body is to be clean and pure when you enter here."

She nodded in understanding, then scrunched her face. She had not learned much of this sacred ceremony held by Aisharians before battles, funerals, and weddings. "I must ask, how is this ceremony, which seems so heavily based upon myth and magic, still legal? When the First King outlawed other religions and found the hidden truth in the ceremonies of apostates and heathens, events such as this were banned and replaced with holy truths, were they not?"

Lord Tyrrian chuckled, "Found the truth in? Dear niece, I believe you mean appropriated. Stolen. Colonized." His lip twitched. "Lucarius outlawed many things, as did other rulers before and after him, but what he could never take from our hands were the deepest parts of who we are. And this already holy and sacred ceremony is one of them. It is not of myth or magic, but of connection into one's self through the connection with others and natural energy around us."

Sounds like magic to me. She thought.

An elder opened the tent flap as the pair quickly found themselves at the front of the line. She gave the two a crooked, toothless smile and beckoned them inside, along with those who waited behind them. The smell of heavy incense and smoke overwhelmed Princess Arminda immediately. From the back of the tent, a low pipe played long, deep notes that floated on the smoke in the air. Princess Arminda timidly stood behind her uncle as he bowed to the elder, allowing her to run a smoking bundle of herbs over and around his body. The elders' words were incoherent to the princess, as if they were not spoken for anyone besides Lord Tyrrian.

The elder stepped back and touched foreheads with the lord, then let him enter the tent.

Princess Arminda stood in front of the elder and bowed, letting their heads touch as her uncle had before her. The elder mumbled a chant and waved the princess with the cleansing bundle. Several sparks popped from the smudge bundle as the elder wafted it over the princess's abdomen. The elder hesitated briefly and continued her routine before stepping back, bowing quickly at Princess Arminda and avoiding her eyes.

The princess was not phased by the woman's avoidance of looking at her. Servants and others below her station often acted the same way and avoided looking too much at the princess.

She walked down the rows of floor pillows and kneeled at the setup beside where Lord Tyrrian kneeled. Below her knees, the pillow offered a reprieve from the stone and earth ground, and the woven rugs tossed about the floor kept her dress clean from dirt and sand. A mortar and pestle sat in front of each kneeling pillow, but there were no herbs to grind into paste or powder. A wooden cup, wide and narrow and meant for holding in one's cupped palms, sat beside the mortar, pestle, and other tools.

The low flute continued its ghostly notes as Princess Arminda was finally able to take in the space. Floor pillows were arranged in circular rows pointed to the center of the tent. Heavy lanterns hung on posts and the tent poles, emitting incense smoke and heavy scents of sandalwood and myrrh. Faces that were vaguely familiar to her were scattered about the room; many from the gladiator showcased the past season, dinners, and celebrations with the joined families.

Her wandering eyes met with Sir Marion, who nodded firmly at her before returning to his conversations with the other gladiators.

From the darkened corners of the tent, more elders appeared. They wore the same subdued robes as the woman who greeted the princess at the tent's entrance, and many had shaved heads or long hair pulled back into thin, intricately done braids.

As the elders made their appearance, the room settled into complete silence. Conversations ended mid-sentence, and even the most rebellious-looking among those gathered firmed their backs and bowed their heads in respect as they kneeled on their pillows.

Lord Tyrrian's normally firm and authoritative demeanor had dissipated, and in its place, a calming presence overtook him as the flute melody changed. The elders retreated back to their places against the tent's walls. A metallic clang rose through the room and continued in differing decibels. Metallic bowls hummed out their melody as they were struck, and their edges sang.

Princess Arminda hid her shock as the new notes hummed throughout her skull and down her neck, a feeling she had never felt before. Different tones vibrated throughout different parts of her body.

What was this sensation?

The robed elders slowly made their way around the room, holding out stone bowls to each kneeling guest and sharing a deep bow with them as the guest reached into the bowl and pulled out a share of the contents. An elder paused in front of the princess and bowed to her. Princess Arminda gave a soft smile, nodded, and then looked into the bowl held out for her. Inside was a gathering of small brown beans and remnants of dried mushrooms.

Her eyes flickered to her uncle, who leaned over to whisper, "Cacao beans and mushrooms, princess. You pick what calls to you and set them in your grinding bowl."

"How do I know which to choose?" she whispered back, the tones of the singing bowls distorting her thoughts and mind.

The elder slightly nudged the bowl forward and glanced between the two, clearly unsatisfied with their breaking of the ceremonial silence.

"Just trust your instincts and choose." Lord Tyrrian said before giving an apologetic look to the impatient elder.

Princess Arminda hurriedly selected a small gathering of mushrooms and beans, one by one, each picked with worry over how long she was taking to choose and what could happen if she selected the wrong ones. She batted away the annoyance humming at her for not knowing properly what to do. Still, her uncle insisted that her experience should not be spoiled by too much foreknowledge and that true Aisharians would find their way through the experience using their instincts and internal guides.

The princess was a true Aisharian. She may share blood with her father, the king, but her blood was that of the Isles. She knew it, she felt it.

Her uncle had informed her that only true Aisharians would be able to partake successfully in such ceremonies of the foreign culture, and it made her wonder if that was why Prince Percy would not come today. Maybe he knew he did not belong among the people, their mother said he could lead one day on the island of Thelimor.

Maybe that was why he so loudly and passionately turned down her offer of inheritance.

The princess tried not to scowl at the thought. Prince Percy may have hung his shoulders in mourning his entire life over being the second son, but he knew little of what it was like to be the eldest daughter, the one given passed down leftovers and made to priss and preen over in court.

The elder moved on to Lord Tyrrian, who chose his items much faster than the princess had and sent the elder on their way down the row. He leaned back over. "I should have explained perhaps a bit more, but we are not to speak. Just follow what I do."

The head elder centered herself in the room. She raised both hands in front of her body, one with her fingers pointed skyward and the other hand with her fingers forward, and brought her palms together, wrapping her fingers around her hands. As her hands clasped, she bowed, and all in the room returned the gesture, then began to grind the mixture in their bowls into a fine powder.

Princess Arminda clunkily followed suit, never having had to grind herbs before, and continued her nervous glances between her bowl and her uncle's. Lord Tyrrian smoothly and calmly set his pestle down and poured the ground mixture into the wooden cup before him. The princess did the same, hiding her shame at how poorly hers had ground and crumbled.

The singing bowls rang out their melodies again as the robed elders appeared from the shadows, now with kettles of steaming water. They repeated their routines, bowing in greeting to each person who knelt and pouring the water into their cups before moving quietly to the next person.

After Princess Arminda's cup was filled, she eyed the Aisharian stranger beside her, who had set their cup down and began whisking the cacao, mushroom, and water together with the wooden whisk that had been hiding beside their cups. She did the same, feeling a drunk-like fog begin to take over her mind as more bowls and flutes sang their hypnotic tunes. The vibration from the flute and the bowls, and the heavy smoke, held her in a trance, quieting her mind and making her feel weightless. She had no room for thoughts, memories, emotions, worry.

She was just there.

The elder who had greeted her at the door stayed at the center of the room and took a deep breath before joining in with the singing bowls. But she did not sing in a way the princess had ever heard; instead, a guttural, deep droning came from her. The elder continued her throat singing and raised her hands up at her side. As she did, each gathered began to drink from their cup.

Princess Arminda took a polite sip and was startled by the bitterness of the mixture. But she would not, could not, stop. She closed her eyes and gulped down the bitter cacao and mushroom drink.

And then, she was gone.

CHAPTER 40

Princess Arminda felt her flesh and bones fall away and her body become weightless as a phantom of herself stood outside a ramshackle shed. Within a quick blink, she recognized the dilapidated building that stood a half night's walk outside the walls of her father's city. She had visited it once before as a little girl and went back to it many times in her dreams.

The door creaked loudly against the call of the night's creatures and the moon's beckon. The princess held her hand out and rested it against the worn grain of the door. She knew she was not truly there, but still, she felt the grain against her hands, the chill in the night, the anxious beat in her heart.

Princess Arminda gently pushed the door open, the dark interior no better lit than the quarter-moon night sky that she stood under.

"It has been some time, my dear. You are much taller now," the old crone's voice scratched against the quiet of the inside. "And yet no closer to your fate than you were when you were a desperate little thing."

A harsh wind yowled from behind the door and slammed it shut, pushing Princess Arminda back two paces to the woods outside.

A twig snapped beneath her foot, and a wolf growled behind her.

Princess Arminda felt no fear as she slowly turned to face the ruddy brown creature standing tall enough to nuzzle its nose to hers. She met the wolf's blue-green eyes and bowed to him as the wolf did the same before it turned and calmly walked into the woods.

Each time she had the vision, the wolf had been the same- ruddy brown fur and large blue eyes made of snow and ice.

She followed the beast as the forest floor began to crunch with snow and ice under her feet, the dirty forest floor disappearing with the chill of each step she took north. Princess Arminda shivered and crossed her arms over her chest to warm her bare skin against the fabric of her dress. She still wore the elegant, revealing red dress she had worn at the Aisharian ceremony; this vision offered no change to her attire or appearance.

The wind began to rip at her hair and burn her skin as she continued following, the beast occasionally stopping to beckon her to hurry her leisurely pace. She looked up from watching her steps to find the wolf waiting at the edge of a wall of blowing snow, so thick that one could not see the back half of the creature as it backed up into the storm and howled as it escaped her sight.

Princess Arminda quickened her pace, pulling up her dress skirt and running through the powdered hills, following the path the wolf called her on. The wolf disappeared into the blizzard, sprinting as fast as the snow fell and the wind blew.

The snow around her stilled as her steps came to a halt, and she stood at the foot of a throne carved from broken bones.

She knew what happened next. The vision gifted to her by the Seer at a young age, and now a recurring dream, had always followed the same actions and ended the same. Beside the throne of broken bones, the wolf growled but remained resting in the snow, waiting for her to step forward and sit in the chair.

The beat of far-off leather-skinned wings accompanied the wolf's rumbling growl.

And then the princess woke.

Chapter 41

The red sands of the beach were dense under Sir Marion's bare feet. Crystal-clear waves lapped against the shoreline and cleared away others' tracks. Various sticks and shells had been washed ashore by the current and littered the red sands.

He found his way up the waving pathway that gradually turned from thick red sand to dirt and rocks, the new texture cutting and scratching against the bottoms of his bare feet. He paid the pain no mind; his life was filled with worse pains than cuts on calloused skin.

The town that came into his view stood empty, a sight his imagination could have never come up with on its own. The city he had called home had been a livelier part of the Aisharian countryside, with many coming and going from the town to find their way to Castle Red on the central isle or farther south for the annual Blood Rite on their island's southern shore.

Sir Marion stepped under the white stone arch of the city's entrance and instinctively turned left towards his childhood home. He made it two steps before he heard the whispering and turned.

"Who are you?" he demanded of the woman standing before him.

The figure said nothing and stared at him with empty eye sockets.

Her skin transformed from a light olive to a lifeless white. Blue and purple bruises covered her skin and encircled where her eyes should be, and empty veins rose to the surface of her taut and crackling skin. Her pale mouth dribbled blood, and the gash at her neck opened and closed as she spoke, blood bubbling and pouring out from where she had been cut open.

"There are so many of us; perhaps we should ask which of us you remember?" She let out a wet cackle, and her body unnaturally jerked and moved. "Should we count ourselves lucky if you do recall our names or luckier if you don't?"

"Do you at least remember me?" A tiny voice beside him queried and stole his attention.

A young boy, no more than ten, stood with his arms politely held behind his back and stared up at Sir Marion. It was not until the boy turned his face, a face so familiar to Sir Marion, that he recognized the boy from the Blood Rite.

Maggots feasted on the child's busted open head, where chunks of rock still remained stuck in his skull.

"I was your first, remember? You didn't want us both to win the Rite. We could have both survived, you know." The boy looked down in sadness and shame. "I thought we were friends."

Sir Marion's face crinkled in disgust and anger. He felt the heat from the sun coat his face and burn his entire body. He turned and stormed off, leaving their ghosts behind. He made his way quickly past the market stalls, ignoring the ghosts and bodies that appeared and reached out for him, crawling over tables and through windows, calling for him

Calling out with bloodied mouths and hard-beaten souls.

He turned a corner and found himself much too quickly at the door of his old home, abandoned and worn with time and lack of use. A red x was painted on the busted door, a sign on buildings containing evidence of crimes that were not to be touched.

Sir Marion knew what lay inside the home. He had been the one to leave them all there.

It had been a rite of passage, a test of loyalty by the Lord of Aishar, who knew a man of Sir Marion's caliber would be more useful outside of the standard guard.

Even though he knew exactly what lay out for him, Sir Marion still held his hand out towards the broken door so that he could look inside. He hesitated, then set his hand on the worn handle.

Just for a moment, he wished to finally be home.

From behind, his father's baritone voice sent a stiffening shiver up his spine and set his hair on edge.

"Not until the job is done. Not until you bring Aishar glory."

Sir Marion felt blood cascade from his hand wrapped around the doorknob, blood stained his side as the other bled, too. No cuts adorned either bleeding hand as he dropped them both and turned to his father's voice; Sir Marion knew the blood was of the countless men and women whose souls he had turned to memory for duty.

Not for honor.

Never for honor.

But for duty.

Necessity.

For his country. His oath.

The skeleton he had made his father into glared at him, the bones covered in gashes from blades, and the skull bludgeoned by revenge and blood-sworn duty. Despite this brokenness, his father's carcass still spoke.

"Aishar still owns you, boy."

CHAPTER 42

L ady Kathilla tossed the fur blanket off her bare torso. The chill of the night had left the tent as the sun rose, and the heat from her body tangled with her lover had begun to make her sweat. A small, callous hand, delicate in size but not in its ability, ran up her side where it had been resting on Lady Kathilla's hip.

"Good mornin', my queen." Sabine crooned in Lady Kathilla's ear. "I am surprised you could rise so early, given our night."

Lady Kathilla inhaled, "The heat from the mornin' is not all that woke me." She moved Sabine's hand to the throbbing heat between her legs.

Before Sabine could work her fingers where Lady Kathilla lay, the queen threw herself on top of her body, Sabine's hand moving with it. Sabine smirked up at her queen and began slowly rubbing the tips of her middle and pointer fingers back and forth between Lady Kathilla's lips. Sabine opened her legs more, straddling one of Lady Kathilla's thighs.

Lady Kathilla let her head roll back as she sat mounted on top. "Our camp is leaving for Thindell this mornin'," the Craigie queen said with a low, gasping moan as she felt Sabine's wet heat grind against her leg. "We cannot take all day as we usually do."

Sabine plunged her fingers inside Lady Kathilla and grabbed her hip, holding her down as she rapidly stroked her from the inside while grinding herself against Lady Kathilla's thigh, "You are our people's queen. They shall wait if you desire, and I shall make you cum as fast or slow as you demand."

Lady Kathilla's chest rose and fell quickly as she gasped and moaned. Her own hands rose to her breasts to rub her nipples as she rode Sabine's working hand.

"They will wait a thousand days for you, my queen." Sabine said, moving more fingers inside Lady Kathilla and pumping her hand to meet Lady Kathilla's grinding hips, gasping as Lady Kathilla's free hand came down to stroke Sabine's clit, "We will follow you anywhere. Now come for me. Come for me, my queen."

Lady Kathilla's sweating body slammed down as she broke apart. She barely let her body stop shaking before she crawled off of Sabine's hand and moved her face down between Sabine's legs.

Lady Kathilla ate as if she had been starved her entire life.

Lady Kathilla stepped out of her tent into the mid-morning sun, casually pushing aside the flap. Stretching her arms wide, she rolled her neck, feeling the satisfying crackle of tension easing from her shoulders.

The camp was almost entirely packed, and her people were sitting about awaiting her. Their heads bowed as they noticed her leaving her tent, the sole remaining one standing upright.

"My queen, your horse is ready," a warrior who had been by her side since her ascension to the throne, greeted her. "We have kept a fire to warm your mornin' meal."

"I appreciate it." She rested a hand on his bicep and firmed her grip on it. "I will take my meal as we ride. I have held us up long enough with my private needs."

He smirked, "No man would blame you for allowin' a woman to take up your mornin'."

They shared a laugh at the jest before Lady Kathilla prepared to move towards the front of the deconstructed camp. "If we could get extra hands to finish tearin' down what remains, I would appreciate it greatly."

"Yes, my queen." He nodded as he stepped away from her. "Your children await you at the front as well."

Lady Kathilla found herself quickly within earshot of her waiting children, a crowd of warriors and aides surrounding the two as they all took moments of leisure.

"She makes us wait while she—"

"Barron, enough." Gladys shot at him.

"She is wastin' our time again. We have been wastin' our time for too long, and now we run back with our tails between our legs to visit elders hidden in a forest. And for what?" he snapped in a harsh whisper at Gladys.

"For guidance." Lady Kathilla firmly said as she stepped beside her children. No anger or emotion was in her voice. "For assistance. Our elders have asked for my presence, and we will grant them that. And I need their guidance in the coming times."

Barron stood up from where he sat casually lounging on the back of a cart. Lady Kathilla raised her hand to quiet him.

"I know I am changin' our plans with little guidance or information but returnin' our holy lands back to us will not be easy, and even with the guidance and strength of the Vahar behind us, there is more we- more I- need to lead us to victory, to our freedom." she raised her chin, "I have learned as of late that fightin' only with weapons and bloodlust will not grant us victory. We keep tryin' the same tactics to no lastin' success. When the veil was thinned between worlds…" she let her voice trail off, noting the widened eyes and leaned-in posture around her.

They cannot yet know what I saw on Des Mortem.

"We head north," she ordered. "The Forest of Whispers awaits us. Prepare your minds for what hides in its shadows and trees. And prepare your bodies for little rest until we have passed through into Thindell."

Chapter 43

Sister Ora could not help but be enamored and taken aback as fire dancers from Odessin swept flames across the stone floor and throughout the charged air while she watched their bodies move elegantly in sync with the flames they wielded. Fire breathers inhaled flammable liquid and spat it onto their torches, breathing flames as if they were scaled beasts to fear. They wore gold-crafted bands and chains around their semi-sheer-robed bodies

Each of the dozen tables lining the main dining hall of the King's Keep was overflowing with ale, wine, herbed dried meats, and seasoned vegetables and cheeses piled high atop one another. Guests ripped and broke chunks of warm bread, accompanied by rowdy shouts over the music of the desert flutes and ringing bells.

Genderfluid bell dancers from the Isles of Aishar flicked their wrists in different formations and jutted their hips in tandem with the drums and flutes. The delicate bells adorning their body added to the cadence and kept time with the songs of celebration.

The music alternated fluidly between songs of the Isles, Odessin, and traditional bardic ballads of Britia, with the musicians occasionally riffing off one another's melodies and blending each country's music.

All except for the music and dance are often sung and performed in Ayeshire.

On the stage at the front of the dining hall, a separate dining table stood at an imposing length. Seats were left empty for the king and queen, Princess Arminda, Sister Ora, Prince Percy, Father Figgins, and the rest of the King's Council.

No seats were left for the bride's missing family.

The guests of honor were spread out among the crowd, sharing drinks and conversation. The noblemen and prestigious acquaintances of the royal family shared copious amounts of phony laughter and congratulations on the following day's nuptials. Prince Percy and Sister Ora remained separated throughout the hour, mingling with their preferred and sometimes not preferred guests.

The several days of marital celebration had been long, arduous, and excessive in waste, pomp, and circumstance. They would reach their final crescendo tomorrow night after their post-ceremony feast ended.

"Do you not find it a bit... odd that at your pre-wedding feast, they are showcasing acts and melodies of cultures that are not your own?" An upper-class noble lady, short and stout in demeanor and intelligence, crooned at Sister Ora.

Sister Ora softened her face into a dutiful smile as the gossiping woman set the obvious trap before her. "Not at all, my lady. In fact, I find it quite beautiful to see so much of the kingdom celebrating the prince and I's nuptials."

The woman leaned in, feigning a whisper, but her voice was too booming to speak in secrecy, "But do you not find a lack of decorum in their disregard for your country's music and ways? These celebrations are about you, after all."

Sister Ora's tongue ran along her teeth; she threw on another toothy smile. "Why do you ask, my lady? Do you find any discomfort or a lack of pleasure in their majesty's celebration?"

The woman gasped and rested a hand on her chest, leaning away from the bride-to-be. "Of course not! Goodness, no."

"How lovely to hear. Please excuse me; I must find my betrothed and discuss our dance cards for the evening." Sister Ora curtsied, her face finding a scowl as it turned to the floor, and her manufactured ease returned as her spine straightened.

The King's Guards that stood close behind her turned with her every movement as she left the conversation to find another to be suffocated by. Sister Ora swept through the crowd of vipers dressed in their finest clothing, plastering on lovely smiles and chortling with others before sneering behind one another's backs. She had once wistfully dreamed of a life at court in Ayeshire, a future she could find contentment with despite the displeasure she held with much of the duties she had to endure due to her Divine House.

She had once believed a life adjacent to a noble court could bring her into the circle of the most intelligent and bright minds to commune with. After such a short time in the king's court, she realized that many of the noblemen and women were not as bright as they made themselves seem from atop their pedestals. In fact, after the dull conversations she had to endure tonight, Sister Ora realized she had had more compelling discussions with the stone walls of Middleton Landing or the stray castle cats roaming the halls.

The flute and bell music heightened and softened into its ending as Sister Ora followed the sounds of Prince Percy's voice to the front of the room. She found her betrothed in deep conversation with nobles she did not recognize. To her relief, Prince Percy, despite his turned back, seemed to be having a riveting conversation with his guests. His shoulders lifted and fell in chuckles, and his arms moved in the air with his words.

Finally, a conversation she would not suffer in.

"Your Highness." Sister Ora curtsied as she approached. Prince Percy's back was to her for much of her bow, but she did not miss the small sigh and drop in his eyes as he turned to her.

"My lady." Prince Percy greeted her plainly. Sister Ora had spent her night and the past days smiling until her cheeks ached, masking her true self behind a persona of thankful bride and loyal future member of the Royal Scott house, only to see that her betrothed so carelessly showed how he did not care for her presence, did not wish to play the role he should in this court to ensure...

Oh my gods, she thought as she ended her string of thoughts, I do sound like his mother.

Polite and, to Sister Ora's annoyance, dull conversation ensued as she was brought into the fold. She tuned out their discussion of the upcoming season, their hopes for the harvest, and their predictions about winter weather. She tilted her ears to the conversations surrounding her, hearing snippets of court gossip, whispers of the war, and what they had heard from travelers returning to the city.

"My son is with the prince's army. I heard from a trader near the lakes that..."

The man's voice faded from her ear as he lowered his tone to whisper. Sister Ora pricked her ears to another conversation, stepping back slightly and turning her head to pick up their feminine tones laced with Aisharian accents nearby.

"Between you and me, Sir Marion is a more generous man than he seems. The other night, my friend and I found ourselves on either side of him and..."

She grimaced and shook her head, having no interest in hearing more of that gossip.

"Sister Ora." Prince Percy's voice called her, and she turned her attention to him as he spoke, "It is time for dinner. Let us go sit."

As the betrotheds excused themselves and took their seats at the head of the table, the prince surprised Sister Ora by speaking to her without pressure or force, making him.

"I heard of the letter you received from your family. I am sorry that my father decided to send word with a disguised courier to your family in the south. That he and Father Figgins felt it appropriate to tell them of our wedding and how they could not come," he whispered to her.

She cleared her throat and adjusted the cloth napkin on her lap. "I could not decide which was more cruel, their act or my mother's response. Both I was not surprised by, but neither hurt any less."

Sister Ora did not know why she so easily let the vulnerable words fall from her.

Prince Percy's eyes flicked up and down her face. Sister Ora swore she saw worry and pain in his eyes. "What did she say?"

She scoffed and took a sip of her wine. "Did her words not make it around your Council table? As I am sure it was read before it was given to me."

"If they did, I did not listen," he replied, his words hard and his tone sharp.

Sister Ora sighed, "She said the usual. How I am a disappointment to her again, that their inability to attend our wedding was all my fault somehow, that my mother deserved," she gestured to the grandness of the event, "- this. And how once the wedding is finished, I need to," she paused to remember the exact words, "remember the family that made me."

Prince Percy let out a long sigh and shook his head. "I am sorry she said those things."

Her eyes flickered at the sincerity in his voice. She shook her head, "And she informed me that I am to tell the king how they are loyal to him always and that they fear for their safety in Ayeshire... that I need to arrange for them to move out of Ayeshire and preferably into the castle, of course."

The prince took his turn fidgeting in discomfort and mumbled. "I can find them somewhere else to live if they fear for their safety. They don't need to be close to you."

Sister Ora almost choked on the wine she had been drinking, shocked at his response, his seeming defense of her. "What?"

Prince Percy held another moment of silence and shrugged as if the weight of her confessions bore down on his body, and he needed to remove the heaviness. "They don't need to be here," he mumbled. "We don't need more conniving people in this court using one another."

"Oh," she said, not even trying to hide the disappointment in her tone. For some silly reason, she had thought that his words came from a place of care for her, not of hatred of politics and scheming.

Around them, the room settled into the opening of the meal. Cooks began to carry out trays of the feast- the food stacked on tables merely an appetizer and starter for what was to come- and make room for each steaming plate on the crowded tables. As the first plates were set, the clanking of metal and the groaning of wood called attention away from the servants and moved all eyes to the back of the room.

Lord Tyrrian Priscius stood centered in the threshold of the opening doors.

A bright ivory-fitted tunic flowed down his legs, hugging his body's muscles. The fitted sleeves loosened into billows of embroidery at his biceps, where detailed golden stitching gave way to the pristine white fabric that ended at his wrists. Crashing waves, laurel leaves, florals, and krakens danced in gold, weaving into a mighty tale around his arms and onto his chest.

The vassal beside the door cleared his throat, and his voice boomed. "May I present Lord Tyrrian Priscius, Lord of the Isles of Aishar, Head of House Priscius, Lord of the Waters."

"Several moments too late," the king grumbled in aggravation from his seat.

Lord Tyrrian soaked in his moment and slowly sauntered down the steps, his hands clasped behind his back, his chin held high, and his movement casual. Over his tunic, a long chlamys was draped and dragged on the floor behind him. The red fabric covered one arm and left the other free. The deep, blood-red fabric was beaded on the edges with stones reminiscent of the autumn sky at sunset.

He made his way down the central aisle and stopped at the dais steps before the head table. The tyrant nodded at the king and everyone who sat beside His Majesty.

"Your Majesty, Your Highnesses, please accept my congratulations on this celebration," he crooned and let his eyes linger on Queen Onetta before shooting them back to the king, who rigidly sat beside her. The lord dismissed himself to sit at the head of the noble table set for the guests of the Isles. The room had kept its quietness, the guests' eyes following Lord Tyrrian as he made his way to his seat.

King Ivan waved two fingers to a well-dressed vassal standing beside the stage. The man approached and shared in harsh whispers with the king before the Master of Ceremonies moved to stand in front of the royal table.

"Ladies and gentlemen, as we commence with the feast, let us give thanks to the most gracious King and Queen of Victarius for their generosity this night, and let us celebrate the union of Prince Percy and his betrothed!"

They won't even say my name.

Sister Ora worked every muscle in her face into a pleasant smile despite the fact that each muscle wished to form a scowl.

A chorus of cheers and applause broke, dissolving the tension in the room and restoring a more relaxed atmosphere. The servers returned to moving between the tables, filling goblets, and serving the array of new dishes.

Dried meats and small dishes meant for snacking were replaced with quail and wild boars on heavy, decorated trays; dark berries, green leafy vegetables, and citrus from the Isles were laid atop the animals' bodies and stuffed into them. Herbs patterned the skin of the fowl and the heavy potatoes and leeks they were served with.

Each guest received their own heavy plate filled with the tiny bird and roasted vegetables. Those who wished for boar were given heavy cuts of the pink meat; the boar's head was left attached to its body as it was wheeled about the room.

And then the stag came.

Sister Ora's jaw shook at the sight of her people's noble and holy creature laid out on a rolling cart, roasted until crisp, surrounded by an early autumn bounty. The servants lowered their eyes to the ground as they presented the beast to Sister Ora first.

"My- my- my lady," the cook stuttered and stammered with fear, "we- we were asked to offer you the first cut of meat, to ensure you got the best of it."

Sister Ora did not control her arm as it slowly moved for the knife beside her plate. She did not control her mind as she wished to slice and cut at the royal family, sneering down the table.

"Take it away. Now," she heard a man beside her growl. She had never heard such vitriol and rage come from the second prince before. She had not recognized the voice as his at first.

As the meal progressed, Sister Ora found herself picking at her food, her appetite completely dissipated, her emotions having drained her. She glanced at Prince Percy, who seemed equally distracted, his fork idly tracing patterns on his plate while he mumbled to himself and shook his head repeatedly.

The Master of Ceremonies returned to his place at the front of the hall as bellies became full and plates began to empty.

"As we drink and dine until our bellies cannot take any more," the man smiled as he rubbed his bloated belly. The room laughed at his gesture, "- let us be entertained!"

He clapped twice before exiting the center of the room and being replaced by court jesters. The jesters tumbled and cartwheeled into the hall, their brightly colored costumes a whirlwind of motion and joy. Bells jingled at their wrists and ankles; these bells were louder and harsher than the delicate ones that the prior dancers wore. Their movements were synchronized yet chaotic and individual in each turn and twist.

Sister Ora forced a smile as the dancers looked to her for approval. Prince Percy feigned shyness when the jesters pleaded with them to kiss. When the attention fell away from the pair, Sister Ora glanced at Prince Percy again. His eyes were empty and dead as he watched and nodded at the entertainment.

Select jesters made their way around the room, picking unlucky noble guests from the crowd and laughing at their portly bellies, balding hair, and overly ostentatious dress. They gained laughs from those around them, and some guests joined in on the jesting of one another.

A youthful jester with blonde hair and blue eyes gained the most laughs with his quiet miming of lords and ladies. He jumped and tumbled to the front of the room to gasps and applause. He bowed deeply to the king and queen, so far that his nose touched the ground. As he lifted his face, he rubbed it, and brown makeup smudged onto the tip of his nose.

He let out a clownish laugh and shook his body with over-ly done laughter as he pointed to his brown nose. The crowd laughed at the sight. He shook his skinny stomach with his hands before taking a deep inhale and pushing his belly full of air. He pointed at the king and then his stomach and mimed their similarities.

Nervous laughter followed.

The young jester did not pick up on the king's tightening pos-ture nor the tension behind the chuckles. He continued his act, miming drinking from a large chalice and stumbling about in faux drunken clumsiness. The jester stuck a hand in his pants, then unzipped them, his pinky finger poking out and falling limp. He mimed a gasp and used his other hand to try to lift his limp pinky, faking cries as it did nothing.

The Master of Ceremonies stepped forward, his gaping face shocked and appalled by the crudeness, and intended to stop it. He made it three steps before King Ivan stood without haste or urgency.

The room stopped.

King Ivan's hardened stare burned at the young jester, whose face lost all color and joy and fell into fear. King Ivan turned to the King's Guards lining the room and nodded once at Sir Marion.

The king stood as a group of King's Guards dispatched from the wall and held the young jester between them. They did not exit the room with his body in tow, nor did they beat the man into an apology; instead, with another nod as he slowly sat back down, His Majesty commanded the jester's head.

No one dared to cry out or protest; even the fellow entertainers held back their fears and opinions on the act. The young jester knew quite quickly that fighting would be fruitless, that apologies would be silenced. He hung his head for the last time as a sword was unsheathed.

The feast continued on as the blood was mopped from the ground. All too easily, the nobility moved on from what occurred. All too easily, they ignored the blood.

CHAPTER 44

"You found them where?" King Ivan snarled. He sat upon his throne of gold, hunched forward with his elbows on his thighs, not from exhaustion, but from rage that weighed him down. The king glared down at the citizens, broken and beaten, dripping dirt and blood onto the floor of his throne room. It angered him how they seemed to show no remorse for attempting to steal from their king.

"Attempting to break into your private gardens, Your Majesty." The newly minted castle guard said. "They had empty sacks, several of them. Seemed they were going to pick the gardens dry of food."

King Ivan pinched the bridge of his nose, stifling a yawn at being woken so late in the night. He shook his pounding head. The night's rest had not been kind to him. He had attempted to let go of his need for drink for one day. As he sat on the throne, he knew he would not make it to his chambers before breaking his promise to break from the bottle. "You are fucking joking, yes?"

"No, no, sir." The same guard nervously replied. "They almost got in a lower gate, but we stopped them in time."

The king inhaled deeply, "You woke me in the middle of the night for this? For what? For me to tell you what you already know you must do?"

"Well, we just-" The other guard cut in with a shake of his voice.

King Ivan threw a hand up to silence their talk. He stood up, his eyes nothing more than orbs reflecting into a lost consciousness, a broken final straw. He heavily stomped down the dais steps. His voice not yet shouting, but hard and vicious, firm and mocking, "Must I order every little thing each day? Would you like me to tell you when to piss and shit? How to fuck you husbands and wives? Yes?!"

He pulled the sword from the closest castle guard's sheath, "Must I take care of them myself? Or are you capable of doing your job?"

He brandished the sword wildly as he mocked his own guards. The citizens on their knees ducked and shivered in fear near the king.

The doors slammed open, and hard, armored steps rushed inside. "Your Majesty." Sir Marion quickly greeted, "I received the call regarding the break-in."

King Ivan held his arms out, the sword still in one hand, "Oh, and here he is! The one you should be pestering with this bullshit!" King Ivan threw the sword on the ground.

No one dared move to pick it up.

"My apologies, Your Majesty. These guards are new to our ranks." Sir Marion calmly replied and slowly stood between the king and the rest of the room. "I will handle their punishment for this misstep."

"I should not have been woken for such a tiny thing, and these thieves should not have been able to get as far as they did." King Ivan grabbed Sir Marion's armor and pulled him in. "How is your king supposed to rest soundly when you and your men allow traitors so close to his chambers?"

Sir Marion's lip twitched. He hardened his face but nodded in submission, "My apologies, my king. It will never happen again. I will see to it myself. You have my word."

"Your word, Sir Marion? Your word?" King Ivan chuffed an amused laugh. "I want action, Sir Marion. Not words."

His grip tightened on Sir Marion's armored collar. "Take care of this and take care of any others who may wish to be so bold as to steal from the king." King Ivan snarled, shoving back Sir Marion and storming out of the throne room. "Do it. Now!"

The red cloaks of the King's Guard clashed against the black cloaks of the City Watch. Despite their differences, they stood as one united front. Sir Marion adorned himself in his complete Master of Armor regalia, including his rarely worn helmet. He stood at the front of the anxious group, feeding into and on their energy.

"There are many, including myself, who are to set sail for battle soon," he shouted. "The last of the warships of Aishar have arrived, and with that, more gladiators and more warriors, hungry for victory. And for blood."

Roars of applause ruptured from the field of armor.

"And with that leave comes the possibility that some may decide to rise up, to go against the Crown again while they think it is weakened." He chuckled and smiled, "And we are here to warn them of what will occur if they dare to try. To remind them of our strength over them."

More applause roared, and armored fists banged against chest plates.

"If they run, chase them. If they beg, make them bleed. If they fight, kill them." Sir Marion ordered.

The King's Guard and City Watch all too eagerly made their way out of the castle's gates. The torch flames they carried and the candlelight they walked beside illuminated their path of fury in the night.

The heavy marching woke citizens from their restless sleep, and onlookers peered at the parade from the open edges of their curtains. Eyes bulged in fear as the guards made their way down the streets; gathered citizens rushed out of their way, spilling the ales that they enjoyed, disposing of their card games on the cobblestone as they tried to flee.

Noises from a lowly tavern were silenced as citizens from the street fled inside for shelter. The armor-clad men and women split into groups, some following those inside and others marching down different alleys.

Screams erupted everywhere, and armored footsteps followed.

Sir Marion shouted at the tavern many ran into, directing his armored guards to enter. He took the lead, slamming through the door and stepping aside to allow King's Guards and City Watchmen alike inside.

"Harboring criminals, are we?" Sir Marion sneered at the barmaid.

She shook her head in fear, her trembling hands raised in front of her.

"Then swear fealty to the king, all of you," he demanded.

The barmaid bowed her head and swore her oath to the king as did the shaking crowd in the tavern. Down the bar, a lone man stayed seated and hunched over his beer, ignoring the guards who entered and their demand for fealty.

"You!" Sir Marion shouted at the drunk, "Raise your head and plead your fealty to His Majesty."

The drunk ignored his demands. Sir Marion shouted again and took two hard steps forward, "I said, swear fealty."

"Oh, piss off!" The drunk slurred as he wavered in his seat.

The crowd's shock was tangible, their murmurs spreading like ripples on a pond. Yet Sir Marion remained intent, focusing solely on the drunken man slouched in the corner. The onlookers' whispers and stares were mere background noise as he strode towards the stool, his hand closing around a bottle of liquor, its smooth glass cool against his palm.

He stood before the drunk and held out the bottle to him. But just as the man's hand reached out to take it, Sir Marion flipped the bottle over with a flick of his wrist, spilling it in the drunk's lap, then splashing it on his face.

The drunk's face transformed; hope for another drink replaced by confusion and disappointment. Sir Marion held his smug smile as he looked about the room. He walked backward away from the drunk, splashing a trail of the remaining liquor on the ground, a crooked line running from the back corner to the doorframe.

Fear overtook the crowd. It did not take a mastermind to know what he was doing. Sir Marion's guards, now turned loyal soldiers, held their spots at the door, not allowing anyone to exit.

Sir Marion smashed the bottle on the ground and turned to stand in front of the only exit. The King's Guards and City Watch moved outside the building as he took up the frame of the doorway.

A King's Guard handed him a torch.

"You will not speak out against the king. You will be loyal. You will be obedient. Or you will face the fire."

Sir Marion hurled the torch to the ground, right where the trail of liquor ended. The trail sizzled and cracked as the flames consumed it. He slammed the door behind him, shattering the doorknob as it closed, rendering it useless.

Piercing screams and the sound of shattering glass erupted alongside flames as panicked patrons tried to escape. Citizens threw themselves against the door; others used barstools and fists to shatter the windows and crawl outside.

For some, it was enough.

For others, it was too late.

"Thief!" a King's Guard shouted at a fleeing man.

The man turned to look at the raging King's Guard, causing him to collide with a black-cloaked City Watchman who grappled him.

"No! No, I have not done anything!" the man shouted.

"Then why do you flee from us?!" The City Watchman gritted back.

"I- I- I- don't know. I was frightened," he stammered out.

The King's Guard grabbed him by the throat and threw him on the ground, stepping on his forearm to hold him in place.

"If that is all, then you can serve as a lesson," he growled. From his pocket, the King's Guard pulled a jagged dagger.

"No! No! No!" the man on the ground screamed and flailed. His movement stopped when the City Watchman stepped hard on his back.

His screaming continued as the King's Guard sawed off his hand and left it in the street.

CHAPTER 45

Parchment flapped in the light breeze that made its way through the streets of Isilria. Homes and businesses, once thriving with colorful flowers and well-attended care, now stood as simple stone structures to hide in.

There were no moments of laughter or liveliness as there had once been in the king's city, even when many were restless and whispering thoughts of rebellion. The Renaissance that came after the Dark Times had finally, fully, and truly come to an end.

Nailed and adhered to posts and doorways of every square of the city were parchments posting rewards and warnings. Rewards for information on traitors and treason-makers and warnings for those who wished to fill those roles.

The king had lost his mind when he sent his men throughout the city to beat and bruise the city into submission, and even more when he turned his knights into bird killers and closed them off from the rest of the world earlier in the season. He lost it again when he shouted commands at Sir Marion to take revenge on their starving people for daring to steal food from the king.

The king knew what Sir Marion was willing to do. What the men loyal to Sir Marion, the king, and their coin would do to keep the city in line and their coffers full.

Good men never donned armor that was often stained with blood, no matter how kind they were to you before they beat you into loyalty. No matter how much they preached, they were just doing their jobs and keeping the peace.

The king had lost his mind, yes, but no one dared admit it, not even with a subtle look or a simple thought. The king had gotten his obedience, but the price of it would haunt whatever parts of his soul still felt anything other than malevolence.

At the market stand in the middle city, an elderly woman's jaw trembled alongside her voice, "Six copper for the bread, sir?"

She held out a frail hand with four copper coins inside it.

"Yes, ma'am." The bread maker's deep tenor held its own shake despite his best attempts to hold it steady. "Prices changed and all that."

His eyes quickly darted to the armored guard standing a few paces away.

"But it was only three when I came here last." Her voice was beaten and worn, tired and lost.

"I know, ma'am." his eyes darted to the guard again, whose helmet had turned slowly in their direction. "This is the price now."

"But I—"

"Is there a problem?" The guard shouted at them, stepping forward and sending a jerk up both their spines. He cocked his head slowly at the woman as he met beside her, leaning in and making her face turn red in worry, "Do you have an issue with the king raising prices for the new taxes?"

Her eyes shot to the ground. "No, no, I do not. My apologies: I swear I do not. I just do not have the coin, sir."

"Well, that's too bad then, innit?" the guard sneered.

"I can cover it, sir. That way, the king gets his money, and she can feed her family." The baker begged, his eyes also not meeting the guards.

An armored glove shot from the sword it held as the guard snatched the bread off the stand and threw it to the ground, "No. If she cannot afford it, she does not eat."

"Yes, sir. I understand, sir. I apologize, sir," she cried, her tears falling as she waited for his hand to rise against her, her eyes meeting the sigil on his suit— a sigil that once meant protection and servitude to the people but now meant brutal policing and obedience without consequence.

"If you cannot afford the food, crow, then you do not need to loiter. That is a crime these days."

Her head nodded quickly as she bowed at the guard and rushed away.

The baker looked at the bread, broken and crumbling on the cobblestone. He let out a deep breath as his eyes fell closed in defeat.

"Pick it up," the guard barked before returning to his post in the marketplace. "Littering is a crime."

Defeated, the baker moved from behind his stand, a basket and broom in his hands, and swept up the loaf, picking up the larger pieces and shunning away his shame in knowing he would eat it that night as his dinner. For his wife and daughter, he would only give them the pieces that did not touch the stone; he would take the rest.

He stood and turned, nodding to the new customer who had appeared by his stand.

"A loaf, please, sir." The new shopper, a built man with olive skin and a worn face, asked. His large hand tugged at his hat, pulling it back down over his forehead. "And a biscuit as well, if you can."

"Eight copper, sir," replied the baker as he set down his items and began wrapping a new loaf in paper and twine.

The shopper dug into his pockets, pulling out the money and being careful not to let the rest rattle. The baker exchanged the coin for the bread, dropping it in his own pocket, and reached to wrap the biscuit the customer had ordered.

"Oh, save yourself the paper, sir; I will eat it on my way."

The baker nodded, slowly meeting the shopper's eyes and giving him a tiny smile as he handed over the biscuit. "Thank you, sir."

The shopper nodded. "You as well."

The shopper set off, keeping his pace somewhat quick, appearing as a man running a quick errand. His steps took no time to meet up with the frail older woman rejected from the bread stand. He approached behind her; her back turned as she very timidly tried to purchase a meal from the vendor in front of her, with little luck again.

"Grandmother," Sedrick's voice shocked her as he leaned into her, gently setting his hand on her arm. "I got the bread for you as you asked."

The very pale and tiny white woman looked up at Sedrick's olive-toned face in extensive confusion, "Child, I am not your-"

Sedrick's eyes shot down at her as he shoved the bread towards her.

She cut off her own words, realization overcoming her somber expression. "Oh, my sweet grandson, yes, thank you for getting the bread for us."

Her shaking hands reached out for the bread, resting on top of his for a moment. They exchanged silent gratitude with only a touch.

"I'm off to work, grandmother. Are you alright with shopping alone?"

"Yes, yes, I am. Thank you again for helping me today." She smiled through the new tears welling in her eyes as Sedrick turned and walked away.

He made his way through the too-small market crowd, his eyes straight forward as he passed each guard on the street again. He minded his business, ripping apart and chewing the dry biscuit to keep his hands and body busy. As he left, his eyes began to wander, noting any glaring eyes or suspicious followers. He mistakenly drifted his glances towards the guard standing near the bread stand he had visited.

His eyes shot away too quickly as he passed by.

"Hey! You there!"

Sedrick did not stop; he continued walking.

"You! I said stop." The guard's voice quickly made its way directly behind Sedrick, and at the exact moment, an armored hand grabbed his shoulder.

"Oh! My apologies, sir." Sedrick bowed his head as he lied, "I did not know you were speaking to me." He gestured around at the almost empty street, "It's just, you know, you could have been talking to anyone."

The guard held his grip on Sedrick's shoulder. "Where you off to?"

"Work, sir. Heading off to work."

"And where is that?" The guard's hard drawl exaggerated with the tightening of his grip.

"The docks, sir." Sedrick nodded. "I'm a dock worker."

"Show me your hands, then."

Sedrick shrugged as he lifted up his hands, one still carrying the biscuit and the other sporting biscuit crumbs. "Fully intact, as you can see."

The guard snatched the hand with the biscuit and held it up by the wrist, causing Sedrick to drop his meal.

"Right, right. Not a fan of jokes." Sedrick mumbled.

"Intact... for now," the guard laughed, "See? I like jokes."

Sedrick reeled back without breaking the grip. He opened his hand more for the guard to inspect. "It's just a hand, sir."

The guard threw his hand down. "Those are the hands of a worker." His eyes squinted under his helmet. "A little soft right now, like a woman of the night. Seems suspicious."

Sedrick shook his head quickly and rubbed his hands on his clothes. "Work's been spread thin a bit as of late, what with the sanctions and the Aisharian fleet here working on their own boats."

"You complaining about the king's orders? About the king—"

"No, no, no, nope." Sedrick quickly cut him off, waving his hands in front of his chest. "I would never. The king is a just ruler doing what he must to save our kingdom."

The guard smirked. "That is what I thought." He patted Sedrick on his chest, pausing his hand as he felt the unnatural shape of parchment underneath his vest. He snagged Sedrick by the cloth. "Take it out. Whatever it is you have hidden on you, take it out."

"Sir, it is just simple parchment for note-taking and map-making for work. Nothing important." He shivered.

The guard's grip tightened on him as his head jerked around to order more guards to surround Sedrick. "Take. It. Out."

"Okay," Sedrick sighed, "ok, I will."

Sedrick pulled out the papers folded in his vest pocket, careful not to tear or rip an edge. He unfolded them just as another guard snatched them from his grip.

The guard's eyes stared at the paper through the slits in his helmet, squinting and turning the pages. "They are blank."

"Yes, see, as I told you. Blank papers for my work." Sedrick nodded one too many times, remembering himself, then stilled his body and his mouth.

The first guard glared more before finally stepping back. "Watch yourself next time you're on the king's streets."

"Yes, sir." Sedrick averted his eyes.

The other guard did not bother to properly fold the parchment before handing it back to Sedrick. Instead, they slapped it into his chest, not even giving him a moment to take hold of the pieces before dropping their grip and walking away.

"Where is a back alley bucket when one needs it?" Sedrick swallowed the bile in his throat that had risen when he was forced to speak kind words of the king. He folded the parchment carefully and tucked it into his pocket. "I have to get out of here. I cannot wait any longer for more information or more tasks."

He turned his head uphill, where the highest turrets of The King's Keep could be seen. He swallowed the pain in his throat. Not long ago, just under two moon phases ago, he had been forced to witness what was meant to be his own execution. Instead, he watched a man, looking too much like him, lose his life over the sins Sedrick had committed against the crown. He had watched Sister Ora shriek and her chest heave as she watched the man lose his life, believing it was him.

He had wished to shout at her, "I am here! That is not me!"

He had wished to run to her, to grab her wrist and jump into the ocean beyond their reach, to make for the waters and save themselves from this wretched place. To abandon it all to the seven hells.

Instead, he watched her be hauled away in chains as she shrieked and cried over the second man being killed. Those tears had been much different than the ones she shed for the man she thought her friend. Those tears were of a heart shattering so much that only ashes were left behind.

Sedrick swore she met his eyes before she disappeared, kicking and screaming behind a wall of armor, but his shadowed face would not be easily seen by anyone so far away from his trembling body.

He brought himself back to this moment, to the aftermath of what they had done.

"I'm sorry, Ora," he mumbled as he turned to leave for the harbor.

With each step he took, anxiety and paranoia engulfed him. His fingers repeatedly moved to the center of his chest, where he could feel the faint outline of the parchment beneath his clothing. A copy that he had created from Sister Ora's confidential findings, delivered to him in the shadowy back streets of the castle.

A parchment inscribed with a peculiar ink that was invisible to the naked eye, a product of Sister Ora's keen knowledge of old scribes' secrets. Secrets she had shared with Sedrick over time to satisfy his curiosity about her life.

The life he wished he could have had.

Every step he took was filled with unease as if each would be his last. He knew where the original copy lay hidden beneath dusty bricks shoved back into place in the most downtrodden hostel he had boarded at. Although he knew it was unlikely that anyone would uncover the secrets of what he held, every passing body became an enemy, a spy, the one who would bring him to his end.

He refused to mentally paint the dead man's face any longer. The ghost of his doppelganger stood over his shoulder, haunting him alongside his worry about how Sedrick had gained his freedom, weighing the likelihood of it being merely a coincidence or something sinister that spared his life and took another.

The day after the execution, Sedrick had dropped a bag of coins in front of the dead man's humble home. He dared not knock, the screaming cries of the fatherless babes inside being too much to bear witness to.

"Please understand," he whispered as he adjusted the small pack on his back and boarded the trading caravan heading east. He spoke not only to the ghost trailing behind him but to his friend locked in the castle.

And perhaps, he spoke to himself, too, convincing his heart that leaving her behind was the right choice, that moving forward was not only best for the kingdom, but for her, too.

Chapter 46

Pyria 1, 690AC

Kaylah ran the end of a comb down the center of Sister Ora's scalp, ensuring that her part was perfect and not a single strand of hair fell on the improper side of her scalp. The lady's maid traded the comb for hair pins that she gripped between her teeth and shoved them between strands behind Sister Ora's ears. Their eyes met in the mirror as Kaylah ensured that she had laid the bride's hair properly over the tops of her ears and down her neck. They shared a sad smile as another lady's maid brought over the tiara Sister Ora was to wear: a circlet of pearls, diamonds, and dark blood-red gems that fit her like a large headband, holding back her pinned hair.

"The queen did a lovely job picking out your jewelry, didn't she, m'lady?" The borrowed lady's maid asked innocently, "Such a shame that the one you wished to wear had broken."

"Yes, it is." Sister Ora replied flatly. She stared up at the ostentatious and sad excuse for a headpiece; while it was worth twice its weight in king's coin, the gaudy precious gems and stones that made up the piece would have been more beautiful had no laborers taken them from the mountains or the sea.

Kaylah leaned down to whisper in Sister Ora's ear, "Perhaps I tell Her Majesty I got confused and assumed the veil was to go over the headpiece to cover it?"

Sister Ora scoffed in amusement. "No, there is no need. I will wear it proudly and show the kingdom how lovely Her Majesty's personal taste is. This was from her personal, private collection, was it not?"

The borrowed maid chimed in, "No, actually, m'lady it–"

"Oh, oh, but I am so sure of it being from her own collection. I swear I heard that somewhere as well, that this was a piece so near and dear to her heart." Kaylah added.

"No, it–"

"Hush, child. Go tell the rest of the maids that our bride will be ready in a moment." Kaylah quipped and dismissed her.

Kaylah silently pinned the short ivory tulle veil into Sister Ora's hair, the clips hiding underneath the combed-out bump behind her gaudy jeweled headpiece. "Up," she said to Sister Ora. "I'll finalize everything once I see you standing as you will in front of them all."

Sister Ora stood and stepped in front of the large mirror that had been brought into her chambers for today. She took in the beautiful gemstone red semi-sheer tulle that lined her chest and arms, then fell onto the floor behind her, the excess fabric forming a train. The tulle continued down her chest until it meshed with a heavier satin fabric in a softer, nobler red that bustled at her natural waist and fell to the floor, puddling into a nest around her. Covering the torso of her dress were gold-stitched strands of vines that climbed from the center of her chest up onto the tulle and down onto her legs.

Had she not grown to loathe the color red, she would have been awestruck at the ensemble.

A soft knock came from the door, quickly followed by the knob turning and opening to reveal an elegantly dressed Princess Arminda, in her signature soft pastels and florals, her dress capped at the shoulders and her skirt falling in perfect alignment at the floor.

"Your Highness." Sister Ora greeted as she and Kaylah bowed to her.

"The dress is gorgeous, sister." Princess Arminda said as she met beside Sister Ora in front of the mirror. "What a beautiful bride you make."

"Thank you." Sister Ora nodded at her through their stares in the mirror.

"Oh, but this hair," Princess Arminda tutted, "I must correct it."

She turned to smile sweetly at Kaylah. "You did a fabulous job, but I just would love to give her my personal touch and talk to my future sister in private if you please."

"Of course, Your Highness," Kaylah replied as she bowed and dismissed herself, closing the door behind her.

"Thank you, Your Highness," Sister Ora said as they both stood in silence. Princess Arminda took her in and looked up and down at every bustle of fabric and strand of hair.

"Of course, I thought we could also use a moment of privacy before today begins." Princess Arminda played with the placement of strands of Sister Ora's hair. She smiled as she curled a wave of Sister Ora's hair around her finger and held onto it. "I must say, I am quite surprised that we got to this day."

"You and I both, princess." Sister Ora replied with a soft chuckle, Princess Arminda's quiet kindness offering her a breath of air on such a suffocating day.

"I wonder how long they will let you live." Princess Arminda mumbled as she reset Sister Ora's veil and adjusted it. "Maybe they will wait long enough for you to be with child, then let you bleed on the bed, claiming the babe was the only one able to be saved."

All color drained from Sister Ora's face as she became a ghost, petrified and held in place.

Princess Arminda stepped back and walked around Sister Ora, observing her gown and each accessory. "Or maybe they will not allow you to get so far- to let your blood taint my family's legacy. My parents' desires confound me when it comes to you." She tapped a finger to her lips and pursed them, then stepped forward to take off Sister Ora's necklace.

Sister Ora jolted at her touch.

Princess Arminda smiled without her teeth as she unclasped Sister Ora's delicate necklace and set it on the armoire, replacing it with another one. A short strand of pearls held a golden 'S' in the center, and a second, longer strand of pearls fell beneath it. Princess Arminda admired it as she spoke, "If it had been up to me, you would have already been killed or truly imprisoned instead of this farce my family calls proper punishment."

Sister Ora quickly raced through her memories of the princess: the kindness she showed her at their first meeting, her soft smiles, curious looks, and sisterly gestures. Has the princess always been like this?

"Then perhaps I should be grateful that it is not you who gives the orders of execution." Sister Ora kept her hands clenched. The princess was unlikely to cause a scar or inflict a wound on a day when all eyes would scrutinize every pore of Sister Ora's face and each stitch of her clothing. But still, Sister Ora kept her defenses ready.

Princess Arminda shrugged and looked at her through the mirror in front of which the two stood. "Yes, perhaps. It is not as if I hate you, I truly do not, emotions such as that are frivolous and take up too much of one's mind. But you have proven yourself quite a liability that we must now waste so much time watching, and I do not see much of a benefit to our family's reputation or our war in keeping you alive- who knows what you could do while you still breathe."

Sister Ora looked up into the mirror before her, watching as Princess Arminda looked at her. "It is easier to hold control over a corpse than a living traitor."

"It truly is. But you need not worry, I will not kill you. I have several ideas on how you can be of use to me personally. But if I did kill you, it is not like anyone would suspect me." She squeezed Sister Ora's shoulder, not in softness or care, but in a reminder of the grasp the royal family held on her. "That is what is so fun about this game you and I both play, sister."

Princess Arminda stepped back, admiring her work and the shock on Sister Ora's face. "Perfect." The princess's false kindness and courtly behavior came through with the simple word.

Another game. Another pawn. Another piece to be moved around.

"And what game is it that we are playing, princess?" Sister Ora narrowed her eyes.

"The game you started before I watched you run through the shadows of the tunnels underneath our feet. I knew you would be up to something long before that night. I started doing such things before your name was even a whisper on Father Figgins' lips." Princess Arminda stepped forward and cocked her head to the side. "I perfected the act of the meager, quiet girl before I first bled, and I have gained much since then and saw right through your act."

Princess Arminda walked around Sister Ora again and tossed herself down on the bed, grabbing a wine goblet and taking a large swig from it, then dangled it at her side with her hand holding it from above the opening. "And I learned early on how not to get caught, unlike you. Your friend from home and your armored lover were not the only ones sneaking around the night you passed off those hidden parchments." She pointed a finger at her. "The only problem is that I have not been able to figure out exactly what it was you gave to him. My eyes around the castle told me you were reading up on our castle's history just days before the exchange," the princess swallowed another swig, "but I truly have no idea why that matters to you and your little traitorous friends."

"Why are you telling me this?" Sister Ora slowly stalked toward the princess- a pawn playing as a predator. "Why this long confession of your secrets? No one confesses their sins and plans simply to talk about their schemes. What is it you want?"

The princess laughed. "Do you know how hard it is to have kept this all a secret? To sneak and snake around these halls for ages and have no one to tell about how great you are at it all? How you outsmart these... imbeciles every day?" Sister Ora began to open her mouth to retort, but Princess Arminda tutted at her, "But now, I finally have someone to tell. Someone who will never be believed if they speak of what I say."

The cunning princess smiled with all her teeth. It was not kind, nor was it that of a predator bearing its teeth as a warning; it was completely mental. "And that is why I will not interfere with whatever mother and father have planned for you, because I finally have someone who knows who I truly am and who gets to watch me win."

"Win what?" Sister Ora bit out.

"Everything I've ever wanted." Princess Arminda got up and began walking. "And you will be such a help now that you are to live. Did you know my stupid brother, your betrothed, was not only offered to teach at the citadel in Odessin that you are moving to, but was also given the chance to take the throne of Thelimor?" She shook her head, "Meanwhile, I've been given nothing but leftovers. Oh sure, I will get mother's inheritance of the Thelimor throne since he now wishes not to take it, but I should have been offered it before him."

Sister Ora followed the princess's footsteps, turning slowly in place. The soft swishing of her large skirt gave away her movements.

"You're right, you should have." Sister Ora jutted her chin and held her ground in the princess's path. "You seem the type to fit in quite well with men like your uncle, better than Percy would."

"Thank you, sister. I would." The princess brushed a hair away from Sister Ora's shoulder. "But... I have a destiny much too large for that old island." Princess Arminda waved her hand dismissively and set the wine chalice down on a table.

"And what is that?" Sister Ora glanced at the door. How have they been left alone for so long? Surely she was late for her own wedding.

"You don't get to know everything, not now, not yet," she tutted.

"So you wish for Thelimor and hold anger over Percy and your mother for it being granted to him and not you, but now you wish for something more? Something bigger?" Sister Ora tilted her head. "And I will help you achieve this. How?"

Princess Arminda stood in front of the chamber doors. "By becoming one of us. Come, sister."

Prince Percy's skin itched and burned under the heavy sleeves of his tunic; he had already been corrected about his fidgeting several times when he had found himself at the head of the packed church, standing in front of the pulpit and staring at the empty spot across from him on the dais.

King Ivan and Queen Onetta had taken up much of the crowd's earlier attention as they entered the royal chapel last and took their spots in the front pew; gasps and quiet whispers accompanied their entrance, some over the queen's elegant gown that many whispered risked outshining the brides, while others mumbled over the king's oddly quiet demeanor and blank staring as if he were not mentally present.

The loud whispers and murmurs quieted as the church organ took up a deeper tune, elongating the note and carrying it over the talking, gently hushing each parishioner. The doormen at the end of the hall pulled open the cathedral's double doors, and silence befell the people.

Light poured in alongside small cheers and shouts from outside onlookers. Sister Ora stood in the center of the light, her hands clasped at her waist and gripping a bouquet of white flowers and fern-leaved greenery.

Bodies shuffled in the pews as they turned to watch Sister Ora walk herself down the aisle. Few paid any mind to the plethora of guards anxiously resting their hands on their swords' pommels as she walked by. Even fewer listened as the cathedral doors closed and locked behind her, drowning out the mixture of cheers and restless shouting from the streets.

Prince Percy pulled at the tunic button at his neck, needing to feel a sense of freedom from the stiff fabric choking him and taking his air. He moved his grip to pull at the curved cutaway wings on his collar. Father Figgins took a deep breath beside Prince Percy, a silent reminder to stop his fidgeting and movement.

The prince clasped his hands together at his waist, his nervous energy manifesting in the anxious wringing of his fingers. His gaze fixated on a painting adorning the lower dome vault ceiling, just above the aisle where Sister Ora made her procession. Ornate gilded carvings framed the artwork and cascaded down the balustrades and along the coffered ceiling, creating an ostentatious and rich ambiance to the church's entrance before opening into the heavenly high expanse of the cathedral's lofty heights.

Each of Sister Ora's steps echoed through the hall. The organ tune accompanying her march was full of deep, elongated notes. To Sister Ora, Prince Percy imagined it became the soundtrack to a death march. To him, the feeling was mutual.

The tension and dread in the room reached their peak as she stepped in front of the dais steps. Queen Onetta and King Ivan turned to her, standing in the pews on the side of the stage. Sister Ora's hesitation before her bow lasted too many breaths but was the only act of rebellion the bride offered.

With a graceful bow, she honored the king and queen and ascended the steps, the train of her dress ending in a puddle on the floor as she shuffled herself opposite her groom. Around them, the congregation held their breaths. No one dared voice their disapproval or question the betrothal. No one dared cough or clap.

Prince Percy clenched his jaw as he kept his head straight, looking just above where his ensnaring fate stood dressed in red. He prayed for a crazed outburst from his father, for His Majesty's descending state to reach its crescendo and interrupt the ceremony.

But the milky glass over King Ivan's eyes matched the heavy dose of the poppy's milk that coursed through his veins and kept his behavior reined in as Father Figgins began the ceremony.

"Your Highness?" Father Figgins whispered to the prince.

Prince Percy blinked and stared back at Father Figgins, mouthing the two words he was waiting for the prince to repeat.

Prince Percy cleared his throat. His voice was froggy and rough, filled with defeat and sadness. "I do."

The prince closed his lips into a thin line and glanced forward, taking in the sight of his bride again. The pair held one another's eyes, both devoid of the warmth and glimmer they had once known. Father Figgins' droning words wisped away in the moment, only returning to their minds when Prince Percy flickered his eyes away from hers and tightened his jaw again.

"I do." Sister Ora murmured. Her voice rough, too.

The pair quickly exchanged their rings with barely audible mumbles and with minimal touch.

Father Figgins beamed as Sister Ora finished placing the ring on Prince Percy's hand. "By virtue of the authority vested in me under the laws of the monarchy and the eyes of The One True, I now pronounce you husband and wife."

He turned to Prince Percy, his smile becoming a sneer in the young prince's eyes. "You may now kiss your bride."

Applause slowly filled the cathedral at the announcement, and the organ played its long and deep notes again. Prince Percy took a gentle step forward and gave a curt nod at Sister Ora. His heart raced as his eyes traced the curves of her full lips, imagining how soft they would feel against his. He banished the thoughts from his traitorous mind and forced himself to remember what she had done to him, to his family. He raised his hand and leaned forward as if to cup her face, only to hide them both behind it as their lips moved together.

Before they could kiss, Prince Percy turned his head away, allowing her lips to only burn the side of his mouth.

Prince Percy opened his bedchamber door. His eyes stayed attached to the floor as his new wife timidly shuffled through, her eyes also admiring the stonework at her feet. The newlywed prince felt nauseous despite only imbibing slightly in his cups at the dinner and reception.

Prince Percy's feet shuffled behind her as the door creaked and latched closed. As the latch clicked and the silence fell over them, she swallowed hard as her lead-filled feet moved her toward the bed.

No lady's maids or assistants followed them in the room to assist with their undressing; neither party desired to be around others any longer.

Prince Percy's bed chamber looked like someone had created a miniature Grand Hall of Archives and shoved a large canopy bed against the back wall out of need and last-minute remembrance.

A heavy bronze-and-glass telescope stood on a pedestal in front of the large bay window, centered on the far wall, its floor-to-ceiling doors leading out to a private terrace. An open door to the right of the room led to a smaller room of books and plush furniture, a space one could lounge and read in if the bedroom furniture did not suffice.

"There is a partition set up there for you to undress behind if you desire." The prince said, "I can undress out here while you change there. I have grown quite tired and would like to rest immediately."

"Of course," she replied, "but are we not meant to... consummate?"

Prince Percy sighed, "Meant to, yes, but I do not desire to, nor do you, I imagine."

She shrugged and left to stand behind the dressing curtain, "At least we are both on the same page on one topic."

Prince Percy felt a surprise jolt of pain at her lax words. He did not wish to touch her or be wed to her, so her rejection should not have struck any chord within him, but it did.

"Right," he said. The prince undressed quickly beside his bed while his wife undressed behind the partition. His sleeping trousers and long blouse hung loosely on his body, giving him back some of the freedom his ceremonial clothes had taken away.

Husband. Wife. A pained prince and his reluctant lady. Despite her being granted a lowly and in-paper-only title of Lady of the Court, Lady Ora was still the same woman he could not love or look at.

"Umm..." he heard her uncertainty despite her low tone, "shit."

"Are you alright?" he asked as he rolled the cuff of his sleeve.

"Well, it is just that dresses such as this require assistance with the corset and buttons, and I am without a lady's maid at the moment," Lady Ora grunted, and Prince Percy saw the partition move as she bumped into it. "Could you help?"

Prince Percy's eyes bulged, and he stuttered, "Yes, I mean, yes, I can go find a lady's maid or someone to-"

Lady Ora's head peeked out from behind the partition, "For hell's sake, it is a few buttons and some ties; you do not have to take the dress off of me."

Prince Percy forced the excitement that parts of him felt to stop at the thought of undressing her. His body straightened as he hushed the warmth in his chest.

"I know you hate me and wish not to be close to me, but please, could you help so we can please just put this day to an end?" she asked softly.

He swallowed and nodded, "Yes, of course."

As he stepped behind her, the partition hiding them from the rest of the room, Prince Percy ran his fingertips gently over his thumbs and closed his eyes as his heart beat loudly. He was not supposed to feel any of this. Not with her of all women.

He had worked hard to rid himself of any care for her. When she betrayed him and slept with Sir Loren, she showed him that his care was pointless and would never be reciprocated.

Prince Percy's eyes shot open as he remembered her other betrayal, the one to his family and the throne. The betrayal that was meant to weigh equally, if not more, on his heart than her betrayal with her body. Perhaps after his own betrayal, when he sent the Psalms to those wishing to dethrone his father, he had unconsciously let what she had done go.

If he pondered it too long, he would remember that they both acted with the same intent—to end the war and stop the tyranny, to create peace.

But he was meant to hate her.

"Your Highness, could you just loosen the ties and unbutton the hem?" Her soft voice broke the spell he found himself under as he stood a hair's breadth away from her. Her round eyes, so dark and full of emotion and expression, looked up at him from over her shoulder.

She smelt of cinnamon and sweet vanilla, of whiskey and wine.

The conflicted prince pulled at her corset strings, slowly loosening them so she could slip out of her dress. He ignored the sigh of relief she moaned as the corset came loose on her body. He ignored even more how that sound made him feel.

The buttons at the hem of her corseted top ran down her backside, ending just where her curves rounded the most. His hands hovered over the buttons.

"Red is a nice color on you," he found himself stupidly saying.

She laughed, "Thanks. I hate it."

"Oh," he said as he began to unbutton her dress.

"I prefer shades of dark jewels and greens." She huffed, "Not that I am allowed that color anymore, thanks to your mother."

The prince's fingers paused against the fabric around the last button, now undone. "I'm sorry," he softly said. He felt his body stepping closer to hers, but then he stopped.

"Goodnight," he abruptly said before turning and quickly leaving her to undress.

Later that night, after showing his wife the bed she could sleep in while he slept on the couch, Prince Percy found himself in his private privy, the door well locked and his mouth biting into his bicep to stifle his grunts and moans as his hand tightened around himself. He could not close his eyes as he found his pleasure, for each time he did, he imagined her face looking back at him as he stood behind her, her dress on the floor, and him inside her.

Chapter 47

The Odessian Dragons and foot soldiers made their place in the Crown Prince's army camp without asking for permission or waiting for acceptance from those already stationed there. The Britian army had left the outskirts of Clardin behind, but Ravenhall still stood a few quick days away and surrounded by Sebern and Ayeshire soldiers holding the land from a siege.

The army of gold and orange moved at a relaxed pace. Their finely chiseled desert horses pulled large contraptions carved of wood and forged with metal into the edges of camp, and began constructing their own tents. Black-ink tattoos adorned the skin of many of the fighters: marks for battles won and lives taken intertwined with many House sigils, family mottos, and crests. For those honored with the high ranking of Dragon, their bodies bore the winged beast.

In the homeland of Odessin, any person who lost their Dragon title through dishonor, if allowed to live, would face the fire to burn the mark of the dragon off their skin and carry their shame into the afterlife.

"You act as a dragon yourself, Kairos." The Odessian woman laughed as she stroked the long snout of her horse. The sorrel coat of Kairos shone in the sunlight as the Dragon rider patted her neck to calm her snorting and huffing. She unhooked the horse's bridle and removed the saddle, tossing it to her aid. She patted Kairos again, earning a happy flick of the mare's high tail, "Go, friend. Join the others in your roam and come back with the moon."

Kairos flicked her tail as she trotted off to the open field where the other Odessian horses roamed and rolled.

The woman rested an open hand over her heart and bowed at the neck to the Dragons around her, signaling her leave. They returned the gesture, and she quickly turned on her heel and moved gracefully through the camp.

She quickly approached the camp's center where a larger tent stood. She knew it housed the prince and his officers- Brits always laid their camps in the same fashion, making it easy for any enemy or ally to guide their way through the fabric and makeshift homes.

A Britian guard shouted at her as she hastily approached, both she and the guard moving a hand to the pommel of their blades.

"Report your name!" he shouted as he moved towards her. "Or you may not enter."

"Oh, hush," she said as she quickly swooped under his broad frame, his jutted elbow feeling the breeze of her hair as she swooped and turned. She pulled a small blade from her belt, tapping it at his lower back where the metal plates held a gap.

She did not cut or slice, her movement a simple warning to how he so easily left himself open to a kill shot.

"Poorly trained. If you were my guard, I would slaughter you myself," she said dismissively. His mouth lay agape as she threw open the tent flaps and stepped inside. Behind her, the other guard joined in storming into the tent after her.

Her complexion was a dark olive that had tanned in the harsh sun of the season. Bits of her black bangs clung to her forehead, the sweat of a long, tiresome travel wearing on them despite the bronze circlet she wore to keep her hair in place. She wore her hair pulled back, but unlike Dragons older than her, she was only honored with two war braids. Each began above her ears and swooped back together to the crown of her head, where they were joined before falling back into one united piece of dark brown, nearly black, strands.

She stood at the tent's entrance, her large hazel eyes carrying an aggression that startled many men, despite her soft, kind look.

She looked to Prince Elion and nodded once. "Husband."

The officers in the room shuffled and straightened their spines.

"Wife." Prince Elion nodded back.

"You called for aid," she raised her hands. "And here we are. Now, what is our plan?"

She strode forward, making her own place at the strategy table beside Prince Elion.

"Officers, this is Princess Easter Mete. Your future queen." Prince Elion could not help but let his mouth twitch into a snide smirk at his stunned men. "Some of you know her, most of you only know of her."

"Princess Easter Mete, Leader of the Sand Dragon Brigade, Heir to the Dark Dragon Blade, Lady of Dragon Tower, and future Queen of the Six Kingdoms," she corrected the prince. She raised her brow and her chin. Despite her stature compared to the soldiers around her, she managed quite adequately to look down upon them.

The prince nodded his head in apology. "My apologies, my lady."

She carelessly shrugged.

Discomfort suffocated the air. The officers in the room were unsure what could be discussed with her present, and the guards she had embarrassed outside stood at the tent's entrance, unsure whether to dismiss themselves or take her with them.

Prince Elion quickly noted the discomfort and dismissed the room, demanding privacy for him and his wife.

In the privacy of the tent, the pair shared a soft smile. They both placed their right hands on one another's shoulders and squeezed, then rested their foreheads together. An old greeting from Princess Easter's lands that was often done between family and friends.

"Please tell me that you have that delicious honey mead I enjoyed at our wedding somewhere in this tent," she said as they parted.

"I may have a bottle or two stashed in here somewhere," he smiled and turned, rummaging through his personal stash and finding an unlabeled bottle of golden magic. He pulled two empty glasses, possibly used and unclean, given their worn nature, from the scattering on the table and poured for the pair.

"So this," Prince Elion gestured, nodding at her armor and attire, "is what you have been studying? Battles and fighting?"

Princess Easter took a glass of the golden drink. "More or less, yes. The Citadel taught me much about war strategy and the intertwining of field tactics into court leadership. I thought," another careless shrug, "Why not apply what I learned about battle in the classroom in real life before I must apply what I've learned of court politics and ruling."

Prince Elion laughed under his breath. "Yes, why not? Going to war and becoming an officer, just like that."

"And let you have all the fun? That is not like me, princeling." She sat down in an abandoned chair, and Prince Elion followed suit in another.

He shook his head and took a long swig of wine. "Thank you for coming. But you must excuse my confusion at seeing your face and not that of another officer."

She took a long sip of the sweet honey wine, then let out a breath. "You know that this battle is not the only reason why I led my brigade here, Elion."

She flicked her eyes up at his, and he timidly met her look. "Straight to business, then. It is almost time, isn't it?"

She nodded. "While His Majesty... theoretically has much time left in his reign, we were to begin attempting to bear children this coming winter."

Prince Elion took in a deep inhale and held it. He rested his head on the back of his chair and slowly let the breath out. "While you are a wonderful woman, I have not been awaiting this time with hope and joy."

"And neither have I," she snorted. "You are much too small for me. I prefer my men more well-rounded."

"It is not an ideal time, Easter. War and all that." He waved his hand and shook his head.

"I believe this poor timing has more to it than this simple war," she said matter-of-factly.

Prince Elion lifted his head and looked at her. Solemness fell over his expression.

"We were warned via letterbird of what occurred. I'm sorry about your loss. I truly am. He made you happy, that much I knew."

Prince Elion chewed the inside of his cheek. He rubbed his face and then nodded quickly. "Yes. Yes, he did."

She leaned forward and rested a hand on his knee. "I hope one day you find another who will give you that again and more."

Prince Elion set his hand on top of hers. "And I you."

She loved Prince Elion; she always would. As odd as it may sound to some, she loved her arranged husband as a friend, a brother, never a lover. Neither of the two wished to ever love one another in any romantic way.

They shared the quiet for a moment before Princess Easter leaned back in her chair. "I have a plan to delay the inevitable, which is why my Dragons and I are here. My brigade and I will aid you in whatever battles come next, and when we are victorious, you and your officers will write to His Majesty explaining how my Dragons and I were instrumental to your success and how it could not have occurred without us. My fathers will support those statements and, knowing the portion of our marriage contract that comes due this next season, they will suggest a delay in any familial joining. After all, I cannot lead and aid in a war if I am with a child. And you, as your letters will say, cannot win the war without my help."

Prince Elion smirked and slowly shook his head. "Always with a plan, always scheming and plotting. You are going to be a terrifying queen."

She smiled crookedly. "Respected and beloved by all, but most of all, terrifying." She raised her glass to cheer. Their glasses clinked, and they both chuckled and sipped.

"The kingdom will know you as the Swordbearing Queen reincarnated," he jested.

"Aye, but they will know Queen Daiyin is still in her grave when they see me in a dress."

"That woman did hate dresses. I do not know why the history books cared so much to remind us of that fact so often," he laughed. "I'm surprised that during her dark ruling, she did not outlaw their wearing."

"It would not surprise me if she did, and history simply forgot it or chose not to write it down. The First King and First Queen did much after that war, perhaps too much to ensure their rule and loyalty," she said reflectively.

The sweet wine had quickly made its way into both their systems. Prince Elion wavered his head back and forth, enjoying another sip. "Perhaps not. After a war where loyalties sway, and hard decisions must be made, the victor must do anything to ensure the bloodshed ends."

Princess Easter gave him a disagreeing look over her raised glass.

"The First King and Queen made some hard decisions, but you must agree, they were not terrible in all they did." He gestured with his hands. "They gave your ancestors their freedom and broke their chains after the war."

And there it was. One of the many points of contention that would always keep a wall between them.

She angrily replied, "My people were not given their freedom. They earned it. A right they fought and died for that should have been granted by the very breath in their lungs, not granted by some king who turned out to be another monster with a crown."

Prince Elion adjusted his posture and realized his tipsy error. " I will not contest that."

He flicked his eyes up and down her body, then slowly raised them to her face. His eyes squinted as his head tilted as he ran over her words again, "From what we know, Lady Montarian raised her banners- quite poorly in secret- to fight against my family, to demand my father's crown- my future crown- claiming he was beginning to rule in tyranny, many also calling him a monster with a crown. One born from the history of freedom fighting and breaking chains could easily find empathy in a cause such as theirs... Do you find empathy in their cause?"

Princess Easter took a long pause and shared an unamused stare with the prince.

"While they may speak of chains, ours were literal where theirs are mind-made." Her eyes became lost in a foreign landscape, and her hand stiffly rubbed the handle of her wine glass, threatening to break it had its metal been able to shatter.

Her nostrils flared as her words were freed, "If you are asking where I stand in this war, Elion, let me be very clear. My people deserve to rule just as much as yours do. I deserve to rule and wear the crown I was promised. I will fight and sacrifice for my future throne—" she let the gold in her eyes flicker to life and match the glimmer of the candle flames around them, "and anyone who tries to stop me will become my enemy, no matter who they are or why they stand in my way. Through fire and flame, they will be ended, and the blood of the dragon will rule."

The flames died down in her heart as she felt Prince Elion submit to her fury. She inhaled more wine to steady her breathing, letting the drink be her excuse for a delayed response to his next query.

"Anyone? Even if it is the crowned lion you have joined Houses with? You would fight me then, Easter?"

"Such questions are stupid to ask, especially moments before we fight alongside one another. Do not sow division where there is currently unity, prince."

Chapter 48

Gerald's bare feet left deep imprints in the wet sand as he trudged ashore. He caught his breath as he made it onto drier sand; the hems of his pants rolled up well past his ankles, now speckled with golden grains of the southern beach known as the Crabs Claws. He ran his hand through his wavy golden hair, tussling it to shake out the water trapped in the locks as he approached the small group gathered on the beach.

"Anchor should keep it in place while we set up the test cannon. With the current, any debris should float east before hitting the shoreline, so we should be alright over here." He squinted as he looked out onto the waters at the small, abandoned boat bobbing in the light waves, "You think I took it out far enough?"

Ephraim looked at him, pausing their gaze at his broad shoulders and bare torso glistening with salty water droplets.

"Leaf, did you hear me?"

Ephraim shot back to reality. "Uhhh, yes, yes, I did."

"I know you worry, but I have full confidence that this will work. If anyone can accurately recreate Hellfire, it is you." Gerald gave them a half-smile, trying to offer comfort and familiarity despite the emotional wall now standing between the two.

"And worst-case scenario, I just do the king's job for him and accidentally kill all of us standing here." Ephraim's weary and sad spirit pulled at them from the depths of their soul. The edges of their words trembled, the exhaustion of their sorrow breaking each syllable apart.

They did not wish to be here, taking on this task that they pushed so hard against, and yet here they stood, perfecting a weapon of mass destruction for a bloodshed they wished to have no part in. Before Ephraim, there had lain two diverging paths that screamed their desires: one endangering the lives of their less experienced colleagues by allowing another to take on this deadly task, while the other compelling them to compromise their principles and go against their oath to cherish life and the very earth that gave it to them.

Lives would be lost either way, and Ephraim would prefer to bear the burden themself rather than allow another to be weighed down by the blood. And perhaps, taking lives could guarantee the saving of others.

When Ephraim wrote to Lady Montarian, confirming they would create Hellfire cannons and bombs for the war and asking her to send aid and supplies southeast to the beaches of the Crabs Claws, they had not expected such eager excitement from their fellow Herbalists or Gerald's accompaniment.

Ephraim had yet to decide if Gerald's acting as if nothing had ripped between them was a courtesy to their current mission or an annoyance to their emotions. They let their eyes fall as they walked to the small cannon pointed out to the sea and the small cannonball on the table beside it. They let out a slow breath and inspected the weapon for any cracks, dents, or defects—a task they had anxiously done at least a hundred times that day—before setting it back down with the small opening staring up at them.

"Prepare the cannon for use and position it towards the target." Ephraim's flat voice ordered. They focused on the opening of the cannonball, imagining burying their emotions inside it and then placing the stopper on top.

They set their shaking hands on the table and swallowed the hard dryness in their throat. Their voice shook as they whispered, "Lives will be lost regardless of what I do. But this is the right path. This must be the right path."

Their soul and conscience remained silent.

They firmed their feet on the sandy beach, feeling the warmth rise up from the grains and through their simple laced shoes. "Forgive us all, Mother," they pleaded to the earth beneath them.

The warmth of the sand and the sun on their back hummed through their body, a gentle and warm embrace that echoed understanding.

The gathered crew took their places: one loaded the small canvas bag of pre-measured gunpowder down the muzzle of the cannon's barrel, and Gerald checked the wind and the positioning of the boat. He ordered others to adjust the muzzle to the correct angle, and the remaining worked together to move it into position. After being satisfied with their tasks, the crew ran weighted chains throughout the cannon's wheels to weigh it down and hold it in place.

"Ready," Gerald called to Ephraim.

Ephraim stood straight and nodded slowly.

Their fingertips tingled as they moved their hands over the cannonball. The tingling prickled as they picked up the small vial of liquid—the final and most sensitive ingredient to Hellfire—and poured it into the opening. As they poured, the hard mass in their throat grew more solid and choked them, smothering the life from the hope and happiness that flowed through every inch of their being.

The power they felt at their fingertips grew as if it enjoyed the task ahead of them—as if it was a darkness that fed on the future souls that Ephraim would take from this realm.

Ephraim tried to hush it, but reminders of what the king's soldiers had done to their fellow citizens played through their mind. The gasping wind of soldiers' last breaths blew across their face—patients they could not save. Sister Ora's boisterous laughter carried on the wind, followed by the fear of never hearing it again. Their knowing that even if she survived, His Majesty would be so cruel as to ensure she could never laugh again fed into the crackling in their body.

Ephraim took a deep breath, their heart beating so hard it felt as if it would burst through their chest, and picked up the now-prepped cannonball with hands that barely managed to stop shaking. They slowly walked to where the cannon lay, glaring down at the weapon in their hand as they carefully stepped to the cannon base.

Sensations that now felt like lightning poured through their body.

Ephraim turned their unblinking gaze from the bomb in their hand to the small open door on the cannon. Because of Hellfire's volatility and delicate nature, the group had to modify a cannon to be loaded from the base instead of the neck, fearing that the impact of the cannonball rolling down the barrel and hitting the base of the ignition chamber would cause it to explode.

The scientists were anxious about the task ahead of them and carefully prepared for, considered, and analyzed every precaution, pause, and scenario that could occur. There was no room for mistakes with such an experiment, no space for carelessness.

Inside, a wad of cotton cloth was placed to create a tight fit of the cannonball in the barrel and ensure that, when ignited, a maximum amount of pressure would be created to launch it properly at its target. Ephraim slowly, through sweaty palms and nerves, set the bomb down in the nest and delicately removed their hands.

It was only after their touch left the sphere that they noticed they had not taken a true breath since picking it up.

Around them, they heard small exhales of relief escape their colleagues.

As Ephraim closed the door on the cannon, the crackling within them rattled with giddiness. They motioned for the pick stick to push through the touchhole to rupture the bag of gunpowder. After breaking open the powder bag, they stepped back and turned towards Gerald, nodding at him to light the long fuse he held and ignite the cannon.

As the fuse Gerald held sizzled with life, the slightest breeze fell over the beach again, barely enough to cool the heat on the group's faces but still strong enough to strike anxiety among the crew. While they all understood their careful nature was exaggerated and their movements could be less pristine when utilizing this weapon, none wished to test the limits of Hellfire's strength on their own mortality.

"Fire in the hole!" Gerald yelled as he stepped beside the cannon and transferred the flame he held to the massive iron weapon. After several excruciatingly long moments, the tense silence on the beach was filled by the sharp whoosh of the cannonball escaping the barrel.

Upon the crash of impact, the beauty of the crisp blue land-scape of the sea and the clear, cloudless sky was disrupted by sharp white flames engulfing the boat. The flames held on a singular blinking moment as pieces of debris attempted to float away before disappearing into nothingness in seconds.

The crew on the beach remained silent, unsure whether to cheer in celebration of their successful creation or mourn what this success meant.

The light breeze on the beach whistled again, and in it, Ephraim heard the dying shrieks of the victims this weapon would be used against. Their mind shouted angrily at the satisfied warmth running through their body.

They saw Gerald's shadow fall over them as he stepped beside Ephraim.

"Why did you come?" Ephraim mumbled; their eyes stuck on the horizon.

"Because I knew you'd need a friend. And even if I am not that anymore to you—" Gerald cleared his throat and shook his head, leaving his words unfinished. His breath caught and shook as he released it. "Shall we head back home today or tomorrow?"

"Today," Ephraim's voice cracked, "we can head back today."

Gerald set his hand on Ephraim's far shoulder, wrapping his hand around their back in comfort as they both continued to look out to the water.

"Ok," Gerald replied.

Waves crashed against the shore and pulled sand away as they receded back out to sea. Neither the wind nor the waves stopped the screaming in Ephraim's mind.

"A lifetime of work, now diminished down to this, to how I can best slaughter those ordered to raise their weapons against us." The life left Ephraim's eyes. "Just imagine the world we could have if we were gifted time to spend creating tools to bring us together instead of weapons to rip one another apart; what a world we would have."

They gave in to the darkness.

But they held onto the hope that they would someday emerge with light.

CHAPTER 49

The grey-speckled mare pranced around the ring; her long, slender legs moved swiftly to create a rhythmic sound. Her tail hung high behind her as she ran, and her coat shone in the sun. The handlers waved their flags to guide her, and she precisely followed their cues. Her long, slender head flicked, and her mane tossed as she thundered around the enclosure, her powerful hooves kicking up a cloud of dust that swirled in the air. She came to a sudden halt, skidding to a stop, and turned sharply, almost colliding with one of the handlers clad in a white thobe. Without missing a beat, she sprinted off again, running another lap around the ring.

Lady Ora rested a soft hand on the stone and wood fence, watching the animal let loose in front of her. The day had a chill, the last speckles of autumn falling away like the yellow and orange foliage that had finished its journey to death. Lady Ora pulled the dark cloak closer to herself, hiding the slight shiver that came over her as a breeze weaved through the open space.

She had been forbidden to wear green but still refused to wear the royal family's rich red. Her bell-sleeved cloak was a foggy grey, the edges trimmed in black thread sewn in a stem-stitched pattern with fishbone leaves growing from the twists of thread. The sleeves fell below her knees, where the skirt of her grey dress skimmed around her waist and fell gracefully to the floor.

Her free hand fiddled with the toggle, keeping the cloak closed around her chest.

"She is wild," Lady Ora said to Lord Shaital, standing beside her. Her whisper full of wonder and awe.

"Would you like her?" Lord Shaital asked, keeping his eyes on the mare.

Lady Ora's mouth fell open, and she tore her eyes from the horse for a moment. "I- why are you offering me one of your horses?"

Lord Shaital chuffed, "It is a wedding gift, my lady. Tradition dictates among noble houses that we are to gift one another luxurious things—horses, gold, jewels, and, in some instances, homes." He shrugged, "Meant to symbolize our happiness for the betrothed, but truly a symbol of our own posterity."

He turned to look down at her, her eyes still on the mare. "So, would you like her or another? We have plenty of others we could offer."

Lady Ora drummed her fingers on the fencing. She could not tear her gaze from the horse. She felt the wind running through her braided hair as if the white mane whipping in the wind were her own locks. The mare ran past them again, Lady Ora's eyes locking with the horses before the mare turned and continued her run.

"May I be brash, my lord?" Lady Ora asked.

Lord Shaital smiled. "Of course."

She turned to him, breaking her fascination with the mare. "What is it you are up to?"

"Excuse me?" He may have let himself look taken aback, but Lady Ora knew better by now.

She held her chin high. "Everyone in this city is playing at something, has some agenda, and you are no exception. You have offered me nothing but kindness, empathy, and care since you arrived. So what is it you are playing at?"

He looked at her with astonishment. Fake astonishment, and they both knew it.

"Did you ever think that maybe my husband and I offer you those things because you deserve them?"

Her response came fast and cracked like one of the horse trainer's whips. "What benefit do you get for treating me with kindness?"

Lord Shaital laughed and nodded his head at the running mare. "It appears you and the mare have more in common than your coat color, my lady. You are as wild and sharp as she."

The mare whinnied and reared before settling back onto the ground, kicking up more dust as she paced backward and forward in the far corner. Handlers waved their flags and hands to corral her into the pen so she could be bridled and taken back to the royal stables behind them.

The handlers spoke words meant to calm the mare as they enclosed on her. She kicked at one that approached from behind her. The dock of her tail flicked in agitation as she shooed the men away, darting for a path between them and forcing them to let her continue to run free.

"I am but a pawn in this game of nobility, my lord. I have had my quarrels with such things and accepted them. So," she again jutted her chin, "tell me what it is you are up to. If it is to my advantage as well as yours, then move forward with whatever plan you have brewing. You have my consent. But if it is not to my benefit, I will add your House to my list of ones—" she corrected her words, "You are not the only one with vengeance burning in their eyes, my lord. I see it in yours most of all."

Lord Shaital slowly tilted his head, a pleased smile crawled across his face. "My my. It seems there is much more to you than what you allow to show on the surface."

"Only a woman so weak and stupid would show this world who she truly is." She stepped back and turned to leave, prompting her guards to step forward, "And I will never allow myself to be so vulnerable again. I will take the mare, my lord, and I give you my deepest gratitude for this gift."

She flicked her eyes at him. "Many noble families also gift one another items of luxury as a bribe and a thing to hold over another's head. I learned such basic things in my early schooling. I am grateful you would not stoop to such basic and overused manipulation tactics. We are both above that now, aren't we?"

Only when Lady Ora disappeared behind her wall of armor did her mare calm and return to the stables of her own will.

Princess Arminda stepped out of the hallway's shadowed cover and entered the courtyard. Her gaze fell on her mother, Queen Onetta, seated on a stone bench with a look of calm contentment on her face. The queen's usual steely and cold demeanor had softened, her expression gone warm, as she watched her youngest daughter, Princess Kalia, in her autumn lessons with her governess nearby.

A faint smile graced the queen's lips, and for the first time in what felt like an eternity, Princess Arminda felt the subtle pang of longing wash over her. Princess Arminda's steps slowed as she took in her mother's warmth—a feeling she could not recall being gifted to her recently or perhaps ever. The queen had always held an otherworldly softness for Princess Kalia that neither Princess Arminda nor her brothers had known.

It took little thought to figure out why the youngest princess was set apart from the rest of the children in the queen's heart. Princess Arminda knew; she had known since she was young and had taken detailed note of her younger sister's darker complexion, richer hair, and different eyes, none of which looked like the traits of the other Scott children.

With a quiet inhale, she pushed those feelings down and approached her mother. Only the slightest chill of the upcoming winter air brushed her cheeks—it would surprise many if the king's city saw frost or snow. Most winters, they only saw a slight chill in the air, with a rare snowflake spotted throughout history before it quickly melted away.

As she made her way to the bench, she cleared her throat and bowed her head, "Hello, mother."

"Arminda." The queen barely turned to meet her gaze, her focus still on Princess Kalia, her smile kind and unreserved. A treasure Princess Arminda wished to pirate for herself.

Princess Arminda nodded towards her little sister and governess, "I see Kalia is doing well with her winter studies. Do you think she will be taught well enough to begin dining and socializing with the family this holiday season?"

Queen Onetta inhaled and let her breath out slowly, still watching Princess Kalia across the courtyard, "No, she will not. I want to give her more time before all of that must begin for her."

Princess Arminda halted her jaw before it fell open or let out a scoff. "When I was her age, I had already come out into society." Her eyes slitted as she looked at her mother with annoyance and sparks of frustration. She turned her emotions into embers and let the breeze carry them away before her mother could see.

"Times are different now, Arminda. And she does not need to be out in society so young."

But there was a need for me at only eight? The princess thought before politely smiling and saying, "You're right, mother. She deserves to be a little girl for a bit longer. All girls deserve that."

"Mmm," the queen said. Princess Arminda knew she was half listening if that. Her mother was often found inside her head these days, especially since the king had begun to fall ill and Lord Tyrrian had come to stay in the castle in her mother's bed when they thought no one was watching. Her mother had never been one to be so subtle, a trait Princess Arminda learned quickly from.

"Mother..."

"Yes?" another absent-minded reply.

"Percy is wed now."

"Yes, he is."

Princess Arminda's heart sank as she met her mother's eyes, the aching desire to share her feelings suffocating under the weight of silence. They turned away from each other, trapped in the unrelenting storm of unvoiced sorrows, as the world continued to rush past them.

"Come, Arminda. Let us stretch our legs and speak." The queen firmly ended the silence as she stood and began a slow promenade around the courtyard.

The two royal women walked side-by-side, their mixture of guards watching the perimeter of the space while a set followed directly behind them as they moved down the interweaving stone paths.

"Percy is wed now, which means I am next." Princess Arminda sighed and let sadness cover her expression. Her eyes fell to the ground they walked upon, "Have you and father decided what you will do with me? Which ally will I marry? Which minor lord will gain a new title because of me?"

"It is tiring, I know. Waiting around to see who you will be forced to marry so you can finally plan your life. Finally start to become who you can be in the marriage." The queen offered no kindness or comfort, no soft touch or shared look, but Princess Arminda still heard understanding in her mother's words. And that, she thought, was something she could have and hold onto.

At least it was something.

"Will my inheritance of Thelimor's throne change anything regarding the bartering for my hand?"

"Perhaps, but Percy still must decide if he wishes to take it or not." The queen ran her eyes up and down the sculpted statue centered in the courtyard, their pathway curving around its base.

Each courtyard corner held a grand stone statue of one of the four Alvarian siblings who conquered the land. Still, those statues, which were as old as the forging of the Golden City that Isilria once was, were not as giant as the one the queen and princess now stood in front of. The First King's stone face looked down upon the princess and queen from where he sat mounted on his war horse, his sword drawn, and his face contorted in heroic anger.

Princess Arminda crinkled her eyes at her mother and twisted her face in innocent curiosity as she lied. "I just assumed he had turned it down since nothing was said at the wedding."

She knew he had spoken with their mother in a heated conversation before the wedding and turned down the title before his wedding day. She knew her mother was still lying to her. But she could not see why.

Queen Onetta shook her head and walked around the statue. "No, he has yet to say anything."

Their path crossed where Princess Kalia and her governess sat in a lesson. Princess Arminda watched her little sister as the governess painstakingly ran through the words and noble names of the various houses of the continent with the young girl, "May I be brash with a question?"

"Of course."

The princess thought carefully over her words despite her desire to use them to sting, to break her facade, to snarl and bite at the woman she emulated—the woman whose attention and praise she would kill to have. Princess Arminda glanced back over to Princess Kalia. She did not hate her little sister, but she envied the childhood she got to have—the pawn she was not molded to be—yet.

"Arminda–"

Princess Arminda shook her head and turned back to her mother. "Apologies, mother."

"Where is your mind these da'es? Since your brother's wedding, you have been absent often– both in mind and body." Queen Onetta leaned into her daughter, "Your uncle told me that you took part in the smoke and cacao ceremony– did you see something during it that startled you? The herbs used in those ceremonies can lead to odd hallucinations and visions."

Princess Arminda cleared her throat and did what she had always done. She turned the truth into a mangled lie mixed with pain and deception to get what she desired. "I saw—" she gulped and pulled her shoulders inward, slouching and looking to the ground, "nothing. I saw nothing, mother."

The queen stepped closer to her.

She smiled weakly at her mother and let wetness gather in her eyes, "I promise. It was nothing."

"Arminda," the queen softly said, reaching over and wiping a tear from Princess Arminda's cheek as it fell. "Save the tears for someone they will work on. I know what you crave and desire. I know you watch rooms much closer than the men leading in them." She cupped her daughter's face and let out a small breath, "You cannot play this game against me. Not when I am the one who taught you the rules."

She dropped her hand from Princess Arminda's face, the tears now dried and the act falling off, "And next time, perhaps do not divulge that you know information that has yet to be shared. Percy has turned down the title to Thelimor, yes, but no one has spoken of it outside of he and I's private conversation."

For a moment, Arminda faltered. She had thought herself clever, thought she had learned the rules well enough to out-maneuver her mother. But the queen had already seen through her before Princess Arminda could gain even a crumb of information, a half step of advantage. Had her mother always seen through her act each time the princess batted her eyelashes?

"Then why–"

Queen Onetta raised one finger to silence her. "There are much bigger things at play in this kingdom right now, darling. Give it time to grow, the changes time to settle, and then push your way into your rightful place in it. I tell you this as a warning, darling. I see the moves you make, for they are the same I did when I was just a girl like you."

Queen Onetta gave her daughter an inkling of the love and tenderness the princess craved. The queen returned her hand to her daughter's cheek and kissed Princess Arminda's forehead, "You must watch who else you play this game with; not all who see it will let you keep your head."

Good, Princess Arminda thought, let her believe she knows of what I wish for.

CHAPTER 50

Madam Fury trekked through the dark tunnels underneath The Black Fingers. Glass and metal lanterns adorned the walls every dozen steps, adding only small spots of light throughout the space, just enough to guide those familiar with the twists and turns beneath the burnt dirt. Her steps were confident and sure; she knew which turns to take and where small gusts of wind might blow out the pillar of flame she held.

In a time since forgotten, a massive crater had been lit aflame and burned for over one hundred seventy epochs. The fires within it had taken the blended landscape and turned it into what became The Black Fingers, a land of stone columns, caves, and cold desert nothingness. Natural and man-made tunnels, vegetation, and desert grass caught fire as the crater burned, consuming everything within the flames' reach and burning the lands from underneath.

By dragon fire or man-made flames, the stories still disagree on what had lit the land.

The ending of the burning was seen as a sign from The One True that the continent had finally begun to move in the right direction. But just like the unity of the Rominia-Scott Houses, the regrowth that had begun during The Age of Unity did not last long, and only small seedlings and patches of grass as brown as the mountain sands were birthed from the black soil.

And so, while the rest of the continent rebuilt above ground, Odessin rebuilt what was burned beneath in secret and in silence.

They built the True Citadel of Odessin, the one so few knew existed.

Madam Fury's rich orange cape flowed behind her in a breeze she created with her swift stepping. On her shoulders were metal scales of dark bronze that formed a horned cap on each shoulder, reminiscent of the horns and spikes of the dragons whose blood coursed in her veins.

Her weapons clinked lightly against one another with each movement of her hips. The dark belt cinched together the dark leather clothing she wore under the cover of the cape.

Madam Fury took another turn, moving through the last steps of the corridor and into the grand chamber hidden beneath the land that once burned. She nodded in greeting to the other Odessians roaming the hall.

No words were spoken, the silence not deafening but comforting.

On either side of her head, she wore three heavy braids, each of the total six ran along the sides of her scalp and fell down her back. An additional braid of finer hairs framed her face and fell in front of her ears. Unbraided hair atop her scalp was styled into a bump on her crown before it became a heavy braid falling down her back.

While she wore her war braids proudly, she did not come to shed blood, but to pay tribute and honor. Even a woman born to make others bleed knew when to halt her sword.

The underground hall rivaled that of the grandest castle. Pillars several stories tall were carved in the stone and told tales of old leaders, Seers, and dragons. Stalactites had been carved into ornate art- some as daggers and swords, others as falling stars or ornate spears, some simply sanded down and rounded off to form textured trim on the ceilings and walls.

The carved stone bodies of past lords and ladies stood firmly holding on to symbols of their past reigns and formed pillars throughout the hall: broken chains were held by those who led the Odessian people to freedom, dragons sat behind those who once rode the beasts, orbs and scrying bowls were held those who saw the future and led their people towards their glory.

Metal-forged rails helped keep structures in place and created staircases and partitions, and below Madam Fury's feet, if one bent down to listen, the sounds of trickling and rushing water would sing to them.

A ring of burning candles, several deep, framed a large, circular stone dais that was centered prominently in the space. Stone worn by bent knees encircled its edges. Madam Fury set her candle on the shrine to join the others and kneeled, bowing her head at what lay in the flames.

A hard, oval stone, its top narrow and nearly pointed, was heated by the fire burning around it. The stone was a deep, earthy orange with natural stripes and waves of deep brown—coins of gold and gems of all colors lay around the flames and the ancient egg.

Madam Fury unloaded the Dragon pins from the pouch at her side, the clinking of the metal echoing up the balustrades of the tall hall.

"For you, child of Riomiar." Madam Fury whispered as the last of the pins fell into the pile of tributes and offerings. She bowed her head. "Men of flesh and bone unworthy of your honor, sacrificed in your name. I ask forgiveness for not seeing through their facades and bringing dishonor to the memory of your kind by naming them Dragons."

She bowed her head deeper until her forehead rested on the warm stone. "For you, god of fire and flesh, I owe my life."

Shuffling fabric and a shifting body gave Madam Fury cause to raise her head and turn to the one who joined her.

"Lady Silu." Madam Fury said, seeing Lord Shaital Pathis' blood daughter kneeling beside her. "My gratitude for meeting me here."

"Of course, Madam." Lady Silu Pathis wore a delicate marigold-yellow dress, the fabric soft and the top layer sheer, showing her fawn-beige skin beneath the long, thin sleeves and skirts. Her father's caramel hair was darker on her, more copper than his. Lady Silu lit an incense stick on one of the candles, blowing out the flame and letting the incense smoke in one of the many tiny holes on the dais.

"I am surprised to see you light an offering to the egg, my lady." Madam Fury said, her eyes stuck forward at the stone.

"I light it out of respect for my heritage," she nodded to the side and shifted her eyes to Madam Fury, "to our heritage."

Madam Fury lit her own incense, blowing out the flame and setting it beside Lady Silu's.

Lady Silu continued. "It has been nearly seven hundred epochs since Riomiar had drowned in the sea. If it has not hatched by now, one would not be blasphemous to believe it may never."

Madam Fury shot her head at Silu. "Dare not speak of such things in front of a dragon unless you wish us to be its first meal when it hatches."

She laughed, "Do you know how many simple stones we find within these lands of similar pattern and differing size and shape?"

Madam Fury huffed in anger. "We will not continue this talk."

"Very well," Lady Silu replied.

Footsteps shuffled around them while Madam Fury gathered herself.

"You are a keeper of knowledge, my lady, and knowledge is what my Dragons and I need. The South will soon engulf itself as the North once did, beginning another civil war that eventually will rise to our lands. We have already been dragged into the south, distracting us from what we deserve to take here and what we must do."

"If knowledge is what you seek, then I must ask my own inquiries, Madam."

She sighed and adjusted the weight on her knees. "I would expect nothing less from a woman of your caliber."

Lady Silu smirked at the comment. "Why must we continue the fruitless battles in the Holy Lands when, in due time, my half-sister will become our queen and can simply grant the lands back to our people?"

"What if she is killed in battle? She has now gone to her husband's army with her Dragons to lead with him. If not killed, what if she and the prince lose and the king is usurped? Our enemies would not simply grant us the land when they win, given our alliance with those they wish to take from power," retorted Madam Fury.

"When they win?" Lady Silu cocked a brow.

"You know of what I speak. And you know my concerns over the future of this war are not to be ignored." Madam Fury hissed and leaned to her to avoid her words from echoing too far. "You have your own inquiries, and I have mine. What if they win, and a peaceful way to grant our lands back to us fails?"

"Yes, and what if the earth were to crack open and swallow us whole? What then?" Lady Silu turned to her, the corner of her mouth cocked up, "These strips of riverrun land are not the true battle, and neither is the distraction in the south. Come, Madam."

Lady Silu stood and turned, no hesitation in her leave, knowing Madam Fury would follow behind without pause. She led them past others dressed in similar soft yellow garb as Lady Silu. Many were gathered in their quiet groups, talking so low the empty air did not catch any echoes. Others sat or stood in solitude, peering down at parchments or small bowls of water or sand on carved stands.

Lady Silu spoke again, "My sister, as prideful and sure as she is, will find her way to be queen. If she has to slit the throat of her prince at the end of a lost battle and marry a usurper, she will, just as she will fight alongside the prince to ensure they are crowned. Our people will never accept defeat or chains again, Madam. Ruling and power are in our blood. Our Dragonblood"

"Yes, but—"

"Shhhh." Lady Silu calmly hushed her.

They reached a stone table with open scrolls and books, organized in perfect squares and cleanly pressed free of wrinkles. Lady Silu nodded her head at the table and gestured with her arm.

"You need not worry of Odessin's loss. We will not lose what is precious to us. Our eyes across the kingdom have gathered much information for our country, as they always have. The Guild Lord in Ryanar is inciting his own petty fighting against the king, threatening to allow the pirates freedom to steal and pillage any ship with the king's banners, charging double the port fees to his ships, and triple the boarding fees to His Majesty's sailors.

"What a shame my fathers cannot do anything to stop it, try as they might," she smirked. "Across our burned lands, the dowager Lord Lisarian is working to divide his own house despite no longer holding any station. We chose him to marry the late lady, knowing no matter what occurred, so long as he breathed, Odessin would have dutiful eyes in neutral lands. And you paid such a helpful visit there, too."

Madam Fury nodded and grunted, showing Lady Silu she knew of what was occurring at Broken Tower.

"The Dowager Lord can do much damage without power if he causes those around him to question his son's agency and ability to control his own House." Lady Silu continued.

Madam Fury replied, "Lord Lisarian asserted his authority quite well on the battlefield and over at the border camp. He likely knows of the damage his father's deceit could do if he does not act and remind all who holds the title."

Lady Silu nodded, casting a glance around the room at the other Keepers. "Yes, our network saw that as well."

"What else?"

She tapped her finger on the map over House Torrin. "Lady Torrin is doing her best to rehouse and lend aid to those who have left the cities around the Grovelands and Lake Lahere to seek shelter away from any upcoming battle. Her babe grows restless in her belly, and she battles with herself on many heartbreaks with her old home."

She took a pause.

"And all the way in the reborn Golden City," she ran her fingers across the map to the outline of Isilria- the King's City, "is a king going mad."

Madam Fury cocked a brow. Lady Silu nodded and continued, "He and his Council have done their best to keep it quiet, going so far as to shield him from the public, keep him as silent as they can in meetings our lords attend, and to kill, or keep from flying, all the birds not kept by his royal messengers."

"But our lords have sent their own messages north?" Madam Fury questioned.

"All the messages our Lords have sent from the king's castle have been monitored, which is why they have contained useless information." She lifted her eyes, "All the ones sent by bird, that is. His Majesty pays little attention to those dressed in servant rags who come and go on errands throughout the city."

Madam Fury took note of the mass of papers Lady Silu had gathered, messages from her information network around the kingdom. She knew there was much more than Lady Silu had to say about the kingdom's happenings.

"Lady Silu, I appreciate your thoroughness, but the true information I seek is what your Seers have found to be our path to finally take back our lands and rid ourselves of those barbarians. And finally bring about the new age. The Age of Dragons."

Lady Silu nodded, understanding Madam Fury's light impatience and desire to learn what she came for.

"We need to fracture our northern enemies. Craigie has stood too long and spilled too much of our blood and tainted the world with their fighting. We must also weaken the Houses that would aid them if we were to lay them to waste." She ran her fingers down the map, over House Lisarian and House Torrin's homes. "Drive those Houses to such distraction and anger that they lose all logic, all thought, all care about what we do here. Fracture them. And then, we wait."

"And how would you suggest we do that, Lady Silu?" Madam Fury asked.

Lady Silu once again looked about the room, her glances pausing on each person standing in front of the raised bowls of water and sand, their fingers drawing patterns in the sand and pouring vials of tinctures into the waters, "The Seers have many ideas. Many end with the same outcome. Others end with teetering fates that hang by delicate threads even I may not be able to control."

"What is the outcome that many end with?"

"Total destruction of this kingdom as we know it. For the Psalms, the king hid from us to come to life on a catastrophic scale. For the age of man to end and be reborn, as the Psalms of Fire and Fury state. There are many interpretations of old words and poetically written prophecies, so many bent to the will of man over time, influenced by ambitions."

Madam Fury shifted. "There is no other way but to allow the prophecies from the age of dragons to come to life? Lady Silu, while I prefer to stake my claims on the battlefield, is there not a way we could gain what we desire without so much loss?"

Lady Silu ran her fingers delicately across a bowl of scrying water on her table, sending small ripples across the surface that met one another on the stone bowl's edge. "We could always give a few more eons of political bargaining a try." she said, then shook her head, "But to change the very fabric of time, one must not politely ask, but demand."

Chapter 51

L ady Catherin Torrin held her husband's Lord's Council in her grasp. Not that she needed to grip them so tightly, but these days, she felt her resolve and control slipping as her hormones raged with the babe inside of her, and her anxiety increased with each passing day of this war.

"My husband promised these people refuge under our banners, and we will not turn them away out of fear or anger," she firmly addressed them. "We do not have to let them into these walls or these meetings, but we do have to— we must— let them within our borders and show them safety."

She only slashed every few words with hard emphasis, not needing to shout or beg them for their agreement, only needing to remind them of what their country stood for.

"We agree, but..." Sebern's Master of Coin tilted his head back and forth as if his head were the scales he balanced each day. "There is a cost we worry about, especially knowing our trade with Britia is now non-existent, and Ayeshire likely will not have much to trade this season, given the attack that may soon ruin their lands."

"Our lands are fit for good huntin', even through the cold season. Where we cannot feed them grain and fruits, we shall feed them meat. My people," she did not let the sad flicker on her face stay for even a moment, "spent many long winters in the North livin' off of the blood of the land and little else. When reserves run dry, we hunt, we ration, we survive."

"Perhaps we..." she shook her head and let the words disappear. An idea brewed in her mind. If their stores of food from the season and final harvest were not enough, and they could not trade with Britia as they once had...

It wouldn't work. It would be fruitless.

"Perhaps what, my lady?" said the court's High Scholar, an elderly woman draped in robes in the color of the court. Her thick white hair, all color drained from it over her long life, fell down her back and over the cowl around her neck. She cocked her head, "Perhaps we ask the North for aid?"

It always startled Lady Catherin how Mother Yennen could do that—guess what she was thinking, finish her sentences for her, and solve problems before they were spoken.

Lady Catherin's hands were held together in front of her where she stood, having tried to sit in comfort in the meeting only to feel her ribs and spine ambushed and assaulted by her babe each time she settled in her chair. She let her hands fall apart and open in front of her as she timidly nodded to the Lord's Council.

"We have talked for many ages since my husband took the lordship about makin' amends and attemptin' to rekindle our

Houses... perhaps now is the time," the Lady of Sebern said, letting her Northern accent come out more.

Lady Catherin's eyes flicked to Mother Yennen before scanning the room. Mother Yennen had quite impressive foresight and intuition, though some days Lady Catherin wondered whether it was something unnatural that enabled the elderly advisor to provide such exquisite counsel.

Mother Yennen's eyes watched the ceiling and the flames of the chandelier above them, her lips pursed into a thin line as she contemplated. The rest of the Lord's Council who stayed at the castle, Lord Bentin, the Lord's Hand, and Master Sandoval, the Master of Coin, were not shy in how they directed their attention to the women in the room to provide their insights first.

This Council has come far since my husband's father ruled over them all. Lady Catherin thought.

Mother Yennen nodded, "Perhaps it is time to rekindle with the North; given Lady Lisarian of Broken Tower's Northern lineage and how we ally ourselves with the crown's enemies, it may not be fruitless."

Mother Yennen did not know, although Lady Catherin thought perhaps she had managed to find out, that they also allied themselves with the man that Lady Katherine wished vengeance upon, the man who turned the Battle of Broken Tower into an infamous and dangerous tale to talk of. Mother Yennen had not been on the Lord's Council when Broken Tower occurred, but Lord Bentin and Master Sandoval had.

Lady Catherin looked to the two men, "And what say you?"

Lord Bentin sighed, "I have little faith in Craigie ever coming to our aid after our histories changed with one another, but these are new times, and with that, new desires are born. It would not hurt to see what payment Craigie may request if we ask for aid."

Master Sandoval nodded in agreement.

There had been a letter Lady Catherin had never finished that she had wished to send to Lady Kathilla, her former sister through friendship and sister through marriage. The letter was an olive branch and confession of her broken heart after all this time away from one another.

She could not send it, not now that her country would ask Lady Kathilla's for aid. If she did, Lady Catherin knew that her former sister-in-law would not see her words for what they were- a genuine apology and wish for amends- but she would see them as a tactic to manipulate her into giving in to their request.

Lady Catherin held onto her desires and heartbreak a little longer, knowing someday she could try to rebuild what she had lost with the woman she had grown up with and the family she had lost. But for now, she could not tell Lady Kathilla all she wished.

Lady Catherin rubbed her stomach where her unborn daughter grew fiercer every day. Maybe another time would be best to ask for forgiveness.

Maybe another day, she could tell Lady Kathilla everything she regretted.

Chapter 52

"Do you know when you will die?" Elder Aelan asked.

"Soon. Long before the war in the South ends." Lady Kathilla replied from where she sat opposite the elders of Craigie. "But our people will know freedom," she nodded solemnly, "I just will not live to see it."

"Your blood has always been birthed for sacrifice." Seer Feriae nodded, looking in Lady Kathilla's direction but not directly at her. "It has taken many generations for the gods to call on your blood again. Sir Wallace knew his fate as well."

Lady Kathilla's eyes shot up at the elder Seer, "Sir Wallace knew he would die in the Great Civil War?"

A pleasant smile fell on Seer Feriae's hard-aged face, "He knew well before he first called for our freedom. He ran into each battle knowin' his death would come, but so would our freedom because of it."

"But we lost the war and gained no freedom." Lady Kathilla countered.

The shadows within the dark and fire-lit room glared down on the group gathered within the sacred elder hall. This was not a space meant for politics and arguing, but for discussions of fate and destiny. It was holy, as were the whispering woods; their ancestors built the tiny village of Thindell within.

In the small northern village of Thindell, nestled between the boughs of the Forest of Whispers, magic and the old ways held more weight than any king-made rule or law.

The Edgel clan and their warriors had followed the orders of the Lisarian bannermen and returned to their lands. They picked up their down-beaten warriors who had been removed from the Odessians' camps they had overthrown and found themselves in the ancient village of elders and seers, hoping, perhaps, that their return to the old ways would be better blessed than the path they had forged recently.

"Ahh, yes, but he saw the far-off future, many, many generations after his, livin' in their own lands under their own rule." Seer Feriae's foggy left eye stared at Lady Kathilla; her right eye had turned pure white long ago, "Some believe he saw you."

Lady Kathilla shot up out of her chair, "And you kept this from me?"

Seer Feriae rocked back and forth in her chair, "It was not our vision to share with you, our queen, not until you knew yours. And there was no certainty behind our thoughts, just hope."

Elder Brenainn added, "What is important for us to know?" He leaned forward. "What will you choose to do with your vision?" With what the fire of the vale showed you?"

Elder Aelan spoke up again, their voice stern, "Tell us in detail what the fire showed you as you walked through it."

"Do you not trust me to decipher what the gods themselves have told me of my fate?" Lady Kathilla argued, still standing.

Elder Aelan clasped their hands, the flickering firelight from the pit at the center of their round table casting a glimmer on their shaved head. "For one who has come to seek our guidance and forgiveness, you speak to us with much venom, especially so in this sacred hall you disrespect with your shouting."

Lady Kathilla bowed her head in apology and returned to her seat at the round Elder's table. She watched the flames in the pit, internally willing them to play out their story again for those gathered so she did not have to speak it.

"It happened so quickly- many things danced across the flames and showed themselves to me. A queen's crowning, but her face blurred."

"Lady Belva has been crowned Queen of the People by those she fights to free; perhaps it was that." Elder Brenainn speculated.

Lady Kathilla shrugged in uncertainty. Sometimes visions provided insight into things already unfolding, and other times, into events yet to come. "A dark tower crumblin' as bodies fell from its windows. Ghost ships sailin' below a black sky. A blade in my body." She moved her hand to rest on her chest, where she had felt the blade in the flames. "One that felt familiar to me. I do not know how, but I knew the blade that pierced me and took my life."

She looked up at the Elders and tried to blink away the glisten in her eyes, "But then I saw it. A white flower- a snowdrop-

bloomin' in the cracks of frozen earth. And I knew what it meant for all of us."

The Elders looked at one another and nodded in agreement; the symbolism was clear to their knowing eyes. The white snowdrop flower appeared in many tales of heroes and villains—a white flower that bloomed with its petals facing the ground, but those who encountered it knew to look up—to hope. Snowdrop flowers often bloomed in dreams and in real places where rebirth and new beginnings were on the rise. They bloomed in spring, bringing with it the renewal of the lands after death.

Lady Kathilla swallowed and shuddered, "I do not wish to die. I wish to see the world I have fought so long for, that my ancestors have fought for." She held a pause so long that worry fell over the Elders, "But if my death grants our people our freedom, I will fall on my own blade for it."

Relief walked through the room, followed by contemplative silence.

"No one is to know of this." Elder Brenainn shook his head as he reflected on her visions, "We must let the world play out as it shall. If too many know, too many will interfere or change course, forcing this vision and destiny to fall to ash."

Agreeing "ayes" were spoken by all before another long silence was held. It was the stoicism of Elder Aelan that broke the crackles of the fire.

"Freedom or death." The elder said the words that the people of Craigie spoke between one another, a casual modification of their official words: Freedom, honor, glory.

A reminder for their people that death was preferred over chains, that freedom was the virtue worth dying for.

That if one must choose, death would be a welcome sacrifice for freedom.

"Freedom or death." Lady Kathilla said, accepting her fate.

Barron walked down the frost-dusted forest path, brushing branches of weighed-down pine out of his path. The dilapidated shed came quickly into sight, the winter-worn wood of its door and structure blending it into the woody surroundings. He did not need to knock on the Elder Seer's door to let her know he had come down her path in the middle of the night. As he raised his hand to announce his presence, a creaking voice from the other side ushered him in.

"Come in, young lordling; you are a bit later than I expected."

He pushed open the broken wooden door and stepped inside. "I am no lordling, m'lady."

"Neither are you a king." Her large left eye blinked at him several times while her milky white right eye did not move. "Well, not yet."

Seer Feriae gestured a hand out for him to sit opposite her, a place setting already awaiting him. A small cup void of contents sat next to a small bowl of tea leaves. As he sat, the kettle on the fire rang out.

"You see me becoming a king? "He asked with curious excitement over the kettle's whistle.

The Seer hobbled over to the fire to take the kettle off the flame. "I see many things for you, as I have for many curious noble children across this continent. And since the day you were born, red wolf, I have seen much that could happen with you– or because of you."

"What have you seen of me?"

She set the kettle in front of him and shook her head. "Not all I see is meant for mere mortal eyes, white wolf. And much of what I have seen has come true or has been avoided by choices the stars and gods did not predict or believe or to choose."

"Like what?" his already gruff voice became more hostile and demanding as she seesawed through her words. Seers never spoke directly, and he always hated that about them.

Seer Feriae folded her hands on the table as she sat. "Like you letting your sister live that day on the lake when you were but a boy, and you could have simply pushed her farther in. You knew she could not swim, and the water would chill her to the bone in but a moment."

Barron's eyes bulged, but he spoke no response.

"Ahh," she let out a small laugh, "I knew you were resistant, but you came anyway. You could not help but hope there was some truth to the elders' folklore you still treat as mythos. I knew one small push would remind you of our ancient ways, red wolf."

"Why do you keep calling me that?" he gruffed in annoyance.

She smiled with her teeth, the gaps in her mouth hiding secrets. "In time, you will know."

"I must know what you see in my future. If you see…" he clenched and unclenched his fists on his lap.

"If I see you becoming King of the North… or the realm?"

Barron kept quiet, unable to decide if his silence was due to embarrassment and shame or something else.

"You must pour the tea yourself for me to See your future best." She gestured at the kettle, now calm but still steaming. "Pour the leaves first, then the water."

Barron hesitated but did as he was asked. He looked down at the cup, then up at her. "Now, what do I do?"

"Bring it here to me."

He gently set the cup in front of her and stood by her side as she rested her hands around its warmth. The light ceramic had been stained by past readings, and lines were carved into it, marking sections where the leaves may fall. The seer ignored his presence and looked into the cup. She swirled it gently on the table before quickly and without care throwing the tea out onto the floor at her feet.

Barron jumped back a half step as the hot tea splashed his boots.

She leaned farther forward and intently stared at the cup, rotating it on its side in her hands and nodding and squinting as she read the leaves. Barron leaned forward, attempting to make images out of the chunks, swirls, and knots of leaves.

"You will conquer the world, red wolf, but..." Her voice trailed off as she clicked her tongue at the tea leaves.

"But what, old witch?" he ordered out, his words a harsh demand, surprising even himself in the silence.

Her eye squinted at his brash rudeness, but she continued her reading. "But it will come at a cost. You will conquer the world, yes, but if you do, it will be nothin' more than ash, and you will do terrible things to get it."

As her words sank in and Barron felt his anger come over, the hunched-over Seer gasped and chucked the cup into the fire, sparking new flames around the hearth and filling the air with embers and crackling pops.

"What else did you see?!" he shouted.

She shook her head in a panic and refused to look up at him. She got out of her chair and stepped away from him. He followed her too closely.

"I do not speak on all I see, both in the leaves and in my eyes." Her milky glass eye moved around. She shook as she rested a fragile hand on his bicep. Her voice shook as hard as her hands. "Heed this warning, red wolf, do not turn this into a kingdom of embers and ruin. Do not pursue this path."

Chapter 53

Lady Belva had forgotten how beautiful Middleton Landing looked from above.

As she sat amidst the graves on the southern hills outside of town, the first light of dawn weaved its gentle shadows across the quiet landscape and she thought over why those most honored were laid to rest upon the high hill. Though books and historical leaders spoke of the hill as a vantage point from which the deceased could watch over their loved ones and the Landing for all eternity, Lady Belva saw it differently today.

To her, their final resting place was a different deliberate choice—to ensure that the beauty from which those buried had come would never fade from their memory, so they could watch the rolling hills of green for all eternity. While each passing soul ascended to the stars, each one left behind fragments of their essence, lingering to walk beside their families and to remain a part of the living world long after their departure.

And what better place was there to rest than here upon this hill?

Lady Belva could not recall the last time she visited her father's grave or spoke to his spirit in the church pews with a bowed head in her solitude. She had long since stopped taking advice from dead men whose words she could no longer listen to.

Each burial site had a carved stone bench opposite the headstone for visitors to sit on while they talked to their lost loved ones. Every bench was carved and engraved to match the grave markers they sat opposite of. Her father's set was inscribed with their noble House sigil, freesia flowers, and oak leaves on vines crawling up the legs of the bench and around the curves of the headstone.

She left her hands in their familiar place, joined on her lap, and looked down at his large headstone and the others of her ancestors. A quiet thought flickered through her mind—she should remember to thank the gardeners and landkeepers for their diligent care. Their work was so meticulous that it infused the place with a sacred stillness.

"The shadow you have left behind still looms beside me, father. A constant reminder of all the words you warned me with before you left us." Lady Belva finally spoke after sitting in silence for so long. Her words were not clear, not meant to be heard by any mortal ears that may be lingering around.

"I sometimes find myself reflecting on my childhood, on the doting you and mother did on me, and the pressures you put on all three of us girls." She wiped a stray tear, "And then I remember how I no longer have two sisters. Lydia treats me as nothing more than another noblewoman, and Magolin... Hells, I do not even know where she is anymore or if she is even alive.

She left almost as quickly as Lydia did, before you could decide for her what her future would entail. After she saw my fate with Theo, she could not leave fast enough.

"I hope she is near the sea. Magolin always loved the water and watching the boats sail away. They are free, Bel, she would say to me whenever we sat on the docks. They get to decide where to go; the wind and their captain are their only lords. I wish we could be like them."

Lady Belva sniffled and wiped a tear that broke her waterline.

"You were an amazing father and leader, and mother was everything to us, but still, the pressures of this world that you had to place on our shoulders did not make that love enough to prepare us for what was to come." she hesitated, "And some of the things you were forced to do, to put us through so young, I have begun to question if it was the world forcing your hand or if you so freely moved it for your own gain."

She swallowed, "For our family's own gain."

The fingers on her right hand twisted the wedding band on her left ring finger. "I do love Theo and our boys. I learned to love Theo quite quickly to save both him and I from the misery of my anger over your decision for us to wed. I am grateful to be leading our people. My life is quite lovely despite," she waved her hand around in the air and returned it to fidget with her ring, "everything happening now. But it didn't have to be this way."

She stood, walked over his grave, and rested her hand on the top of his gravestone. "None of it had to happen this way.

Theo could have been forced to face punishment for his sins. His Majesty could have ended the cycle of tyranny when he inherited his father's crown and lies. I could have told the king no when he promised Sister Ora to his son. I could have hesitated to set myself apart and not begun this war until I knew more of what we were fighting against.

"But I didn't say no. None of us did. We chose paths that were easier for us. We chose propriety over what was right. We chose to uphold instead of breaking apart." She flicked her hand off the headstone and back to herself, "But this ends with me. It must. If I am to be Queen of the People, I must be of the people and do what is best for them, not our name."

She looked to the skies and hillside. "If the world is to end and begin again, then let us build it with and for the dreamers, the oppressed, the silenced. Let it be their voices that reign."

Emaline sat in the pews of the small cathedral; her heavy armor weighed her down as much as her constantly wavering faith. She held her broken gaze at the stained-glass windows behind the dais; colorful depictions of miracles throughout the ages were aglow in the daylight.

Centered above the abandoned pulpit was a painting of a star within the moon, its glowing light shedding down onto the darkness below. Worshippers knelt and fell in prayer and gratitude, and new life formed where the light eradicated the darkness. Within the shadows of the night, demons and dark creatures lurked; red eyes glared from the depths of hell, and pointed teeth hung from their foaming mouths. They all stood waiting to pounce once the faith would fall, and they could once again devour the earth and His creations, reforming the world back into the first circle of Hell.

Emaline's hands were held together in prayer and resting on the pew in front of her. Between her palms, she held on tightly to her mother's coin. Her mind painted new pictures as she continued to sit silently, attempting to pray to a god she had never known to be real or false. The harshness of her life made her eternally ponder if any god, forbidden or not, was worthy of her praise and worship.

If The One True so loved His creations, why did he allow them such sorrow and put them through such pain?

If He loved her so much, why did he never answer her cries as a child, an orphan, a broken girl?

Why did he make her work for His approval? His love?

Why did any god?

The stained glass turned to life, the moon and star moving farther upward in the sky, retracting its light from the people below. The demons cackled and sprang forward, the once faithful people fell to the ground in terror; shrieks of death rang in Emaline's ears as the darkness danced around them, and the demons ripped the hearts out of His creations and devoured them whole.

The faithful fell again in prayer, asking for mercy and aid from the light as it ascended to the sky and drew itself away from them, ignoring their shrieks and begging. The faithful shouted blame at one another for their god's leave and turned on one another, devouring each other wholly and aiding the demons in their quest for the consumption of the beautiful life that once was.

Blood stained the windowpanes and dripped down the stone, puddling at the pulpit, threatening to turn into waves and swallow the cathedral whole.

The pew beside Emaline creaked, shocking her from her visions.

Her head snapped to the side, meeting the soft eyes of another coming for prayer. The woman at the end smiled at Emaline, nodding in greeting before turning to face the altar and bowing her head.

Emaline gathered herself, shaking her head and clearing her throat as she stood up. Pocketing her coveted coin, she walked to the other end of the pew and exited the cathedral. Besides herself and the woman she left behind, the church remained empty, as it had often been in the days since the Psalms were brought to Ayeshire's people. Even the most devout that Emaline knew from her time alongside Sister Ora hesitated at the church's steps.

Outside the church, a diverse crowd gathered: young children, their parents, and the elderly, all gathered while bards played classic chimes usually reserved for celebrations. The children danced carelessly, streamers in their hands as they ran around and clumsily moved their bodies. Their parents and those gathered stood looking on, clapping to the beat of the instruments and whooping and hollering each time one of the children leaped in the air, spun around, or danced with more freedom than one had ever known.

Behind the adults' smiles, they hid a somber knowing. The king's ships were almost upon them; they had been sighted with the moon rising. The barricades on the streets and boarded-up homes of Middleton Landing showed all what this greenlit home would become within the coming days.

The pain in Emaline's eyes lifted as she watched, nodding her head and smiling somberly as she made her way to where her life and this war may come to an end. She was always destined to die in war glory; giving her life in defense of others was in the oath she spoke when she was not much older than the children giggling in innocent joy behind her.

And now, after years of resentment and anger toward her holy House and life of service, she found a sense of pride in her wounds and happiness in her acceptance of her fate. Like her, many of those she would face in the war were not soldiers of choice but of force, fighting for causes that would harm them no matter who the victor was, causes that most benefitted those in power, those in control.

Even Lady Belva, the future Queen of the People's, kingdom would surely have suffering, surely have pain, starvation, hierarchies and division.

Despite knowing this of those on the warships coming for her home, Emaline would still put her sword through them with no hesitation if it meant that the soft laughter of the children would not be extinguished by the men who made themselves monsters and disguised themselves as saviors.

Emaline would fight, yes, she would pick up the sword that weighed too much for her heart, but she would not do so for a kingdom that still created crowns. She would do it for those like her. Those like Sister Ora. Those like the ones risking everything for a kingdom that may still wash its hands of them if it benefitted others.

Emaline would fight, but it would not be for a new queen.

A new queen that seemed content to trade lives for power or victorious battles.

Who seemed so quickly to care for politics over people despite the words she had preached for so long.

A new queen who seemed to trap so many quickly under her spell.

Emaline spent her entire life fighting: fighting to survive, fighting to live, fighting battles and skirmishes under banners carrying another's name.

Another's glory.

Another's victory.

She would fight again, yes, but not for Lady Montarian.

Not for the Queen of the People.

But for the lost.

The burdened.

The broken.

Herself.

Chapter 54

Pyria 27, 690 AC

Queen Onetta plucked an ivy leaf from the stem crawling up the balcony's baluster and wrapping itself around the rail. Tossing it dismissively over the side, she set her hand back on the balcony, now undisturbed by the leaf that dared to tickle the edge of her hand.

The clink of a goblet being set beside her took her attention away from the waves rolling in the endless blue waters of the Ina Gulf.

"My ships do not enjoy the task of sailing inland and trapping themselves between shorelines. We crave the open waters." Said Lord Tyrrian, taking a sip from his chalice as he studied the specs of sails in the distance. His battle carracks were far enough on their journey into the Ina Gulf that, to the naked eye, they appeared as tiny dots and not the battle galleons that they were.

"Their sails will turn west soon enough. If your fighters are truly as great as Aisharian gladiators once were, they will make quick work of destroying Middleton Landing and be able to turn back to the sea before the moon rises on the morrow." Queen Onetta said flatly.

Lord Tyrrian let out a long, slow breath, then replaced the air in his lungs with more wine in his belly. "We do not enjoy bringing ourselves into disputes on the continent."

"Yet you do not seem to mind when we set our sails for your lands to aid when you need it the most." King Ivan corrected as he stepped behind the two.

Lord Tyrrian's eyebrows rose at the comment as he turned to face the king, considering a petty retort in response. Instead, he held his tongue, nodded in polite greeting, and turned back to the balcony overlooking the city and the Ina Gulf. He set his chalice down on the ledge.

Queen Onetta knew what would happen next. These two men were always predictable with one another.

"Do not forget that my ancestors aided yours ten generations ago when you were tearing apart the continent over the crown on your head. If not for our aid, this continent would have destroyed itself, and we would have fallen, too." Lord Tyrrian stayed calm and spoke into the wind. "We saved your crown."

"All of that rescuing, and yet you still managed to lose your independence." The king paused at his snide comment, meant to strike a blow. He squared up to Lord Tyrrian's lax demeanor. When no reply came from the Lord of the Isles, his eyes darkened, and his tone lowered. "I know the history and the tales of my ancestors, Your Grace. You need not recite them to me as some poor attempt of patronization."

"Do I not, Your Majesty? You have been oddly forgetful as of late." Lord Tyrrian smiled and sipped his wine. He struck a nerve so hard that even the queen felt it.

"Enough, you two," Queen Onetta hissed, "We stand here to celebrate what is to come thanks to the work of our united Houses. Do not tarnish that with your egos and squabbles."

King Ivan took two steps towards his wife. He feigned ignorance at Lord Tyrrian's rigid posture and stance that hardened the closer the king leaned into her. The king wobbled slightly as the stench of wine poisoned the air between the two. "You do not give your king commands. It would be wise to remember your place here."

"Or what?" she hissed. She shot her eyes at Lord Tyrrian, a warning not to interfere.

King Ivan's jaw shook as he caught the shared look between the two. He raised his chin and stepped back by the balcony edge while taking another drink. "I may be forgetful on some days, but I still recall the fate of Talar and Oriana and what happened to their House- your House- because of my line."

One push. Queen Onetta considered—a stern grasp on his tremoring arm and a shove with all my might.

She shook the treasonous thought from her mind as she mentally heard the breaking of the king's bones on the rocks below.

The lineage that would become the queen's house, House Kavistia, predated recorded history, originating from the bloodline vaguely shared by the Priscius noble line through the lineage of Talar Vistus, husband to the usurped Queen Oriana Rominia. During her first pregnancy, Queen Oriana faced severe health complications and, on her Healer's advice and husband's blessing, chose her life over her unborn child's, ensuring stability on the throne and her chance to bring another heir into the world. While some praised her decision, others, including her brother Prince Jacquard, saw it as selfish and dangerous, leading to a smear campaign that fueled the Royal Civil War.

When the war dragged on with no end in sight, Queen Oriana and King Talar ceded the throne to the usurper prince, leaving for Talar's home on the Isles of Aishar to preserve their kingdom's survival under another's rule. In the ancient city of Thelimor, they adopted the local tradition of combining surnames, and two generations later, their line became House Kavistia, the House now led by Queen Onetta's father.

The queen scowled, not bothering to look at the king. The full balcony around them held its breath as it watched the glares exchange and the anger pulsate between them. She cleared her throat. "I recall it quite well, Your Majesty."

"You may be the queen, but I am the king and the man you owe for the crown you enjoy wearing." his tone was dangerously calm and even, an attempt to feign calmness to those who looked on.

Queen Onetta worked to shoot her anger at him, her words failing as she looked into his eyes. Eyes that looked more like his father's predator-like glare than her husband's blue gaze.

He held her look for a moment before walking away. Even on his worst days, King Ivan rarely ever spoke to her in such a way.

Her hands shook as she set them back down on the ledge, her voice barely at a whisper as she collected herself. Lord Tyrian attempted to rest a hand on her shoulder, but she jerked her body away and stormed for a quiet corner of the space.

"Everything I am, I owe to no man," she seethed through clenched teeth.

The dim town lights of Burnsley greeted Sedrick as he huffed his way down the last stretch of road before nightfall would make it too hard and dangerous to continue his travels. He needed rest to clear his mind and learn more of what was occurring around him before deciding what route he would take next. He had made it out of the king's city, which was hard enough by evading patrols, bribing bored watchmen, and taking to the woods and lesser-known roads, all with no sleep.

Sedrick knew there was safety in Ravenhall, whose stone pillars were much closer than those of Tower Bridge and his home across its waters. The silence from Ayeshire had left his mind still and unsure. He had no certainty of his use in the war once he delivered the parchments he had been tasked with retrieving and giving to Lady Montarian.

He had also yet to decipher if the comfort of home at Middleton Landing was where he was needed or if plans had since changed.

"Where is a poet born to sail meant to be?" he asked himself quietly as he approached the fence line around the edges of the small village.

The trees blocking the shore view of the Ina Gulf grew thin and disappeared as the fishing village took over the landscape. He fixed the backpack he had slung over his shoulder, the weight irritating his muscles as he headed down the road, hoping to find Royland again and instead spotting a small gathering of villagers nearby.

As he opened his mouth to call after them about an inn, they turned and bolted for the docks, shouting accompanying their movement. More villagers popped out of doorways, and everyone abandoned their duties as they all took for the shoreline.

Sedrick stopped.

His heart pounded over the sounds of running feet, and his head spun in circles as he turned toward the shoreline. He saw nothing more than growing darkness and ripping waves, a familiar vision for the few moments after sunset. He found his feet moving toward the nearest shoreline as more excitement grew around him.

He did not peel his eyes from where they squinted in the direction of his home.

He patted his pockets for a viewing scope, finding the familiar curve in his vest, and retrieved it. His pack fell to the ground, and he shifted to look through the lens out past where the naked eye could see.

His vision adjusted, the distant view slowly morphing from blurry splotches of color into clear shapes and movement.

Sedrick's stomach fell as he scanned the length of the Ina Gulf.

Where there had once been clear water free of obstruction, there now sailed Aisharian warships—too many to count and too many for any battalion to stop.

CHAPTER 55

The dull glimmer of the crescent moon drew a white line in the waves as if it were pointing the battleships to their destination before it disappeared behind clouds and turned the sky black. The sun had long lain itself to rest far in the depths of the Ringhar Sea, and stars hid behind the dark blanket of the night sky; only a few dared to peek out from its protection. The gods that commanded those stars eager to peek out behind their cover and watch the night's battle.

The warships bobbed in the silent waves, their sails flapping with each crash of water as small dances of wind wove around the canvas.

But the decks remained silent.

Line after line of redwood ships filled the Ina Gulf, overwhelming the waters meant for trade and fishing and blocking views from the shoreline. Periscopes held to the eyes of those on the land were quick to notice cannon holes and damage to some ships, a sign that those in the Spotted Isles did not allow easy passage for their enemy.

But the ships, they still came.

Crackling fires held a steady heartbeat on shore, lighting paths of vision for those armored behind barricades and giving aid for when the ships would wreak their havoc upon the shore. Barricades and blocked passages ran along the winding main roads of Middleton Landing, holding the line if the blocks on the beach were to break.

Inexperienced civilians found themselves pauldron-to-pauldron with the most elite soldiers of Ayeshire, holding the same swords and knocking the same arrows as they. There were not enough bombs to eliminate the Aishar fleet before their ropes were dropped and their passenger ships found their way to shore. The battle would inevitably find its glory and climax on land.

Closest to the fortress, trebuchets were lined, and their large infrastructure towered over those stationed downhill. Standing beside the towering weapons, Ephraim swallowed the lump in their throat and adjusted the House of Healer pin on their chest. They had not stopped fidgeting with it since the building of their destructive weapons had begun. Their eyes scanned the mixture of cannonballs and the black iron orbs containing Hellfire, specially marked with painted-on blue flames.

Ephraim held the glare of one of the Hellfire cannonballs, remembering the blue flame that erupted upon the initial creation of this batch of weaponry.

Their batch of weaponry.

Ephraim's imagination filled in where memory could not; screams erupted in their ears as they turned their gaze back to the waters, their mind continuing its journey and desecrating each ship with Hellfire, murdering hundreds in one of the most catastrophic ways.

Lord Montarian stepped beside Ephraim, tilting his head as he spoke, his tone frustrated and hard, "Why are they not unloading their ships? Our scouts to the west could see them loaded to the brim with men. Why do they wait?"

Ephraim shrugged. "I am not versed in battle strategy, but perhaps they wait for us to initiate? To draw upon our impatience and nerves?"

"Perhaps." Lord Montarian mumbled. The Lord of Ayeshire continued his stressful pacing.

Archers stood at the ready along the fortress wall, fully loaded quivers on their backs and drink barrels at their sides. Repurposed from holding ale, the barrels now held an overflow of arrows for each archer and spears for throwers. Extra bows were strapped to the barrels, a precaution in case of damage to the ones in use or for sword-bearing fighters to grab in times of need. The north and west walls of the fortress had little walk space left, each path taken up by armor, blockades, and fighters. The south and east walls were well blockaded as well, but held hidden escape routes in case the worst were to occur, as well as hidden traps for enemies that may sneak around the Ayeshire soldiers' cunning glares.

Lord Montarian paused his pacing and rested his hand on a wall. He copied the breathing techniques his wife often used in her times of turmoil. With each deep, recentering breath, he sent his love down the stone lines to where his beloved and others hid in the dark from the upcoming throes of battle.

He knew she wished to be at the front of the fight, but even her stubbornness knew when to recede and allow him to lead their soldiers in her stead. She was to be the face of total command when victory was in their grasp or defeat bloodied their doorways.

More fire crackled as time crawled by without movement or sound.

Stand up straight. Don't let them see the worry. He thought to himself.

Lord Montarian's hand fell from the stone, and he shot around to once again look at the ships quietly bobbing in the waves. No amount of calming breaths would stop the worry that overwhelmed his entire being. He needed to be in the chaos of combat, but he could not adequately lead a battle so widespread if he could not even see the enemies in front of him.

He hardened his jaw and jutted it at those nearest him, "Eyes up. Don't strain your bowstrings yet. Don't freeze yourself in place; your legs will quickly grow stiff. Be ready."

Emaline walked the line of soldiers she commanded by the shoreside. The barricade offered enough protection for an initial clash, but that would only buy their forces time to understand their enemy for a brief moment before needing to fully engage. Her eyes ran down the trenches they had dug downhill, the outline only visible in the dark if she held her eyes on the space and concentrated. Beneath the threshold of the dug trenches were buried cheval de frise made of wood and metal.

Their enemy only needed enough of their fellow invaders to fall onto the spikes below before that defense became nothing more than an annoyance. The wet rocky shoreline around the ports would provide trouble for the footing of those who came on shore, but knowing the finesse and experience of who they were facing, Emaline knew the rocks would not make enough enemies stumble.

She continued her pacing, overanalyzing every single tactic they had created and every defense they had erected. It would not be enough; she had continuously told herself for days, each time she walked the city and strategized new defenses, nothing would be enough.

As the silence dreadfully continued, her own anxiety fell onto the shoulders of those around her. The green fighters who had once been innocent bakers or teachers, the well-versed battlefield-ready soldiers, all stood anticipating the worst and feeling less at ease each time her boots thudded behind them, and orders did not fall from uphill.

They all could die the same. They all would be her responsibility.

She stopped pacing and scanned the town before focusing back on the quiet shoreline. The voices of past trainers and officers flooded her mind, Sir Rainey's firm tone standing out and stinging most as she searched for words on what to do and how to lead.

She glared at the bobbing ships, Sir Rainey's words of advice from prior battles shifting to memories of his lies and his betrayal. Her anger clouded her mind as she recalled how he snuck among them like a venomous serpent while they were distracted by the enemy in front of them. Her head slowly cocked to the side as the map within her mind drew more paths to walk or steps to avoid and found what it needed.

Somewhere among the hundreds of threads of thought Emaline worked through, realization stunned her.

"There is no movement at all. It is almost as if—" her eyes widened as she searched the line for someone to shout her words at.

Overhead, a cannon flew from Middleton Landing, crashing against the large warship nearest their shore. The sounds of splintering wood and breaking metal sang as shards of the ship flew in the air, and a quick eruption of flame illuminated the empty ships around it.

"—as if they were empty."

What their scouts had seen filling the ship's decks was nothing more than a trick: dummies placed on the boats to hold the place of a real enemy.

"Eyes up!" Emaline ordered.

Chapter 56

To the west of the city ports, Gerald's wall of archers held steady as the flames shook the night sky, and Emaline's orders echoed uphill towards where he held a barricade in the middle of the city. His head snapped back to where Sgt. Pell held command of their unit and was waiting for an order to deliver to the archers looking at him.

The silence of the western barricades was broken with the call of battle.

Three arrows whooshed through the air and stuck in the side of the blockade wall, a warning demanding attention to be turned to where the units' green-caped backs had been facing.

Aisharian soldiers did not count kills made by striking at an enemy's back; their methods required watching their enemies' lives fade from their eyes. Blood-stained Aisharian and Britian fighters now ran shouting towards the blockage; no care taken to avoid tearing apart the properties they leapt and tore through in their descent.

"Charge!" Sgt. Pell bellowed down the line. "Move out!"

"Fire!" Gerald ordered as he raised his bow towards the enemies behind them.

Arrows fell quickly enough upon the Aisharian and Britian invaders, to give the Ayeshire archers time to begin reloading and for their swordsmen to turn on foot to charge and begin the fight to defend their home.

This was not meant to be the front of the battle, but the blood and fury already erupting did not care that their plan went awry.

Bellowing descended from uphill, and Gerald turned in time to see the shadows of movement as an enemy unit broke off and made for the stone castle.

And with them, strapped to packs on their bodies, were bombs.

The echoes of fighting came down the hill seconds after the wreckage of the cannonball calmed. Lord Digarius threw himself into action, storming along the line of his soldiers along the waters and shouting for different squads to break from where they held and move to defend the western support blockade that fell under attack.

"Green squad fall out! Blue squad, fall in!" His baritone voice reverberated and carried no pause or hesitation. "Red squad support!"

"Kingery!" he bellowed over the footfall of moving soldiers, as he shoved his way through the crowds, "You hold this line! It is yours now to command!"

"Yes, sir." She calmly replied as he approached her. Her eyes barely turned to his stance as he marched toward her, her focus held on the shoreline, daring any movement to come from it.

"Prepare for an attack on either front; you know what to do." He shouted over the building noise, clasping a gloved hand on her pauldron, "This is what you were made for."

Her eyes flickered at his last words, a harmless comment meant to aid in confidence and provide certainty in her abilities, but instead, they choked her.

Now is not the time. She thought. Now is not the time for reflection on wants and memories.

Lord Digarius did not catch her shift in expression or her silent contemplation. He quickly marched forward with the soldiers heading west.

There was no order to how the unit holding the west fought. Their backs were quickly pushed against their own walls, forcing their line to form into knots and waves to hold back the overflow of red capes that had snuck up on them.

The stock of arrows the fletchers had prepared diminished as archers reloaded as fast as they could, some defaulting to wielding the metal-tipped arrows as daggers and stabbing into the flesh of those who came too fast and too close to be shot. Other rations were destroyed by malicious fires set by their enemies, who let the city burn.

Small explosions sounded from all directions. Smoke clogged the skies, and flames turned the cold city night into a sweltering hell.

Gerald knocked another arrow and loosed the bow on instinct, operating on a well-ingrained sense of his craft. The feather fletching barely moved past his fingertips before he reached for another, knocked, and loosed it again. His eyes searched for shades of red, aiming only for those wearing the favored color of both enemy countries, holding back his aim when a green-caped or shielded ally came too close to his target.

Armored footsteps jostled his attention behind him as he instinctively reached for another arrow and shielded himself behind a busted wall. He allowed himself a shallow breath of relief when he saw the aid responding to their call.

Gerald did not ask permission to give orders. "The fortress! They are heading for its walls! Move!"

His head jerked uphill where he and others had been fighting to clear a path; Lord Digarius's familiar figure busted through his unit at Gerald's voice.

"Green squad, defend here! Blue, move uphill!" ordered Lord Digarius, offering Gerald only a quick nod of acknowledgment before moving past and ordering him as well. "Ackley! You and your archers are with me."

Gerald swooped a foot from under his hunched body and spun to stand. Two arrows knocked and pulled back as he stood. A quick flash of leather-clad tan skin threatened his vision, and Gerald released, both arrows penetrating the neck of the seething Aisharian gladiator.

He walked backward, his hand already loading more arrows as the chaotic line of allies reformed and moved, giving up a single slice of land to protect the rest of the town.

Gerald held back his breaking. He chose to lead the western blockade because the farming sector had been his home. He sniffed the air as he shot more arrows, the smoke of burning barns and fields of crops bringing stinging tears to his eyes.

But he kept moving, letting his home burn, and kept following Lord Digarius without question or fault.

Chapter 57

Emaline and her soldiers waited in heavy anticipation, hate boiling through her blood at having to hold a line that had yet to be touched while the sounds of pain and death echoed so closely by. She focused her anger on what was before her: soldiers and civilians awaiting command and a shoreline of enemy ships that had yet to move.

She approached an archer nearby who straightened up immediately at her presence. "Fire a flaming arrow at the nearest ship. This quiet still does not seem right." She continued as they lit an arrow aflame and knocked it, glancing to their side for her command to fire. "A Gulf full of ships covered in blackness and not a single soul aboard. They are out there; they must be. How else would the ships have sailed so easily here?"

She nodded to the archer, prompting them to fire. "Light it up."

Their longbow hit true, bursting one of the canvas sails into flame and restoring sight to the shoreline and the Britian and Aishar on passenger boats creeping to shore.

She stepped back, addressing those around, "They hid their loaded ships behind those that were empty, hoping we would find ourselves too distracted with those who came in on foot. Fucking sneaky bastards.”

She mumbled, “And we are fools.”

“Fire again! Light those ships on fire to give us sight!” Emaline ordered as the flames died down on the enflamed ship. “Now!”

The three empty warships within range turned into bonfires on the water, their flames and falling debris taking out some of the smaller boats as they sailed inland, no longer shrouded by the darkness of the nearly starless night. Enemies dove from the safety of their ships, swimming for shore with terrifying speed; others picked up the pace of their rowing, no longer needing to be silent. The blaze of the warships showed the littering of cog and caravel ships racing for the shoreline; their appearance minuscule compared to the ships that had once blocked the view from the shoreline.

“Archers! Spearman!” she continued, “Ready to fire! When they hit our mark- take them down.”

Her heart palpitated and would not rest.

This is what you were made for.

Lord Digarius’ words echoed again in her head. Instead of lowering her chin in shame and disgrace at the fate she was handed, she raised it and snarled.

Through the flames and waves, she glared down at the soldiers sailing in. She stood with her hands crossed behind her, staking her claim on each enemy that lay ahead. In her flickering glare, her soul swore she saw a familiar, cunning face that haunted her nightmares and enraged her every being.

Her lips snarled at the memory of Sir Marion.

She spoke to herself as she unsheathed her sword, "If he is here. He is mine."

Lord Montarian's shouting sounded miles away as Ephraim stood stone still on the fortress wall. Flames flew from the arrow slits along the wall and the internal staircases below, engulfing soldiers before they could rip the arrows from their bodies and continue their barrage of the fortress.

"Block the stairways! Do not allow them to make it up! Save the flames for groups, not single men!" Lord Montarian continued to shout.

Ephraim's breathing grew harsh and uncontrollable as they watched the bloodshed and flames take over their home. The fire on the shoreline and town gave them a clear sight of what was occurring below.

They rubbed the Healer pin on their cloak, hands trembling as they did so. The oath they gave as a young apprentice echoed over the noises of war around them.

With my ancestors and God as my witness, I swear to carry out this oath and promise.

In front of them, a green-cloaked soldier fell from the wall and screamed as they plummeted to their death below. Another ran to take their place without hesitation.

I will abstain from causing harm and only heal.

I will protect life, not take it.

Shouting and clashing from the stairwell jerked their mind back for a moment. Blood splattered in front of them as a stray arrow made its way into the head of an archer near them.

They could stop this. Help put this to a quicker end.

I will prevent pain and sickness where I can.

The soldier fell to the ground, screaming in agony and holding his eye, his fingers wrapped around the arrow. His body convulsed for a moment before his shrieking stilled.

I swear to uphold this oath and my obligation to all: the sick and the fallen, the healthy and newborn.

A bomb erupted on the side of the castle, shaking the stone where they stood. Their memory raced back to where they had said goodbye to civilians and their children who could not flee or fight, who hid inside the fortress that was steadily being taken.

"Ephraim!" Lord Montarian's voice broke through as he ran for them. "Can you not hear? We must fire! Load the Hellfire and aim for the ships! Aim for the outlying parts of the west! Aim for their bodies!"

He did not give Ephraim a moment to reply before rushing for the upcoming fight that pushed through the stairwell.

May I always act as so to preserve life and the traditions of my calling. May I experience the joys and abundance of aiding those whose call I answer.

Ephraim rubbed the Healer's pin on their chest before gripping it in their fist and ripping it from their chest as they marched for the Hellfire in front of them, preparing the cannonballs with their final ingredients.

So help me, God.

Chapter 58

King Ivan stood on the balcony with his family and Council. They all watched the dark night, looking southeast toward where the siege of Middleton Landing was to take place. There were no images or sounds coming from so far across the water, but he could not turn his eyes away.

Laughter came from around the balcony, servants refilled cups and plates of food, devious and arrogant conversations took over. Beside the king stood a quiet and contemplative Prince Percy. His eyes did not watch the waters as his fathers did, but the sky.

Prince Percy's eyes kept scrunching in contemplation as he looked for constellations and signs in the empty sky.

Lord Tyrrian wove tales of what his Aisharian gladiators were likely doing to the Ayeshire army at the very moment, his words falling onto the unamused and bored ears of Lord Nesima Mete and Lord Shaital Pathis. As he spoke, his eyes flicked to where Queen Onetta casually lounged, smiling at him as her eyes danced up and down his body, the wine flowing much too easily in her cup.

King Ivan sipped his wine and stared down the waters. "Do the skies say anything?"

Prince Percy swallowed, and his breath shook. The nights leading up to the battle had seen too many starfalls, and now the sky stood lightless outside of a single blinking star. There had been others, but they fell, too. "It says too much," the scholarly prince said.

Laughter erupted from behind them, turning into shocking gasps and shrieks as an explosive boom shook the air. The balcony shook as they all ran to its edge to find where the sound erupted from.

Another eruption rang through the sky.

Then another.

The king gripped the balcony ledge, keeping his eyes on the far east shoreline while others watched with him.

Sister Ora stepped up beside the group and looked out at the waters and the far-off flickers of blue flame shooting upward and quickly disappearing, only to be replaced with another seconds later. From where they stood, the flames were a distant glow that pulsed on the skyline.

Anger flickered around the kingdom's leaders, knowing the weapon being unleashed was not of their army. But Sister Ora smiled and let out a breath as she stepped near the king and watched the blue fire flames in the distance..

King Ivan mumbled to himself amid the shocking gasps and conversation around him. He took his eyes off the blue line to look into the sky, where the Eye of the Lion flickered and began to dim.

"When the eye of the world has dimmed, and stars have fallen as if made of rain," the king mumbled.

Prince Percy added a breathless whisper, breaking his shock, "Of solid gold and stardust rulers shall remain—"

The king continued, "—forevermore until burned in fury and in flame."

King Ivan felt the world fall apart and clutched his heart. His chest constricted in pain, and his entire body felt loose and weak.

The king saw total darkness as he fell to his knees.

Chapter 59

"We do not falter! We do not fail!" Emaline shouted over the crashing of boats against the rocky shoreline and the war cries of their enemies, "We do. not. yield!"

And the arrows of Ayeshire did not yield as red-caped bodies poisoned their lands.

But behind the fallen foes came more rushing with reckless abandon and little care for the comrades they stepped over.

"Cannons! Fire!" another officer ordered; the sounds of whistling cannons followed the last gasps of his words.

Waves exploded in the air as the cannons impacted the water. Only a select few that were haphazardly shot made contact with empty and unloading boats. Two lucky shots took down a small boat of enemies, throwing their bodies and armor around. The Aisharians did not care for the loss; their adrenaline fueled by the explosions and debris, their rushing stampedes pumping with more blood lust.

Emaline's line held their position, not daring to move, egging on the enemy to continue to rush them and fall to their deaths in the spiked pits separating them. Their hope was answered as the first line of fighters failed to notice the dug ditches and fell with painful shrieks and crunching bones.

But Aisharian gladiators were used to much more torturous war and were disciplined in their movements. A rushing line of gladiators halted in unison, steps away from the ledge of the pits, and took several paces backward. Loud shouts of command carried over the pit, the Aisharians holding steady as the voice commanded a change in tactic.

Emaline concentrated on the shouting man centered among them, his chest painted in blood and scars. Vengeance overwhelmed her sense of hatred for war, for killing. Even in the chaos and recklessness of battle, she recognized his tenor and hard face.

She swore Sir Marion met her eyes across the carnage and smiled at her.

She no longer wanted the war to end.

She wanted blood.

His gladiators rushed for the pit, as did he, and cleared it with ease as if it were part of an athletic game and not a battle. Their exposed bodies took on flying arrows and spears, but wasted no effort stumbling or showing pain at the nonfatal hits many took, snapping the arrows off and leaving the points under their skin.

Armor-clad Britian soldiers, their suits too heavy to allow them such free movement as the Aisharians, held their own line behind the pit and offered cover with their own returning arrows and flying weapons.

Around Emaline, soldiers who were not quick enough to move or simply unlucky, fell as arrows and flying spears flew from across the barricade. Allies snagged their bodies and moved them, letting the Healers who stood with them on the wall render aid.

Emaline continued with orders, her hand gripping her sword in anticipation and anger as she waited, carefully watching the approaching enemy from behind their cover and the slits in her helmet.

Her eyes kept looking for Sir Marion among the gladiators.

I will have him. She promised herself.

Though the king had ordered Emaline back to Ayeshire before the war began, stripping her of her duty as Sister Ora's personal guard and handing the honor to a man loyal to the crown, Emaline knew the decision hadn't come from His Majesty. No, this was the work of that spiteful, sick man who led the King's Guard—Sir Marion. He had despised her before he even knew her, seeing her as unfit for her duties.

Emaline had been warned about Sir Marion, told to watch her back around him. But she had been too naive, too arrogant, too focused on her duty to see every drip of venom in his eyes.

Anger surged through her— he is mine, her thoughts growled.

It was only a matter of time before the barricade broke; the Ayeshire arrows were not endless in supply nor were their reserves of soldiers. They were meant to hold the initial line with units further inland backing up their losses and aiding their offense. But their backup was held off elsewhere as Emaline blocked out the screaming and clashing from behind her.

Britian soldiers rushed forward with ladders and busted ship materials, throwing them down across the pit and joining their Aisharian brethren in their rushing. Bodies fell in flame and blood as Ayeshire refused to pause their defense for a moment's breath.

Two more cannons fired down the defending blockade wall, one aiming for the ships left in the water and another for a nest of armor-clad fighters rushing for the makeshift bridge. Both exploded on impact, the boat in the water now a mess of debris, and the rushing soldiers falling into pieces as mud and dirt exploded around them, taking down more as the flying mess of body parts and earth impacted them.

The groupings of Aisharian's blended together as Emaline forced her feet to stay put in her command position. Her eyes kept straying to the mess of the men and women laying siege to her allies. Sir Marion was centered among a circle of Aisharian gladiators that worked as one unit, twisting, turning, and rotating as they slashed and cut down her people. When one Aisharian fell to a blade, their body was kicked and moved out of the way for their allies in arms to continue their movement.

"Jam! Jam!" a deep voice shouted across the line, "It's fuckin' jammed!"

Emaline's head snapped to where the voice originated from as a cannon's lit fuse counted down the seconds before the explosion.

She screamed at the arguing men fighting over whose rushed carelessness caused the malfunction, their anger allowing them to forget what was coming, "Move! Fucking move!" she screamed as she ran for them.

But it was too late. The explosion took out those who did not rush from the impact and left a hole in their barricade, now covered in body parts and blood.

Gladiators and soldiers rushed for the exploded opening as another cannonball sounded from the opposite end. The crashing of wood and shouting of her own soldiers shocked Emaline as she jolted around. Another hole had been blown in their blockade. Their remaining cannon went in a heap of wood, metal, and fire. Out on the water, a cannon ship continued turning on its side, the sound of more cannons being loaded haunting Emaline's future nightmares.

She shouted to no one other than herself, "We do not yield!"

CHAPTER 60

Prince Elion wiped the mud off his face and threw his helmet back on. His horse lay on the ground, taking its last breaths, whinnying and kicking in pain as the arrow pulsed more blood from his body. The prince rushed over and grabbed his dropped weapons. He rested a soft hand on his horse's neck, a silent apology, before thrusting his sword through its heart, ending his pain quickly.

Prince Elion's officers around him offered cover as he collected himself.

Their attempt to take the Sebern army by surprise in the night had failed miserably from the first sword draw. Lord Torrin had either predicted their attempt or tried to do the same to them. Both armies had held their hard formations after the glow of sunset turned into darkness, but both armies were too well-matched. When both sent their calvaries to the opposite side of the field of green, perfected military commands fell to the side as Prince Elion ordered all to charge.

Even with the Dragons by their side, His Highness' army still struggled to gain ground. There was no cohesion, no unity in Prince Elion's lines.

The Crown Prince shoved forward to aid his soldiers in drawing blood, their push into Sebern's lines gaining better traction with each exhausted swipe. The push and pull of the battle was hopefully coming to a victorious end.

Desert horses whipped around the outskirts of the armored armies, their riders yipping and shouting as they whipped spiked slingshots at soldiers and threw spears across scuffles. The battlefield had drawn allies too close to enemies for the Dragon army to use their weapons of fire without losing too many of their own.

Prince Elion threw down the dead enemy soldier in front of him, his sword sliding out of their shoulder after he plunged it into their neck to finish the slaughter. He scanned the field for the next clash, his feet grounding him in place as an explosive boom shocked the battlefield.

Surprise waved through the clashing crowds, and fighting stopped as every head- red, blue, and green-caped- turned to where the explosion came from as two more shook the air. Blue flames shot skyward miles across the shoreline before disappearing and sucking any light away with it. More flames erupted as another boom rattled the fighters on the field.

Prince Elion's breath paused as he watched the blue flames shoot for the starless sky and disappear. Each returning breath was accompanied by the echoing words of the prophecy long feared, the words that the crown prince had never held much weight in.

Until now.

The blue flames in the sky brought forth mentally painted images of the parchment on which the Psalms of Fire and Fury were written. Blue flames and dotted stars decorated time-worn, yellowed paper. Centered under the script of the Psalms of Fire and Fury sat a melting gold throne- the gold throne Prince Elion was destined to sit upon.

Prince Elion almost dropped his sword as he gasped out the last line of the prophecy that haunted his family line. "And the world of men shall be made to begin again."

Chapter 61

Children screamed and burst into tears as their mothers and those around them attempted to soothe them while pushing away their own fears. The fortress shook as each trebuchet unloaded above them and bombs exploded outside.

Lady Belva held herself together by a thread as she moved continuously throughout the room, offering hugs and smiles to those who needed them and relief for worried parents who needed to step away from their children for a moment.

"Taylian," she mumbled as she spoke to a boy about his age, "come here and introduce yourself."

Lord Taylian obeyed, learning from her to hide what was running through his body. The Montarians were meant to be a sign of strength and virtue, especially in times like these. He sat beside the boy, his composure shy and inwardly drawn, and Lord Taylian led the conversation by asking about the game he held and challenging him to play a round of it.

Lady Belva stood up and wrung her hands, nodding slowly and keeping her face firm.

Another explosion burst out, and the castle shook more vigorously. She darted for the door, where guards were gathered inside and outside, where they hid.

Whispers and conversations stopped as the crowd looked again to her for guidance. "It is nothing, I am certain. We are well and safe. Do not worry."

She glanced for the door again as rushing footsteps approached. Her breath hitched for a moment, and the guards facing her tightened their stances. A murmuring conversation came through the door, and coded knocks followed.

Lady Belva nodded at the guards and stepped forward, opening the door enough to hear the message. Lord Samwin sat nearby against the wall with other children his age, sharing their wooden toys and books with one another. She gave her youngest a quick smile.

"The front western tower was hit with a bomb, my lady. They are working to put out the fires now." The messengers whispered through the crack in the door.

She nodded, smiling as he spoke to calm those who watched eagerly. "And what else?"

The messenger paused and swallowed the stone in her throat. "They came from the west on foot. Then they snuck in by hidden boat. It is... your army is doing everything they can, my lady."

Lady Belva's chest and stomach tightened, and she held her breath before replying with niceties, "Yes, yes, thank you."

She shut the door and turned to the watchful eyes, "Our families are the fiercest fighters in this kingdom. We should all be proud."

She smiled as she tightened her clasped hands. Mothers smiled at their children, calming them with words of praise and excitement over what she told them. Breathes loosened in tight chests as Lady Belva continued to smile and sat down in her seat beside the door. She turned away and closed her eyes, counting her breaths to calm herself.

Lord Taylian held a close eye on his mother, watching her compose herself as she always did so well. He moved to comfort her and gather Lord Samwin to help, looking to where his little brother had sat with friends. Lord Taylian jostled in worry as he searched for where his brother had been sitting, his fear growing more as he noticed his absence from every corner of the room.

"Shit". Lord Taylian took a careful gaze around the room, his eyes stopping on the servant's entrance doorway tucked in the corner. The handle of the doorknob finished turning shut as he let out a breath, "Shit."

Gerald loosed an arrow at the Britian soldier climbing the fortress wall, their fall taking down two more on the ladder below them. He knocked another into place and shot it through a female Aisharian fighter that had made her way for him as he ducked behind crumbling remnants of the castle of Middleton Landing.

Gerald focused all his effort on keeping his breath steady. He had only been called into battle once before this day, back when he was barely a man and when the beast of men came down from the mountain pass and into the village of Wolfsden looking for a fight.

Defending the mountain pass outside of Wolfsden was an unofficial rite of passage for those seeking expert markings in archery or defense, just as hunting the great mountain wolves had been. Gerald had simply done it because it was what Lord Digarius had asked of him back then. He had not wanted to kill a man nor see battle, but his future lord, his closest friend, had asked for his aid then, as he had now.

Gerald reached for another arrow, his quiver now bare.

"Fuck," he mumbled, quickly glancing about for any weapons.

Lord Digarius shot forward for him. "Here!" he shouted, throwing a blood-soaked quiver of arrows at Gerald before running forward for incoming fighters.

Gerald threw the quiver over his back, checking his surroundings and fellow archers beside him. They shared a nod, knocked their arrows, and moved forward to continue pressing onward.

Gerald kept watch over the advancing group; double arrows knocked as he moved just behind the sword-bearing group. Lord Digarius slammed his shield into an oncoming Britian soldier, sending him to the ground, just as an Aishar gladiator swung for Lord Digarius' neck. Lord Digarius ducked and swung before Gerald could even raise his bow, the lord's sword finding resistance in the exposed thigh of the blood-soaked Aisharian.

Lord Digarius struggled for a moment to tear his blade from their flesh as he stumbled away and out of Gerald's line of sight. The lord heir stepped over countless fallen bodies, and his footing fell along the uneven and slippery terrain. Lord Digarius' soldiers, fighting alongside him, faced their own struggles and enemies, just as he did.

Gerald cursed the battlefield regulations that dictated leaders and lords to be decorated differently from common foot soldiers. His closest friend was clearly marked and decorated as one of importance, an easy target to hound and aim for. Meanwhile, the Aisharians cheered for the standing order, knowing who to focus their attacks on.

An enemy group rushed for the stumbling lord- the last cluster of killers in this area that Ayeshire defended well. They had picked him out easily among the rest of their prey. Gerald loosened the arrows at the charging enemies, taking one down with ease as he already readied another shot.

He raised his bow and pulled back the string to kill the man raising his sword at Lord Digarius's turned back.

But Gerald's world stopped as heat erupted from his right shoulder, and his loosened arrow shot into the ground, his bow falling alongside it. His body stumbled to the side as pain emanated from his shoulder. He reached his left hand to grab the arm muscle, searing in pain, only to find no muscle to grab.

No arm to grab.

Gerald's vision turned blurry and black as he watched Lord Digarius and his soldiers continue to race forward, leaving behind Gerald's falling body without a turn or knowing what he had sacrificed for his lord.

For his friend whom he had always followed.

CHAPTER 62

"How many left?!" Lord Theodus shouted at the men loading the trebuchets and cannons.

"Not enough!"

Lord Theodus fisted the man's shirt collar from under his chest armor. "That is not a fucking answer. How many?!"

The man shook. "Four."

Lord Theodus threw the man back with a hard shove and released his grip. He shot his hand at the cannon. "Launch them all. Aim as true as you can to our enemies, but if we must lose some of our own to survive, then so be it."

Lord Theodus rushed down the wall, continuing his manic pacing as he attempted to lead from every front.

Each one fell apart despite every order he tried to give.

The western wall had fallen. A cannon from a ship had aimed so high that it shocked the city as it made its way so high up the hill. While it did not hit the fortress, another did that had come by land. Brought in under the cover of a mass of soldiers, a land cannon had been shot from the western assault and took down stones older than Ayeshire's naming. The exploding and flaming mess was too catastrophic for Lord Theodus' soldiers to rush down and protect; their paths on the wall destroyed by the explosion.

And the ones that came after that.

Ladders thrown onto the wall by Britian soldiers were shoved away with reckless care, and molten metals were poured down the wall at those who made it too high. Arrow after arrow, spear after spear, were shot and thrown down until there was nothing left to fight with on the wall but their fists and swords.

"There are too many." Lord Theodus croaked as he heaved himself over fallen barrels, spending arrows to the shouting fight. Foes had made their way up the winding staircases, only to be stopped by a barrage of the lord's men. He let himself feel relief as he met with his soldiers and heard scuffling behind their enemies, a sign that other defenses had come for the fortress and fought at the other side.

When the staircase had cleared of enemies, and Lord Theodus met familiar faces in the middle of the carnage, he allowed himself a slight ping of victory amidst the shouting and fire.

Unfamiliar war cries and screams caught his ear as he rushed over bodies left on the steps. Lord Theodus stepped foot on the bloodied grass as they successfully took back a sector of the castle, but every breath and second of relief had left him as he watched the slaughter outside the fortress and felt the flames down the far side of the crumbled wall.

Amidst the ongoing slaughters, more faces joined in. Unrecognizable soldiers rushed from sturdy steeds and threw themselves into battle before Lord Montarian could make out any coat of arms.

He did not know if he should scream or cheer as a horde of black-clad warriors rushed into the fortress, the flames swallowing them whole as they followed behind red-clad and leather-armored foes, and others split off to join the fray.

The stampede through the halls of Middleton Landing could be heard from the depths of their underground cells and buried rooms. Prayers to every god, old and new, forbidden and revered, were shouted and cried. Armed citizens stood from where they sat, slowly walking for the doorway to step outside and die with honor and the hope that their slaughter would mean the saving of the innocents.

Even if she could surrender, the Lady of Ayeshire knew that, given the fury and chaos above them, it would not be heard. She stood beside the door, silently praying for each person who stepped outside to defend the room.

She beckoned the attention of the guards in the hall.

"Is there any chance of us escaping? A clear path away?"

The guard beside her held his hand on the doorknob. "Best barricade the door, my lady."

The defeat and mourning in his voice gave her every answer her unasked questions begged for.

Outside was a slaughter.

The end was nigh.

The door closed before her, and she untucked a knife that had been hidden in her skirts. She would not go quietly or let the monsters do far worse things to her than simple throat slitting.

Lady Belva Montarian, the Lady of Ayeshire, the Queen of the People, would not let her people die without placing herself before them. She turned to them. "It has been my honor to be your lady," she swallowed hard and let her voice shake, and the tears formed. "To be your queen."

The room held one another as she turned back to the door, the knife shaking in her hand. Screaming and unsheathed metal silenced the noises in the room. The crying stopped; her people would not whimper or beg as they were slaughtered. They would stare down their enemies and make sure their eyes haunted them for eternity.

A few more steps and their end would be outside the door.

Lady Belva counted the dancing steps of the fight outside. Their movement growing closer.

Armored steps stopped in front of the door, and it burst off its hinges.

The barricade of chairs did nothing to stop their entrance.

A tall, lanky man led the sea salt-stained soldiers. Long braids ran down the sides of his head, and black was painted across his eyes to match the charcoal of his armor. He met Lady Belva's fear-filled eyes as she raised her knife in defense.

He smiled and sheathed his sword. "Lady Nilkimm sends her regards, my queen."

Lord Digarius stepped in behind the black-clad leader, with Lord Montarian following closely behind. Her tears would not stop as she dropped her knife and embraced her family.

"We won. We won. We won," she cried into her husband's chest. "How?"

"Iron Bay ships and horseback soldiers followed behind the enemy and came for us." He comforted her.

Lord Digarius pulled back from the hug, allowing his parents a moment. He scanned the room for his brothers. "Where is Taylian?" He paused. "Where is Samwin?"

CHAPTER 63

The crumbling of stone and fire did not stop as Lord Taylian screamed for his brother. The voices of foreign soldiers outside were muffled by the flame and the room collapsing before him. The moment he saw Lord Samwin duck out of the hideaway they all hid in, Lord Taylian knew his brother would so stupidly sneak across the fortress to the room housing his experiments and toys.

A room held in the corner of the fortress that had been hit first.

"Taylian!" Lord Samwin shrieked from down the hall. His arms were full of supplies and parchment, and his body shook as he stood in the hall, flames burning far behind him.

"Samwin! What are you doing here?!" Lord Taylian shouted as he met with his brother.

"I- I- I. The fire, I did not want our things, our experiments to be ruined," he cried, realizing what he had so carelessly done.

Fighting made its way inside, and soldiers rushed down the hall just outside where the two were tucked away. Pounding footsteps and shouting made their way to the two young boys.

Lord Taylian shook his head at his brother. "Go back, now, it is not safe. Run!"

Footsteps echoed too close in the hall. Lord Taylian gripped Samwin's shoulder.

"Run!"

Little Samwin did not move. Lord Taylian shoved him repeatedly, trying to get him to move and run with him.

"Run! Run! Run! Hells dammit!"

Samwin cried out and finally burst down the hall back to where he had escaped from. Lord Taylian turned before he began his own run, but it was too late. He had to stay. He had to let his brother escape. If he ran now, they would surely follow. They would kill little Samwin.

Lord Taylian could not allow that. He drew the sword at his side. "I cannot stop them all, but I can save him."

A party of Aisharian and Britian soldiers turned the corner just as Lord Samwin completely disappeared down the opposite way. Lord Taylian steadied his breath and firmed his stance- just like Lord Digarius and his father had taught him. He stood tall and ready as the soldiers met his stance.

The company paused their rushing and slowly prowled for him. Their postures were lax, and their weapons were held loosely. The Britian soldier closest to Lord Taylian opened his mouth to speak, but was cut off as an Aisharian gladiator covered in blood shoved past and made his way forward.

"It is a child!" The Britian soldier shouted as the Aisharian stormed.

Lord Taylian's fear of the man twice his size did not take over. He charged, too.

The gladiator pulled a second sword from his back, swinging the first to knock Lord Taylian's sword out of his hand and send it clattering down the hall. The second went straight through Lord Taylian's chest.

The Aisharian sneered as he slowly sank his blade in further. "It is an enemy."

"A dead enemy," he laughed.

Shouts for retreat came from the outside as steps of a different echo came down the hall. The Aisharian removed his blade from Lord Taylian's chest and carelessly let his body fall to the ground, backing up and rushing back to where they came.

Chapter 64

Lord Digarius was the first to see Lord Taylian fall to his knees.

The image slowed in time, his footsteps not fast enough to prevent the fall as he sprinted down the cobblestone for his brother. Lady Belva's shrieking pierced the air as she ran for her son. Lord Montarian bellowed out as his feet hit the cobblestone when he turned the corner.

Lord Taylian fell on his hand, kneeling and sputtering for air as he watched his own blood drip from his mouth and chest onto the stone below.

His body was jerked to the side as Lord Digarius pulled him to his lap.

Lord Digarius choked out, "Healer! Healer! Someone help!"

His hands ran down his brother's face, his entire body shaking as he held him.

"I'm sorry." Lord Taylian sputtered, blood sprinkling over Lord Digarius' already soiled and stained face.

"No, no, no, no. Don't be sorry. Stay with me. Stay with me. Please," Lord Digarius cried. He shook his body back and forth as he held his brother.

Lord Taylian reached a trembling hand to touch his brother's shoulder, a grasping hold they often gave one another in times of comfort.

"I did what I thought you'd do," he coughed, and his hand fell. "I wanted to be—"

More blood.

"—be like—"

"Shh shh shh." Lord Digarius crooned. He did not need to hear the rest of his words.

Be like me.

What a ridiculous thing to try to be. Lord Digarius thought as he put more pressure on Lord Taylian's hopeless wound.

Lady Belva fell in front of her sons, her screaming still overtaking the halls as her hands jerked out for her dying son. Lord Digarius let her pull his body from his lap.

"My baby! My baby boy!" she screamed, pulling him to her chest and putting her hands onto his wound, "Help us! Help us!"

"Mama," Lord Taylian spat out, "I wanted to fight—"

More blood sputtered out of his mouth.

"— fight for you."

Lord Theodus stood behind her, his entire body heaving with each breath. The Lord of Ayeshire slowly descended to his knees, wrapping one arm around her shoulders and the other around their dying son.

And he sobbed.

"I'm... sorry," Lord Taylian spat out and heaved more blood.

Lord Samwin stood behind them, the supplies and toys he came for falling to the ground. He did not move to be with his family.

"Shhhh," she comforted Lord Taylian, "You're okay, baby, shh shh."

Lady Belva felt the last breath escape Lord Taylian's chest as his body turned limp in her arms. Voices behind them shouted as Healers made their way too late to them.

"Taylian, baby, wake up. Honey, wake up, they're here to help you," she sobbed, "Baby, wake up."

She rocked back and forth with him in her arms, like she used to do when he was a babe crying in the night for comfort and his mother. Her husband squeezed her shoulders as she rocked their son to sleep for the last time.

He knew.

She knew.

Taylian was gone.

Flames took over Lady Belva's eyes, darkness shrouded her face, and her entire body radiated heat.

They took her son.

He took her son.

"He killed my baby. He killed my baby," she choked out, still holding tight to Lord Taylian's limp and lifeless body. "He killed my baby..." her words continued until they faded into nothing but sobs.

And then she screamed with such fierceness that the final moments of battle ended.

Chapter 65

"You fought so carelessly, with too much anger hanging over you. If not for my Dragons, Your Highness, we would have lost ground, not gained it." Princess Easter said to Prince Elion as they walked through their broken-down camp. Around them, soldiers in red, orange, and gold regalia packed up wagons of supplies to prepare to move east, past the shores of Lake Lahere and the outskirts of Clardin and into the hills of Ravenhall. One more successful clash and they would regain Ravenhall's fortress.

"We should gain Ravenhall by the time the ground frosts, if not sooner. Madam Fury has written to me about her plans to join us." Her words paused briefly, and her eyes flickered down before she quickly jutted her chin again. "She can send soldiers soon through the Three Sisters. If we coordinate properly, we can attack from the north and the west. I think it is time we properly push forward. No more waiting. No more timidness."

Prince Elion responded with a simple hmph.

Her hands wrung together behind her back, and she stopped their walk, firming her stature and jaw as she looked up at him. "I had wondered how our enemies managed to retain control over Ravenhall. But after seeing how you battled, I now understand."

"Excuse me?" Prince Elion replied. He was too tired to show proper anger; the restless night after the battle and the exhaustion he faced from tearing through enemies wore heavily on him and his patience. Despite feeling bone-tired and drained, he felt a fire simmering inside him, bubbling below the layers of exhaustion.

"There was a clear lack of discipline, of direction. I did not fully realize how poorly your actions had affected your soldiers until now. Even my eyes and ears around camp did not see it fully until we fought alongside you the day prior."

Prince Elion stepped forward and let loose what anger he could muster. "You were spying on us?"

"No. Gathering information. There is a difference, prince."

He had no reply.

"They are afraid of you," she said, her tone a warning of the news she set to reveal.

"Good. They should be." He would not look at her. He scanned their disassembled camp. He wanted to be gone and on the road now.

She stepped to his side, ensuring his wandering eyes would find her firm glare. "They are uncertain of you. And after witnessing the blue flame fires exploding over the horizon and us yet to know who lit them, they grow more worried."

"Then I shall set them right," he gritted out between clenched teeth.

"Elion, will you listen?" Princess Easter hissed, "Enough with this posturing and this ego. You are leading an army in a war that was started against your father. You are fighting a war to win the right to inherit his throne against a woman named Queen of the People. A title granted by your own people turned against us and her people who have been inspired."

Prince Elion looked away again.

Princess Easter stood tall, her expression determined as she held her ground with unwavering conviction. "Meanwhile, you have murdered enemies that you kept in your camp all on an assumption you made in," she snapped her fingers, and he jolted. "- a second of anger because you assumed they murdered your lover."

"You do not get to set me right," he sneered. His eyes threw daggers at her, and his anger threatened to do worse.

She continued her hissing, her tone still low enough to be heard only by him or those nosing close by. "Someone must. I will not lose my throne because of your insolence, and I will not allow you to bring shame to me through our association."

"Yes. Our association that could, through careful work on my part, be dissolved before either of us gets our crowns. Kings have done it before. Kings have also found other ways to rid themselves of their wives." The anger boiled over; Prince Elion felt it burning his flesh and bones.

Princess Easter shook her head slowly. "You would let something so simple, so trite, erase who you are inside. A logical, well-thought-out prince and leader, gone just like that because you had to send a few unruly citizens to their graves, fight a few battles, and lose your fuck toy to revenge or an accident." She scoffed in bafflement. "What a disappointing arc, prince."

His eyes narrowed with a growing fury that pierced through the veil of fatigue that had settled upon him. A wave of anger surged through his body, threatening to consume him and all around him. He could feel the tension building within him, like a storm gathering on the horizon.

Princess Easter noted the storm clouds in his glare. But she would not stand down.

"Change your path, Elion. This will not end well for you, nor the kingdom, if you do not stop." She jammed a finger downward between them. "Return to who you truly are. Become the king who will proudly rule this kingdom when his time comes, or lose that future."

Princess Easter turned sharply, her braided hair whipping behind her as she stormed for the gathering of gold and orange. Her Dragons greeted her with respect and excitement. Prince Elion surveyed the moving camp around him, the clouds of red and silver avoiding his looks and working with furor.

As he stood there, surveying the camp, his chest still heaving with anger, he let out a deep, rough sigh. The anger that had been crackling through him like a fire out of control had finally dissipated, leaving him feeling drained and exhausted again.

Despite the armor he wore and the armor he had freshly built inside himself, her words penetrated his very being and found the parts of himself the fire had engulfed. They were but ashes and burned remains, but there they remained.

Chapter 66

"You will calm yourself now, father, or you will find yourself in chains," Lord Digarius snarled at Lord Theodus, his voice full of authority. "The soldiers have surrendered and will be evacuated to their homeland, peacefully, as the laws of war demand."

"They murdered my son!" He screamed, his voice one of pure rage and grief. He turned to Lady Belva, who appeared more ghost than woman as she sat in her chair. Her shoulders were slumped, and her dressing gown, now covered in a restless day's worth of stains and sweat, crumpled over her slumped body. Her eyes had dug caverns into her face and sat atop deep circles. Her braids, once perfectly twisted and laid, were already coming undone; her gaze, once hardened and concentrated, had her lost in a world no one could reach. Lord Theodus lowered his tone as he looked at her, "They murdered our son."

"I know," Lord Digarius snapped back at his father, demanding his attention again. His grief cracked through his anger as he fell forward and placed both hands on the table. He hung his head and loosened a breath. "I know he is dead. I held his body as he took some of his last breaths. But these soldiers were not all responsible; the ethics of law demand their return, not their deaths. We cannot let ourselves resort to the senseless violence of the king."

"No." Lord Theodus said. "They need to suffer for what happened to Taylian."

"And they will, but not in this way," Lord Digarius shook his head and straightened up. "Father, you know we cannot simply slaughter everyone in our wake. We cannot become the thing that we fight against."

"Look at her." Lord Theodus jabbed a finger towards Lady Belva, "Look at your mother and tell her that you will not find vengeance for what they have done to your brother, to your mother. Look at her and tell her that if I, your lord father, get revenge, that you will stop me."

Lord Digarius's mouth fell open at the low blow his father threw. He turned to his mother and kneeled beside her. "Mother, mother, we need you, please."

She did not reply nor move.

"Mother, your people need you."

She slowly reached a hand atop the carved table of their lands, the map they used for battle strategy and to count the armies around the kingdom using carved figures and place markers. She gently pointed a finger to the stag figure that bore her family crest and sat atop Middleton Landing. Her finger shook slightly as she touched the stag's antlers and pushed it over.

Her hollow eyes stayed frozen in place as she shook her head.

Lord Digarius rested his hand on top of her outstretched one. He turned to his father, looking to him for help. Lord Theodus shuffled on his feet and clenched and unclenched his hands- he had no understanding of what to do with silent pain, of sorrow and sadness.

"Do you really believe she would want more children dead? More innocents taken? More bloodshed?" Lord Digarius asked. "If so, then behead the prisoners now and kill their sons while you swing. Otherwise, perhaps we fix our home that has fallen before we raze another one to ashes."

Chapter 67

Ephraim found themself sleeping in their office again. This morning, they had woken with their head resting in their folded arms on their desk. A mortar and pestle spilled over beside their elbow, and the ground herbs had fallen into a mess of a pile beside the tools.

They groaned, brushed the pile of lavendula, chamomile, and lemon balm back into the stone bowl, and returned it to its place on their paper-laden desk.

Death records with blank lines where a Healer's name was to be signed stared up at them.

They could not decide which records hurt the most to sign, the ones with familiar names or the ones with names they did not recognize.

Ephraim pushed the papers away and rubbed the rest of the grogginess from their eyes. When their eyes closed, the memories came again.

Screams, explosions, and the clashing of metal rang in their ears. They found themself on the high wall of the fortress again among armored fighters. Bloodied soldiers cried out for help as enemies rushed the steps, and arrows took down allies. The city screamed of war.

Their eyes shot to the battlefield below as another Hellfire bomb flew overhead. Green and red capes disintegrated in an instant, and bodies were turned to ash by their hand.

They refused to take their eyes off what they caused. They refused to look away as the terror in the soldier's eyes flashed for only a second before they met their end.

"I did this. I did this." Ephraim shook their head and tried to wipe away the memories. Their heart raged in their chest, and their breath came out in harsh gasps; Ephraim clutched their chest as the anxiety worsened. Their hands shook as they reached for a vial of infused liquid. They ripped the cork off with their teeth and downed the vial's contents.

The harsh burn of the liquor was soothed by the herbs infused with it.

Ephraim dropped the vial, and the glass clinked against the desk's surface. Their hands still trembled as they impatiently awaited the relief the herbal aid would bring to their mind. They dared not close their eyes as they worked to steady their ragged breathing.

With each inhale, they remembered the breath they had taken from others. With each exhale, they felt hollow.

Gerald's head lolled to the side as he slowly woke from a sleep that felt like a thousand ages. His eyelids were heavy, and the fog around his mind hid his last memories. His shoulders rolled under him as he moved to sit up; an uncomfortable pain throbbed through his back.

He pushed his body up and leaned to his right to rest on his elbow, only to fall onto the bed; no arm was there to support him.

Gerald let out a pained and confused grunt as his face met the cotton sheets of the Healer's house bed. The pain radiating through his body cleared his mind and brought back the memories of battle. His breath was lost and found in short bursts as he began to panic, and a scream built in his throat.

"Mr. Ackley, breathe. It is okay." A soft voice spoke from beside the bed, and shuffled footsteps stopped inches away from him. Small, calloused hands gently gripped him and moved him onto his back.

Gerald's eyes dilated as he was turned over and looked upon the ceiling above his bed. His vision was blurred as his left arm was grabbed and thrown around the neck of the Healer, who pulled him up to sit up in bed.

Gerald settled and turned his gaze to where his right arm should have been. His eyes focused on the stitched and swollen flesh; bruises and redness dotted the tanned skin wrapped around a short nub protruding from his shoulder.

"It's gone. It's gone. It's gone." His mumblings became more coherent as his voice found its place. He began to shake and heave, "Gone. Gone. Gone. Gone. Gone. Gone."

"He's doing it again," the Healer said as more came running over, "Should we put him to sleep again?"

"Mr. Ackley, you are okay. Yes, you lost your arm, but—" a strange voice tried to soothe him.

"Gone. Gone. Gone." Gerald continued, now shoving at the Healers and kicking and crying in his bed. "Gone. Gone. Gone. Gone. Gone."

"Get the rag and douse it. I will hold him down," the phantom voice said.

"Mr. Ackley, please take a breath. It is okay. You are okay."

"Gone. Gone. Gone. Gone. Gone."

Arms reached for Gerald, but he kicked and shoved against them.

"Gone! Gone! Gone!"

Strong arms held Gerald down despite his thrashing, and an ether-like odor overwhelmed his senses as he breathed into a wet rag placed against his face.

He found himself in familiar darkness again.

Chapter 68

Sedrick walked with urgency down the worn wooden docks, his eyes darting to the horizon of home. Royland sat on a crate, his fishing line in hand, puffing on his pipe. Sedrick stopped abruptly and leaned in towards the familiar fisherman without wasting a moment.

Sedrick spoke in a hushed tone, "I need a horse, and I need the fastest one you can find me."

Royland raised an eyebrow, still focused on his fishing line. "Where to?" he asked.

Royland had aided Sedrick when he first docked his boat on the shores of Britia and quite poorly disguised himself as a fisherman heading to the king's city for work. Royland saw through Sedrick's guise and reminded him that many ordinary people under the king's eye held no love for their ruler and oppressor.

Sedrick scanned the docks around them, wary of prying ears. "I can't make it across the Gulf, not after that battle. But I can travel by land. I heard that the Sebern army is still stationed around Ravenhall. That they still hold the fortress. For now."

Royland put down his fishing line and removed his pipe, letting out a long puff. He looked at Sedrick. "But the prince's army is still in those same lands. Between you and your allies."

Sedrick shuffled and twitched his hand to his breast pocket, feeling for the parchment still tucked in its place, his anxiety needing to feel it again. "I know. But I need to get to the Sebern army. I did what I needed to do in the city, and now I need to get back home."

Royland put his pipe back in his mouth and gruffed, "King still kickin'?"

Sedrick squinted and shook his head in confusion. "Yes, that wasn't my—"

Royland raised a hand to hush him. "As long as he's alive, I'll help ya. Come on, I know of some horses that we can get you." He paused his words and his steps. "But, I hope our new queen gave you enough coin to pay for some discretion."

"Our new queen?" Sedrick whispered.

Royland chuckled. "Queen of the People, they call her, your Lady of Ayeshire. Seems now she is fightin' for a new throne and not just against the king."

"Lady Montarian has declared herself a queen?" Sedrick rushed the words out in a too-loud gasp as Royland stood up and guided him down the dock.

One monarchy to replace another.

Another head to wear the same crown that has inflicted so much harm.

Royland shook his head at Sedrick's comment, then nodded in greeting at the other fishermen they passed by. "She has not, no, but the people have. Rumors made their way up the waterline that she revealed some big secret of the king's, and now everyone doesn't just want him gone, but wants her in his place."

Royland paused and turned to look up at Sedrick, then flicked his eyes at Sedrick's breast pocket. "That secret got anything to do with what you were doin' in Isilria?"

Sedrick instinctively put his hand against his pocket and stepped back from Royland. "No. That was—"

"Ah, I don't care, doesn't matter to me." Royland chortled and returned to walking.

"What are people's thoughts about her possibly replacing His Majesty?" Sedrick huffed out as he made to walk beside the older man.

Royland shrugged, "An ass in the throne is still an ass in the throne, no matter who it belongs to. But," he grunted as he leaned to open a rickety door of a small tavern nestled behind a building at the port, "it's not like our people know any different. Someone's gotta lord over us all in the end."

Sedrick followed behind him into the quiet and dimly lit tavern. Only two other patrons sat inside, hunched over in the corner at a booth. They paid no attention to the new men coming inside. "But do they? Before the Conquest, we were all free."

"And look how well that turned out," Royland grumbled as he sat down at the empty bar.

Sedrick felt a familiarity wash over him at the quick back-and-forth between the two. A familiar feeling of comfort he felt when talking to Father Robb or Sister Ora about all of his ideas and knowledge, conversations that would turn quickly into debates and friendly arguments of ideals.

He knew he had little time to find comfort in his days, but he craved it so deeply amongst the heaviness.

"From the rumors and theories found in old scholarly journals, the freedom and open borders were prosperous, healthy, vibrant for the people of The Continent. But just as many, if not more, speak of how important it was for the people to gain law and order and direction. One still must wonder how much the victors of The Conquest worked to change the narrative and ensure–"

Royland cocked his head to the side and blinked several times at Sedrick as the young man turned in his stool and caught the fisherman's eye.

"For a simple sailor, you sure know a lot about journals and Scholar work." Royland turned as a barmaid came from the back of the tavern to greet them. "Lots of folks would be very interested in that information. Could make a lot of money off that if they told the right people."

All Sedrick could manage was to stutter and stammer. He had been so stupid to divulge too much to someone he barely knew he could trust. While Royland hated the king and acted against him as far as Sedrick could tell, Sedrick never did stop to learn if it was a ruse or a trap.

He had always been too quick to trust.

You, stupid, stupid boy! His mother's voice screamed in his head.

He still carried the scars from his boyhood, where his knuckles were rapped with reeds for secretly holding books instead of sailing rope, his heart was sliced into shreds when his family sent him to the streets for betraying His Will and dooming their souls with his scholarly curiosity.

If he had not trusted his closest friend to know his secret, he would have never been abandoned. And now he had possibly done it again.

"Hah! Anyway, not like it matters in the end. I heard something about Her Future Majesty ridding us of the Divine Houses."

"What?" Sedrick choked out.

"Yeah, turns out it was all bullshit." Royland pushed a full stein over to Sedrick that the barmaid had set in front of the old man. Royland looked at the barmaid, "Anyway, my friend here needs a favor, my lady."

Royland set a coin on the counter for her. "And remember, just like the other ones, he was never here."

"The others?" Sedrick leaned in and whispered.

The woman with no name held out her hand to Sedrick and smiled. "There have been many things happening in the kingdom for some time. Not that we know anything about that, man with no name."

Chapter 69

He had killed Lord Taylian.

He had killed her soldiers.

He had tortured and executed countless men.

And he certainly would be playing a part in Sister Ora's current torture and pain.

Sir Marion may not have held the sword that took Lord Taylian's life, but he was the man who led the army that did it. Who trained the Aishar soldiers who did. He may not have drawn the blood from each of her soldiers, but he ordered it to be taken.

Lady Montarian may want the king's head, but Emaline needed Sir Marion's.

She sat on the bench at the end of her bed in the barracks she had been staying in at Middleton Landing, admiring the new sword she had forged after hers had taken too many hits in the battle. She sharpened the blade again and again.

On the blade, she had engraved three names, all of which would meet its steel when she had her chance.

Sir Marion.

For being the bastard he is and for everything he has done to her best friend since he forced their separation. Emaline may not know exactly what pain he has caused Sister Ora, but Emaline will make it seem like kindness when she is done with him.

Father Figgins.

Because she knew his will and words moved many to do treacherous and terrible things. While they were not covered in blood, his hands were certainly not clean.

King Ivan Scott.

The man who could end all of this but chose to add to the death and pain— who chose to start it. The man whose life she would save for Lady Montarian to take herself if she asked.

Sir Rainey's name was also carved closest to the hilt, her justice upon him already met before the blade was cast aflame.

The rest would soon follow.

She had a list now, and if she were destined and made to be a soldier, to draw blood and take lives, then she would do so in her own way— for her own form of justice. If she were born to kill, she would take the most wretched. If she were made to defend, she would save the most helpless.

With every sing of the sharpening stone on her blade, Emaline heard the word her vengeance and anger would bring to this world.

Justice.

Justice.

Justice.

And when she was done, she would decide whether the name etched on the decorative cross guard would meet the blade, too, or if that name could live after all this was done.

Emaline Kingery.

Chapter 70

"Your Majesty?" an old, male voice sounded from a distance, as if it came from a land of dreams or called down from the souls that spoke to King Ivan in the sky.

"Your Majesty?" the voice sounded again, this time closer.

King Ivan's head lolled as the voice called him back. A bony hand touched his shoulder, and the king jolted.

"Hmm? Yes?" King Ivan said to the hand on his shoulder. The fingers were short and stubby, swollen around the joints, with slight crooks near the tips of each finger. Brightly polished golden rings covered in stones and engravings drew attention to each digit.

The king's lips smacked together as he opened his mouth. His dry lips hurt to move, and his throat felt raw, like bile had stained and burned his throat.

"Your Majesty, it is good to see you awake," the male voice came clearly into the king's mind. His Majesty turned, and his eyes fell on the Hand of the King pin on the wearer's tunic.

"Lord Orville." King Ivan's voice cracked as if he were to weep, and he rested his hand on the crooked fingers still resting on his shoulder. "Oh, my friend, where have you been all this time?"

The hand he held stiffened.

"Your Majesty, it is I, Father Figgins. Your new Hand."

A memory fell over the king. Shame followed close behind.

King Ivan quickly removed his hand from Father Figgins and pushed himself up out of his chair. The blanket on his lap fell to his feet as he rose stiffly and cleared his throat. He pushed away the fog that continued to swirl in his mind, a fog that created echoes of memories, half-formed thoughts, and pain.

"Yes, of course, a slip of the old tongue, Father." King Ivan replied. He forced his words to carry harsh command. The short effort exhausted him quickly.

"Yes. Of course, Your Majesty." Father Figgins said.

"How long has it been since the battle? Since we..." the king trailed off.

"Since we lost and began to await the return of our soldiers? It is the 29th of Pyria. You slept in fits for two da'es after you fell during the battle."

King Ivan hobbled to the sideboard lining the wall of his chambers. He searched for a stiff drink but found none. A decanter of herbal water—a boiled and cooled mixture of lemons and thyme many Healers used to help those in their care drink more and refuel—sat half full. Sweat-soiled rags sat in a small basket beside a pile of fresh towels. Oily stains dotted the wooden counter—the scent of medicinal herbs mixing into a stink that disgusted the king.

King Ivan shook as he poured a glass of water for himself. "Do the Master Healers know what caused my fall and slumber?"

He pushed his mind to its limits again, forcing command into his tone and sanity into his words. He sat again to recover his strength.

"The fog may take some time to be lifted, Your Majesty. You hit your head," Said Father Figgins. As he spoke, King Ivan touched his forehead and felt the stitching that held a scar together. Father Figgins continued, "They believe the stress you have placed on yourself lately, alongside that of the battle, had put too much strain on your heart."

King Ivan took a deep breath and found his chair again, taking deep breaths as he sat.

"I believe it wise, as does the Council and your Master Healer, that you spend your time resting and recovering fully." A vial clinked onto the table beside the king's chair. "The poppy-induced slumber they put you in helped you heal quicker, but we all worry about the pains below the surface, more so now than we did before."

King Ivan flicked his eyes between the medicinal vial Father Figgins had set on the table and his face, "The pains below the surface?"

Father Figgins hesitated and thinned his lips, "Your mind has become a subject of concern."

The king spat, "I hit my head when I fell; smaller men have been hurt worse in battle and recovered without a care."

To emphasize his point regarding his health, King Ivan shot up out of his chair. He stepped forward and hurriedly walked to the window- an attempt to cover up the dizziness that hit him and sent him reeling forward.

"Yes, but those men are not the king." Father Figgins said, "And... there was not an existing worry of their mind before their fall."

The king started, "Do you dare question your king's mind? His sanity?"

"I do not, no. It is— perhaps I have spoken too much, Your Majesty. Please forgive me." Father Figgins quickly blurted out.

King Ivan's lip curled, and he turned away from the window ledge that held him up, "You have not said enough. If conspiracy and conversation are occurring about me under my nose, then it is your damn job to tell me! You are my Hand- act like it."

Father Figgins nodded sheepishly at the sick and shouting king.

"Perhaps they only converse out of concern, but..." Father Figgins's head bobbed side-to-side as he contemplated his next words, "You know how Lord Tyrrian is, and the lords of Odessin, always plotting and talking. I fear their worries may have also fallen to Prince Percy's ears." Father Figgins swallowed and carefully stepped forward, "Your Majesty, I tell you this not to startle or anger you."

"What do they say?" the king interjected.

"Your Majesty?"

"What do they say, Father Figgins?" his words shot out like venom. "What does my own Council say of their king's mind?"

Father Figgins squared his shoulders, took a deep breath, and let it out, "They fear that you have gone mad."

"It is not possible for us to know every potential move our enemy might make or every weapon they possess. Had they not had Hellfire—" The chamber doors swung open, cutting off Lord Nesima Mete's words. The Council members immediately rose from their seats as King Ivan entered the room. The king acknowledged no one as he made his way to the head of the table, taking his seat with cold authority.

"Go on, sit." King Ivan said to his Council. His tone was flat and straightforward.

"Your Majesty," Lord Nesima said, "we were not expecting you at this meeting."

"You did not expect the king to be in his own Council meeting, Lord Mete?" King Ivan snipped in Lord Nesima's direction before helping himself to the wine and spirits laid out on the table.

Lord Nesima could not help but be taken aback. He had a brief, uncertain glance with his husband, who wore the same intrigued expression he had maintained throughout the meeting. "Apologies, Your Majesty. We thought you were still recovering."

"Your king is fine. I am of sound body and mind and do not need to spend more time in a bed, drugged on some concoction that only makes me sleep." King Ivan joined his hands on the table- a tremoring shake preceded their tight clutch on one another- and scanned the room, "Unless any of you have some sort of concern?"

Another glance was shared between the Lords of Odessin.

"Your Majesty," Father Figgins calmly said. Lord Nesima looked deeply at the expression Father Figgins wore as he spoke. One bushy eyebrow was raised, and his chin dipped to the side. "Perhaps we can recap for you what we have already covered?"

King Ivan cleared his throat, "Yes, do."

"The returning ships are a few da'es away from returning with the dead and survivors. We lost at least a dozen ships-"

"An expense my people are not happy to bear." Lord Tyrrian snarled. "We do not build ships to be destroyed in a battle we should have won with ease."

Father Figgins continued, "— and the remaining ships all have some damage to be repaired upon their return. Iron Bay was more resilient and prepared for our ships than we expected and did much damage before many could pass, and the Hellfire bombs... we are still awaiting a true count of who survived."

"Lord Barker, how much did this cost us?" King Ivan turned to the Master of Currency.

"That depends, Your Majesty, on how we assess the value of the lives and property lost, including Prince Elion's casualties," Lord Barker replied carefully.

"And what has my son said of their battle?"

"It was a hard-fought success with the aid of Princess East-er's brigade of Dragons," said Lord Nesima Mete proudly but with caution in his tone.

King Ivan's gaze slowly shifted to the lord, his eyes narrowing as he leaned forward. "Whose brigade?"

"Our daughter, your son's wife, Princess Easter." Lord Nesima said.

The king shot out of his chair, almost throwing it off its feet, "And you all call me mad?! When you send the future queen to battle alongside the Crown Prince? Without a child in her belly or on her tit to ensure they have an heir to solidify their claim?! Are we content to let my line die in this war?!"

Prince Percy quietly cleared his throat.

"Sending the future queen into battle is no riskier than send-ing just the future king." Lord Shaital Pathis calmly replied. "They do not command their soldiers near one another and do not fight beside one another on the field. The risk is low that both would be killed on the same field in the same battle. And outside of our men, no one knows she is even fighting."

"It is a risk. She could be killed. Hells, they both could be taken and used to ransom a victory in this war!" King Ivan's voice trembled with a mixture of fear and fury. "Imagine that the future king and queen in a battlefield cell crafted by our enemy?"

Lord Shaital finally looked directly at the king, his eyes nar-rowing more, "She is at as much of a risk as any warrior under her banner, no more. It would take a snake in the grass for our enemy to know she is there. Do you have concerns, Your Majesty, that not all snakes have been found?"

"She is the future queen of this kingdom—"

"And she is my daughter first," Lord Nesima interrupted, a surge of anger rising in his chest. Every word the king had spoken since entering the room had been laced with accusation and suspicion as if they were fighting a battle among themselves rather than against their common enemy. "Easter is a skilled warrior, trained by her own choice and determination. Her Dragons respect her and follow her commands without question. To keep her from the front lines would be to waste one of our greatest assets."

King Ivan returned to his seat, "And where are your other assets, Lord Nesima? There were to be more of your Dragons and fighters coming to aid, yet here we sit, with only a small sampling of what you all create in the desert."

Lord Nesima took a slow breath to calm himself, "Madam Fury has faced many complications at the border. We have called upon her to stay north and keep her eyes on those that continue to rip apart the Holy Lands. We have sent for others to join the battle here, and she will join us soon."

King Ivan had no satisfaction with that answer. "When you were brought here, you were told to bring your best fighters to this battle. Your king demanded-"

"Your Majesty," Father Figgins cut the king off. " Hard decisions have to be made every day to keep all corners of this kingdom in their delicate balance. Please forgive us for having to make so many without your guidance on every one."

"These decisions—this lack of consultation—are reckless at best and treasonous at worst," King Ivan snapped, his voice cold and sharp. "You are not to act without my permission. You are not to make decisions without my involvement. I am to be included in all meetings, in all discussions, in all considerations now and until the end of my rule."

Heads nodded in understanding around the table. Lord Nesima also nodded politely, though he silently pushed aside the questions he longed to ask about the king's concerns and his current state. Most pressing of all was the question of why the king suddenly seemed unwilling to allow his own Council to carry out their sworn duty—running the kingdom alongside him and in his stead if he were unavailable.

For generations, it had been said in jest that 'the king whores while the Council rules' and that the true rulers of the kingdom were the men who sat behind the drunk king and informed him of which parchments to sign and which marriages to approve.

"What is our next proposed strike?" the king asked, his tone brooking no further dissent.

"We were waiting on Sir Marion's return and his battle report before we plan another strike." Lord Tyrrian said. "His field report will provide us with the intelligence needed to plan our next move carefully and strategically."

The king grunted. "And what else?"

"There have been disturbances within the city, Your Majesty. The people are restless after the recent taxes levied to fund the war efforts, and watching their families be separated between home and battlefield- or grave. And after the King's Guard and City Watch went into the city to" Father Figgins found the right words "show the strength of the throne, one might say, there have been many disturbances. But they are being handled."

King Ivan's eyes narrowed. "Handled? Or suffocated?"

"There is a delicate balance to quelling angered citizens, Your Majesty. Perhaps we may suggest a kinder hand than what was given just before the battle." Lord Shaital spoke up. "Especially since our soldiers come back bearing losses, it may do us a favor to calm the iron fist that has been wielded against our people."

"I concur, Your Majesty." Lord Nesima nodded, sparing a glance at the pondering Prince Percy, who nodded in agreement.

"What exactly is it you would recommend, then?" the king asked as he swung back another drink. "Walking out onto the street and giving them hugs and kisses? Coddle them and ask them kindly to stop?"

Lord Nesima flicked his eyes to his husband, knowing Lord Shaital would be eager to quip and argue and rise against the king's ignorant comments. Thankfully, Lord Shaital did not speak.

"The people are poor, tired, and hungry." Lord Nesima spared a look at the king, hopeful for an understanding to be found with few words.

No such connection was made.

The king truly had gone off a cliff. He had always been a bit short-tempered and short-thinking at times, but even in those moments, he had always seemed to care beneath it all. Had his fall, or something more, truly changed him that deeply?

Lord Shaital sighed, finally letting his tongue loose, "Feed them, Your Majesty. Show them that the crown is not to be fought against but fought for. Feed them before the winter freezes their bones, and you have nothing left to rule over but skeletons. Feed them before you repeat last winter, where your Reapers buried bodies alongside crop seed when the ground thawed."

The king snapped again. "I tried! Do not dare imply I did not! And look what it got me- citizens still speaking blasphemy, allies warring against me, and your Guild Lord fining my ships for sailing into his ports! All because I did try to help my people and the sea took the ship!"

Lord Nesima had never seen so much red before, not in the halls adorned with curtains in the king's colors, not in the battlefields his Dragons and soldiers slayed upon, not in the sands of their western shores.

The king's face was due to burst and light aflame if it did not stop.

"Father," Prince Percy now stood and firmly stared down his father, but spoke like a true prince, not a Scholarly second son too shy and troubled to avoid stammering in such rooms. "We are only wishing to help. I am certain the lords meant no implication by their words. Let us try. One more time, let us try goodness before we finally say goodbye to it."

Lord Nesima was shocked by how the prince's words broke through the king's volcanic anger.

King Ivan swallowed, cleared his throat and took several breaths. Finally, he spoke calmly and quietly. "Okay, son, one more time. But no more."

Chapter 71

A light knock came from the door as Princess Arminda entered Lady Ora and Prince Percy's living chambers. The princess did not wait for any proper greeting from the maids and servants who were busy dressing the room and moving furniture while Lady Ora directed them.

The princess smiled and nodded kindly at the help. "Please, no formalities, I am here to speak to Lady Ora."

Lady Ora watched in annoyance as the princess sat down on a couch haphazardly strewn in the space, her prim and proper act on full display for the audience. Lady Ora's lips thinned to a straight line as she let out an annoyed breath through her nose. She turned to the working servants. "Please excuse the princess and I."

"Your Highness, what can I do for you?" Lady Ora asked, her tone formal and polite, masking her reluctance to be anywhere near the scheming princess, or near anyone from her bloodline. The bloodline that destroyed her home and killed so many of her people.

As the doors latched shut behind the departing servants, Lady Ora remained standing in the same spot across the room, her fingers intertwined and resting in front of her, fighting the urge to pick at her already bloody nail beds. As she had for many days, Lady Ora wore neutral tones often meant for those in mourning. Forbidden ever to wear green again, she opted for mourning grey and black, her only option of rebellion.

Princess Arminda spared a glance at the open wardrobes strewn about, scoffing at the pile of red dresses tossed to the side in crumpled balls.

"I have a task for you," the princess said as she sank into the back of the couch, making herself comfortable.

"So now that you have dumped all of your secrets on me to bear, you are assigning me jobs?" Lady Ora scoffed, a dirty look shooting across the room at the princess.

"All of my secrets? Please, what I told you was barely a scratch." Princess Arminda picked at a loose hair hanging on her soft, white, and pink dress, a signature palette of the princess that Lady Ora now knew to be covering what lay beneath the surface. "This task will be to your benefit as well, and I'm sure you would like to be of use for something, since you had to stand by and watch my father and uncle's armada destroy your home across the Gulf."

Lady Ora balled her hands into fists where they still lay crossed on her chest. She had not been given even a moment to mourn over her country's losses or cry over the tales she overheard. While she knew the stories were likely false exaggerations since the army had yet to return, she still felt a need, a wish, and a desire to let them burn through her bones and turn her into a heap of ash.

But instead, every moment of her day had been filled with obligations: lunches with the noble women of the court, meetings with aides to design her and Prince Percy's chambers, tea with the queen on the very balcony they sat upon during the battle, and where the king fell. The blood where His Majesty had hit his head still stained the stone. God, she hoped the cut would scar.

Lady Ora composed herself and slowly walked to the couch, standing beside the rolled arm. She stared down at the relaxed princess lounging on the side of the couch. "And what task would that be?"

"I know that after the war, you and my brother will head north to Odessin to live your lives away from this court. You will convince my brother- who will convince my father- that you wish to bring me to assist you in getting your household settled."

Lady Ora's eyes slitted as her face crumpled. She cocked her chin up as she questioned the princess. Why would this scheming princess wish to be away from the very court she enjoys playing games in?

Lady Ora asked, "Why?"

"My reasons are mine alone; just know it is important and needs to be done," said Princess Arminda flatly.

Lady Ora scoffed and chuckled. "Why would I want to help you with whatever this is?"

"Because it will benefit you, as I said." Princess Arminda gave a cocky grin. "If you don't, I will use my power to force my father to make you two stay. And if you are stuck in this castle, how else will you get to your friend whom you thought executed? How else will you possibly find a way to escape our grasp?"

"What?" Lady Ora straightened, only hearing the first question.

Sedrick.

"No, I saw it, he was…."

She lost her ability to breathe. Lady Ora had worked so diligently to shove every memory of that day down into the dark pit she had dug into her mind, where she hid everything she could not handle in hopes they would eventually evaporate from the core of her soul.

"Executed by beheading? No. Although, from our angle, that random man did look much like him. The sun was bright that day, and you were standing in such a spot where you could not see the differences between him and the man they brought in, believing him to be the right one." The princess's tone was careless and saturated in power and arrogance.

Lady Ora's hands flexed at her sides. She had every desire to rip and pull at her skin again, to pull out each hair in her scalp to find release from the building tension in her body.

She felt a voice call her to do the same to the princess.

"What happened?" Lady Ora managed to get out between gritted teeth.

"Me. That is what." Princess Arminda laughed at herself. "I planted some information in the ears of those who owed me a favor, and they found another man in the docks who looked eerily like your friend."

Lady Ora's chest rose and fell as steam came out with each of her breaths. She stormed around the couch and snagged Princess Arminda's arm. "So it was you who told His Majesty of that night. It was you who got Sir Loren and an innocent man murdered."

Tears coated her face as she shook Princess Arminda. The princess gave no energy back to Lady Ora's anger and clawed grip.

The princess blinked in annoyance and loosened a breath. "You are not as insightful as I thought you were, sister. For a High Scholar, you are—"

Lady Ora squeezed her arm tighter, "Shut up. Shut up. Shut up!"

She threw Princess Arminda back onto the couch.

"You fucking imbecile." Princess Arminda angrily replied to her turned back. The princess stood. "If you would let me finish, I was going to tell you who to truly direct your vitriol at."

Sister Ora shook hard. She felt herself plummeting again. The pit in her mind opened up into a wind of words that slashed at her skin from the inside. She stood at the edge of the pit, being whipped and slashed by its contents and battling the voices coming from above and below the darkness, one begging her to jump into the comforting numbness of the dark, the other begging her to stay in the illuminating light of the pain.

"It was Sir Loren."

The princess's words were barely heard over the drumming in her ears. Lady Ora's hand caught onto the bedpost, preventing her from falling. In her mind, she felt the slithering of the waking serpent she buried inside the pit, the part of her that snapped and bit at any kindness or care, the one that her mother put inside her long ago when she was taught to hate herself by the first woman she had ever known.

The angry beast that had slithered its way through generations of women in Lady Ora's lineage.

"What?" her voice cracked out. Her jaw trembled. The serpent yawned awake.

"You knew Sir Loren was loyal to the crown all his life. Our family saved him from a life of squalor and poverty. A life of being a simple foot soldier, forgotten in battle, or a bodyguard watching cargo, or a tavern. We could have let him die in his puddle of vomit and ale when he came back from the Aishar war, but instead, we invested in him, knowing how bravely he fought, how great he could be again if given a chance to right his life."

The serpent snapped at Lady Ora's chest, a fang cutting through her ribs and piercing her heart.

"A man does not give up loyalty like that for some woman he thought he loved but knew he could never truly have. A woman who never bothered to ask him about his past. Because if you had, you would have realized what he would do for us."

"You do not know of what you speak." Lady Ora set her hand on her heart, shoving the serpent away from the precious organ in her chest.

"Yes, yes, I do. Sister, I have grown up in this castle and know more than you of what it takes to be here." The shuffling of her dress broke the silence that followed her words as Princess Arminda walked towards Lady Ora.

Lady Ora shook her head in disbelief. "No, he wouldn't have done that."

The serpent clamped its jaws around her pounding heart. It began to shake and thrash it like a hound dog with a ragged toy.

"Yes, he did." Princess Arminda's voice was still firm, but even in her state, Lady Ora heard the cracks of sympathy and sadness in her voice. "I heard it myself when I hid in the private passage outside my father's Council chamber. It broke his heart to confess, but he knew for the good of the realm, he had no choice but to. He did not wish for more death when he could potentially stop it with his own actions. Not after all the death he saw in Aishar. He hoped confessing would stop your plans and stop the war. But he did not know that in doing so, he would be walking to his own death."

Lady Ora clutched her chest. The serpent did not let go of her heart; the blood from it trickled down the snake's locked jaws. It threatened to swallow the heart whole if she did not fight back.

"No, he…" Her words were lost in the memory of Sir Loren, who confessed to killing the one who spied on her that night, snapping their neck and throwing them off the wall. Then she returned to the weighted goodbye Sir Loren had given her moments before everything fell apart. "But why would he…"

Princess Arminda set a soft hand on Lady Ora's back. "Even Sir Loren knew how cruel one must be to survive here."

Lady Ora turned and smacked the princess's hand off of her. She stepped back and sloppily wiped the tears off her face. "If you must be cruel to survive here, then why did you plant false information so Sedrick would survive?"

Princess Arminda cocked her head to the side and blinked at Lady Ora.

Lady Ora's eyes widened softly, the understanding washing over her. She threw her hands up and shook her head. "So that you could have this conversation with me, right? So you could come here and tell me how you helped ensure he lived so that I would believe I owed you a favor."

Princess Arminda's chin raised. "There is the great mind I had heard so much about."

Lady Ora shook her head, her eyes stung with angry tears. She blinked them away.

She would not shed another tear because of this wretched family.

She recalled her conversation with her lady maid, Kaylah, about how the proper way to sleuth and slither around this court was by acting the part of the proper lady, to obey in public and rebel in private. To not let them see you fight.

Fuck it, Lady Ora thought, *let them see the monstrous woman they created.*

A coldness fell about the room as Lady Ora transformed into a vicious lady of the court; her face cold, calm, deadly. Her posture perfect, her movement slow and deliberate. Lady Ora felt the serpent swallow the bleeding lump in its mouth. Her heart disappeared down its throat. The pit inside her breathed in satisfaction as it grew larger, taking up the space where her warmth and love had once been.

"Tell me something, princess, since you know so much that I do not. Do you know how to field dress a kill?"

I will not be forced to survive them. They will be forced to survive me.

Princess Arminda gave her an odd look.

Coldness coated each word of Lady Ora's. "I grew up in a family that learned to hunt on our own because we were too poor to pay for already prepared meat. We had to fight starvation often, but it taught me many skills. You need a sharp, sturdy knife to cut the deer hide and muscle of the belly, from crotch to breastbone, without puncturing the gut. Accuracy and deliberate intent are required- one cannot be sloppy. One must not faint or falter at the smell and sight of cut flesh and insides."

She held up two fingers as her voice dropped to a chilling whisper. She was standing inches away from Princess Arminda now. "Then you put your fingers inside alongside the knife.

You see, when you field dress a kill, you must get your hands dirty and bloody, and I hunted and dressed many kills when my father took ill, so I know how carefully and slowly you must cut so you do not puncture any organs. And I know how to pull out all of a kill's organs and use them for traps, trade, meals, and many things. I am quite resourceful, patient, and skilled."

Princess Arminda had not realized how close Lady Ora had gotten to her. The princess swallowed in discomfort and a bubbling fear as Lady Ora met face-to-face with her. The princess looked disgusted and confused. She tried to hide her fear.

She failed.

Lady Ora stepped back from the princess. "You look quite ill, princess. Are you okay?"

The princess swallowed. "Why do you waste your time telling me this? I do not care for learning about hunting and butchering."

Lady Ora chuckled. "I tell you this not as a lesson in life skills that I wished to share with you- a woman who so clearly does not desire to get her hands dirty, but forces others to do her dirty work for her." Her glare intensified. "I tell you this as a warning, *dear sister*."

CHAPTER 72

"You're awake!" Lord Digarius cheerily greeted Gerald as he took up a spot on the edge of the hospital bed. He smiled, "Ephraim told me that it took some time for you to calm these past few da'es, but I am so glad to see you awake and not thrashing about, good friend."

Gerald's eyes showed no life as he listened to Lord Digarius loudly speak. Gerald sat silently, his arm resting on his lap and his chest barely rising and falling with his breath.

"They said you were lucky that the cut was clean and happened so close to the fortress. Healers were able to find you quickly and cauterize the bleeding before getting you to safety." Lord Digarius rested a hand on Gerald's blanket-covered leg.

Gerald finally turned; his head angled as he glared at his once-friend. "Yes, I am so lucky, aren't I?"

Lord Digarius gave a puzzled look. "Yes, you are! Many men would have died from that injury."

Gerald fell back into the headboard and scoffed. "Do you recall how I got this injury? You were right there when it happened, my lord." He took a harsh breath and jerked his head back up to glare at Lord Digarius, "No, there is no need for you to confess to me that you do not know how I got this injury, so I will tell you."

He grunted with exertion as he leaned forward, his voice turning from a stern tone to a shout, "I lost my arm because of you. Because I was too busy defending you and watching and protecting you to watch out for myself!"

Ephraim rushed over from a nearby patient, "Gerald, please be calm."

"No!" he shouted at Ephraim. Then shot his words back at Lord Digarius. Gerald choked on tears and words, pain he did not know he held until he saw Lord Digarius saunter into the hospital bay unharmed and untouched by the war. "You did not even see me as I fell. I was risking my life for you, and you did not even notice what happened to me. You never have, have you?"

Lord Digarius stuttered. His simple joy was gone, replaced with the shadows of sorrow. "Gerald, I am sorry. The battle was a mess. We were overwhelmed."

"How many scars do you bear from that battle, my lord? Any at all? Or do we, do I, bear them all for you?"

"Gerald!" Ephraim gasped.

Lord Digarius jumped up and stood. His finger shot down with each statement. "I received plenty that dae, many of which will never heal, not with time nor medicine."

Gerald refused to listen and shook his head. "How many times have you come before now to visit me? Even when un-conscious, did you come at all to check on your 'good friend'?"

Lord Digarius did not answer.

"I know the answer to that, as well." He swallowed, "I have always been there for you, my lord, always, and when I needed you the most, you were not here, nor there on the battlefield. You did not even turn around to see me as I was saving you." Gerald murmured, then turned his back to Lord Digarius and laid down to rest his eyes.

Lord Digarius excused himself with shaking hands and wet eyes.

Ephraim sat down where Lord Digarius had once been. They spoke in an even tone. "Lord Taylian is dead."

"What?" Gerald said.

Ephraim clenched and unclenched their hands on their lap, and their teeth crushed together between his words. "Lord Tyrrian is dead. You asked Lord Digarius if he bore any scars in this battle, and I am answering you. His brother is dead. His brother died protecting little Samwin. And Lord Digarius could not stop it and watched him as he died. Lord Digarius held his brother as he died, then he held his mother as she shrieked until she could no longer breathe."

Ephraim stood up and forced Gerald to look at them. "You are not the only one permanently scarred or changed because of what has happened, Gerald. Do not dare to go down this path believing you are the only one deserving of pity or sorrow. We are all ruined by what has happened to us."

Gerald hated everything. The bed he lay in, the smell of the ointments and tinctures. He hated how his body felt, how it was now uneven and useless. He hated his past, his future, his friends, his enemies.

He hated how Ephraim's past words echoed at him when he had passed out from his injury that night. How Gerald remembered their conversation in the spring, where Ephraim called him an obedient dog tied to Lord Digarius. How Ephraim had been right, that Gerald did follow him around like a loyal dog without question or fault.

"All of us? And what scars do you carry? What parts of you have you lost?" Gerald's teeth clenched.

Ephraim's chest heaved up and down as their breath came in slow, deliberate inhales and exhales. Gerald ignored the rage on his friend's face. In this moment, he did not care why his words struck Ephraim.

"I have lost my entire identity, Leaf." Gerald pushed himself forward to sit up. He gestured to his lost arm, "What am I without this? I cannot knock an arrow nor pull a bowstring."

"Alive." Ephraim's jaw was solid and hard. "You are *alive*."

Gerald's face fell as he studied the stitching of the blanket on his lap. He considered how much less painful it would have been not to survive, to succumb to his injury. Then, at least, he would have died a hero in battle. He would have had an identity, a purpose, until his last breath. He had been born with a bow in his hand, and now he would never wield one again. He had found his purpose in service and duty to Lord Digarius—joy in the mundane life of a common man. And his best friend since boyhood had not even looked when Gerald fell while protecting him.

"I spent my life following Dig around, and he didn't even see me fall," Gerald whispered. He felt the bed move under another body's weight as Ephraim sat beside him. A sigh accompanied the weight of Ephraim sitting down.

"That's what this is about, isn't it?" Ephraim asked.

Gerald just closed his eyes.

"You cannot fault a man for not seeing an ally fall in battle when," Ephraim choked on their words, "- when the battle was pure fire and blood."

"The last thing I saw was his back as he turned and continued on his path," Gerald said. "A familiar sight to me. Always seeing his back and following it wherever he would go."

Ephraim held a soft hand on Gerald's knee and gently squeezed, "Perhaps this is God's cruel way of offering you a chance at a different life."

Gerald let the tears form. The room was already full of muffled crying, and the air was pungent with pain; his tears would not be well noticed.

"Here," Ephraim gently said as they stood up to leave, handing Gerald a bottle. "For your pain, take a spoon of it twice a day for a few more days."

Gerald slowly picked up the bottle of brewed opium, mandrake, and hemlock. He rolled the bottle around in his hand, watching the brewed elixir swirl in the glass. He set the bottle between his knees and unscrewed the cap with his hand.

His shoulder and head pulsed and throbbed. His eyes glistened, and his throat locked up.

Gerald took a swig of the medicine, draining the bottle, and silently sobbed until the poppy overtook him and sent him to sleep.

Chapter 73

Lord Digarius Montarian woke with the sun.

He had lain slumped against the charred remnants of a once-standing home, his crumpled body a testament to the relentless toil of the remaining townspeople. Exhaustion had overtaken him after three days of ceaseless labor, a desperate effort to resurrect the shattered fragments of his city.

"My lord, care for some tea and breakfast?" a well-worked and sturdy villager asked as Lord Digarius walked to the group gathered around a cooking fire.

"I'll just take the biscuit. Do not worry about me, sir," he replied as he reached for a stone-hard lump of bread. Despite its rock-like state, he savored the biscuit, knowing that the fields of wheat they had yet to harvest that season were now burnt to ash. "Where are we working today?"

"Enough progress has been made on the outer west of the city, and we believe we can move inward more. We repaired the little that was left standing well enough. Iron Bay sent notice that they were bringing what supplies they could soon, and their soldiers are staying to aid in the rebuild. We still believe getting the largest homes rebuilt is best before winter- families can share homes for the season until we can recover all that was lost. The chill is already here." A middle-aged woman in worn-out maroon pants and a stained cream-colored top said. "We need basic shelter and food, above all else."

Lord Digarius ripped at the biscuit with his teeth and chewed the dried crumbs as she spoke. He swallowed hard. "How long until the chill turns to any chance of frost?"

Eyes shifted in the group; suspicion, worry, and uncertainty were spoken with each movement.

"The Reapers worry that it will come quickly because we did not celebrate the close of the harvest season. Between preparing for the attack and surviving the battle, we did not honor the Reaping as we were meant to. And the Reaping was never completed." The hard-working and tall male villager said.

"And the farmers truly believe that god will punish us for being too busy fighting a battle to plan a festival?" Another one scoffed in response.

The man shrugged. "Perhaps the battle was a punishment. Or the razing of our crop fields. Or perhaps this was all some other holy vengeance brought down by Him."

From outside the gathered group, a laboring young man stopped his cleaning and shouted, gathering the attention of those who had just woken up and stepped out of their makeshift homes. "Punishment for what? His words turned out to be a lie, just as His Majesty's words were. That is what those damn Psalms and Her Grace told us!"

He spat on the ground and jutted his hardened chin at the sky, cursing God with his anger.

"Quit shouting, Trenton! You'll wake the children and the wrath of god!" His wife hushed beside him.

"If God is here, then strike me down where I stand!" He stood with his arms open wide in the street. He threw his arms down and growled at his wife when no strike came. "If god is true, then He would not have let so many faithful die in a slaughter brought on by other believers. He would not have let children-"

"God is not here, not anymore." Father Robb interrupted as he stepped outside the small chapel next door. The stench of dead bodies followed the Father outside. The chapel had become a morgue full of dead things: bodies, beliefs, gods.

Father Robb hung his head and walked away from the broken and burned wood doors. The holy rosary he had always worn no longer hung around his neck; he must have left it behind with all the dead.

Lord Digarius did not wish to think of everything lost. He did not want to wonder where his brother's soul rose or fell to. Lord Digarius stood, shoving away his thoughts and returning to work.

CHAPTER 74

"I'm so lost without you, without our hidden moments." Lady Ora mumbled to the stars. She sat outside on the chilly night; the light blanket around her shoulders and her nightdress clung to her- the only protection from the breeze blowing across the private balcony outside her and Prince Percy's chambers.

She shook her head and sniffled, looking down into her lap, "I can't believe it. You wouldn't betray me like that. You wouldn't. You told me that I had all of you: your past, your present, your future. You wouldn't do that to me, to us."

She tried to find Sir Loren among the stars, to find his resting place where he must be looking down upon her and watching over her.

"I am so lost without you. I had you for but a moment, but you changed every single one after that." Lady Ora clutched her stomach and fell over herself, sobbing in her lap, her despair echoing in the empty night.

"I hate it here. I hate how I must be a monster. I hate how I must be cruel now, must not be kind. I hate how my heart is gone, and with it, you. I hate how I was careless in my hope to show my worthiness to my people, to follow her beck and call when she sent me away. I hate how you died because of me. And I hate so much how I have no place to go to find your body and sit beside where you rest." She wrapped her arms around herself as she sobbed more. "I hate it. I hate it. I hate it. I hate- I hate- I hate myself."

She held onto the last piece of Sir Loren she had with her besides her memories: the braided strands of grass he had given her that day in the garden where she had wept and wept over her fate, her people, her losses.

"I miss you; I'm sorry." She lifted her head and sobbed to the stars, her voice filled with the weight of her grief, begging him to grant her forgiveness for how she caused his death.

She held no care in this moment to act with decorum and respect. To hide her emotions so she could morph them into false ones that would become weapons.

She had no one. She was no one.

She was that little girl again. A scared and vicious thing, so desperate for a moment of love and kindness to be freely given to her, and feeling every ache and regret in her bones for the times she had freely given it to others, only to have it used against her.

"I just wanted to be loved. I just wanted something that was mine. That was real," she cried until she could no longer breathe, until her breath was heavy heaves and sharp, shallow pains. She cried until she could not anymore. She let out a shaking breath, "I love you. I'm sorry."

"You did, didn't you?" a masculine voice whispered behind her. "You loved him. It wasn't- It wasn't some affair to hurt me or to get back at my family. You truly fell in love with him."

Lady Ora jumped from her seat with a hard shock and wiped away her snot and tears as she turned to the open balcony doors and the man standing in their threshold.

Prince Percy stepped beside her and sat down on the bench. He pulled a kerchief from his pocket and gave it to her as she stayed standing.

"I thought that despite the glances, despite the moments, despite... every sign that was there– I convinced myself was not there- that even after I knew of you two, that you must have only been with him because you were tied to my family and me. That you wanted revenge on me for my parents' wishes." he swallowed deeply, "Hells, I am so, so sorry."

She shook her head and let the tears fall, much quieter now that the prince was beside her. As she cried again, she sat beside him.

"I don't believe either of us meant to let it happen. It simply did." she sniffled.

Prince Percy swallowed, "Love is funny like that."

She wiped her tears on his kerchief and shook her head. "What a mess we are, Your Highness."

Prince Percy paused and softly told her, "You can call me Percy."

Prince Percy had read once about a man who was forced to swallow his weight in hourglass sand as punishment from the Vahar for wasting his life and the gifts they granted him to help his plague and bandit-ridden village. Instead, the peasant man used the gifts to control the bandits and send them off to poorer villages and steal riches for him. He used his healing abilities granted to him to heal the plague only from those who put him in power and gave the sickness back to those who did not stand in alliance with him.

The legend said that man did not die from the sand in his belly, but from the weight of it holding him down.

Prince Percy felt much like him in this moment. A man held down by mystical weight and heavy from his burdens and actions.

All of that weight made it even harder to decide where to stand when he questioned his loyalty.

He loved his family, truly he did, despite all that they had put him through and pushed him to be complicit with, it was just... Why did his family have to desire power so much that it turned them into unfamiliar monsters he could not recognize some days? And his wife...

Why did he constantly feel a need to protect her, care for her, touch her, despite all she had done? Despite how much he said he hated her?

Before the second prince knew it, his arm was around her shoulders, and his thumb was rubbing her shoulder in consolation. Her body was stiff at first, likely confused by his kindness, but he felt her relax under his touch and rest her head on his shoulder.

In another life, you would have been easy to love. She had said to him before.

Could she perhaps have meant that in this life, too? Now that it was just them?

He recalled their wedding night, how he felt such uncontrollable desire for her that he could not stop his hands as he began to fist himself in his bed while she lay nearby. How he had rushed to his private room to relieve himself of the lust she filled him with after promising himself to stop feeling everything for her. He recalled the nights before and after that where he...

"Maybe he did not love me nor care for me in the way I did him," she mumbled against his shoulder.

He shook his head and shifted his body in his seat to hide the physical manifestation of his invasive thoughts.

"What do you mean?" he found himself asking.

She sniffled and raised her head from his shoulder.

He tried not to let the cold night air sting him as she moved away.

"If he had truly loved me as I thought, even in our brief time being with one another, he would not have sold me off to the king and Council, right? He would not have done that to me if he truly loved me." She shook her head and picked at the skin on her fingers as she spoke. "He would not have hurt me as all the others have before."

Why did she always destroy herself every chance she got? He wondered.

He gently nudged her, hiding it as another shift of his body on the hard stone bench, the motion causing her to stop her picking and rest her hands.

He loathed his heart, the stupid beating thing, for the words that followed her pain.

"The Council was on your tail. We knew someone within the castle was giving secrets away. It was only a matter of time before we would have discovered that it had been you, and Sir Loren knew that. The entire King's Guard knew they had been placed on high alert to look out for suspicious activity within the castle and listen more closely to conversations they overheard." Prince Percy slowly nodded, watching the stars as he paused. "When he told us of what you did, he made my father swear on the throne that he would not kill you. He traded his life for yours."

Prince Percy's words pierced her chest, where he was sure she held a cold, non-beating organ now. The sob that erupted from her cracked the foundation of the crooked castle the prince and the lady were stuck within. It cracked the prince, too.

Prince Percy held Lady Ora all night as she broke apart into a thousand pieces over and over and over again.

What the prince did not, could not, would not tell her was how his blackened heart had not felt a seed of sorrow when his father demanded Sir Loren's head.

And that, he knew, made him a terrible man.

Chapter 75

King Ivan steadied himself against the dresser; his uncontrollable hacking had made him unstable and dizzy. His tongue tasted coins as he continued to cough. In his frustration, he pounded his fist on the dresser as he keeled over more.

Blood dripped from his open, panting mouth as the coughing subsided. His shaking breath spewed red splatters on the rug at his feet. He gripped the dresser with his tremoring hand as he straightened up and leaned against the wood top.

His hands continued to shake as he reached for the crystal glass beside the medicinal bottles; he shot back vials of licorice root and poppy, chasing it with the burn of liquor that stung his raw throat.

"Will you keep it down this time?" asked Queen Onetta.

King Ivan jumped and turned to her wide-eyed. Fear and confusion carved shadows into his hardened and sickly face. "What?" he hoarsely said.

She stepped into the room, her dress trailing long and dramatically behind her. "The medicine, will you keep it down this time? Your chamber aide informed me you threw it up these past few nights."

"Yes. I am fine," he grumbled and nodded once, twice, then found he could not stop as the medicine fogged his judgment and sanity again.

His head involuntarily nodded repeatedly as if it were connected to his body by a spring or hook, like that of a child's bobbling toy that had been flicked with a finger. The king furrowed his brow and slowly raised his head to the sky, concentrating on the gilded ceiling above him.

"Ivan, you have become even more ill as of late; why will you not tell me, or any of us, what it is that has you acting like this?" she asked. "Perhaps we could aid you if only we knew."

A high-pitched ringing erupted in the king's ear.

"Hush." He snipped at her.

The king lowered his eyes from the ceiling and turned away, walking towards his chamber's balcony. The daylight shone through the curtains that he gently parted, his voice matching his careful gesture: "The stars are speaking again."

"My king, the stars are not out yet," her voice said behind him.

King Ivan's hands gripped the curtains with steadying need; he jerked away from her touch as Queen Onetta moved to turn him away from the window that beckoned him again and again.

Hello, my king. Hello. The stars said to him.

"They know everything, the stars. It is immaculate what they share with me... Can you not hear them?" his voice was far away in the sky. He was no longer attached to his body. He was free.

Queen Onetta sighed, and he felt her step beside him. "No, I cannot. What is it they share with you?"

He smiled and laughed. "They're sharing their stories with me. Oh, there is so much more than you know, than we all know. The prophecies they tell me, the songs that they sing."

"Tell me, what is it the stars tell you, husband?" Queen Onetta rested a gentle hand on his biceps. He felt her touch but kept his attention skyward. Dots danced in his vision.

Not dots.

Stars.

Gods.

The king kept blinking at the sky, his mouth moving in silence and his expression changing as he listened to a conversation between two glimmering entities above him.

Fury and flame.

Forevermore.

"They remind me that my blood must always stay on the throne, or else we will fall."

The stars hissed a warning: *they're out to get you, my king!*

"What?" she asked.

Run!

He turned to her, panic biting at his lips. "Onetta, this is why we have done all of this. The First King knew what was coming, and that is why he went to war. That is why I went to war- to save everyone."

"To save everyone from what?"

She's a monster. The stars hissed again.

"The end!" He gripped her arms and shook her. His hands like bony claws around her. "The end!"

She jerked out of his hard grip and clumsily threw herself back. "Ivan, you must stop this! What has this illness done to you?!"

He began pacing and mumbling as Queen Onetta steadied her breathing. The king looked at the nothingness above him as he paced and chanted over and over to himself, repeating the same words as his throat grew raspy.

Shh, my king.

Don't tell her.

My king, no!

He kept chanting the words, "*When the eye of the world has dimmed, and stars have fallen as if made of rain,*

Of solid gold and stardust rulers shall remain, forevermore until burned in fury and in flame.

And the world of men shall be made to begin again."

"What has gotten into you?" she whispered.

Kill her!

King Ivan's head snapped to her furrowed brow and concentrated stare. "You. You've done this to me! You all have, haven't you?! You conspire in meetings and at my table." He snapped his head around the room and made for her with grace his body had not known for some time. "The stars warned me of this."

"Ivan, that is enough! You must stop this!" She shouted as he stepped for her. Her hand threw itself across his face before he could grab her with his outstretched claws.

She shook as she stepped away from him.

The hissing voices dissipated and quieted in his head.

King Ivan raised his head and brought a soft hand to his red cheek. He looked over at Queen Onetta as his hunched body straightened. His face softened and calmed, the effects of the poppy finally taking hold. He slowly lowered his hand from his reddened face, his vision growing clear again as he blinked at his shaking fingers.

Queen Onetta sighed at his calmness.

He furrowed his brow and dropped his hand to his side, "Why are you in my chambers? What is it?"

Queen Onetta firmed her posture before him. The king watched as an expression of what one might believe was concern disappeared, and her familiar coldness looked at him, "I was asked to come check on you. You seem well."

"Yes. I am. You need not worry," the king replied. His face still stung from where her hand had landed. He had no memory of what he had said to earn her anger, and he did not wish to remember.

Chapter 76

Lord Shaital Pathis walked towards the open window and set the black stone bowl on the short wooden stool embedded with crystal shards. The night's wind was gentle enough not to disturb the ocean water he poured into the bowl. He watched his reflection form, and the full moon's light began to glow on the water's surface, the light he needed to See best for his scrying.

While Lord Shaital had many visions of the past, present, and possible futures without using such tools and rituals to tap into his psychic abilities, when one needed to call on the highest spirits and energies to learn of the kingdom's future, one used all the tools they had available to them, including that of the full moon, ocean water, crystals, and precious stones.

As he had prepared his body and mind for this moment, he had ceremoniously extinguished all flames inside their chambers. At the same time, his husband called for aid to extinguish the torches in the hallway and outside their balcony.

Lord Shaital was not to be disturbed by the flickering flames that would interrupt his Sight as he scried on the water. Only the light of the moon and stars was permitted to illuminate the room.

As he settled into a kneeling position before the short stool, Lord Shaital took several deep breaths, allowing his entire body to relax until he felt his skin warm and his body hum into a trance. He tilted his head back and closed his eyes, inhaling deeply before leaning forward to look at the bowl. In his hand, he held a chip of stone that one of his servants had chiseled from the throne room's walls. This stone served as a conduit for his Sight, linking him to the future he needed to See. He dropped the stone into the water and watched the ripples dance in the moonlight, letting his ability take over as images began to form in his mind, and the movement of the water transformed into a fortune.

He sat in silence until the moon's reflection in the water shifted, and the words and images slowed into blackness in his mind.

Lord Shaital Pathis's voice was not of this world, nor his body. "Rats consume their own flesh, and dragon's fire burns the throne. Vipers live and die, are reborn and lie. Cloaks and daggers out in daylight, in the dark, they no longer hide. The path is as it should be."

The whites of Lord Shaital's eyes rolled back down, and he blinked to bring himself back into his body. "There must be something happening that we did not know before, something causing what I Saw to change, or I could not see in the Dragon's Tower, but I can so close to the golden throne. Before," he shook his head and slowly stood up, rubbing his hand on his chin as he carefully strolled about their room. Lord Nesima walked inside their room from where he had been waiting on the balcony. "Before we came here, my vision showed rats running about in the throne room until one bit the throne, and it died. The other rats consumed its body, and the throne still stood until the vision ended."

He looked out the window onto the star-painted sky. "The rats will still devour one another, but now the throne will also be destroyed, and much more." The weight of this change greatly bothered Lord Shaital. He was used to visions altering as those around him took different paths and made new decisions; however, this change was heavy—a change he did not expect.

"The throne will be destroyed by dragon flames. By us, perhaps?" Lord Nesima queried.

Lord Shaital shrugged. "It would seem that way. You are the blood of the dragon, and our House is that of the dragon as well."

They shared a knowing look that spoke so many words. Within seconds, Lord Nesima queried his husband again. "And our actions, what we have put into motion since our arrival here, since Silu wrote to us —despite this new knowledge and now knowing the condition of the king, we shall continue on this path?"

"It is as the universe tells us- the path is as it should be."

"So be it, then." Lord Nesima said solemnly, nodding as he accepted what they had already done and what they must soon do to secure the right future for the kingdom.

"So be it." Lord Shaital reached a gentle hand over to his husband's and squeezed. "I shall write to Silu and let her know of what I have Seen. Perhaps she and her other Seers have more knowledge than I."

Lord Shaital walked away to relight the candles in the room and dispose of the evidence of his forbidden ritual. Lord Nesima called over his shoulder at him, "Even if she learns more, it is too late to stop what we have done."

"Yes, it is." Lord Shaital quietly replied.

"But it will turn out all right in the end, yes? The kingdom's new path will be properly forged, and the sacrifices will have fed the proper path— to turn this kingdom into what we, our descendants, need it to be, correct?"

Lord Shaital heard his husband's worry and saw the pain on his face without even turning to meet his soft eyes. He turned to look at his husband and offer a final bit of comfort.

"As it was, so shall it be. The dragons require the wrongs of man to be righted; this was the best path we saw to do so."

Chapter 77

Lord Samwin Montarian wiped his sniffling nose on his sleeve. He kicked his feet back and forth, his heels knocking against the boulder he sat on. He sniffled again as his hands ran along the fabric leaf he held, a makeshift House of Healer badge he had created when he took a knife to a patterned jacket he loathed, the fabric being too heavy and itchy, and the sleeves too tight.

The sleeves are not too tight. The jacket is meant to be well-fitted. Lord Taylian had once corrected him when he complained. When his brother later found him in his bedchamber with a torn jacket, the only punishment Lord Samwin faced was a stern lecture from Lord Taylian about childish behavior and respecting the labor of their tailor. Lord Taylian had helped him repair the jacket as best he could before helping him concoct a tale of a tree branch snagging the fabric and causing a tear.

"I didn't mean to." Lord Samwin sniffled and talked to the air, "I didn't mean to make you have to look after me again. That's why I didn't tell you when I snuck away."

He sniffled and wiped more snot onto his sleeve. "Mother and father won't look at me. I mean, they have tried since... since that night, but I think it hurts them too much or maybe makes them angrier at me."

He pushed his eyes shut as hard as he could. His tears fell anyway. "I said I was sorry, but I don't think they care. Mom sends her aides to tuck me in at night. Father yells more, and Dig barely comes home."

More tears came, and he wiped his messy face again. "I know I've been a nuisance for a while and that I need to act my age and like a young lord, but I swear I did not mean anything by how I act. I take it all back. I'll be good. I'll be better."

"Give him back," he begged, raising his head to the sky and crying, begging, and pleading. "Take me. Take anything. Just give me my brother back."

Chapter 78

Father Robb sat alone in the library. The lanterns in the room were long forgotten and created no light; only a few well-burnt candles on the table gave a glow to the sullen room.

He sat staring at the unopened holy text in front of him, as he had each day since Lady Montarian's birds came bearing the news of the Psalms. Father Robb had memorized each gilded line and flick of filigree on the cover of the book, knew the exact count of pages, and his touch held memory of each imperfectly cut edge and worn corner.

He now spent his time counting the specks of dust that covered the book he could no longer open.

Father Robb had tried, many times he had, to open the text that he had once found comfort and healing in, but each time his hands worked up the nerve to crack the spine, a force from beyond his mind held itself like a wall against his efforts.

He could no longer lead services on Solan, preach to others how to live a holy and good life, offer faith to the faithless, or hope to the hopeless. Since the Psalms were brought to life, Father Robb had tried only once to lead a sermon to open the knot.

That day, the congregation had been packed to the railings and doors.

But all he gave to his people were apologies and uncertainty. He could no longer find the truth in the lies his destiny- his very being- was built upon.

Father Robb's mala rosary shook in his hands as he held it on the table. Eighty-four beads joined before thirty-seven strings of tassel.

And yet he found no prayer as he counted them.

He forced his eyes to stay shut, mumbling his attempts at prayer despite the wetness rolling down his face and past his moving lips.

Silent steps came from the doorway and stood waiting at the edge of his table.

"I cannot find it." Father Robb quietly said to the visitor, his eyes still closed and head bowed.

"Find what?" Emaline softly whispered.

Father Robb opened his eyes, red with tears, exhaustion, and sadness. He raised his head to meet her solemn stare. "My faith. It no longer weaves itself into my heart as it once did- not even a mustard seed of it remains. It is gone. Who I am is now truly gone."

Emaline sat in the empty chair in front of Father Robb. She remained silent for several moments of breath before speaking. "I have never been very good when it comes to faith. It has always been a struggle for me. I gave up long ago on finding faith in a chapel. But for some reason, I tried again recently to find it after we spoke under the trees. To find something to believe in again," she nodded her head slowly as she looked down at the table, always avoiding looking at the eyes of those she spoke to, "And I did. Do you remember what you taught us when we were children? When you and other Scholars visited the orphanage?"

Father Robb did not reply.

"You said when we cannot find faith in ourselves, to find faith in others."

She pulled out the worn coin she held so dearly in her pocket and rolled and spun it on the table as she spoke. "Life has not handed me an easy path; no moment has given me ease or grace. I find no comfort in any god." She paused, taking a shaking breath. "I do not wish to believe in a creator who has created a world with such evil in it. Who has allowed children to lose their parents, to live without love, to suffer and die for dark men that He will never strike from power.

"And so I choose to find my faith in others, and now, in myself. I hold faith in what could be and what should be. I believe in others, in finding some meaning coming from this bloodshed. To find my own path and clarity."

Father Robb squinted at a subtle fall of hard darkness that waved across her solemn expression before dissolving.

She rubbed the coin between her fingers before pocketing it. She stood and walked to his side of the desk. She rested her hand on his gathered hands. "Sometimes faith is simply hope for light in the darkness of night. Sometimes faith is simply love for one another."

He held a long pause, mumbling his pained reply. "Perhaps, yes."

She squeezed his hand and got up to leave. "And for me, we are enough to believe in. We have to be."

Father Robb nodded at the rosary still tangled in his grasp.

She paused at the door, "Father."

"Hm?" He looked up at her, his eyes still dark and lightless.

"The funeral. It is starting."

The warrior's broadsword lay across Lord Taylian's cold body. His hands were wrapped together in an embrace of the pommel, forever holding onto the weapon. He had been laid in full regalia of his House: a forest green tunic and pants stitched with silver filigree made of oak leaves and freesia flowers. Over his clothing, he had been dressed in light armor plates to ensure protection if he faced any battles during his soul's ascension. On his head sat a small crown of stag antlers.

During shedding season, Huntsmen would scour the woods for antlers to keep as their own good luck charms or to gift to others as charms. Selling stag antlers was seen as a sign of greed and would spread bad luck to all the parties involved, but gifting them was viewed as a blessing between the parties, a sharing of the holy animal's offerings.

No one dared try to claim stag antlers before they were shed.

For those placed to rest with honor in Ayeshire, an accessory composed of antlers would be set on their body; a charm on a necklace, bracelets made of bits and nubs, crowns, and even, for those with a deeper connection to the forest, antlers adorned upon their head as if they had grown them like the stag himself had.

The noble burial hill overlooked all of Middleton Landing. It had been traditional for past lords and ladies of Ayeshire to be buried on the slopes of the hill, their bodies laid at an angle so that they could watch over the city for all eternity.

Lady Belva Montarian had insisted that Lord Taylian take a place on the hill, closest to the peak and facing the windows of her war room. Specifically, the window that cast light onto her chair that sat in perfect view of where his body would forever lie until the earth took it back and left behind bone dust.

She stood beside the catafalque his body lay on, and looked down on her fortress. She had spent the days since the battle in fits of silent grief. She wore her grief as a veil over her sleeping gown, which she would not change out of without coaxing and care from her maids or husband. Today had been the hardest to convince her to change- the day she had to put on her formal mourning attire and stand before her lost son.

"Wake up, my darling," she quietly spoke to Lord Taylian as she set a hand on his stilled shoulders. "Please."

Lady Belva took a deep inhale and closed her eyes. She willed the tears to come, but they would not.

Lord Theodus spoke the parting prayer for her, "May peace be granted unto you. Let your soul depart in peace. Let the mighty stag guide you to the light of eternal rest."

"No." she trembled, "no."

"Darling," her husband's voice softly beckoned, reminding her that this moment was real and not one of the many dreams that had woken her each night since their son was killed.

She shook her head and gripped Taylian's shoulder, bunching up his clothing under her fingers. "Please, no," she whispered.

"Mother." Lord Digarius beckoned to her next.

Her jaw shook, and her eyes fluttered as tears finally fell. As they coated her cheeks, she flushed with anger. No amount of tears would be enough to mourn him. She could cry for eternity, and the waterfalls she would create would never measure the amount of grief in her heart.

Her son was gone.

Forever taken from her.

Taylian was dead.

He will never wake again.

She could say none of it aloud; she could not let the words fall from her lips.

She knew, but she wished for one more moment in her delusional hope that he would walk up the hill and ask why they were gathered there, that he would jump from the catafalque and laugh and smile at some terrible joke that had been played on her.

Her son was dead.

The son that she had spent the past many days mourning and apologizing to for not being a good enough mother, for failing him in his final moments, for putting too much pressure on him by purpose or by accident.

For choosing his older brother to give more attention to, or younger brother for doting on more. Her middle child, her *dead* child, had always been the easy one to care for. She had never had to worry about him; he was always able to take care of himself.

Her baby, her sweet, precious boy. Her perfect middle child, who always looked to her for approval, honor, love, and care, was dead.

She would forever hate herself for every imperfect moment of motherhood, and every single second she did not spend showing him how endless her love truly was for him.

She cracked apart the piece of her heart that Taylian had always held from the moment he first kicked to life inside of her. She held onto that broken piece, cold yet burning with anger, and she kissed it. She made it all the promises she had never given her son when he was alive.

And to it, she vowed something dangerous.

To it, she promised a path shrouded in darkness and light, vengeance and justice.

"May we find one another again." She laid a kiss on his forehead and rested their foreheads together, letting her tears stain his cheeks. "My sweet boy. Please find me again."

Lord Digarius stepped beside her as she stood and wrapped his arms around her. They embraced deeply. Lord Theodus stood still at the head of the catafalque as his wife and eldest hugged.

"He lived to become a soldier and died a hero. Taylian will be put to rest just as all warriors have before him." Lord Theodus said. He held his jaw tightly and kept it straight as if he were holding something inside his mouth that would spill out if he did not stand strong enough.

He reached a large hand down to rest on Lord Samwin's shoulder. Little Samwin had not yet raised his eyes to see his brother's body. Lord Theodus gently squeezed his son's shoulder and spoke lightly. "Let the peace you see on his face now be the last image you have of him, Sam. Trust me, you do not wish it to be of his death."

Little Samwin shook his head at the ground. "I can't," he murmured.

Lord Theodus moved his hand to rest against his youngest's back, pushing gently and making him step forward. "You must because you must ask your brother for forgiveness, not that it is needed, but because if you do not, you will never be able to forgive yourself for your mistake. You will never be able to move on from the blame you have placed upon yourself."

Lord Samwin stepped beside Lord Digarius. He sheepishly looked up at his brother, who gave him a small, broken smile. There was no kindness behind his eyes nor any emotion besides pain. Lady Belva still held her head down, her pain shadowing the world around her. Lord Theodus walked to stand beside her and wrapped his arm around her back. She rested her head on his shoulder and wept.

Lord Samwin reached into his pocket and pulled out his makeshift Healer patch. He set it on his brother's chest and gently patted it.

"I don't deserve this anymore." He mumbled. "I am sorry, brother."

He stepped back and hid behind Lord Digarius, again hanging his head in shame.

Lord Digarius held all the strength that remained on his shoulders. He straightened his body and gently nodded as the sun began to set. The House of Scholar members and Father Robb waited for his nod to move the body and lay it in the ground.

"I believe we have all said our goodbyes. It is nearing dark, and they must begin the internment so he is laid before the stars arise and his soul chooses which he will call his own." Lord Digarius said.

"No." Lady Belva choked out between cries. "We will stay, even through the night. We will stay with him until I know his soul has left and found his star."

Lord Digarius nodded again to Father Robb. The group of holy practitioners stepped forward and began delicately moving the fabric that Lord Taylian had laid upon. As they moved him to rest in the grave that was open for him, full of flowers, offerings, and letters from loved ones, the Montarian family watched on until long after the last of the soil had been returned to the grave and the last prayers had been blown away into the night's wind.

Together, they pointed to different stars in the sky, asking one another which one they believed Taylian would choose. As the moon rose and illuminated the night, no existing star glimmered with renewed spirit; instead, Lord Digarius pointed to the star cluster above the fortress, noting a new glimmer in the night he had not seen before.

Chapter 79

"It can be just us, beauty. We can survive this place together. We can become what we need to make it out of here alive," Lady Ora whispered to the snout of her grey mare. She stroked the horse's nose as the mare huffed and knocked against Lady Ora's shoulder, demanding more oranges from her pocket.

Lady Ora smiled, a true smile, and fed her another slice of the orange in her pocket. She lowered her tone again as the horse nibbled from her palm, "We may win the war. And then we will be free, and then we can go home."

What is home? Where is home? she wondered. Lady Ora had felt like Middleton Landing was her true home for so long, but now it was mostly gone, to be rebuilt and reshaped. And even if the battle had not taken so much of that city, could she go back there and find a new place for herself when this was all over?

Emaline had been right in the spring when the two women spoke of their pasts and futures. The two would never be those little girls again, the ones so full of innocence, hope, and curiosity.

The serpent slithering inside her hissed in amusement at her curious wonderings, reminding her that, alongside her heart, it had devoured the little girl she had once been and wished to hold and to heal one day.

"My lady," the stable hand greeted from the doorway.

Lady Ora had taken her mare out to one of the running pens just outside the royal stables for the afternoon to let her run free. She looked up and noted the empty pens around her, the movement of more stable hands, and the conversation within the stables.

"I apologize for interrupting, but it is time to feed and put the horses up for the day."

"Of course, no apologies needed. I must get back for dinner as well." Lady Ora gave the mare one last kiss, already sensing the horse's agitation at knowing she would be stabled the moment Lady Ora left, and a reassuring stroke on her nose. She moved out of the pen and let the stable hand inside before stepping beside the gate to see her horse off.

The stable hand haltered the mare and began bringing her up the short path to the stables, but they paused as they began to part ways with Lady Ora. "My lady, we stable hands were wondering, have you come up with a name for her yet? It is just easier for us to know their names, is all."

She thought of how the mare's speckles and grey coat shone like silver strands of moonlight, how the horse felt restless in her tack and stable, and how she felt better being free.

"Ayla. Her name is Ayla."

As she and her guards made their way back into the confines of the castle, Lady Ora felt the flicker of light go out inside of her again. She felt the hard stones around her compress and harden her mind and body. She felt the serpent excited for blood again.

She left the guards behind as she entered her and Prince Percy's shared chambers, preparing a comment to have one of the guards call for Kaylah so she could dress for another suffocating dinner, but then she stopped at the sight within the room.

Her and Prince Percy's shared chambers had a candlelight glow emanating from a dining table she did not remember placing in the room when she had it redone after their wedding. And beside that table, filled with food, her favorites, she noted, was the prince.

Was her husband.

"I am not dressed for dinner," she flatly said when she stepped inside.

The prince casually shrugged, "You're wearing clothes. That means you're dressed."

"I smell like horse manure."

"I lit many candles." One side of his mouth curled up into a half-smile.

Be careful, girl. The serpent and her subconscious said to her.

She glared and carefully stepped forward. "What do you want?"

The prince cocked his head at her coldness, her suspicion. "Nothing."

"Everyone in this castle wants something. Just come out with it."

"I- I want to have dinner with you. I—" He huffed and turned away to grab something hidden from her view.

The prince returned with a ribboned box.

"What is it." Not a question. A statement of aggravation.

"A gift. Open it."

"No," she continued, glaring at him with suspicion.

"Ora…"

She did not let the sadness in his tone break her heart.

She gripped the box tightly, and her arms shook. She gritted her teeth. "What do you want?"

Prince Percy shuffled and looked at his feet and the empty space between them. "I want to apologize- for so much. Please, we need to talk. You were right about many things, especially about us needing to form a strong front and working together to survive this court- to survive my family's court."

Her head slowly tilted as she looked into his eyes. She found no coldness, no venom, no vitriol. She found the sweet, shy prince she had known only briefly before the world molded them into cold enemies linked together.

"I'm listening," she said.

He had to make things right with her.

Everything at court was falling apart. His father was lost to him, and Prince Percy did not feel like he could reach him anymore. The king had truly become a mad tyrant; there was no turning back now. He had finally realized the kind of woman his mother truly was, not just to the world but to him as well.

He had shamed himself enough for taking so long to realize this, for holding out too much hope that he could continue to serve on the King's Council and somehow steer it the right way and influence his father to remember the king he had promised to be.

And the battle.

Her people had won, and his brother's army had barely made a dent in the lands of Ravenhall. There was truly a possibility that his family would lose this war. And even though Prince Percy held no sorrow for how he had betrayed his family by exposing the world to the Psalms, he was still a Scott.

And he doubted that her allies would see him any differently when the gallows called his name.

I have to tell her what I did.

Lady Ora carefully sipped the wine that her husband had poured for her.

Her husband.

God and gods, she was a married woman. She had known her future story would not be traditional, but married to someone who disliked her and the marriage arranged in such a heartless and cruel way was not how she imagined a ring appearing on her finger.

"I propose a truce," the prince's voice cut into her mind.

She set the goblet down slowly before her, joining her hands and intertwining her fingers in front of it on the table. "I did not know we needed one."

He looked stressed beyond belief. As if all day and the night before he had been up and wandering endlessly to prepare for this dinner with her. A simple dinner to try to patch what there was between them should not make a man appear so... out of sorts. So endlessly aching.

The serpent sent a warning shiver up her body; she straightened up and hardened her jaw.

"Yes, well, I believe we do. It is as you said to me before we were wed, we must play along in these wretched games and work together to survive. Even when we leave for Odessin, we will still be tied together; we must become partners, a team."

"I agree."

"So then, truce?" he looked at her hopefully.

Lady Ora remembered more of their conversation from another night, when she had tried to lay an olive branch at his feet, to begin mending something between them.

In that lifetime, would you still have fucked another man under my hospitality? Or would you have not been a whore?

The words stung more than she liked. She still carried them around with her. She couldn't let them go.

"You called me a whore, Your Highness." She would not let her voice crack and show him how much that word had hurt her, but she knew he felt it, knew he saw it in her eyes and in how she could barely whisper the statement.

"I know," he softly said back, "and I will apologize for that for the rest of my life. I am sorry for that, Ora. I truly am."

She swallowed and let out a breath. "Did you mean it?"

He looked down at the table again and nodded. "Yes, in that moment, yes, I did."

"Oh."

"And I would never expect you to forgive me for that. But, still, I am sorry for that, too."

The silence that she met him with was deserved, but still, the prince wished for it to end, for her to say something, anything to end it.

"If your family were to lose this war, would you keep me tied to you?" she asked coldly.

Anything besides that.

His brow creased, and his eyes flexed in confusion, in hurt.

"Married. Would you still make us be married if your family were to lose the war?" she glared.

He swallowed the stone in his throat and looked down at his hand caressing the bottom of the wine chalice. He shook his head, "No. If you wished, we could part."

She gave one firm nod of her head, "Good," and then sipped her wine.

I have to tell him. She thought as she sipped the wine, working not to shake. If we are to hold a truce, to ally, he must know.

Their confessions overlapped.

"I was pregnant-"

"I told them of the Psalms-"

"What?" they both said at the same time.

"Pregnant?"

"The Psalms?" Lady Ora swallowed. "What are the Psalms?"

Even on her worst days, when the pain needed numbing by the warmth of alcohol, Lady Ora had never drunk so much, so quickly, as she had while Prince Percy told her of the Psalms of Fire and Fury and what he did to set those words free.

Prince Percy pushed his forehead into the palms of his head and shook his head.

He had told her everything.

If she wished, she could run to his father now and confess what she now knew and have him hanged for treason of his own, perhaps gain her freedom through his suffering.

While he confessed, she had taken the full bottle of wine from their table and walked around the room with it, taking full swigs as often as she took a breath. She stopped walking and put the bottle in front of him while she stood beside him.

"It was Sir Loren's. And no, it wasn't intentional." She took a shaking breath, "And no, once I knew I was pregnant, I didn't want to get rid of it. I wanted to keep a part of him, to keep a part of the only choice I had gotten to make for myself in a very, very long time."

She walked back to her chair and sat.

Prince Percy took a chug of wine and rubbed the back of his neck.

"You said you were pregnant, not *are*. What happened?"

A long pause, then, "Your mother."

The hand that had been rubbing his neck moved to cover his face as he looked up at her.

Her eyes proved she was not lying, that she was not playing some twisted game of shoving a wall between him and his family.

"I knew she was vicious, but…"

The heart he had promised would never beat for her again skipped several beats and then broke for her.

"No wonder you hate us all so much. No wonder you have—" he did not wish to say it.

"Have become so cold? Conniving?"

"... Yes." The prince took another swig of wine and then asked, "So where does this leave us?"

Lady Ora shook her head with uncertainty, "A team.

Chapter 80

Lady Belva Montarian's hands were clasped tightly in front of her in prayer, her elbows resting on the ancient stone altar surrounded by flickering flames. The heat from the multitude of candles seeped through her early winter cloak, burning her skin beneath. The noble cathedral stood in solemn silence; its grandeur diminished by the absence of worshippers. Services had been long forgotten by many, including the Lady of Ayeshire, yet the faithful few still kept the candles burning for loved ones lost.

The air was thick with the scent of melting wax and aged wood, mingling with the cold dampness that lingered in the unheated cathedral. Even amidst the uncertainty of their people's faith, hope remained—a fragile, flickering hope of being reunited with those taken from them.

Lady Belva's eyes were fixated on a single, trembling flame, the one she had lit hours ago when the pale light of day still seeped through the stained-glass windows. The name she could not speak, the memory she could barely form in her mind, surged through her with an unbearable intensity. Her son's face haunted her every thought.

His first cries as she pushed him out of her body with a scream of her own. His first steps and words, both directed at his father. His boyish laugh that never dissipated, even as he grew into a man. His yearning, longing, and desire to be a force of good. Her failure as a mother to protect him.

The blood bubbling out of his mouth as he held her gaze while life drained from his eyes. The sound of dirt being shoveled over his too-young and too-frail body. Her sobs that kept her awake at night. Her husband's anger that broke furniture. His screams for revenge. Her failure to act on it.

Her newfound anger boiling in her blood pushing her down a path she could not return from if she chose it.

Silent tears wet her cheeks. Strength, integrity, and grace. Her family words were deeply etched in the stone archways of the church where she kneeled. Holy verses, aligning with their House words, adorned the arches as well.

"May integrity of the heart guide them into greatness."

"For He is my strength and my defense; He is my beacon."

"It is through your grace, freely given unto others, especially those who have done you wrong, that you will find salvation and truth."

The cathedral's silence pressed down on her, a relentless reminder of her son's absence and her helplessness. The flames flickered, casting long shadows on the walls, and the verses etched in stone seemed to mock her inner turmoil. She closed her eyes, seeking strength in the darkness, as the weight of her grief and the burden of her choice loomed over her like a storm ready to break.

She knew the path she wished to take. The promise she made as her son died in her arms. But words and angry promises were so different from taking cruel action.

"My queen, my apologies," a timid voice broke through Lady Belva's tears. A young Scholar stepped inside the cathedral, a broom and candle snuffer in her hand.

The Lady of Ayeshire did not flinch or falter at the title used to address her. She wiped the tears from her face with trembling hands and managed a weak smile at the Scholar entering the altar room. "Please, no apologies needed."

"Did you need anything, Your Highness?" the Scholar asked, her voice wavering with the weight of intrusion.

Sorrow and ambivalence flashed over Lady Belva's shadowed face. She held a long pause, her gaze heavy and vacant, before she gestured subtly at the carved quotes. "Do you believe in picking them apart?"

"Picking what apart?" The Scholar asked.

Lady Belva nodded towards the carved verses. "His words. We know much of our beliefs to be a fabrication of lies proposed by false men. But how do we know which to choose as the rightful words? As verses to follow?"

The Scholar shifted uneasily; her face contorted in thought. "It is something those of us with faith still left have considered greatly, Your Grace. But it is an answer we do not know."

Lady Belva's eyes fell back to the candles in front of her. "I see."

"My brother. He died in the battle." The Scholar's voice cracked, and she crumpled her hands together, her eyes no longer meeting Lady Belva's. "He was fifteen but looked much older. It was easy for him to lie about his age, Your Grace. It was easy for him to follow that path, even though he told me how it would end. He knew he would die in the battle, but he knew, regardless, he must fight."

She stepped forward timidly, her voice barely a whisper, "They slaughtered him. Sliced him to pieces. I am but a sinner myself, though I try not to be. But this has all made me wonder if perhaps His written word is not what we should follow, for we know how bastardized it has become. Perhaps it is what our heart speaks of that we should follow."

Lady Belva cocked her head and squinted in curiosity.

The Scholar timidly continued. " *The virtuous care about justice for the heartbroken, but the wicked hath no such concern, nor such care for any but their own.*' That is what He has said to us for so long, and you, my queen, are virtuous. But I fear the path of true virtue may not give the wicked the justice they deserve. Justice, above all else, should be a virtue held closely. I fear God may— I am sorry, I speak too much."

The Scholar bowed quickly and turned to leave, shame washing over her for speaking so long in the oppressive silence.

"Would you blame me?" Lady Belva's voice cut through the silence.

The Scholar paused, her hand resting on the cold stone archway. She turned her cheek, her eyes filled with understanding and sorrow. "No, my lady. Even if your path to justice is darkened, it will still be more honorable than His Majesty's."

Chapter 81

Delova 24, 690 AC

"Betar's claws locked with Malindor's, the struggle dropping them further from the sky where Malindor's strong wings had taken them. The great white wolf and the great brown eagle thrashed and let out their screams of agony and anger as they fell.

"Never had their eternal battle become so bloody as it had on this day." Lady Catherin Torrin turned the page, the crinkling of the parchment and turn of her eyes hiding the subtle shake of her head. Her children always enjoyed such violent and epic stories before bed. She could never quite fathom how they found slumber after such tales of lore and time's past, and how, especially on a holiday night- the fourth day of Lunarius- her daughter wished for a story about such violent legendary beasts and not one themed around the gift-giving and ancestral holiday the castle was trying so desperately to celebrate with normalcy.

Cletta looked up at her as she paused the story, hoping for her mother to continue. Lady Catherin obliged her look of sleepy innocence and continued to read, "Malindor let out another screech as the mountains grew closer. Betar's biting jaws had ripped his wings from his body, and he knew he would not be able to fly again. Nor guard the vast and wide lands without them to take him into the skies and past where the people peacefully slept.

"Malindor drew his head back and reared it forward. If Betar were to take them to the ground, the great wolf, who could leap so high that birds of prey knew to watch for him, then he would take much from the winged beast.

"With a hard jolt and stab of his beak, Malindor took Betar's left eye and swallowed it whole. As their bodies met the harsh and jagged rock, Malindor released his claws from the white wolf and plucked his other eye out."

Lady Catherin flicked her eyes to her daughter's face as she turned the page, hoping she would be asleep by now. But still, her daughter stayed awake.

"But instead of swallowing it, the majestic bird taunted the crying and broken dog and placed the eye in his own neck where Betar had previously ripped a hole with his teeth.

'Now you are forever blind, you miserable beast, except your mind will only see glimpses of what I allow it to see when I part my feathers.'

"Betar rumbled a growl and snarled as his body lay beside the mangled bird. 'But now you are doomed to the ground, never to fly, for I took your wings and with them your ability to fly or to leave these mountains.'

'Then we both are doomed to be at one another's side, prowling these mountains for what one another stole,' the bird said.

"A vicious battle, an eternal struggle that neither of us would put to an end.' the wise wolf grumbled.

"And so, Betar the Broken, The Bloody, The Blind began his eternal trek of the Mountain Pass, yowling in the night in mourning of never seeing his moon again, but growing strong to leap high enough to feel the moon's cool embrace over time. And Malindor the Mangled awoke during the day, venturing throughout the lands in search of his wings, taunting the blind beast by showing his stolen eye what he would never get to truly see again."

Lady Catherin closed the book, wiping from her mind the crude images painted on the paper of the beast's battle and changed bodies. An eternal struggle that neither would put to an end, the wolf's words ran through her mind again. Quite poetic given the times, she thought.

Neither beast of legend won their battle, leaving the eternal fight forever mangled and damaged, never letting go of their pasts or anger with one another.

Gods, she thought, *perhaps the two beasts should have been a bear and a dragon to make the tale a proper warning to Odessin and Craigie of what endless fighting does to those who refuse to end it. Or now, a lion and a stag for Britia and Ayeshire.*

"One more story, please, mum," Cletta asked, her tone sleepy and her eyes droopy.

Lady Catherin smiled and softly laughed, "No, my love. It is late and," she stifled a yawn as Cletta's mouth opened to retort, "- and we both need our rest. Your ancestors will visit tonight and leave you gifts, but they cannot visit if you are awake."

Lady Catherin shifted on her daughter's bed and rose, her hand resting on her large stomach and the other pushing her up to stand.

"Mum," Cletta's tiny voice began, "how much longer until I've got a little sister?"

Lady Catherin smiled. "Any day now, my love, and she will be here." She rubbed her belly that she wished would finally fill with pain and cramping to allow her to be done with this pregnancy and hold her babe. "An Iron-born daughter, born under the fresh Winter Moon, just as her namesake was."

Cletta smiled as her eyes battled to close for sleep. "I can't wait, mum," she said before falling into her slumber.

Lady Catherin hobbled out of her daughter's room. She paused at the next doorway, that of Ennis' room, admiring her son sleeping peacefully before making her way back towards the end of the private chamber hall where her room sat just a few doors away from her youngest children. Evergreen garlands decorated with pine cones, dried fruit slices, and glimmering candles cast shadows on the walls and guided her footsteps through the remaining nights of Lunarius.

Four nights ago, the family and their aides had feasted and celebrated as much as they could while missing their loved ones during a season meant to celebrate family, bounty, and gathering. The Torrin clan and their remaining aides and friends feasted and gorged themselves on wine, ale, and treats. Each day since they celebrated in some way, crafts to celebrate the sun and earth, garlands made of treats left about the castle's exterior walls for the animals to enjoy, and a smaller Wild Hunt early this morning for this night's feast, before the children throughout the continent slept deeply, waiting for their ancestors to visit and their spirits would leave behind gifts for the children.

Lady Catherin rubbed her belly as she walked into her bedroom, smiling solemnly, praying that next season her entire family would be home for the holiday season with their daughter added to the festivities. Her lady's maid, Lula, curtsied at her arrival and finished setting Lady Catherin's bed as the Lady of Sebern sat in front of her dresser.

Lady Catherin grunted as she sat and attempted to bend forward to remove her shoes. "Oh, Lula, I hate to ask, but could you help a poor pregnant lady with her shoes?"

Both women laughed as Lula approached and bent down in front of the noblewoman. "I do not mind, my lady. Do you need any other aid tonight? Your bed is heating, and I have also prepared your night cravings."

"Oh, just a bit of help with this dress lacing if you could, please. Then you must be off to celebrate with your loved ones."

Lady Catherin asked as she reached out to ask for assistance standing up. Lady Catherin wished to bite her tongue at the slip of her words.

"Have you heard any news of my family, my lady?" Lula asked.

The two worked to change Lady Catherin into her nightgown and remove her daytime accessories.

Lady Catherin closed her eyes and shook her head, "I am sorry, Lula, but I do not know. I do fear we would not be given word of your father if he survived or perished fighting against our army. And I am unsure of how to find your family in Odessin."

Lula nodded in solemn understanding, "It is okay, my lady. I assumed as much. I have not contacted much of my family in many seasons; they enjoyed moving a lot. We were a very nomadic people– moving with the tides."

"I'm sorry, Lula. I truly am." Lady Catherin met her lady's maid's eyes in the mirror she stood in front of. Lula let her hand fall onto Lady Catherin's shoulder, and Lady Catherin set her hand on top of it. "I know you chose to come here many seasons ago, but it doesn't make it any easier when our countries fight against one another now."

"I chose to leave the coast behind, my lady. My family chose to stay. So is the life of one born a vassal, always destined to live and serve those of nobility. I simply had to go where I could serve best."

"Well, I am grateful for you, so very grateful, Lula." Lady Catherin tried not to cry but quickly failed. She blinked away the hormonal tears, "Blessed Lunarius."

"Blessed Lunarius, my lady," she replied.

Lula removed the noble lady's necklaces, and Lady Catherin fiddled with her rings and bracelet, both taking turns putting the precious jewels on the dresser stand. Lula's hand bumped against the flower vase on the dresser beside the jewelry box, and the accidental touch sent the glass to the ground in pieces.

"My apologies, my lady!" she let out loudly as she bent over to clean up the shards and fallen flowers.

Lady Catherin cocked her head at Lula's nerves and shout over something so little.

"It is ok. Are you alright?" Lady Catherin waddled forward to lend aid, only to be brushed away by Lula.

"Yes, yes, I am fine." The lady's maid finished collecting the glass and jumped up to stand. She bowed her head before leaving. "Please excuse me while I throw these away. I'll return to clean up the rest."

Lady Catherin finished dressing in her gown, the front lacing easy for her to reach without assistance. She moved for her bed and felt the covers, ensuring they were warm enough for her on a chilly night but not so hot that she would overheat.

As she smoothed out the blankets and moved to pull them back, she felt the presence of a shadow behind her.

She did not move, stilling herself to see if the shadow would announce its presence or if it was her imagination again, tricking her into believing she was being watched. For many seasons now, she had often felt as if she was being watched late at night, that the shadows of the castle often looked at her.

The softest padding on the stone floor confirmed for Lady Catherin that she was not alone. She moved to turn and greet the quiet figure. Her daughter always enjoyed sneaking up on her.

"Cletta, is that—"

The Lady of Sebern's words were stopped by a blade jamming in her back.

The blade slid out of her body as quickly as it stabbed into her. Lady Catherin let out a single stifled shout, the louder screaming meant to follow it stopped by stabbing in her stomach.

Her stomach.

Her baby.

Her baby.

Tears filled her closed eyes as she moved her hands to cover her swollen belly; warm blood covered her hands as she stumbled to the side, gripping the bedding as she tried to escape the one who had attacked her.

She fell to her knees at the end of the bed and began to crawl for the door, feeling the life drain from her womb and her heart. She fell from her knees onto her stomach, the blood pooling too fast for her to stop any of it.

"He-he-he-help." she coughed out. She reached for something, anything to break and make a noise to draw attention.

She continued to bleed out, face down on the blue rug stained red, as she let out one heavy shriek. She reached for the broken glass still gathered on the ground.

The baby. Save the baby. She thought to herself.

Cut it out.

Save the baby.

"Mommy! Mommy!"

Lady Catherin looked up at her daughter, standing in the open doorway, screaming. All sleep from her daughter's eyes was gone, replaced with terror. Cletta's shaking frame turned to the shadow behind her mother, and Cletta screamed again.

Lady Catherin turned to look up behind her and clutched her stomach, the pain taking over every one of her senses. She crumpled back onto the ground; her strength was gone, and so was the babe. She felt the last flutter of her unborn daughter die.

The last vision of Lady Torrin was a blur of a falling body as Lula slit her own throat and fell lifeless beside her.

CHAPTER 82

The towering funeral pyre stood harsh and jagged against the evergreen forest. Beside the large pyre lay another, much smaller in size but heavier in the weight it carried.

One fit for a babe.

The gathered town remained quiet; only sniffling tears and long breaths broke the breeze. The birds dared not speak, though they mourned, too.

Lady Catherin Torrin lay upon the larger pyre, her face resting in soft sereneness. The undertaker took great care to clean her body and reset her face to one of peace and not pain.

Wrapped in soft linen in the smaller pyre was her unborn babe. Her soft face and pudgy button nose peeked out from under the cloth, her body having been cut from Lady Catherin's torn-apart bosom. Both the babe and the late lady had an abundance of grave goods laid with them: Lady Catherin with food for her journey, her favorite jewels on her body, and plenty of coins to pay for passage.

The baby was given toys from the town's children so she would know what play was like in the heavens.

The greenery and florals that remained alive so late in the season had been plucked from the grounds around the entire city and braided into the timbers forming the pyres. Notes of love and support, parchments of prayers asking The One True to receive their souls, and other letters holding words for lost ancestors were stuck into the pyre so that they, too, would ascend to the heavens and fall among the stars.

Lord Lyall Torrin stood at the head of the tonne, his younger siblings held beside him by their aides.

"My mother was the heart of our family, a beacon of kindness and strength when any of us felt lost or weak. Above all else, she wanted peace and unity, a world where all could love one another as she loved my father." His words shook, and he paused to hold himself. "But I believe this world was too cruel and not ready for her, not capable of holding a woman like her in its broken grasp. Its cruelty and darkness is what took her and our unborn sister away from us all."

His body shook, and spittle shot from his mouth as he fought back angry tears. "And I am so- so fucking angry at it for taking them."

"Here here!" stray voices shot up from the crowd.

"And I am so scared," he whispered to himself. He shoved a hand to his face to roughly wipe the tears blemishing his face.

"She loved this country as much as she loved her homeland. And you all welcomed her with joy and love, received her differences with excitement, and when she blended the customs of Craigie into our lands, few resisted or questioned. She gave her everything, and now we will give her to the stars in hopes that her ancestors will care for her the way she did for us."

Lord Lyall vigorously nodded, his attempt to convince himself that he could survive the next moments. He turned to the Scholars holding unlit torches and gave one solemn nod.

They lit their torches on the small fire pit before the pyres.

"Wait!" Little Cletta shouted. She broke free from her aide's arms and rushed for her unborn sister's funeral pyre. In her hand had been the teddy she loved with all her heart and refused to ever be without. She kissed the worn bear's forehead, then her sister's, and rested the toy beside her swaddled body.

"You need a teddy," she sniffled. "He is a good teddy. He likes tea and minced meat pie the most."

She climbed down the branch-made steps and went to stand beside Lord Lyall. She reached for his hand, and her hands enveloped two of his fingers.

Lord Lyall did his best not to break apart at her gesture. "We will send their spirits to the stars with the honor they both deserve. May they be received with open arms and granted peace. And may," he choked and burst into tears he could not stop. Cletta squeezed his fingers and rested her head on his arm, "—may our little sister find the love we would have given her if only we were given the chance to."

His head trembled as he nodded to the torchbearers.

The flames came swiftly.

The fire devoured the dried wood, flowers, and parchment, shooting into the sky painted pink and orange by the setting sun. The fire burned, casting a heated glow over the town. Shadows danced in tune with the flames.

And then came the singing.

A haunting melody rose from the mourners—a song of farewell, of love, of pain.

A promise to find one another again in the heavens.

Little Cletta reached out a hand to the flames and waved.

"Goodbye, mum. Goodbye, sissy."

Lord Lyall nodded, and his lips pouted as more tears fell. "Yes, farewell, mother. Goodbye, sister."

The soft padding of little feet and a subtle touch of Ennis tore Lord Lyall's attention away and down to his other side. Ennis looked up into the sky at the flames licking the stars peeking out at sunset.

"Bye, mama. Bye sissy."

When the flames depleted and the ashes cooled, Lord Lyall returned on his own, seedlings in his hand, and planted his mother and sister's memorial trees beside one another.

Lord William Torrin glared past the silent army standing in front of him and his steed. He stared into the distance toward Prince Elion's army, where their campfires were a glimmer of dots in the bleak night. The blackness of the sky and hilly terrain hid the Sebern forces well from the prince's sleeping army. The moon had reached its descent, and the trees had begun to stretch upward to bring Lunar down to rest so dawn could begin soon.

If they wished for total darkness to hide them, they did not have much time left.

"The prince is mine." Lord William said firmly. "We take him alive, and when I am satisfied with his screaming and his pain, I will rip out his insides through every hole we puncture and put into his body."

"Father, *enough*. Go home, mourn mother, mourn our sister, let Cossius and I lead the fight here. Do not lead us into this battle." Lord Rener began, kicking his horse to block his father's.

Lord William pushed his horse past his son's. "I will go home and mourn her when I have the prince's head to bring to her tree. And then I will return for the king's."

"Father, please. We must not do this. You speak of torture, of mutilation, of war crimes." Lord Rener moved his horse to follow his father as he left the hilltop. Lord Cossius followed close behind, as did their armada.

Lord William jerked his horse around, "The king did not care about his own crimes when he murdered your unborn sister and *my wife*," he snarled. "*That* was a war crime. This," his hands shook as they clenched the reins, "this is justice."

"A crime for a crime, a child for a child, is not justice, father. That is not our way. If you do this, you sink as low as His Majesty." Lord Rener's horse jostled and fidgeted with his anxiety. "A raid on their camp is one thing, but capture and torture..."

"Then so be it," Lord Cossius said, his tone flat and his eyes thirsty for blood. He sat on his horse on the other side of their father, his quick anger and deep passion justifying the acts he wished to commit. His sword was already removed from its sheath. He had spent the day sharpening it while the army prepared for their revenge. "We are not so cruel as to go after his little daughter in the capital; he can thank us for that mercy later. A child for a child is only fair."

"Yes." Lord William nodded and addressed their gathered troops, all rippling with their own anger over the news, "We slaughter them all, white flag raised or not. They will burn, and they will die in whatever way our souls demand. We are the keepers of peace, and there will be no peace until the world is rid of the lion and his loyalists."

Lord Torrin ignored any other retorts and kicked his horse forward, signaling the rest to follow into the silent night.

Bells rang throughout the camp, and shouting quickly accompanied it. Prince Elion woke with a start and threw himself out of bed without a moment's pause. He threw on what armor he could; his breastplate and helmet were put on with haste after he pulled on linen trousers over his sleeping breeches. He had barely gotten the sides of his breastplate tied onto his body when his tent flaps flew open.

Commander Blackley looked the same as the disheveled prince- worse for wear and half-armored.

"Attack in the night, my prince. They carry no torches and have moved swiftly; we do not know how many."

Prince Elion grabbed his sword and made for the tent's entrance, tucking in the laces of his boots as he stumbled forward, still waking from a deep sleep.

Commander Blackley put his hand on the prince's chest to stop him, "We cannot risk you out there; let our men take care of this."

"No. This is my army, and I will fight with it," the prince retorted.

Yipping horse riders blew past the inner rows of the camp, the desert horses speeding past the running Britian soldiers.

"The princess's scouts were the ones to spot them." The commander paused, "The other officers and I were only told after her people had already begun to prepare for a fight."

"Son of a—"

"If they make it past the punji pits and foot traps, we may have an exciting night on our hands, my Dragons." Princess Easter smiled as she shouted at her Dragons riding alongside her. Her riders yipped and hollered in excitement.

As the outline of the Ravenhall fortress quickly came into view, the princess felt grateful for the prior battle where they had claimed several more miles of land. Now, at the right time of day, one could make out the large fortress nestled in the hills that now shadowed their war camp during the sunrise.

The princess smiled, her ears attuned to the distant sounds of crunching bones, echoing cries, and the unmistakable clamor of an army falling into her people's freshly laid traps. She and her Dragons slowed their horses with little effort as the bodies came into view under the stars.

Her scouts had already begun the fight- their arrows and spears piercing the Sebern fighters who had not fallen victim to the pits and metal contraptions that trapped others.

Today I gain another braid and another black mark. The princess contemplated what her tattoo would be to mark tonight's battle victory.

She drew her sword and tightened her grip on the reins, preparing to move in on the fight. She let out a fearsome cry and tore into the battle lines

Chapter 83

Lord William Torrin and his sons burst into the tent with a storm of anger, their faces fuming with fury. The air they brought with them was thick with tension, and their heavy footsteps broke through the quiet space. The men were so intertwined in one another's wrath that they did not notice those gathered in wait.

Lord Rener sidled up to his father, his voice low and full of accusation. "That attack was fruitless. Those lives lost pointless. I told you we should not have attacked."

Lord Torrin stopped his walking and swung his body to face his son. He snapped. "Do not dare speak to me in such a way, Rener."

Lord Rener did not step away. "They died because you refused to listen to anything but your anger! If you had listened to me and taken a moment to plan a real attack, we would not have fallen into a lost battle against the ground we stormed on instead of a true battle against our foes! Foes who barely had to swing a sword once they arrived!"

Lord Cossius looked up between the two, noticing those waiting for them in the tent. "Brother, father, perhaps we finish this another time."

He nodded toward the soldiers gathered around a large man with olive skin.

The arguing men stopped their fight and turned. Sedrick stood, bowing in respect at their presence.

"My lords, I come from the castle with something of impor-tance." Sedrick stepped forward, reaching a hand in his breast pocket.

The three Torrin men tensed, and the room reached for their swords. Lord jerked his attention to their guards, his words of suspicion and menace. "You dare let someone from the castle in our camp? In your lord's tent?!"

Sedrick paused and quickly raised his hands. "I apologize, my lords. I came from the castle, but I am not from the castle. And I," he shook his head, "- and in my exhaustion, I am making no sense. My name is Sedrick, and I am an ally of Lady Montarian, finishing a mission she sent me to the king's city to complete."

The tension simmered down as shoulders relaxed in the room.

Sedrick pulled out a folded parchment in his breast pocket. He held it stiff before him, the corner still hidden in his pocket. He held the room in silence. His face crumpled and softened, contorted and twisted. He sighed, giving in and pulling the paper out completely.

"This was meant for Her Grace's eyes only, but I am unable to return to Ayeshire at the moment to hand it to her, and it is of the utmost importance that what I retrieved be utilized immediately if what I have quite literally just heard of the previous battle is true. I do not know if we have time to await my return to her to put this plan into action."

Sedrick uncomfortably glanced at the others gathered, then looked back at the Lord of Sebern and his sons. His hands still clenched the paper. He emphasized his repeated statement. "This was meant for her eyes only. But I must trust that you lords are true allies." He nodded at the guards. "However, I will not trust anyone else."

Lord Torrin ordered the guards, his voice tight with impatience. "Leave us."

As the last guard left and the tent hushed back to silence, Sedrick opened the crinkled and stained parchment and set it on the table.

"I fear it is not the original. I could not risk being caught with it, but this is a copy I created using the juice of a lemon, making it only visible in the right heat and light." He carefully took the parchment over to a hanging lantern, delicately holding it close to the flame. The Torrin men followed closely behind.

As the parchment warmed, lines appeared and formed an image

A map.

No, a blueprint.

"The record halls have many copies kept in their historical records, some dating back to the time the current castle was first built, to when the Golden City fell and was rebuilt into the Isilria we know today. It is a copy of the tunnel system under the King's Keep. At least, what it looked like when it was reconstructed. From the shores of the Gulf to back alleys of Isilria, this map shows one how to get into the castle from below and behind."

"By God." Lord Rener whispered.

"How did you get your hands on this?" Lord William Torrin asked with confounded curiosity. He gently pushed his way forward between his sons, his eyes scanning the lines in awe.

Sedrick folded the parchment back up as he spoke, his voice barely above a whisper. "A friend within the castle searched and found it. We met in secrecy, and I was given it. That was before..." He swallowed a lump and lost his words. He looked to the ground, then back to Lord Torrin. "Lady Montarian intended this to be used to plan a siege from underground, but only if necessary. I am no war general, but I believe now it may be the only right path to take."

The lantern fires crackled with excitement, as did the three Torrin men. Lord William cracked a smile, a plot already brewing in his head. He reached a hand out for the parchment, his voice eager. "Thank you, son. We will create a true copy of this in ink we can all see, and-"

He crumpled his brow as Sedrick stepped from his grasp and pulled the parchment away.

"Give me the map, please," the lord asked with no kindness.

Sedrick shook his head. "No. No one touches this but me."

Lord Cossius stepped forward, his frame shadowing Sedrick's. "Give my father the map before I force it from your hands."

"No. I have conditions." Sedrick did his best to stand his ground. He swallowed his fear and straightened his posture. He stepped back towards the lantern, holding the parchment near the flame, his voice trembling with urgency.

"This mission, to take the castle from the ground up, will not only be a siege but a rescue mission of the one who risked her life for this. Who has risked her life every day to gather information for our cause and is now... I don't know, but someone must think of her," he pleaded. Sedrick did not care if his worry and the begging in his voice made him appear weak.

Someone had to think of her.

Someone had to save her before it was too late.

Sedrick did not hold much power or control in this world, but he held this parchment in his hands.

Lord Rener became a voice of reason, his voice soft but unyielding. "Sedrick, we are in the midst of a war; we cannot guarantee the saving of one person at any time, especially if it means more will fall or suffer. You must understand that there are larger missions, larger needs for the greater good."

Sedrick shook his head. "So you would not risk your cause to save one life, but you would do so to take revenge on a single one?"

He shot his glare at Lord William.

Lord Cossius squared his shoulders. "We could cut you down where you stand and simply take it from you. You know that, right?"

Sedrick shook his head slowly again, his voice low and urgent. "You could, or you could agree to my terms. And you will agree to this, or I burn this map now and face whatever revenge you deem fit."

Sedrick moved the parchment dangerously close to the open flame.

Lord William rested a hand on his son's shoulder. "We will not harm you. But we cannot promise that if we take the castle, we can save anyone in the chaos of a siege. But we can promise we could try."

Sedrick shook his head again. "We save Ora, or we save nobody."

Chapter 84

The deep thumping of hide skin drums gave a hard beat, roaring and loud as thunder, for the fire dancers to spin and stomp to. Bass-filled chants accompanied the dancers and the drumming; the chanters' voices so loud and harsh one unfamiliar with the ceremony and song would think god-like beasts had descended upon the area and were shouting with fury.

The fire dancers' moves were harsh and jagged. Even long flows and swaying movements held a warrior's edge.

"On this day of Thiran, we give our gratitude to the true gods for never faltering or failing us, for standing behind and beside us. We beg our ancestors for forgiveness and mercy as we continue their path to freedom!" A group of ale-drunk and fur-clad people raised their glasses as the man continued his toast. "We piss in the face of the king as we celebrate the birth of our true queen- The Queen of the North!"

Lady Kathilla smiled crookedly and raised her glass in gratitude for the toast before taking a long sip and setting her stein down. She turned her attention back to the elders sitting alongside her at the head table.

"My warriors and I await your judgment and wisdom on how we can move forward, your honors. We have failed our people. I have failed our people. I should have sought your counsel first, but instead I chose to seek counsel only from myself. And now that I know what the gods hold for my future, I wish to wait for your advisement and knowledge."

"We have all made mistakes by looking only in ourselves or in ways that the false god and his followers would do so. Our ways, the old ways, Kathilla, require more spiritual guidance and insight." The Seer Feriae said, her swollen and milky eye watching the crowd.

"Yes, and I offer myself up for whatever penance and sacrifice is needed to make amends for my wrongs, for how I lashed out at our prior meeting, at how I have misstepped before then." Lady Kathilla's voice had no authority or harshness to it, only docileness and submissive softness. "Perhaps the vision I saw of my future is the proper penance."

Another elder said, "No penance is needed, child. Our gods know your soul more than you and know you will one day act on your imperfections. They are much kinder than they seem and welcomed your sacrifice of wolves and the man from many moons ago. But you must remember to seek their guidance and forgiveness not only when you need something from them, but always. Keep your faith in your heart, even when your heart is full."

"Yes, your honor." Lady Kathilla bowed deeply to the only people she would even show her neck to.

"And you will need them much in the moments to come," Feriae said. Her milky eye darted up and down, then looked straight ahead into the throes of the party.

Lady Kathilla's own eyes moved towards the sidelines of the celebration. She noted the quick movement of her daughter, Gladys, and others gathering to talk; a folded paper shook in Gladys' hand. Her daughter nodded and bowed her head before turning back to the room. Their eyes met for a moment, and they spoke of the terrible words that were to be said.

Lady Kathilla did not wait for the elders around her to dismiss her or offer any more words. She bolted up from the table and met Gladys as their paths stopped together.

"What is it?" Lady Kathilla asked.

Gladys swallowed. Her stoicism, which mirrored her mother's, was shaken and trembling. "It is Aunt Catherin. She-"

The words that were not said stole the breath from Lady Kathilla's body.

"No, no, she cannot be."

"Aye, but she is." Gladys solemnly nodded.

Faces around the room slowly halted their noises and joyful celebration.

"And the baby, tell me that baby did not die with her?" Lady Kathilla's voice shouted, and her eyes softened in sadness that she knew she should not carry in her heart for the sister she disowned.

Gladys hesitated, then shook her head, "The babe was still in her belly."

Lady Kathilla held her stomach as if her own womb had been stabbed. While Lady Kathilla held no love in her heart for the Torrin family, she once had much love for her late husband's sister. They were girls who grew up together and were forced apart by love and hatred, duty and politics. Despite the distance that put them at odds for so long, she growled. "Who did this?"

"It was her lady's maid. She left a note b'fore she took her own life. It bore no words, just a crude drawin'," Gladys paused again, "A lion."

Angered murmurs and hushed curses echoed throughout the space as the news carried through them.

Gladys held out a rolled note. "This is for you, mother. Cousin Lyall said it was left on his mother's dresser, incomplete, but addressed to you."

Lady Kathilla slowly, with a shaking hand that she could not halt, pulled the parchment from her daughter's hands. She did not read the words aloud. She did not trust her voice to hold steady.

~~Lady Kathilla,~~

~~Dearest~~

Sister,

~~I~~

~~How are~~

As you can tell, I have struggled with how to even begin this letter. I do not know how to speak to you, and that hurts me more than anything I have lost.

And I am sorry for that.

I do not know how to make amends or find a bridge between us, but I wish to try. I have wished to try for many da'es and more nights but have fallen into my cowardice each time.

I miss you, sister.

I miss Fraser, too.

I miss his loud laughter and our memories as children. I miss the broken-tooth smile he had each time your name was brought up. He was an odd man and too stubborn for his own good and too hot-headed for any sense, but gods, was he a great brother.

You were a great sister. By choice and love, we found each other as little girls and became so close that it was as if the gods mistakenly made us only friends when they meant to make us sisters.

I wished to tell you something, something I wish I could share in person, but the war, the world, and your rightful anger has kept us apart.

The babe is a girl. I am certain of it.

And her heart beats as fiercely as the war drums of home.

I wish to name her Kathilla so that our family will always have a part of you in it. That is, if you would allow us the honor.

Our families have broken apart when they were meant to be strong together, and as each da'e passes by in this war, I wonder if, perhaps, all those ages ago, I should not have gone so silently into agreement with my husband's family when they chose to

The letter ended abruptly.

The world stopped around Lady Kathilla. The party held no noise; the words of Lady Catherin's death were already well spread through the space, and heads were bowed as prayers to their gods were given in her honor.

Lady Kathilla had been born with a war axe in her hand and unending anger in her body. When she came from her mother, her scream was so loud it deafened the village. For much time, she had not known what to do with it all. She believed that maybe the anger was within her to fuel herself each time her right to the throne was questioned or each battle with Odessin grew worrisome.

As she gathered herself and rolled the letter back up, Lady Kathilla knew why Thirdall blessed her with life and why Niyja did not balance her anger with an equal amount of softness.

It was all for this moment.

Niyja was the goddess of love and watched over all emotions to ensure the world remained balanced between love and darkness and that each soul had a balance of hatred and love, pain and joy, passion and passiveness. Thirdall gave life and took it. Both goddesses blessed Lady Kathilla, especially on this day.

Lady Kathilla walked to the center of the room where the large pyre burned and whipped with flames. She looked to the elders, specifically the Seer Feriae. Feriae nodded her head. The elders held no hesitancy over what they knew was to come with the news that had been broken.

Her people would not gain their land, their freedom, through skirmishes and battles over holy lands with their neighbors.

It would be gained by the king's blood dripping from her axe.

"Great warriors of Craigie! Fighters for the Vahar! It is time for us to return to our glory, to battle for our country and for our people across this entire kingdom. We feast now and leave when the light shines again. We make to the western shores and prepare our ships to sail." Her ice blue eyes were already lost to the seas and the blood she would spill in their waves.

"We move our fight away from our borders and into the south." Lady Kathilla snarled. "Where I'm going to kill the False King."

Chapter 85

Scholus 1, 691 AC

King Ivan had ensured that the cathedral hall was packed full of citizens from every part of the city, even those well below his castle's shadow. His Council told him to show his people the kindness of the crown, to show the city that he would not rule only with an iron fist but with mercy, with justice, with the values his enemies claimed he did not have.

To remind them that fighting for him, fighting with him, was the proper choice.

The king hastily and quickly asked his Council to arrange a feast for the final day of Lunarius at the largest royal cathedral in the city, to take rations from the royal private stores and prepare them alongside a sermon of gratitude to The One True. It had been too long since the city hosted a holiday celebration, and the king believed it most appropriate to host a feast on the first day of the new epoch, his hope being that as the wheel of time turned and started fresh again, so could he and his people.

King Ivan did not let it bother him that the cathedral halls had not been packed with eager worshippers thankful to gather in fellowship alongside His Majesty in one of his private cathedrals reserved only for noblemen and royals.

He had not let himself sneer in agitation as the halls only filled when the doors were flung open for the feast that took place after the sermons concluded, and that many filled their plates, then their pockets, and left.

They came. They will see what we are truly about. He reminded himself. *What my crown is truly about.*

I will show them the kind of king I can be. I will prove to them that I am not a mad king.

I am not a mad king.

I am not a mad king.

He repeated the words to himself until several eyes darted to him in concern, where he sat atop the dais with his family. King Ivan stilled his lips that he had not known were murmuring the phrase over and over again as he looked down from the dais where they sat safely away from the crowd and beside the choir. They had intentionally arranged the pews and tables so the crowd would have to queue by the royal family and walk past them after getting their meals, so they would have to face the king who gave this kindness to them.

It was easier to count the number of citizens who gave him thanks than to count those who did not.

The only sounds in the church were those of silverware clanking and quiet murmurs from those who gathered in community at their tables to eat, of those saying hello to their neighbors and friends before enjoying their free meals and leaving. There was a palpable tension, no joy, no smiling, no happiness at what was given to them by His Majesty.

King Ivan could not hear the whispers exchanged by the new faces who rushed in through the door, nor could he understand the appalled and shocked looks on those who listened to their whispering before glaring up at the king with wide eyes.

"Figgins," King Ivan hissed over his shoulder to Father Figgins, who sat beside him, "get the choir to sing. To do something to make this occasion feel less like a funeral and more like a celebration."

The Head of the Church, His loyal Hand, quickly shuffled to where the choir sat quietly gathered. Their robes shuffled, and their feet brushed against the stone floor as they all rose. Father Figgins returned hastily to his seat as the choir mumbled among themselves, likely deciding which songs to bless the crowd with.

Several singers cleared their throats, and their leader stood before them and raised her hands for the choir to begin.

And so the choir sang as they were asked to by the king. Each member placed their soul on display with each note that rang through the hall.

And slowly, ever so timidly, the crowd joined.

They put down their plates of food provided by the king and harmonized with the singers. Even if they did not know the words, the crowd hummed along, their voices rising into a powerful chorus of defiance.

The king would have been satisfied with the outpouring of alliance, of fellowship, had it not been for the song that carried through the space.

The Anthem of the Stag, a symbol of Ayeshire people's—and now, clearly, many of his own people's—allegiance to a power greater than the king, a reminder of a shared history and the strength they can draw from it.

In time of need and in plenty

When this land knew magic and mercy

The stag took sentry

And protected us fiercely

We proud sons and daughters all

Sing to make it known

The stag has risen to the call

His mighty trumpet blown

Fierce on field

And in halls

The stag is the mightiest

Foe of all

The king knew he could not put them all down.

The king knew he could not strike the entire hall to its knees for such an act.

The king knew he could not stop as Lady Ora joined in from where she sat several chairs down from him, her eyes meeting his, a threat, a request for him to *try*. His jaw tightened, his fists clenched, but he did not look away from her.

Then came the song of his mother's home– of Sebern.

The Flight of the Eagle took his attention away and spread it across the sniffling, crying, angry crowd.

His Majesty did not know why mothers wept while they sang it. He did not know why many held tightly to their newborn babes or swollen bellies while glaring at him.

He did not know.

King Ivan did not know.

"Figgins, *someone*," the king hissed, "What the Hells is going on?"

The King's Guard slowly walked towards the king and encircled him and the royal family while the singing continued. King Ivan ignored the few who hesitated in their steps as they moved to keep the crowd away from the king.

Father Figgins made his way to the king, a nervous servant now standing beside the Hand- a servant so defiant that he allowed his nerves and the news he bore to paint a glare on his reddening face.

"Your Majesty," Father Figgins began, "we must get out of here. Now."

Chapter 86

Lord Digarius sat on the edge of his late brother's bed. The room had remained untouched since Lord Taylian had last been inside. It was still the mess of a room common for a boy on the edges of manhood. Dirty clothing sat in a corner; most of the cloth had padding sewn into various locations, made to protect the wearer's essential organs and muscles during sword practice.

Several swords adorned the walls, and polishing cloths and small repair kits were set alongside the desk that had always been bare of books, except those to do with war and strategy.

Not even the scullery maids had been allowed to cross the threshold after Lord Taylian took his last breath.

Lord Digarius sniffled again and wiped his eyes. His hands joined together in anxious prayer in front of him. His elbows rested on his knees, one leg restlessly moving up and down.

"Why would you wish to be like me?" he whispered. He sniffled again, and his voice cracked, "What a stupid thing to die for."

He raised his head and looked to the ceiling as if his gaze could pierce the stone above and see into the heavens.

"I have few friends, and the ones I do have, I have learned that I perhaps do not treat them as I should. I have gotten men killed and made orphans of babes because I cannot make the right decisions in battle. And the ghosts of the men who taught me what I know now haunt me. I constantly worry if Sir Rainey's shadow of betrayal will possess me or if father's haunted past will become my future."

He cleared his throat and returned his eyes to the floor. "Why would you look up to me? I do not even wish to look at myself."

His hands rubbed through his locks. His words now spoken into his chest as he tucked his chin inward and left his arms wrapped over his tucked head.

"I must be better. If not for myself, then for you. You died doing what you believed I would have done, brother. That is an honor I cannot waste."

Lord Digarius cleared his throat and pushed his emotions away, and stood. He made for the door, swinging it open with determination and headed down the hall only to be stopped by the urgency of a messenger sprinting towards his mother's Council room.

When the messenger caught sight of Lord Digarius out of the corner of her eye, she did not stop running but shouted back at him, "My lord, you must come as well! Please, hurry!"

Lady Montarian shook with rage, grief, and sorrow. "Lady Catherin, she is- she is-"

Her hand covered her mouth as she turned and stepped in front of the open window, her deep breaths attempting to bring freshness to the stale hatred festering in her heart.

Lord Theodus stormed forward and snatched the letter from Father Robb's shaking hands, "No, no, no," he assured himself. His chest rose and fell in great heaves as he read the letter from Berren Castle, "An unborn babe. He murdered a pregnant woman and unborn child!"

Lord Digarius stood on the opposite side of the room. His shock stilled his body, and he and Father Robb dared not move as Lord Theodus' rage ruminated through the space.

The Lord of Ayeshire threw every item of breakable value in front of him. Only when he ran out of items to take his vengeance on did he stop to speak again. "He murdered our child and now another. I will bleed dry every last one of his children and each that is born to a loyalist under his banners."

His breathing came in harsh huffs and spittle.

Lady Belva subtly touched her stomach, remembering the times when her own stomach would flutter with life. She let her hand fall back to her side and looked out onto her country.

Her kingdom.

She looked toward the hill where the fresh soil of Taylian's grave still caught her eye in the right sunlight. Tears blurred her vision, but her son's face stayed clear in her mind. Lady Catherin's smile and laughter, accompanied by the sounds of her army of children, played in Lady Belva's mind as well—memories from past holidays the families had spent together, letters shared between the two, an understanding of love and exhaustion in the same breath, tired mornings and late nights that could never be replaced. It was a feeling only two mothers could bond over and remember when they looked back at their children's youth and newborn days.

She would now only ever see their faces in her dreams, hopes, and prayers.

Lady Belva no longer felt numb. Instead, desire crept in to sit alongside her grief.

For her entire life, all she desired had been peace and justice.

But now she craved something more– a desire for blood-soaked revenge.

"No. No, you will not, Theo," she said calmly and softly, a jarring contrast to her husband's outburst. Her hovering hand slowly balled into a fist at her side. "But I will."

The men in the room stood in silence as the Lady of Ayeshire turned to them. While all three men had known her for much of their lives, if not all of their days, the woman who turned to them was not the noble lady they had all grown familiar with, that they had watched fall quietly into her grief.

The Lady of Ayeshire did not speak to them.

The Queen of the People did.

"I will have every ounce of revenge and more. I will end this crooked kingdom and birth a new one from His Majesty's bleeding and broken corpse. Only then will justice be served. Only then will I be satisfied."

"What do you wish to do, Your Majesty?" Father Robb asked.

"He tried to crumble our home. He took away those we love. And now, I will have everything of his."

"Mother, what do you mean?" Lord Digarius swallowed and stepped aside her, his worry pushing against her thrumming anger.

She turned her hard face to his softened and downfallen expression, "I mean to say, there will be no throne left to take from him. The King's City will fall upon his body and become his grave; his family and his allies will become his companions in the dirt. I mean to say, the empire must fall."

The Queen of the People stepped onto her castle's front balcony, her crown of golden vines and stag antlers caught the glimmer of the harsh sun. The golden crown formed a strong point that rested against her edges and pointed down to her firm face. Smaller cuts and curls of metal and stag antlers were woven together and protruded in jagged harshness. Within the tight curls of her hair were matching golden beads woven into the twisted strands that fell down her shoulders.

Silence fell over the crowd in her presence.

She took a deep inhale and brought her hand up in greeting. The silver and golden threads on the cuffs of her split-sleeves matched the intricacies and elegance of the filigree carvings that ran along her crown and down the train of the dress. It had been her coronation dress, and all these epochs later, it still fit her aged body. The golden buckled straps running across her chest rose and fell as she took in her people's presence and began.

"I have always thought of myself as a good and honorable woman, a merciful and just leader. I was raised this way, as all in my line have been. And I raised each of my sons to be as good and just and honorable as I believed myself to be- as I hoped Taylian would be." Queen Belva Montarian took a shaking inhale and unclenched her tight hands. "But the King That Once Was took him from us, and now I am not so merciful. I am not so kind."

Excitement bolted through the people. Nodding heads agreed with her anger and rooted deeper into their own.

"And now the king will find out exactly what kind of woman I am, and what kind of monster a mother is willing to turn herself into."

Chapter 87

King Ivan took a large swig of his drink. "The ground is frozen, and so much has changed since it last thawed." He covered his mouth with a fist and let out a small fit of coughs and cleared his throat. "And I am not only speaking of the war. The Dragonia Starfall did not bless us this winter- no spirits ran across our sky to bless our new epoch that has begun."

He wiped his mouth on a kerchief, the speckles of blood joining the other dried splotches of red. "And my Healers have now recommended routine changes to heal me from whatever it is that has been torturing my body. They have these ridiculous new theories that it may be more spiritual than an illness of the body. I worry they are right, Father."

"Whatever its source, let us hope their aid finally resolves this issue, Your Majesty." Father Figgins replied. "It is painful to watch this slow descent of your health."

The king watched Father Figgins pour another glass of dark liquor for himself. The king held his grip on his cup of tea. "Among meditation, they have unfortunately recommended I stay away from the bottle for now. Believing that these supposed fits of madness and these physical scars may be linked to too much drink. I fear they may be right, since I've stopped drinking as much and taking more of their theriac, my bloodied fits and horrid visions have lessened."

Father Figgins laughed and took a sip. "If that were true, that drink is the cause, Your Majesty, then all of us within the kingdom would be screaming from rooftops and covered in cuts and sores. As a man of God, I can find understanding in their belief that it's a spiritual illness rather than physical, but I have my reservations on much of their thoughts and treatments."

"Oh, really?" King Ivan said, taking another sip of the fruit and herb-infused drink his Healers had made for him. The hot tea scorched his tongue and throat. The sensation of the low burn did not leave his dry throat even after the heat of the infused water had gone.

Father Figgins looked up at the king, his pointer finger lazily tapping on the rim of his own glass, the beat tapping in an impatient manner. "Well, if The One True did not wish us to drink, then why would he give us the knowledge of its creation?"

"This is true, but, for now, maybe it would be wise to step away. While I do not remember these fits they spoke of, I do feel my mind falling from my control." King Ivan raised a shaking hand to his forehead and rested his head against it. "Even now, at this moment, as the stars wake in the sky, I can hear their voices and feel a pull of fog washing over me. Perhaps the Council was right."

"Do you wish to rest, Your Majesty?"

King Ivan fought through the pounding in his skull and pushed against the edges of hallucinations creeping into the corners of his vision. He shook his head. "No, no, I do not wish to rest. I wish to fight this affliction."

He took a large gulp of the tea, hissing at the harsh burn of the hotness. It did nothing to soothe any of his afflictions and pains.

His head pounded more as he fought harder to quiet the thrumming and the pain. The room swirled in his vision, and his insides felt suddenly raw and on fire. Every surface the tea had touched now burned as if someone had poured scorching water down his throat.

The pain moved to cover every inch of his insides; he burned and itched everywhere his blood flowed. The king jerked his body up and stumbled against the table, both hands slamming down onto the table and framing his place setting. "I wish to be rid of whatever it is that grasps me! I wish to know why Lady Torrin was murdered in cold blood and why my empire is looking to me for their blame! I wish to stop this all- to take it all back!"

He coughed again, the cough bordering on a hacking vomit. His open mouth spewed spit and blood droplets over the table and his hands, the paper, snacks, and drinks now spoiled by his sickness. The coughing did not cease, and the king prepared himself for a longer fit to work through. His tremoring hand reached for a glass of chilled water, the burning of his insides too much to handle. His tremors grew erratic as his coughing grew louder, the glass within his reach falling as his hand wildly knocked against it.

King Ivan slammed his fist against the table and turned away from Father Figgins, who sat calmly waiting for the king to recover. The king's steps stumbled as he stopped using the table to support his body. He clutched his chest, feeling deeper pain take over.

His mind swirled into a panic. He had grown used to his body hacking and coughing these past moon phases, but there had not been one so painful or long as this.

And his heart. His heart had not fluttered so erratically before.

In his realization, short bursts of memories came through. Like jagged half pieces of a puzzle, they still managed to make enough of an image for the king.

King Ivan turned back to Father Figgins, who had not moved from his seat and was watching the king struggle with a bored look on his face.

"You." King Ivan coughed, his mind free from fog and pain for a brief enough moment.

Father Figgins smirked as he unfolded his hands resting on the table. He unbuttoned his shirt collar and reached his spiny fingers inside, pulling out a kerchief wrapped around a small tube. He did not break eye contact with the struggling king. "And here I thought you would go to your grave, never being able to figure out what was so clearly right in front of you. We had to be careful with the dosage, of course. Too much at one time would have led to a suspicious death, but small enough doses over many moon phases and a final heavy one in your tea to speed the timeline up, and well," He smiled again. "few still hold suspicions over Mad King Jacquard's death. In fact, in the end, many were thankful for it, for death to come for The Mad King."

King Ivan choked on blood and air as he attempted to spit words at Father Figgins. The king made his way to the table. Father Figgins did not blink or flinch.

"It would have been better for you to continue to follow blindly, to be the king we were shaping you to be. But you resisted at times, allowed weaklings like Lord Orville or your second son to leech bullshit of righteousness in your ear, and caused you to hesitate when we needed your strength. It would have been better for you not to force us to make you another Mad King." A toothy smile slithered over Father Figgins' face as he set the vial on the table. "No one likes a mad king, but they do love the ones who clean up his messes after he is gone."

Despite his failing body and mind, King Ivan held onto two words Father Figgins said.

We.

Us.

King Ivan attempted to scream, but his throat burned with blood and pain. Father Figgins poured a fresh glass of whiskey. Behind him, the door unlatched.

King Ivan heard the latch and stumbled for the door, his knees hitting the ground in front of the queen. He reached a hand out to her for help, only to have her smack it away.

"Ah, good. You are finally here." Father Figgins said, his back turned to the door.

King Ivan exchanged a look between the two as he hacked and coughed more on the ground, unable to form words, and his throat too raw and bloodied to allow him to scream. His heartbeat slowed, forcing him to slowly waver to the ground and focus his efforts on breathing.

Where were his guards? Why had no one come yet?

"It is done, yes?" the queen asked as she stepped over and around her husband's fallen body.

Father Figgins waved a hand at the floor where the king still battled for his life. He stood and handed a glass to the queen. "It would be if he had drunk the entire glass as quickly as he should have, so now we have this to deal with. The story was that we both were drinking with His Majesty when he quickly seized to death. Take a drink so we are not questioned why only two cups instead of three were drunk from."

She took a large gulp, set the glass down, and then picked up the small vial Father Figgins had left on the table. She stuffed it between her breasts, knowing no one would search for evidence in her bosom. She took the king's cup of tea and tossed the contents onto the rug.

"Yes, well, if he takes any longer, we will have more issues to concern ourselves with than one questioning our corroborations. I sent the guards away for a moment, telling them I saw a strange figure in a window and it frightened me." She took a deep breath, watching as the king gave in to his struggle with the god of death. She leaned down and whispered to him, a sharp finger under his chin holding his head steady. "We remember, we do not forget, Your Majesty. House Kavistia remembers the Usurper King who took our name from the throne, and The Isles remembers the lies you spit to uphold your line."

The king's mouth opened and closed like a fish out of water, gasping for more of the air that it could not live without.

She tutted. "You should have never attempted to make me inferior to you, and your father should have never fallen into marital business with the Isles."

Chapter 88

As the king's last breath left him and his eyes lost the last speckles of light, his body fell to the floor with a sharp thud.

The room stilled for several moments, the two killers waiting for another breath from King Ivan's body.

New breath did not come.

"Finally," she said.

Queen Onetta knelt beside his limp body and set his head in her lap. She poked her eyes with her fingernails, producing tears in the corners of them that would soon fall down her painted cheeks.

The queen took a deep inhale and then let out a guttural, ear-piercing shriek that rang through every stone and crevice of the castle while Father Figgins watched, smiling at her cries.

"Help me!" she screamed, "Help me! The king is dead!"

Chapter 89

Queen Onetta stood before the golden throne, her stark black dress a shadow in the light of the early morning sun. Beside her, Prince Percy, Princess Arminda, and Lady Ora stood in cohesive confusion, their attire disheveled and appearances hurried. Their aides had quickly dressed them in basic court attire and run combs through the two ladies' hair.

The youngest princess had not been called to the early morning gathering. Her aides had been informed to allow Princess Kalia to sleep in and, if she were to wake, to keep her busy until the queen called for her.

The entirety of the king's court had been ordered to the castle at dawn's first light. All within Isilria's city walls were rushed with haste to the throne room to hear the mysterious and urgent news.

"Do you know what it is they have called us for?" Princess Arminda whispered to Prince Percy. She kept a keen eye on the room and the whispering groups of lords and ladies.

"No," he shook his head and scanned the room alongside her. "There was no Council meeting called before this. I was rushed here just as quickly as you were."

He leaned back, his eyes locking onto his mother's attire. "Mother is wearing all black."

"She hates that color." Princess Arminda swallowed hard, her voice barely above a whisper. Panic flickered in her eyes.

Prince Percy nodded slowly, feeling a knot tighten in his chest. He held his breath, the air thick with dread. He let out a shuddering exhale. "It has happened, hasn't it?"

Princess Arminda shook her head, tears welling up. "Please, God, let it not be so."

The doors to the throne room clanged shut, the sound echoing like a death knell. Silence descended over the anxious crowd, and all eyes diverted to the dais.

Father Figgins laid a comforting hand on Her Majesty's shoulder. She nodded in gratitude, but her eyes were hollow. The Hand of the King stepped forward, his face grave.

Father Figgins licked his dry lips and bowed his head. "Last night, during a conversation with Her Majesty and I, His Majesty fell to the ground, seized by an uncontrollable force shaking his body. Despite our attempts and cries for aid," he lifted his head and slowly shook it, "- despite all we did, the king is dead."

Harsh and loud gasps violently stole the air in the room and the windowpanes feared being shattered by the force of the shock.

Princess Arminda's crumpled expression dropped, and her mouth fell open. Her eyes became ghosts of themselves, empty orbs watching the Hand of the King speak.

Prince Percy's eyes mirrored his sister's. His hands ran through his hair and then shook at his side. He held his jaw tightly closed and swallowed the bile and shouts he felt brewing inside of him. Princess Arminda's hand moved to take his, both gripping too tightly, but neither sibling cared.

Lady Ora stood beside the princess, her gaze sharp, watching every nuance of Princess Arminda's reaction.

"You truly did not know, did you?" Lady Ora whispered, her eyes wide with realization.

Princess Arminda swallowed hard, faintly shaking her head. "No," she admitted softly, her voice barely above a breath. "I had no clue."

Prince Percy ignored their words. Why would Lady Ora believe his sister would know of any of this?

"In his stead, the Regency Act asks us to begin our period of mourning." Father Figgins paused dramatically. The queen stepped forward beside him. "And it appoints Her Majesty to take his place until Crown Prince Elion returns from war."

Lady Ora's mouth hung agape as her head jutted back to the princess beside her. "This wasn't a part of —"

Princess Arminda quietly choked out one word as her body started to shake. "No."

Between quiet tears of mourning, Prince Percy caught the two women's interaction and looks of anger and knowing between the two. He caught only a flicker of it before the queen's words stole the room's attention.

"My husband led our great kingdom for over eight epochs. He faced trials and celebrated successes-"

The queen's words faded from Prince Percy's ears as he looked for the expressions of Lord Nesima and Lord Shaital. The two lords stood over her shoulder just below the dais steps. Their eyes spoke of worry and uncertainty. If they held any guilt or responsibility, the men hid it well as they looked at the prince and bowed their heads.

The Queen Regent pushed her shoulders back and kept her joined hands together in front of her. "My first duty as Queen Regent is to extend my gratitude to you all for your grace with my family and I as we take on our mourning. And I thank you for your understanding of our desire for privacy regarding His late Majesty's death."

Queen Onetta maintained the stoic demeanor the kingdom knew her for, but beneath her composed exterior, her words carried a hidden weight that caught Prince Percy's ears.

The prince glared at his mother through her veil, attempting to decipher her words and what lay beneath those she carefully chose. His brows furrowed and relaxed repeatedly, his head shaking as his eyes darted between Father Figgins and Queen Onetta.

Queen Onetta's eyes bore no redness from tears or a sleepless night. Her mourning dress, an outfit all nobles kept a collection of for sudden times such as this, did not bear the markings of being kept in storage and hastily brought out with only a moment's notice. Her breaths between words did not show exhaustion or pain.

While he always knew his mother as a woman of clean composure- to act properly at all times in and out of the court, even the coldest beast would- should- still shake at the memory of watching their spouse suddenly die before them.

He could not bring himself to hold the same contempt for his mother that he held for Father Figgins. But still, her words and composed demeanor struck a chord of unease within him.

"Why would we announce this to the whole court before the Council? Before our family even knew?" Prince Percy mumbled in wonderment.

Lady Ora did not glance at Prince Percy as she whispered a reply. "Because it was meant to shock us- all of us in this room. To prevent any scheming or plotting before the entirety of the court knew what they were up to."

Queen Onetta's voice resonated through the hall once more. "The regency period will not be without its challenges," she stated firmly. "But the throne will persevere. Together, as a united court, we will ensure the continuation of the rightful noble line. We will ensure our kingdom continues on a just path."

The noble crowd nodded and murmured agreement and content with the new declaration. They so easily accepted this change as if it did not shake the entire foundation of the kingdom, where it sat in such a fragile state. They so easily murmured and began their gossip while Prince Percy and his sister shook with pain over losing their father, as their entire lives changed in a second.

"Long live the queen!" Lord Tyrrian Priscus broke the murmurs with a cheer as he stepped out of the crowd beside the dais and walked up to the dais steps.

The tyrant kneeled before the mourning queen. His knees touched the ground in front of the golden throne for the first time.

"Long live the queen," he said again as he looked up at her, both of them smiling at one another.

Lady Ora's words spoke again to Prince Percy. His mother was always the best at court politics and games and logically, the prince knew they would have to announce his father's death quite quickly whenever it did occur, but this did not add up.

He and his sisters should have been told in private and given a moment to grieve and collect themselves. The King's Council should have been given a moment to plan for a change in their ranks and duties. But they were given nothing as far as the prince could tell.

And his uncle now bowed to his mother as she stood above the throne, the prince knew the Lord of the Isles loathed. This was more than just a simple act of respect for the woman, the entire court knew Lord Tyrrian still loved.

This was...

A slow clap began at the end of the hall. Lord Tyrrian stood and stepped beside Queen Onetta as they both failed to hide their shock at who walked down the aisle.

The man continued his slow clapping as he sauntered with a satisfied, smug step. He wore a deep blue tunic robe with a sash of gold medallions shaped like the sun. The robe flowed and moved around him like dark waves dancing in the wind. Behind him, his guards wore rich blue pants and long matching shirts underneath breastplates made of cream-colored metal, a large sun hammered into the center of the plate. Their pauldrons were forged of moveable mail that appeared as glimmering fish scales, their tassets fashioned in the same fish scale cuts.

"Father," Queen Onetta said.

The Lord of Thelimor, the oldest and grandest city in the world, stopped his clapping and leisurely continued his walk down the aisle, his guards filing in behind him.

"You neglected to reply to my letters- many of which I assume went unread- and now I see why. You have been quite busy, daughter." Lord Orilion Kavistia, the wealthiest man in the kingdom, the lord who oversaw the Golden Bank that kept all the kingdom's finances in order, stood before her. "I would finally tell you I am proud of you, but that would be a lie."

He raised his chin at Lord Tyrrian, shook it, and tutted in disappointment. Lord Orilion somehow managed to look down at the two despite their standing on the dais above him. "You two really could not help yourselves, could you?"

"Why are you here, Father?" the queen asked.

"I am here to collect on the crown's long overdue debts and, it appears, attend a funeral and a coronation." He looked around the room of gathered spectators. "I do say it will be hard to celebrate, seeing as the new king just so happens to be missing."

"Prince Elion is on the battlefield." Father Figgins stepped beside the queen, "As the laws of ascension dictate –"

Lord Orilion flicked his hand up, silencing Father Figgins and ignoring the offense on his face. The lord slowly curled his fingers into his palm and joined his hands behind his back.

"You need not tell me of the laws you twist and contort to your desires; I know them much better than you could hope for." He looked Father Figgins up and down in disgust. "Now go get the Council chambers ready. The Hand of the Queen would like to meet with his daughter in privacy."

"Hand of the Queen? You think so highly of yourself that you take and give titles at your leisure?" Father Figgins sniped.

"I think if my daughter knows what is best for her, she will gladly rip that pin from your chest and place it on anyone else in this place," he replied without even looking in Father Figgins' direction.

"Leave us. Now. All of you." Lord Orilion did not turn to the crowd of minor lords, ladies, and people of importance as he addressed them all. The room was emptied except for the Thelimor noble guards, Lord Orilion, Queen Onetta, and Lord Tyrrian, who refused to listen to his lover's father. Father Figgins glared as he began to leave, only for Lord Orilion to pause his leave, "Actually, I changed my mind. You may stay. You were involved in this stupidity as well."

Lord Orilion stepped up on the dais, stood far too close to his daughter, and lowered his voice to be just above a whisper. "Do you wish this entire kingdom to know what you did? That you three killed the king. Because soon, they likely will."

"I can assure you—" Father Figgins cut in.

Lord Orilion rolled his eyes and ignored him, still addressing his daughter, "Our people failed at taking the throne when Mad King Jameston took too quickly to the same mercury you fed your husband. An idea quite likely fed to you by this fool in no-bleman's clothing." Now, the great lord spared Father Figgins a glance before looking back at the queen, "You have tarnished generations of work to restore the Rominian line back on the throne, all for you to sit on the same throne you stood beside. Your marriage was instrumental in granting our people what was always ours."

"I have taken what is ours!" she gritted out.

"No, you have not. You have now given the enemy and any other with a desire for power more reason to stand against this throne- to take away what we have been working in silence to take back. Your son, who is half Aisharian- half the blood of the Usurped Queen, was set to rule after your now-dead husband. And in a few generations, after more careful planning and more marriages arranged like yours, we would have claimed the throne in its entirety. Queen Oriana's blood would have fully ruled the empire once again."

Queen Onetta stilled her jaw that began to shake.

Her father shook his head, "Had you bothered to read any of my letters, you would have realized I learned of your plans and was writing to you to stop them. You would have come to realize that your fury and your lust for a man too hot-headed and simple thinking in his desires would be the end of what our ancestors began. Why do you think I was rushing you to name an heir worthy of Thelimor? I needed another to continue this work when I die."

"You had me. You could have told me, could have told Tyrrian—"

"When have either of you proven yourself cunning and smart enough for something as dire as this?" Lord Orilion looked at Lord Tyrrian, "And he knew- as did his brother. Why do you think the twins really waged war against one another? Hmm?"

The lords of the Isles glared at one another, "Perhaps the wrong twin won the civil war. Kilarus was always more patient than you ever were, Tyrrian. He worried deeply that you would pull something like this and ruin what we planned. He told you as such before he raised an army against you. I'm surprised you didn't cut his tongue out instead of cutting off his balls."

Lord Tyrrian reached for his sword only to pause at the sound of dozens more being unsheathed.

"Fucking my daughter and siring her bastard princess wasn't enough for you?" Lord Orilion turned his back on both of them and slowly descended the steps, "You are both fools if you think for a moment that your deviousness went unnoticed, that I did not help keep those who knew of this quiet."

"What?" the queen's voice shook.

He turned back to face her and straightened his spine, "You have not been as careful as you thought. You let your cunt and love of that one—" Lord Orilion jerked his chin at Lord Tyrrian, "expose you to ones you now owe favors to. And you let that one—" he nodded at the fuming Father Figgins, "whisper sweet lies and promises into your ear that he knows he can never keep."

"No one knows. We made sure of it." Queen Onetta worked to sound sure of herself.

Lord Orilion looked at the blackened doorway beside the dais and nodded at the shadows.

"Did you now, daughter?"

"Your father speaks true, Queen Scott." Lord Shaital Pathis smiled from where he stood, having now stepped outside of the side doorway he had previously walked into. He ignored her bulging eyes and looked to Father Figgins as he and his husband returned to the throne room. "We warned you upon our arrival that you were not the only snake in the garden, Father."

ACKNOWLEDGEMENTS

There are so many people to thank and I do not know where to begin. Truly, I do not know who to thank first becauuse there are so many people who have made this series what it is today. From those who literally made the pages possible: Sharina my editor, Rachel my cover designer, Cassandra my map designer, Kayla and Hannah my alpha readers, and Ashe my artist for all things Victarius.

To Benjamin and Hermione, my furry kids, thank you for very promptly reminding every day me when dinner time is so that I did not spend 14 hours every day writing and forget to eat. Even though, let's be honest, you were doing it for yourselves, not me.

To the Margin Mavins, Kayla and Steph, TPoFaF series would not have a wider audience at this point without the podcast feature you two did. Thank you from every part of me for loving this series and sharing it with your listeners.

To Kayla of MM specifically, your obsession with this series and constantly sharing it with your Twitch community has helped my confidence so much and helped this series grow.

Thank you to everyone who read book one and supported the series, thank you to those who support the series even if you don't read it, and thank you to all who have left reviews and feedback for me to sneak online to read and torture myself with.

And much gratitude to my very committed team of Lexapro, wine, Poppi soda, desk naps, Takis, and iced caramel lattes with oat milk. You all were major players in this series and in keeping me alive.

About the Author

Ever since she could pick up a pen and scribble, Kristina has always been up to something. She has been writing stories, poems, and novels ever since she was first able to form sentences and spell (most) words correctly. Throughout her life, her nose was always stuck in a book and her mind was always wandering and creating fictitious tales that helped her escape life's struggles. She lives in Illinois with her living room library of books and her furry friends- Benjamin and Hermione.

Follow on TikTok, Youtube, and Bluesky @ KristinaMBarbee on all platforms

Photo © NoxNichelle Photography